I0818317

Charge of the Beast

A NOVEL

Charge of the Beast

A NOVEL

ROSALIE KING

Published by Safe Haven Press
Houston, Texas

ISBN: 978-1-7351432-1-7 (Hardcover)
ISBN: 978-1-7351432-0-0 (Paperback)
ISBN: 978-1-7351432-2-4 (Ebook)
Library of Congress Control Number: 2020909647

Cover design by The Book Cover Whisperer:
professionalbookcoverdesign.com

Published by Safe Haven Press | Houston, Texas

Printed in the United States of America

IN MEMORY

1st Lieutenant Phillip Isaac Neel
United States Army
27 November 1979 – 8 April 2007
Killed in Action
Operation Iraqi Freedom

"Ascent of the Willow"
For Phil

Under the gaze of the towering Cottonwood Tree,
Grew a young willow strong and free.
Rooted by the river so desired the youngling,
To touch the Great Branches of the Cottonwood Everlasting.

Aware of the impossibility to reach so high,
Still continued the willow its fullest to thrive.
Impenetrable by insects, its trunk was built.
Solid branches with bounteous leaves were filled.

Whilst surpassing all others in its glorious ascent,
Followed by a tempest did an East Wind rush in.
When the faithful willow suffered a fatal blow,
The fight went on. The trunk did not hollow.

As the wind gusted and leaves fell one by one,
The willow sought once more the Cottonwood to gaze upon.
He gasped in awe as the Great Branches around him spread.
His mission had been accomplished. He laid down his weary head.

The remaining leaves fell, and only a lifeless trunk remained,
But the Eternal Cottonwood would recall the warrior again and again.
Then in sight did appear a fledgling willow of the same kind,
Who in its upward call to duty its fruits shall also find.

To fallen military warriors of the U.S.A.
You loved your country.
You paid the ultimate sacrifice for our freedom.
You will always be remembered.

To our heroic combat veterans,
Past, present, and future.
You were willing to die for your country.
This nation honors your service.

INTRODUCTION

In September 2001, world leaders announced a Global War on Terror against al Qaeda and all terrorist organizations. Four years later, I sat in my living room, shocked by yet another attack. Our servicemen and women were dying by the numbers in the Middle East, nearly 600 Israeli citizens had been killed in suicide bombings in the previous five years, and reporter Daniel Pearl's execution in Pakistan still lay heavy on my mind.

I felt compelled to put my thoughts on paper and decided to write a novel. In my twenties, with little life experience, I did not get far. It would take five years of writer's block before completing the first full draft of *Charge of the Beast* in 2010. Ten years later, after much personal growth, improvements on the craft of writing, and global events to weave into the story—including the most recent historical crisis—*Charge of the Beast* is ready at last!

I hope you love the characters, their unique stories, how they come together, and the ways in which they grow.

Enjoy!

Rosalie King

PTSD WARNING

For those who suffer from post-traumatic stress related to war, be advised that there are two brief combat flashback scenes in *Charge of the Beast.* While the flashbacks are relatively non-violent, they may trigger feelings of anxiety.

Please read at your discretion.

If you are in crisis, please call the following hotline immediately. A combat veteran will answer.

877-717-7873

PTSD Foundation of America

PART I

The Vow

December 2009
Outdoor market, Jerusalem

Who has the bomb?

Rina glued her heels to the last step of the city bus, paralyzed by fear. At full capacity, everyone lined up behind her. They wanted off. Now.

Unwilling to leave the relative safety of the cramped vehicle, Rina scoured the surroundings at the open-air market. On the eve of Hanukkah, a killer prowled, determined to make a statement of martyrdom. Underneath the disguise of an ordinary shopper, they plotted revenge.

But who was it?

An elderly man with soft mounds of wrinkles chuckled in pleasure. His eyes spelled a story of malice. No doubt, he was up to something shady.

A lanky teenaged boy tugged at his baggy shirt, fanning sweat. Why wear oversized clothes for any other reason than to conceal a weapon?

"Mama, go." The gentle voice of Rina's ten-year-old daughter intruded upon the search.

"Eliana, turn around. We're going home." Rina's grip on the cold, greasy handrail weakened.

"I can't." Impatient passengers pressed against Eliana.

"Le'azazel eem zeh," Rina grumbled and led Eliana from the bus. A cloud of black smoke heaved from the muffler, leaving a stench of diesel in its wake.

Over a year and a half had passed since the last suicide bomber hit Israel. Many citizens had abandoned their fears, but Rina did not share their complacency. Evil lurked wherever the sun and moon revealed their splendor, and Rina would risk everything to preserve her late husband's only child.

A sudden breeze prompted the hair on Rina's arms to spike. Was it Seth's spirit, warning her not to go into the market?

Too late. Rina busted through the mass of bodies. Only a 360-degree shield could protect Eliana from harm now.

Ignorant of her vulnerability, Eliana smiled at vendors and took in the sights, never asking for the things she wanted. Long, amber wavelets bounced over her shoulders and down her back.

I will shield you from harm, my child, until death stops me.

In search of the killer who wanted them dead, Rina met eyes with two Israeli Defense Forces soldiers. Anguish struck. She relived the nightmare. Again.

IDF soldiers break through the door.
Frozen still, Rina watches. Waits.
She knows her husband cannot be saved.

"Seth." The word hissed through her lips.

"Mama."

Rina snapped from the memory. "What's the matter, my Love?"

"You're crying." Eliana's face twisted with worry.

Rina dabbed the cold moisture from her face. "I'm sorry."

"It's going to be okay." Eliana tucked loose tangles behind her ears. The depth of her jade eyes matched her father's. She had inherited his inner strength.

A group of tourists crowded the entrance of a famous bakery. Rina grabbed Eliana's arm and pushed through. The nectarous scent of piping hot pastries gave her a smidgeon of comfort.

"Rina," the cashier waved her in, "good to see you and little Eliana. Not so little anymore!" Joshua's shoulders bounced with exaggerated laughter.

Rina offered a wooden smile.

Joshua knew about Seth's tragic demise. It was on every news channel for weeks.

"Mama, here." Eliana offered a paper bag for their purchase.

Customers snatched tongs and hovered over massive trays of sweet confections. Gooey dough, powdered delights, and bite-sized morsels distracted Rina from looming flashbacks.

"How many rugelach will we get?" Eliana pointed to the bakery's famous chocolate pastry.

"Ten for Aunt Naomi's Feast tomorrow. Plus, one for us tonight." Rina ached with love for her innocent daughter, hopeful for a taste of her favorite treat.

Four celebrations in December made this Eliana's favorite time of year. Her birthday on the 2nd, her best friend Shamira's on the 14th, multiple Hanukkah celebrations, and best of all Christmas.

Rina had celebrated only one Christmas with Seth before he died.

"Eliana, let's go." Heat from the steamy rugelach warmed the thin paper bag.

"Will we make the bus?"

Less time at the market meant less time in danger. "I'll make sure of it, my Love."

Rina linked elbows with Eliana and plunged into the congested alleyways. Mounds of colorful produce, tangy kosher olives, and fragrant herbs streaked like motion-blur in a photo.

Something terrible is going to happen.

Sharp rays from the morning sun blinded Rina. She had no choice but to single out suspects. A dark-skinned man wore a thick coat. Winter attire on a crisp morning? Where was he from? What was he doing in Israel? He could only be an enemy. An insidious bomb waiting to explode.

The man shot daggers with his eyes as if he'd read Rina's discriminatory thoughts. Perspiration on his hairline glistened when he pivoted to face the sun. He slid out of the jacket. Nothing underneath but a skinny man in shorts and a short-sleeved shirt. Still strange.

Pop! Pop! Pop!

Booms echoed through the alley.

"Get down!" Rina pulled Eliana to the ground and cocooned her body.

"Ouch!" Eliana sucked air through her teeth. "My head!"

Rina withdrew from her daughter's delicate frame. Blood streaked her left temple and dotted the curb. "I'm sorry, my Love."

Eliana turned away.

An apology would not be enough to make amends for her frantic behavior today.

"Stay down." Rina inhaled a sharp breath and crouched to survey the area. Fear engraved creases into the foreheads of every other shopper who dared to look.

"What could this be?" A fish merchant scowled as he climbed the bottom steps of a folding stool and scanned the corridor.

Rina studied his face for clues. Eerie silence preceded shouts and arguing, then noisy laughter.

"Something fell down," the ornery man snarled. His tone matched the stench of the glossy, limp fish displayed over crushed ice. "That's all it is."

"What about the scream? I heard someone scream." Rina pressed a palm to her chest. Her heart thumped against her hand.

"Who knows? A frightened woman?" The man sneered with slanted brows. "Like you?"

Rina ignored him and dabbed Eliana's scrape with a tissue.

"I'm fine." Eliana rolled her eyes. "Can we hurry?"

"Yes, let's go."

Rina pulled Eliana's hands to help her stand. She bumped shoulders with shoppers in her path and snapped at those who wouldn't move.

"Mama." Eliana tugged the hem of her shirt. "You didn't stop at the cheese store."

"Right. I can't make cheese latkes without the cheese." To show up at Naomi's Hanukkah feast without her signature side dish would raise serious questions. "Here, hold the rugelach."

Rina waved a pliant shekel and shouted her order ahead of others who waited. "My daughter is feeling ill." The statement did not convince the offended shoppers who watched Eliana sniff the package of sweets with a smile.

"Try to keep up with me." Rina forced her customary manners aside and shoved through the line. It was rude. She didn't care. She would never see these people again.

"Mama, are we too late for the next bus?" Eliana's eyes deepened with hope.

"Not if we hurry. We have enough olive oil at home." A lie. She wouldn't be able to make the fried cheese pancakes. Naomi would complain. Whatever. Eliana's safety is more important.

The exit came into sight. The terrifying trip to the market was almost over. Soon, they would be home.

An IDF soldier stood tall, ready to fulfill his valiant oath to combat all forms of terrorism. He was sure to catch anyone who wanted to harm the people he aimed to protect.

Or would he? Everyone has bad days.

This isn't over yet.

The plastic bag handles bit into Rina's fingers—now swollen, purple, and numb. The bags would break if she didn't set them down soon.

A city bus roared around the corner.

"Look." Eliana bounced on her tiptoes. "There it is!"

The lift at the corner of her almond-shaped eyes mimicked Seth's when he smiled. Rina needed a reminder from him now more than ever.

"I'm sorry for acting like this today." Rina smoothed Eliana's frazzled hair. "I love you."

"To the stars in the sky and beyond?" Eliana assumed an expression of confidence sprinkled with affection.

"To the stars in the sky and beyond."

"I love you too, mama."

"Come on, let's go. We have a rugelach to share—this time *before* we start cooking!" The delight in Eliana's face nourished the famine in Rina's soul. It gave her enough sustenance to walk the last fifty feet to the bus.

An amalgamation of body odor, perfume, greasy scalps, and stale smoke tempted Rina to back away from the flock of bodies at the entrance of the bus. She ground a foot on the bottom step. Their immediate passage home was now secure.

"Go ahead." Rina pivoted to allow Eliana's entry.

Eliana wasn't there.

Instead, a gasping teenager shouldered through the crowd.

Outfitted in traditional Muslim clothes, the girl's dark eyes darted in every direction. In search of someone. Or something.

Rina clutched the cold handrail, determined not to lose her place. Impatient strangers stared her down.

"Mama," Eliana cried from the market entrance. One of her bags sprawled on the ground, its handle split in two. She cradled the rugelach package, making all attempts to collect the fallen groceries futile.

"Do you want me to help you?" Rina yelled with her foot planted on the bottom step.

A vendor with a brown paper bag crouched next to Eliana and packed the goods.

Rina felt a nudge in her ribs.

The Muslim girl, seventeen years of age at most, plucked at her cloak. Something underneath bothered her. Like an itch on her belly. But she didn't scratch.

She felt for something with her finger.

A loose button?

No.

A detonator.

She's the one.

Seconds became minutes.

Rina made eye contact with the human bomb. Wordless pleas accomplished nothing.

"Don't do it," Rina shouted in Arabic.

The girl took no notice of her words.

"I'm coming," Eliana yelled, oblivious of the looming catastrophe.

"Stay there!" Rina's heartbeat thrashed under her breastbone. If she were to get off the bus now to shield her daughter, it would be too late. She had seconds to act.

Rina dropped the bags. Hands free.

Ready for the counterattack.

Ready for a fight to the grave—a vow she had made moments before they entered the bakery.

The trained killer slipped on the milk that now dripped from jagged steps. She stumbled backward when Rina yanked her head covering.

A burst of adrenaline pumped Rina with more power than ever. It was almost too easy to lift the girl and slam her down.

Rina dove on top of the skinny body and immobilized the girl's arms.

Determined to become a successful Shahida, the brainwashed teen doubled over and writhed to break free. Angry groans rumbled from her chest when she became entangled in her robes.

People yelled to run. Some screamed.

Shoes pounded on the pavement. Voices became distant.

No one volunteered to render aid.

It was all up to Rina.

Like a commander would fall on a grenade for his troops, Rina crushed the time-fused bomb for Eliana.

In tandem, they bumped down the steps.

The suicide-bomber screeched and flailed in mania. Tore free to finish her mission.

Double-edged daggers of flaming coal seared Rina's legs.

Sweeps of Seth's lips landed upon her. They were together again.

PART II

America

ELIANA

August 2019
Nashville, Tennessee

Teardrops traced Eliana's cheeks like fresh mist on windowpanes. Fatigue from the multistate drive did not plague her. Angry rush hour drivers hadn't sent her into an emotional eruption.

One truth ruined the moment: her mother's death. And she was to blame. She should be six feet under too.

Eliana wiped her eyes for a clear view of the breathtaking campus. Time to get out and face her second year at an elite university in America. An honor she did not deserve.

Muggy heat fell upon her like a hot towel when she opened the door. A lengthy gulp of flat Coke compounded her thirst. "I have to find a water fountain," she said to the empty bottle and slammed the door. The noisy alarm chimed amongst peaceful quietude.

Rural Mississippi had been Eliana's home for eight years, then Vanderbilt University after high school. Its beauty was more of a culture shock than the move from Israel. She never got used to it either.

A canopy of trees over the lush campus beckoned Eliana to explore, regardless of her unworthiness. Gothic, Victorian, and modern style buildings perfected the architectural variety. Bronze sculptures, expansive lawns, and colorful blossoms created an oasis adjacent to downtown's bustle.

If Eliana were still in Israel, would there be a campus so beautiful? That's where she wanted to be. But she had no one there. No family. No friends. Not even Shamira, her best friend who disappeared after the bombing.

Unnoticed by busy groups of students engaged in conversation, Eliana faked self-confidence as she navigated the grounds. The first week of her Sophomore year culminated in the most embarrassing experience. Dozens of students stared when she sprinted into Jewish Studies ten minutes late. She shuffled up the steps to an empty seat in the semi-circular lecture hall.

"Here." A well-sculpted man with a crew cut and close-set eyes stood from the end of a row. "Take my seat."

"Thanks." Eliana glanced back as the gentleman jumped steps two at a time to the top.

"Not a prob."

"Welcome, dear," the professor greeted Eliana in a delicate French accent. "I'm Professor Ramzi. You are?"

"Eliana Gibbons."

A female student in the front row twisted her body to make eye contact.

"Nice to meet you." Professor Ramzi strutted to Eliana's side of the room. His short, sculpted afro, vintage eyeglasses and formal blazer made him look far too debonair for the college classroom. "When you came in, we had just started introducing students from overseas. I am from Morocco. A young lady from Israel just introduced herself. Who's next?"

A low grumble resonated from the person next to Eliana. Without turning her head, she made out the figure of a male wearing a black trench coat.

A petite girl with a purple head covering raised her hand. "I am Jazmin from Palestine," she said in a thick accent.

Eliana gained a better view of her neighbor, who nodded at Jazmin in approval. *He likes the girl from Palestine. Did the grumble mean he didn't like the one from Israel?*

How is he going to feel when he hears there are two of us?

Thick boots thudded on the floor when her neighbor stood up. A slim, midnight beard lined his sharp, angular jaw. Dark-ringed eyes contrasted from his smooth sandstone complexion. "Hakim. From Iraq." Folds of his coat swept Eliana's desk when he sat back down. A strong odor of cigarette smoke followed a lengthy sigh.

Professor Ramzi scanned the rest of the room after three other guys introduced themselves in almost incomprehensible English. "Anyone else?"

Eliana wanted to connect with the Israeli student. As much as she hated the thought of returning to the spotlight, she had no choice. This could be the single opportunity to regain a piece of her homeland. "I'm Eliana, originally from Israel, but I've been in America since I was ten." The statement rolled from her tongue with more confidence than expected.

The girl in the front row corkscrewed her body. Her face hung limp in a classic open-mouthed stare.

Hakim's throaty rumbles verified Eliana's hunch. He grazed a thumb along a metal object in his massive palm. Prolonged pauses allowed her to distinguish what resembled a set of claws adhered to inverted brass knuckles. As Professor Ramzi enunciated his closing words, Hakim pitched his belongings into a black duffle bag.

"Pitiful race." He shot to his feet and bumped Eliana's chair. A large bulge seesawed under his coat when he jostled down the stairs.

"Ouch!" Eliana rubbed the prickly vibrations from her funny bone.

"Hey." The gentleman who had offered his seat waited in the aisle. Fine creases fanned the corners of his eyes, which were as blue as aquamarine gemstones. Wind-weathered skin evidenced extensive outdoor activities. The cowboy boots, jeans, and plaid shirt totally gave him away. He had to be a rancher or farmer, although his black leather jacket made no sense. "You okay? I saw that guy hit your chair on purpose."

"I didn't notice." On the contrary. Hakim had intended to make a statement.

"Might want to stay away from him," he said and turned sideways in a fluid movement. "By the way, welcome to the States."

"I've been here a long time. In Mississippi, to be exact."

"Best of both worlds. I'm Brian Draeger."

Eliana gripped Brian's outstretched hand. "Nice to meet you."

"Someone else wants to talk to you." Brian pointed to the bottom of the steps. "It's the other student from Israel."

The girl from the front row hugged her bag. She peered at Eliana, waiting as if to say, "*Will you be my friend?*"

"Thanks again for your seat."

"Not a prob." Brian shuffled down the steps with a final glance over his shoulder.

The girl studied Eliana with narrow eyes. Not out of contempt or judgment. This was head-scratching bafflement. She looked familiar. It was like Eliana had already met her at some point. But when? Where? She could be an old friend from school.

"Eliana," the girl said in a shaky whisper, "you're from Israel?"

"Yeah." Eliana slid her purple backpack in place.

"I'm also from Israel." She probed each side of the room. Nerves, uncertainty, or fear made her jumpy. "I moved when I was ten."

"I did too! What's your name?"

The lecture hall cleared. Except for Professor Ramzi. "Time to turn off the lights, mademoiselles!"

"My name is—"

"Outside, s'il vous plaît!"

The room darkened. Faint beams shined from elevated ventilation windows.

Eliana stepped from the room and held the door open. "Now, you were trying to tell me your name."

"Shamira."

Eliana's shoe hooked on the door's bottom corner. Her knees hit the tile floor full force. On her hip, she studied her friend's features. In a flash, she recognized the deep-set eyes, broad lips, and frizzy curls. A charge of memories ignited her senses: downy pillow fights, yawns amidst late-night sleepovers, syrupy chocolate rugelach for Hanukkah.

In simultaneous unrestraint, the long-lost friends launched into an embrace.

"I tried to call you so many times." Eliana retreated from Shamira's slackened arms. "What happened?"

"My father made us move to Chile." Shamira's eyes reddened in a glassy haze. "I don't know why. The day you didn't come for Hanukkah was terrible. Papa left and searched for hours. He took mama to their room when he came home. She screamed. I can still hear it." Shamira cupped a hand over her face. "Papa brought me a suitcase, told me to pack, and a few hours later we went to the airport."

"Then you don't know about..." Eliana felt the faded memory gaining ground. A brutal awakening in the hospital led to an abrupt beginning of life without her mother. "Let's get some air."

BRIAN

Brian slid a hand through the coarse edges of his high and tight haircut. He trailed Hakim, thirty feet ahead. What kind of prick would treat a woman like that?

With his background in the Middle East, Brian knew without a doubt that Hakim was up to no good. The scumbag had watched Eliana and the other Israeli student leave the classroom with a look of hatred just like the insurgents. Brian had come face-to-face with that a time or two.

Hakim shoved a slim phone to his ear, shoulders rounded in animated discussion. He gouged at the grass with his combat boots. The trench coat made no sense in this heat. There was only one explanation for it.

The ring of Brian's phone alerted the Iraqi.

They engaged in a stare down.

Eyelids peeled, unwavering, Brian fished for the phone from his pocket.

Hakim muttered under his breath before he turned foot to leave.

Brian zipped a thumb across the screen. "Hey Cabrera, perfect timing."

"What's up, bro?" Jay's metal lighter flicked. His Philippino mother forbade him to smoke cigarettes. His CIA dad, white as a white man can be with a Spanish last name, lit up with him in secret. A way to reform a bond with his son, a United States Marine, changed forever from three tours in Afghanistan.

"I need you to look someone up for me." With Hakim out of sight, Brian headed back to the lecture hall in hopes of catching Eliana. For what reason, he didn't know. He just wanted to talk to her again. Make sure she's all right.

"Details?" The phone crackled as Jay exhaled a deep drag.

"Don't got much, man. Foreign dude in my class. Name's Hakim. From Iraq."

"As long as there isn't more than one Hakim from Iraq there, it'll be easy." Jay hacked a moist cough in the background.

Brian glanced at the yellow stain on his fingers from cigarette use. He kept cancer sticks in ample supply in the desert. It was the one request when the family sent care packages. Tobacco-free for three years now. "Man, you should chunk the smokes. For good."

Jay ignored Brian's advice. "Any other suspicious foreigners?"

"Not suspicious. Two female students from Israel. Totally innocent. A dude from Pakistan and a Saudi seem harmless. There's an older lady from Luxembourg. I talked to a guy from Venezuela who's pretty cool. A chick from Palestine is questionable, although I think she's safe. Looks can be deceiving, as we've seen." In the desert, sly Taliban insurgents were experts at blending in with ordinary Afghani citizens.

Typing fingers clicked. Jay mumbled, most likely with the cigarette hanging from his lips. Something about research on social media and the Net. "What the hell are they doing in a Jewish Studies class?"

"Got me."

"Sounds fishy."

"Roger that."

A series of lighter flicks signaled Jay's eagerness to get to work. He was already on smoke number two after a minute of conversation. "Whatever, bro. I'll get back to you pronto. Just don't do anything stupid. We're not in the Middle East on deployment."

"Nah, man. Talk at you later." Brian slid the phone into his pocket and stopped short when he rounded the corner of the building. Eliana shuffled from the white steps, the other Israeli student in tow. Rather than happiness with the connection, the girls seemed disturbed. Especially Eliana when she sank knees first onto the lawn. Odd. Did Hakim torment them in some way before Brian had a chance to stop him? He'd put a stop to that mess.

Everything in Brian's gut told him that guy was a threat.

ELIANA

Visualizations from the waking moments in the hospital erupted when Eliana closed her eyes.

"Hey!" Shamira, the most beloved person Eliana never dreamed of seeing again, stood over her. Hands planted on her hips. Eyes cold. Sculpted brows arched. "Tell me what happened! Why didn't you come for Hanukkah?"

Eliana returned from the flashback. Shamira waited for news that would send her into devastation. "This isn't easy."

"Is it Aunt Rina?"

"We went to the outdoor market." Eliana folded her arms over her torso to hide the guilt in the pit of her stomach. "It's all my fault."

"What's your fault?"

"I knew I'd get a rugelach if we finished cooking early, so I convinced mama to hurry to the bus." Eliana covered her face with clammy palms. "There was a suicide bombing. She…died."

Shamira allowed her canvas bag to slide to the grass in a single movement. "Why didn't my parents tell me?"

A random breeze cooled the sweat on the back of Eliana's neck. "I tried to call so many times after I moved here. Now I know why there was no answer."

"You've been in America all these years?"

"Yes. My grandparents have given me a good upbringing."

"I'm glad things went well for you." Shamira sneered with a cruel smile. "My life has been bad."

"Why?"

"Too much to explain. It's all because of your selfish motives. Thanks a lot!" Shamira spun. Fine grass clippings wafted into the air as she ran away.

Eliana fell to her knees and allowed her body to land backward in the prickly grass. Lawnmowers hummed in the distance. Sunrays shot through openings in branches and lit green particles ablaze as they danced above her.

Joined by the swaying of leaves, nature's elements transformed into a blur. Her mother's shaky voice at the market resurfaced for the first time since that day.

"Put your arm through mine."

Eliana grabbed a handful of cool, spiky grass. All these years, she hadn't dealt with the loss.

"Eliana?" An unfamiliar voice echoed.

She unclenched her fists and released the grass. Brian towered over her. What did he want? She didn't need someone bothering her right now.

SHAMIRA

Shamira slammed the small wooden chair into the wall for the second time. It split into pieces, fueling the anger.

Her roommate's fishhook eyebrow posed a serious question. "I hope that's yours." Leah sawed her fingernails with a cardboard file. "I bet the school would charge a pretty penny if it's theirs."

Where had the violence come from? Nowhere. Like a temper tantrum, she'd lost the ability to control herself. She never did that. Her father, on the other hand, after they moved from Israel. That was a different story.

Shamira refused to follow his patterns.

Crackles of splitting wood deepened Shamira's self-reproach. She collected the pieces and flung them in the corner. The cheap dorm mattress bounced from the momentum of her belly flop.

On her final day in Israel, she had plunged into bed, in the same manner, three times. Eliana and Rina were missing, her parents were scared, and she was forced to stay in her room for hours. Rumbling wheels had woken her from a fitful nap. Her father walked in with an oversized suitcase and said, "*Pack this with everything you can. Stuff it full.*"

The happy life Shamira once had never returned after the move. Her latest attempt at happiness—relocation to America two weeks ago. Here she was, with the sweetest taste of Israel in her reach. Eliana, the person she dreamed of reuniting with someday, turned out to be responsible for her family's destruction. All because she wanted her mama to hurry home.

"Hey!" Leah yelled over her hair dryer. The sulfuric smell of burning hair made Shamira want to leave the room.

"What?"

"Wanna go have some fun?" The howl of the blow dryer distorted the subsequent details. "...party in the woods..." Leah brushed her blond main sideways as the blast of air whipped it into stormy waves. "...fun to be had by all." She finished the wild blow-drying session and waited for an answer with a hand on her hip.

A fun party sounded good. Maybe she could rely on Leah and her friends to help shatter the misery from the past decade…and make it easier to forget about Eliana's presence on campus.

Like that was going to happen.

ELIANA

The lecture hall's solid doors budged to a dark room. Automatic sensors awakened buzzing fluorescent lights.

Today Eliana arrived ten minutes early. In control, she had the first pick of seats.

Far from the suspicious Iraqi guy, Hakim.

Far from Shamira, who would rouse the bad memories that had tortured Eliana every night.

Close to Brian for support and protection. He had offered both last week.

The furthest seat in the top row would do.

Eliana made a beeline for the stairs when she heard the door open, but she tripped over her feet. Her knees and hands smacked the stone tiles before landing face-first on the bottom step.

Sandals flapped behind her. A female voice murmured foreign words. Slender, delicate hands branched across the tile. "I help!"

Winged eyelashes void of mascara boasted the most prominent feature of the girl's face. Fine tufts of black hair had escaped her floral head covering. "You have bleeding on your nostrils," she said in a thick accent. "I have tissue."

A warm trickle surrendered to heavy drops from Eliana's nose. Had she really hit the step that hard? She squeezed her nasal bridge and accepted the tissue. "Thanks."

"I have oil to stop bleed nose." The student pulled a small brown bottle from her pocket. "May I anoint you?"

Eliana giggled despite the soreness. The girl had announced she was from Palestine last week. She hadn't been in America long. "Yes." Vapors from the liquid forced Eliana's eyes shut.

"Check now." The girl smiled in satisfaction.

Eliana released the pressure. No blood. Only a woody scent remained.

"See? I have medical problem and must anoint my nose every day." The young student tended to Eliana in a motherly fashion. "I am called Jazmin," she said and yanked another tissue from the pocket pack.

"I'm Eliana." Just as Jazmin wiped the floor clean, Professor Ramzi darted through the door. "Use the word *apply*, not anoint. Anointing implies a religious ritual."

Jazmin faked a laugh to hide embarrassment. "Thank you."

"Welcome. My English was bad when I moved here."

"You're not American?"

Doubt crept in. Eliana thought of the Palestinian suicide bomber who killed her mother. According to her grandparents, terrorists in Palestine are a minority contrasted to the five million citizens who don't commit such crimes.

Which group did Jazmin belong to?

"I'm a naturalized American from Israel. I moved here after my mother died." Involuntary huffs broke Eliana's tone. "December will be a decade. I've been with my grandparents since then."

Jazmin's body squared. Her eyes narrowed to a crescent form. "Ten years in December?"

Eliana nodded. What was the deal with Jazmin's tension?

Movement and chatter enlivened the room. A tall figure emerged into Eliana's eyesight.

"Hey." Brian's stack of books slid like dominoes from the neat pile he'd made on the table. His lips hooked into a half-smile until he saw her face. "What happened?"

"I tripped. I'm okay now." Eliana hoped Brian would sit by her today. They had talked for two hours at the coffee shop last week. Basic conversation got her mind off painful memories and the unpleasant encounter with Shamira. Good thing he was here to distract from another uneasy situation.

The seat next to Jazmin swiveled.

Eliana craned her neck.

Hakim slammed a palm onto the table and distended his ribcage with a cocky laugh. He threw a vicious scowl in Jazmin's direction. They knew each other. No doubt. And he was mad at her.

Hakim flared his nostrils in disgust when he zeroed in on Eliana.

"Dude," Brian leaned over to address Hakim, "what the hell's your deal?"

Hakim spread his hands to say, *Nothing*, but the tiger claw in his palm gave a much different notion.

Jazmin clasped her hands together and pressed them to her forehead. Was she praying? Or mentally removing herself from the confrontation?

Unaware of the imminent showdown, Professor Ramzi clapped his hands to shush the commotion. "Let's get started!"

Brian eased into his seat and plugged earbuds into his phone.

With a victorious chuckle, Hakim whispered into Jazmin's ear.

She had to be one of them. Another constituent in the league of individuals who hate Israelis and Americans.

Eliana texted Nannie. Her grandmother always knew how to bring her out of a funk.

Right now, all she wanted to do was pack up and leave.

BRIAN

The prof's lecture faded as Brian scrolled through Jay's texts for the quintupleth time.

No history to make Hakim suspicious.

Yet, no history to make him unsuspicious.

In fact, with no other background info than a valid F1 student visa, Brian made up his mind. Hakim came here with bad intentions. But the law would find zilch on the creep. They'd do nada.

Brian had to take matters into his own hands. Make up for past failures.

Sounds of warfare shattered the pretentious notions. Great. The precursors to a panic attack. They almost always interrupted internal pep talks.

Audible memories of combat jolted him.

Why the hell does this have to happen now?

He'd have to sweat it out. Keep the commotion quiet….it was only in his head.

Don't yell out, dude. This isn't the battlefield.

M240 machine guns open up, unleashing an ungodly amount of fire. Empty shells clink on thick mud walls. More fire. Bullets pass within inches of his body.

Tanks. Blasts. Choppers.

Shouts of anger. Cries of agony from fellow brothers in arms. Forever scarred, inside and out, by a war that wasn't theirs to fight.

Noise-canceling earbuds didn't tune it out. Pillow over his head, useless. Watching TV, pointless.

Only music blocked the inner pandemonium—really loud and really heavy music.

Metallica's "No Leaf Clover" always did the trick.

Brian pressed the earbuds further in and forced his hands to stop shaking long enough to pull up the video.

A duel began. Heavy metal masters verses symphonic perfection. San Francisco Symphony's introductory notes serenaded the opponent. Metallica's heavily distorted guitar notes thundered a retort, a match to the pounding in Brian's chest.

Vigorous vocals put him in tune with reality.

"Good day to be alive Sir…good day to be alive."

It didn't feel like a good day to be alive when First Sergeant Brian Draeger had been assigned as assistant patrol leader. It didn't feel like a bad day, either. Another day in a string of 210 spent in the Wonderland known as Helmand Province, Afghanistan.

The mission: foot patrol out and back, no artillery or air to worry about except Casevac. Just a milk run op. Snatch some High Value Targets out of their trashy little hut and drag them to the Combat Out Post. Capture was preferred, but dead was accepted as a high probability. At the COP, someone from Higher would take them back to Kabul for processing.

It was the same damn thing they had done millions of times.

Brian jacked it all up. Let his best friend and battle buddy down. Neil Phillips had deserved better leadership. Brian should have kept him safe. That's what leaders are supposed to do.

Phillips had certainly upheld his end of the deal. Even when he got hit, he didn't give up. He kept fighting. Maybe shock or something kept him going. The stubborn Jarhead kept firing while his blood drained out into the thirsty dust. Brian should've known…should've done something.

The ambush had come from nowhere. With Neil on point, they were crossing one of the main supply routes when the snap crack of incoming fire split the hot air. Neil collapsed in the middle of the road. All the Marines except Brian dove into cover in the roadside ditch.

Brian stood stunned for a brief second, somehow, without getting hit. He ran to his friend and dragged him to cover. Neil yelled something unintelligible with a hand clamped to his neck.

Just as Brian hauled his injured buddy into the ditch, his left leg crumpled underneath him. He had taken a swift hit to the thigh. His first thought was for Neil, who wormed his way up the berm to get in firing position. Back in the fight.

The bullet must have grazed Neil's neck. Brian would patch him up after they killed all the SOB's.

Without a glance at his own wound, Brian climbed the berm and fired.

Taliban fighters dotted the hillside. They played this one hard and maneuvered to kill or capture this small American patrol. They must have known the Marine Raider squad would be coming through here. OPSEC was worthless with the locals working on base.

Brian chose his targets carefully. He and Neil knocked down man after man. Neither would let the discomfort stop them from their mission.

When Brian realized he hadn't heard Neil's rifle for a while, he looked over his shoulder, saw the blood first, then the limp body. It was all over for his buddy. Neil died a hero, shooting till his lifeblood depleted. Brian reached for him, to say goodbye, but his vision dimmed.

"Man down! Man down!" Sergeant Major Jayson Cabrera's voice tried to pierce the haze around Brian's mind. Dirt and rocks crunched under his boots as he whipped a tourniquet around Brian's leg and called for a corpsman and Casevac.

Another Marine stood over Neil's body and repeated over and over, "Phillips, can you hear me? Phillips!" He had a semblance of hope that there was still some life in the lifeless body.

"Draeger!" Jay Cabrera yelled as he secured the tourniquet over Brian's blood-laden trousers. "Hang in there, bro. I gotcha bud. It's gonna be okay. I'm gonna get you outta here."

"No," Brian had mumbled. "Let me die."

Jay spat curses, telling Brian he was crazy. But Jay didn't understand. He did his duty. He's not the one who failed to help his fellow Marine.

Brian, Jay, and Neil had been a trio. Brothers in arms. Respectful of rank of course, but more like younger brother respect for an older. Brian could only watch as four Marines lifted Neil's body by the limbs and carried him to the hasty landing zone.

A hot knife of pain from his left thigh jolted Brian when they put him on a stretcher. Venous blood flow. Bad, but not as bad as fatal arterial damage. Then, he would have died. He should have died. Killed in action was the honorable way out.

But he lived. Wounded in action. And completely responsible for Neil Phillip's death.

The squad killed twenty-two Taliban, but Brian let his friend down, leading to the company's first casualty. The Situation Report for this patrol would include one KIA and one WIA. The KIA meant Staff Sergeant Neil Phillips had given his all for his country. The WIA meant Brian had not.

The months blurred together in Brian's depressed state. He had been evacuated. Kabul first, Germany, then all the way back to the States. He didn't care. Not even when they delivered the medical retirement orders fresh from the Med Board. None of it mattered now. He was on borrowed time.

Metallica's aggressive shifts and the symphony's powerful replies unified into a perfectly woven masterpiece.

Monolithic. Euphoric.

A soothing guitar riff, high-pitched violins, and soft oboe notes provided a break from the intensity as they fell in line with subdued vocals.

The lyrics reawakened a purpose Brian deserted years ago.

> *"Then it comes to be that the soothing light at the end of your tunnel,*
> *is just a freight train coming your way."*

Brian yanked the earbuds before the song finished. A first.

He hardly knew Eliana, but she needed protection. So did everyone else Hakim planned to harass. Brian was up for the challenge, even if it meant a new enemy rushed his way like a freight train.

Failure would not be an option this time.

ELIANA

Eliana wedged behind the seats and darted down the steps. Blocked by students who hustled into the aisles, Eliana gave up on the hopeless attempt to reach Shamira.

"Bye, Eliana." Jazmin's voice epitomized innocence. She waved with a disappointed frown. A show of deception. She had an association with Hakim in some form. He followed her trail within inches.

I can't be murdered by terrorists like mama and dad.

"Can I walk you somewhere?" Brian had been in another place during the lecture. The music from his earbuds was heard by half the class.

"I'm going to talk to Shamira."

"Change of heart?" He glared at Hakim, who shouldered through the crowd in pursuit of Jazmin. "I'll go with you."

A subtle thunk resonated from Brian's heavy boots on the sidewalk. "How can you walk so quietly in those?"

"Habit." Brian arched his brows and surveyed the perimeter.

"Don't you get hot in that jacket?" May as well ask questions while he's giving answers.

"Nah. It's nothing compared to the desert."

The desert? Not that he had an accent, but Eliana thought Brian came from the country. "It's just that I've never seen someone wear boots, jeans, and a leather jacket in this kind of heat."

Brian wiped sweat that slid from his temples. "I have my reasons. Where is Shamira's dorm?"

"I don't know." Eliana stopped at a fork. Dense trees entwined their branches, creating a leafy canopy. "This is pointless."

Brian ceased his strange scrutiny as the sidewalks cleared. "Where are you going next?"

"My dorm."

"I get a big red flag with the way that Iraqi guy looks at you."

"You really think he's that dangerous?"

"Possibly. Can I take you to get some pepper spray?"

In the sanctuary of her grandparents' country home, the significance of danger had dematerialized over the years. Now Eliana stood face-to-face with someone who wanted her prepared for violent circumstances. And he was right. Hakim and Jazmin may have the same hatred as those who killed her parents. "Sure."

"Come on, my truck's this way."

The irrationality of her decision unveiled numerous questions. Why, for one, follow a stranger so worried about her security? "I can take my own car if you just tell me where to go."

"That's exactly the kind of thing I want to hear from you." He pointed to an old, semi-refurbished Chevrolet flatbed pickup. A United States Marine Corps sticker on the back window explained his protective behavior. "You're all right with me."

Eliana wanted to trust the Marine. "Why are you doing this?"

"I'm one of those pro-Israel Americans. The country gets bullied. I get all bent out of shape when I see stuff on TV." Brian raised the corner of his mouth in a lopsided grin. "Ready?"

A dull coat of imperial blue marked early restoration stages on Brian's time-tested truck. "What year is this?"

Brian held the passenger door open. "Nineteen fifty. It was my grandpa's. Sorry about the smell." The interior reeked of musty carpet and stale autumn leaves. "I had to fix the engine first. Exterior is second priority. I'll do the inside last."

The winding freeway bred a peaceful twenty-minute ride. Brian pushed the limits of the croaky engine while describing the 'awesome store' with a good selection of pepper sprays. He depicted stories passed on by his WWII veteran great grandfather, his Vietnam War veteran grandfather, and a brief mention about his dad who served in the Gulf War and early Afghanistan War.

"What about you?" Eliana hoped Brian would recount his own experiences.

"Afghanistan. Medically retired three years ago." The engine shuttered to a stop when Brian pulled into the parking space. The store's exterior resembled a mahogany country cabin large enough for a family of giants. "Wait there."

Brian tugged the retro, push-button door handle. Hinges screeched like an elderly grandpa who protested a trip to the doctor. Brian offered a hand to help Eliana from the truck. She certainly didn't mind the display of appreciation for her womanhood. "What *is* this place?"

"Bass Pro."

Eliana's jaw hung slack when she entered the store. "Is this a museum?"

"No. The one in Memphis is a museum." Brian led Eliana past the store greeters who looked like wildlife park employees. "It's half a million square foot big. Bit of a drive, though."

Body mounts of wildlife brought the store to life. Or death as far as Eliana was concerned. "Are all of those real stuffed animals?"

Brian choked and laughed at the same time. "It's taxidermy. And yes, they're all real. Mind if I stop over there first? I've gotta blow off some steam."

Eliana followed Brian to a small archery range where he shot five rounds perfectly in the bull's eye. "Feel better?"

"Somewhat. Now to the camping section." The choices of pepper spray were limited, to Brian's dismay. He chose the smallest bottle. "You can hide this in the palm of your hand if you hold it right. They'll never see it."

Bold red letters dominated the package. "Hottest formula by law? Will it burn someone if I use it?"

"It will feel like it to them. The effects last half an hour at most." Brian tossed the plastic package in the air, followed by a quick retrieval. "Long enough to get away and go to the police. Always go to the police if you have to use this."

This form of defense brought Eliana one step closer to reality. Danger was everywhere. Here. At a famous campus in a historic town. One of the most beautiful areas of the United States. What would it be like in Israel? Worse, but now was as good a time as any to prepare. She planned to go back someday.

"Thanks for your service," Eliana said when Brian pulled into her dorm's parking lot.

Brian laughed. "You call what we did today a service?"

"No, I'm talking about Afghanistan." Eliana rested a hand on his shoulder. "I'm so sorry you had to go through all that."

Brian nodded. Eyes vacant. "Text me if you need anything."

BRIAN

The bulky key chain clanked on the laminate kitchen counter. Something about Eliana calmed him. Engaged in everything he said, she didn't prod or ask questions. Not even the reason he joined the Corps.

Good thing. As far as Brian was concerned, he'd never tell anyone.

Apart from head nods, Eliana listened with no response. Truth be told, he thought she didn't care until she thanked him for his service. It was beyond sincere, unlike others who acted according to ritual.

Eliana wasn't the most beautiful woman he'd seen. Not that it mattered. Long since healed, pinstripe scars on her face were visible only when standing within inches. Likely lacerations from a car accident. A sprinkling of fine freckles, cherubic rosiness, green eyes, and long lashes made her the cutest girl he'd ever met. Beautiful in her own way.

The old PC groaned when Brian pressed the power button. Mom gave him a new laptop last Christmas. "*You deserve it. All those medals,*" she had said and pointed to his display case, "*they speak volumes.*" That was great and all, but Little Cousin Millie, a freshman in high school, needed the laptop more.

A headline with a gruesome picture popped up on the local news website. Ten men dressed in shabby clothes kneeled with their hands tied behind their backs. Masked men surrounded them. Automatic weapons in hand. "Not again."

Uncanny to see that on the sixteenth anniversary of his father's capture. Captain John Draeger became a Prisoner of War in 2003 with no clues on his whereabouts. His remains were found a week after Brian's 17th birthday in '09.

The next morning, Brian showed up at the USMC recruiting office.

A wet nose nudged Brian's palm. Sterling, his faithful cat, always knew when he was becoming agitated. "You're my best buddy." The Russian Blue answered with a soft meow. Sterling's sandpaper tongue scraped Brian's arm with the intention to groom the hairs.

The late afternoon sun gleamed through the blinds, creating a warm reflection across frames on the wall. Brian cradled Sterling in one arm and went to the only picture that caused him grief. Jay and Neil stood on either side of Brian with an arm around his neck. Covered in dust, soot, and sweat, their hardened faces proclaimed victory after a battle in which Brian put down three hundred rounds of ammunition.

It was Staff Sergeant Phillips' last full day on Earth. They were a tightknit group. Brothers. Family. No other camaraderie could come close to theirs.

Brian hadn't tried hard enough when they were ambushed. He should have done something different. Or something better. Or at least stopped the damned bleeding.

A series of meows interrupted Brian's breakdown. He relaxed as Sterling nuzzled into his upper body and began a melody of purrs.

The phone vibrated on the counter. An ordinary ring tone blared from the phone.

Someone not in his speed dial.

Brian took two giant steps to reach the phone. "Hello?"

"Is this Brian?"

"Depends on who's asking." The voice of a woman. Not his mother, sisters, aunt, or cousins.

"It's Eliana."

Brian grabbed his keys and carried his boots in one arm. "What's wrong? Are you okay? Where are you?"

"At my dorm. I'm fine."

Brian huffed and slowed his pace.

"Are *you* okay?"

"Yeah, I just thought…something might be wrong."

"I have a question about the pepper spray."

"Let's go get some coffee." Brian shoved his wallet into his back pocket. "Can I pick you up?" *Safer that way.*

"Sure."

"Be there in ten."

Sterling retreated to his position on the bed without a fuss. He didn't know that Brian had someone to protect. "I can't let anything happen to her, little buddy."

ELIANA

The daily search for Shamira dampened Eliana's hope to reconnect. They had to clear things up. In class, Shamira took the same seat closest to the door three weeks in a row. An obvious intention to avoid Eliana.

"Are you going to talk to her?" Brian stroked his fingers atop Eliana's hand.

It was a gesture she hadn't gotten used to yet. Two weeks is all it took to develop feelings for one another. Brian meant more now than a friend.

Morning conversations at the coffee shop distracted Eliana from wavering emotions. Each evening after dinner at the campus café, Brian opened up about his military background. Over the past one hundred years, seven men in his family served as a Marine in all major wars. He wanted to continue his family legacy of service to the United States of America. He described pre-deployment training and his stay at the Marine base in Guam. When he stumbled upon his experiences in Afghanistan, the liveliness in his accounts nose-dived into a hollow void.

In moments of silence, when he returned to the bad event that had scarred him, Eliana caressed his back. It brought him out of the episode every time. Brian said no one helped him with the post-traumatic stress like she did.

On the weekends, they spent all day together. Meals, coffee shop conversations, strolls amongst the greenery, country drives, and some homework at the library filled the hours. Eliana almost felt like she had a boyfriend. She shared plenty about her years in America and a glimmer of Israel. "*Shamira is an old friend,*" Eliana explained when Brian asked. "*She doesn't remember me well.*"

A true statement. Shamira had erased their relationship from her memory in toto.

"Well?" Brian's inquiry brought Eliana out of the daydream.

"I want to talk to her." Shame nabbed Eliana's insides. There was no reason to hide the story from Brian. "I haven't been completely honest. We actually grew up together. When we were ten, something bad happened, and I had to move. We didn't even get to say goodbye. She's mad about something I said on the first day."

"She'll come around." Brian pivoted in his chair and sandwiched Eliana's hand between his palms.

Brian's reassurance gave her a modicum of hope. Still, doubt would remain until the day Shamira welcomed Eliana into her life. "Will you go to her, like you did to me? Get her pepper spray?"

"Good idea."

Jazmin leaned over her notes in review of last weeks' lesson. She hadn't talked to Eliana since they met. No surprise there since she was friends with someone who hated her.

With a pompous gait, Hakim strode through the door. He pelted Shamira with a look that would send Eliana running to call Nannie. Her grandma would offer words of wisdom and conclude with humor to lessen Eliana's fear.

When Hakim directed his attention to Eliana and Brian, eyes narrowed to slits, Eliana resisted the urge to shoot the finger. She'd never done that to anyone, nor had she considered doing so. "He hates us."

"Shh! Don't piss him off even more." Brian curled his lips in cold-blooded contempt. "Sorry, not trying to be an ass. I'm going to get Shamira's pepper spray today."

Hakim snubbed Brian's unrelenting scowl and flicked lint from his shoulder.

Jazmin cracked her neck from side-to-side when Hakim slithered like a snake into the adjacent seat. She carried a new self-assurance in her demeanor. Probably from the time she spent with Hakim. He was already wearing off on her.

Eliana scooted to the edge of her chair for a better look.

"Don't." Brian's grasp strengthened. The muscles in his forearms twitched. "He's staring at us. Got your pepper spray?" Brian pushed his chair backward and arose in a fluid movement.

"It's in my bag."

"In your pocket, please." Brian puffed out his chest and hammered Hakim with steely eyes.

Eliana dug for the canister and slid it into the front pocket of her hoodie.

The room echoed with the beginnings of Professor Ramzi's speech.

"I'm gonna catch Shamira after class." Brian settled into his chair; fists clenched. "Pull out the pepper spray if that prick gets anywhere near you."

The metal bottle gave Eliana a little security when Brian left. He maneuvered through the crowd of students as if he were on a rescue mission. Shamira had the best protection around.

Perhaps they could reconnect through Brian.

Eliana skipped down the last two steps. She stopped short to observe an argument outside the doors. A half-inch crack was enough to witness the confrontation.

Hakim and Jazmin raised their lips, gnashing teeth like dogs as the argument grew louder.

"Why do you think I'm like you?" Jazmin yanked her arm from Hakim's grip.

"We are alike." He sharpened his beady eyes. "We have the same enemy."

"You know nothing about me!" Jazmin fired the retort. "I don't have enemies."

"*I'll* become your enemy if you don't join me." Veins bulged from his forehead. He clamped massive hands around Jazmin's biceps.

Jazmin's head covering jerked as she tried to free herself with what appeared to be self-defense techniques. It didn't work against his strength.

"Let her go!" Eliana ushered through the door and thumbed the red tab on the pepper spray.

Jazmin and Hakim jumped in surprise.

"Get out of here, little Israeli girl." Hakim flashed a snake-like sneer.

Jazmin wrestled in a useless endeavor to break free. Her forearms turned red as circulation slackened. Bright white surrounded the skin where Hakim seized her biceps.

Eliana pulled the bottle from her pocket and raised her arm level with Hakim's face. "This is the hottest pepper spray allowed by law. It burns your eyes and gouges your mucus membranes until you can't breathe."

Hakim raised his face in laughter. "What, are you going to spray her, too?"

A back kick to the shin is all it took for Jazmin to break loose.

Hakim rattled a string of words in Arabic.

"Come on." Eliana incited Jazmin to get behind her with a jerk of the head. "Don't want this stuff on your skin."

Jazmin obeyed. "My backpack."

Eliana compressed the top of the nozzle. It wouldn't take much more pressure to release the stream. "Toss her stuff over here."

"Put the stupid spray up." Hakim threw his hands out like the unfolding events were no big deal. "You don't need it."

Eliana knew better than to believe his charade.

"Your lives are never going to be the same after dealing with me. That is if there's anything left of you." Hakim pitched a hand to the bulge in his jacket.

Eliana sprayed.

Hakim collapsed to his knees. Heaved. Unable to move.

Jazmin's backpack lay next to Hakim's foot. Eliana dared herself to snatch it.

Hakim extended a hand to reach Eliana's ankle.

She punched another spray and jammed her foot in his face.

Foamy saliva sputtered from the corners of his lips.

Jazmin pulled Eliana's hand. "Come on!"

Eliana sprinted through the hall, Jazmin in tow. Their rubber soles chirped on the clean tile.

"We have to go to campus police." Eliana used the sleeve of her hoodie to slide the pepper spray lock in place.

Jazmin declared a lengthy statement of gratitude as they navigated the grounds.

What if the incident was a show or a setup? Did they fake the argument knowing Eliana was still in the lecture hall? Was this a trick?

A church bell version of the National Anthem's beginning notes chimed from Eliana's phone. "That's my friend Brian."

Meet me at the café pronto.

Can u wait? Eliana forced her hands to stop trembling while she tapped the words.

No. She's here. Not sure for how long.

Brian had warned Eliana to go to the police if she used the pepper spray. *What if this is my only chance to talk to Shamira?*

"Jazmin, can you go by yourself? I have to meet someone right now."

Jazmin nodded as she blew a deep gust of air through pursed lips.

"I'm sorry to leave you like this." Eliana typed her number into Jazmin's phone. "Call me later. Tell the police everything. Remember, he threatened us and reached for a gun."

"A gun?"

"You've never noticed the way he walks crooked? There's always a bulge in his jacket."

"No."

"It's a big gun. Or at least I think that's what it is." Eliana recalled Hakim's cockeyed gait. What if he had an impediment? Her assumption would appear judgmental to some. Had she inherited her mother's paranoia? Did she just injure an innocent person? "I could be wrong."

"Do you think I should not go?"

Selfishness willed Eliana to downplay the confrontation. She was the one who used a weapon against Hakim. What if she was right about the gun, though? "Your call."

Church bells rung from the phone.

Almost here?

"Jazmin, I have to go. Call me later."

Had 2 finish something. Be there ASAP.

Hurry

⁂

Eliana slid into the sanctuary of Brian's outstretched arm.

"Does she know I'm here?"

"No, but she's in a good mood. Take the opportunity while you have it."

"Did she get the pepper spray?"

"She wouldn't go with me but accepted when I gave it to her."

"I know someone else who needs one."

"I got a couple extra." Brian pressed his lips together into a slender smile. "Come on, I'll walk you in."

Shamira faced a large window with a view of lush greenery. Eliana stood behind Brian when he approached the table. "I've gotta go, but there's someone else here who wants to talk to you." Brian stepped aside.

Eliana stood helpless in an impossible situation. No one had ever given her such dirty looks.

"Thanks for everything, Brian." Shamira stood to leave.

"Wait. Just hear her out."

"What do you know about us?" Shamira spoke to Brian as if Eliana were not there.

"Enough to say that she's not complete without you."

Shamira's glare strengthened in animosity as her eyes swelled with glossy moisture. "Did you tell him how you ruined my life?"

Brian straightened his back. No wavering on his part. "Your beef with her is not my concern. Call me later, Eliana."

Brian left. Shamira stayed. Eliana held on to hope. "Will you sit down with me?"

"You conspired with your boyfriend to set me up?"

"He's not my boyfriend. I've only known him for three weeks. I had no idea he was going to do that. I just asked him to get you pepper spray because of that Iraqi guy in our class."

Shamira snatched the unopened package from her bag. "He scares me."

"He hates us in the same way the people who killed my parents hated them."

"I know. I've seen him around campus a lot. I feel like he wants to hurt me." Shamira's face tightened. "Yet another thing that wouldn't be happening if you hadn't ruined all our lives. We'd still be back in Israel. Perhaps going to Tel Aviv University."

"America is a safe haven for visitors from the Middle East." Eliana tilted her chin upward. "Besides, I didn't ruin your life. Blame my mother's killer. Or does the responsibility lie on your dad, or mom, or both for that matter?" Eliana stopped before unnecessary words shattered her appeal for absolution. "It hurts bad enough knowing my mother would be alive if I hadn't rushed her."

Shamira squinted at the greenery. "I'm sorry you lost her." Tiny dimples formed on her chin. "I came here to find happiness. When I saw you that first day, I thought my dream came true. Then I found out everything was partially your fault. I got depressed. The exact opposite of what I hoped for. Just stay away if you don't want me to lose my sanity."

Aromatic coffees reminiscent of malted milk balls steadied Eliana's imminent breakdown as she watched Shamira rush to the door. A text from Brian arrived at the perfect time.

How'd it go?

Not good.

Meet me at the truck in 10.

One teardrop broke free, then the rest cascaded like ribbon waterfalls. Eliana convinced herself that Shamira's loss wouldn't be a big deal.

Wrong.

"I didn't do anything to her directly," Eliana stuttered after a sharp recovery breath. "She blames me for her bad childhood after she left Israel."

"There's no way you're to blame for that." Brian skimmed his hands along Eliana's jawline. "Look at me."

Eliana dabbed her lashes, stuck together in wet slivers. Brian's soft, serious expression made her want to release another rush of tears.

"Whatever else you think you did wrong, let it go. You're culpable for nothing."

"You don't know the details." Eliana dipped her head. The patchy concrete resembled the mosaic of emotions in her soul.

"Stop that. Be strong." Brian touched a finger to her chin. "It's not necessary for me to know."

Eliana allowed Brian to nudge her face to the same level as his. He mesmerized her with unwavering, intimate, striking eyes. "Why are you so nice to me?"

"You help me forget the pain. I want to do the same for you."

Eliana's belly tightened as he leaned forward. She had never been so attracted to a guy, but if they were to kiss, now was not the right moment. "How old are you?"

"Just turned twenty-eight." Brian pulled back and slid his hands down Eliana's arms. "Started college late. You?"

"I'll be twenty in December. Maybe a little young for you?"

"Way to make a man feel old." Brian's focus jerked to the left.

"What's wrong?"

"I thought I saw that lowlife." Brian refocused on Eliana.

"Speaking of…" Eliana bit the inside of her cheek. "I have a confession. I had to use the—"

An incoming text from Jazmin interrupted the revelation.

Can you talk?

At dinner. Meet me in the commons?

"That was Jazmin, the Palestinian girl in our class. She's the other one who needs pepper spray." Brian maintained his composure while Eliana explained the incident with Hakim. Whatever he felt remained inside his head.

"Let me know if she didn't report it. I'll do it for her." Brian slipped his hand through the open window of his pickup and pulled out a bag from Bass Pro. "There's another one for you and one for Jazmin."

"Thanks for meeting me. I feel silly for breaking down in front of you."

Brian rested his back on the truck and pulled Eliana into his embrace. "You're beautiful, Eliana, even when your face is distorted and covered in tears."

"I've never had someone tell me that I'm beautiful…except for my mother *all* the time." Eliana leaned into Brian's body as he pressed his lips on her forehead.

"I'm going to check on you later, Beautiful." Brian deviated his focus and cracked his knuckles. "I've got something to do. Have a good dinner and get as many details as possible to make sure this isn't a trick."

"Did you go to the police?" Eliana pushed the tart balsamic vinaigrette salad to the side of the plate. With a steady poker face, Eliana put on a trustful façade.

"No. Too afraid." Jazmin stuffed her mouth full of salad.

Uh-huh! "I don't know how it is where you come from, but don't be afraid of the police. They're here to help us." Steam drifted from the bowl of tomato basil soup in curlicues. "What did Hakim mean when he threatened you?"

"He thinks I have radical Islamic beliefs. My older sister was brainwashed and suffered greatly from her actions. I will never be like her." Jazmin gathered the remaining scraps of lettuce and pushed the salad bowl aside. "I love American food," she said and began to devour her main course. No interest in talking with such a big appetite.

The steam from Eliana's bowl subsided, but the pungent bisque did not hold appeal. "Want my soup?"

"You don't like it?

"I do, but my appetite is ruined for the day."

Jazmin slurped the rusty-red liquid from the bowl. "Now, I'm full." She pushed dishes, cups, and other obstacles out of the way and wiped condensation from the table. "Let's pray together."

Eliana hesitated when Jazmin stretched her hands out. The girl would be praying to someone different than God, whom Eliana addressed in her own prayers.

"Please." Innocence and good-will irradiated from her eyes.

Eliana slid her palms into Jazmin's and bowed her head. Jazmin requested deliverance from evil. Her prayer concluded with a petition for happiness despite sadness. All in the name of Allah.

"Let's get out of here," Eliana said and jerked her hands away. "I have something for you." She explained pepper spray as they walked across campus to the dorms. Jazmin's company was better than being under Shamira's shadow. A striking sunset and pleasant conversation made for the perfect ending of a tumultuous day.

"Can we meet for dinner again tomorrow?"

"I'd love to watch you eat like a horse again." Eliana joined Jazmin in laughter. "I want you to meet Brian, so I'll bring him if you don't mind." Brian's ring tone sounded every time she spoke or thought of him. "That's him. See you tomorrow!"

Jazmin stood in place until Eliana answered the phone and pirouetted to leave. "Brian!"

"Hey, I've only got a minute."

"I have a feeling she's not on Hakim's side. She just wants a friend." Silence followed. He didn't believe Eliana. He's probably right. "Brian?"

"I can't talk," he said in an undertone. "Do me a favor. Go to your room, lock the door, and don't answer to anyone. Keep your spray handy. Tell Jazmin to do the same."

"What's going on?"

"I'll tell you in a bit. Bye, Beautiful."

A crack of lightning burst from the darkening sunset. Eliana hightailed it to her dorm with thoughts of her mother's suspicious nature. She would not carry on that legacy.

BRIAN

"Hey man," Brian said when Jay picked up on the first ring.

"What's up?" The familiar lighter flick accompanied Jay's greeting.

"Look up this license plate for me." Brian pronounced the numbers as Hakim drove away. "I swear this guy was spying on us."

Jay rattled under his breath.

"No worries, man." Brian unloaded a lungful of air. "Trying not to be paranoid."

"No such thing." The keyboard clicked as Jay did his detective work. "I got diddly-squat, bro. Someone bought the car last month on eBay. Fully registered. Everything is valid and up to date. I'm gonna see what I can find on the Dark Web. Gotta be something on him there."

Brian shook off the nerves.

"What's with this *us* business?"

"What?"

"You said he was spying on *us*."

Brian spun and walked in an aimless direction. "I did."

"Well is he a Peeping Tom, or what?"

"Nah, man." Brian choked on his laugh. "We were in a parking lot…"

Jay's bellowing laughter interrupted Brian's account.

"We were standing outside my truck! Hugging."

"Right, and I'm the president of the United States."

"I don't know how she feels about me. Jack-nothing since I'm such a loser." Utter truth having accomplished little in life other than a few meaningless years in the Corps.

"Fool, you'll be married with kids long before I do."

"Why would I bring an innocent human being into this world?"

"Because your wife wants to be a mother, that's why."

"I don't deserve a wife. You know that."

Jay cussed at Brian, half-joking. "Hey, guess what? My old man wants me to get into the family business. Says my detective abilities would be an asset to the agency. I don't know about that."

"CIA? Are you kidding me? Why not?"

"Not sure I'm cut out for it. Maybe I can be one of their secret agents, travel the seven continents, meet a pretty Philippino lady, like dad when he was there."

Not that Jay needed any help attracting ladies. Half white, half Philippino. He inherited his mom's dark features and his dad's blue eyes. He could have anyone he wanted. "Like you need to go overseas to pick up a chick."

"Tssss, whatever. I'll talk to dad about my first assignment—your Iraqi insect."

As they concluded the conversation with more BS'ing, Brian knew he had to trust his gut feeling. The extremists' goal was to bring bloodshed to American soil, and Hakim was one of their tools.

Brian would do anything to stop him. Kill the bastard and go to prison if it came down to it.

SHAMIRA

Twilight blanketed the sky in the dark nook where Shamira liked to escape. The full moon's icy light cast striking spotlights amongst dark shadows in the courtyard. Reflections on nearby trees, still wet from the storm, caused the foliage to resemble a flurry of fireflies.

Shamira closed her laptop and dug into the Chinese take-out bag. She popped open the container flaps, revealing her first and only meal of the day.

No time for breakfast.

Too upset for lunch.

Too groggy for a snack after a two-hour nap.

A divine scent of salty-sweet teriyaki sauce prodded her to dig in. The first bite of gooey noodles and veggies delivered the perfect proportion of nectarous tang. She drove the fork deep into the brown mélange.

Heavy boots echoed from the opposite side of the courtyard. A dark figure in a long coat dipped his head, thumbs tapping his phone. Light illuminated his face.

"You've got to be kidding me," she hissed.

It was Hakim. Eyes now fixated on her. The corners of his mouth raised in a sarcastic scoff.

Shamira attempted to close the flimsy cardboard container, but it slid sideways, and the saucy mess spilled onto her laptop. She jumped at the sound of deep laughter.

Hakim held the phone to his ear. His shoulders bounced. Whether he laughed at Shamira or the person on the phone, she did not know. But he turned his back, distracted.

Shamira stuffed the slimy laptop into her saddlebag and tiptoed to a dark sidewalk. The shadows made her invisible to Hakim. That is unless he carried night vision goggles. No surprise if he did.

"Boo!"

The fright sent her tumbling to the ground, where she wiped out over her bag.

Hakim towered over her. "Scared?"

"What do you want?" Shamira retreated like an abused dog.

"You know what I *don't* want?" Hakim spat the words through clenched teeth. "To be bothered by your presence anymore!"

Shamira's elbows and knees stung. "You won't be! I'm changing schools," she said and bent to look at the scrapes on her legs.

"When? Tomorrow?" Hakim stooped down. His fingers clawed at Shamira's shoulders. "I want you gone toni—"

Hakim groaned.

Someone else grunted.

Still immobilized by fear, Shamira opened her eyes. Brian restrained Hakim from behind and kicked the back of his knees.

Hakim lost control of his legs and fell prostrate on the sidewalk.

Brian rammed his knee into Hakim's back. "Shamira, throw me your pepper spray!" Brian barked the command.

Shamira scrambled to her bag and fished for the tiny canister.

"Hurry!" Brian maintained a remarkable hold on Hakim. "Otherwise, I'll have to knock him out. Or use one of my weapons."

Hakim conceded to the threat with momentary stillness.

Shamira turned the bag upside down. The contents plopped to the ground. "Here!" She tossed the pepper spray to Brian.

In a swift movement, Brian caught the bottle and held it to Hakim's face. "Wanna get sprayed again? Better yet, I have something that will hurt worse." Brian's leather jacket crept up enough to expose a gun tucked into the rear of his jeans.

"No! Please!" Hakim writhed to break free from Brian's unyielding weight. "Let me go."

"Where's your weapon?" Brian patted Hakim down.

"Don't have one."

Brian yanked Hakim's head back. "I'm Marines Special Ops. I know you carry." He pulled a claw-like hand device from Hakim's pocket and threw it aside.

"Okay!" Hakim wheezed as he eyed the pepper spray inches from his face. "I don't always have it on me. It's not even mine. My friend has it at his apartment."

Brian clutched Hakim's shirt and pulled him upright. "Don't bring it back to campus. Or the rifle. Get the hell out of here. And leave the three ladies alone."

Hakim spun and ran into the shadows.

"Good-for-nothing piece of trash." Brian straightened his shirt and adjusted his jacket.

Rocky dirt stuck to Shamira's face. Fine particles grated against her teeth.

"Did you say rifle?"

"Nevermind that. Let me help you up."

The raw abrasions on Shamira's elbows dripped blood.

"Wait." Brian knelt beside her. "You're hurt. I'm calling the police and an ambulance." He reached into his pocket.

"No!"

"He tried to hurt someone else today." Brian gathered Shamira's scattered belongings.

"Who?"

"Jazmin. The Palestinian girl in our class. Eliana was there and used pepper spray. That's why Hakim was so scared when I showed him yours."

Shamira lunged when she saw Brian near her feminine products, but her knees buckled.

"Don't worry," Brian said as he finished. "I have three sisters."

"That doesn't make me feel less embarrassed."

Brian angled the bag over his shoulder. "We have to get this guy on record. I have a feeling he intends to do more than just torture young ladies. Let's at least call the police. We'll use a first aid kit to clean you up."

"I'm tired, hungry, and hurting. No police for me tonight." Shamira's excuse made sense enough for Brian to give in. "Besides, I doubt he'll bother us since we're under your protection."

"Don't rely on human effort to save you. I'm going to pick you up now," Brian said and shifted the bag to his back.

Shamira slammed her eyes shut. She repeated *ouch* countless times in her mind while Brian carried her 150-pound body like a small child. "Eliana is lucky to have you."

"Nah, I'm lucky she tolerates me." Brian bounced to strengthen his grip. "I don't know your circumstances, but I do know something is missing from your lives. That's Israel. Eliana is making friends, but no one except you can give her back a piece of home. Same goes for you."

Brian spoke undeniable truth. She and Eliana needed each other.

"I can't face her yet."

ELIANA

Brian breathed into the phone like he had just completed a half marathon. When he requested Eliana to stay with him for the night, she immediately said no.

"*I'll tell you why later. No funny business*," he had said between gasps. Eliana followed him into the small apartment. An awkward stillness followed as she tried to adjust to his panic mode.

Brian switched on two lamps, which revealed cozy quarters. A slender, gray cat jumped to the top of a camouflage Chester sofa to greet Brian. "Don't mind all the military décor. My gung-ho mom did it."

Olive green furniture, United States flag pillows, and Marine Corps throws completed the interior design of a proud Marine mom. "I think it's sweet."

The feline stretched upward in a hug-like motion when Brian approached. "Meet Sterling. One of my best friends." Brian nuzzled his face into Sterling's downy neck.

Sterling head-butted his owner with a series of vocal greetings. "Rrrrowe?" Throaty purrs coalesced with sweet trills to form a cat language Brian clearly understood.

"Mom calls him my therapy cat. The concept is asinine and a joke, to say the least. Still, he's my little buddy."

The notion did not sound asinine to Eliana, nor would it to any other cat lover for that matter. "You got him specifically for PTSD?"

"Mom did. As a surprise. I was in a really bad place." Brian held his friend in one arm. Sterling hung limp, happy in his master's embrace. "Nothing else helped me, including a service dog. Too high maintenance."

Eliana wanted to scoop up the furry fluffball. "It doesn't sound like a joke to me. Your mom is right. Sterling is a therapy cat."

"Now I have you there for me, too." Brian plopped onto a rugged recliner, Sterling in his lap within seconds. "Take a seat wherever you'd like."

"What is it I do that helps you so much?" Eliana bounced onto an oversized canvas couch and pulled her knees into her torso.

"You listen. I wish I could tell you more, but I'd sound like a freak if I tried to explain what's in my head. I don't want to scare you away."

Did Brian truly feel that way about himself? Or was he trying to be funny? Or both? "I'm not scared. I have my pepper spray with me."

"Good one," Brian said with a puffy laugh.

"Thanks." Eliana welcomed Sterling into her lap when he jumped onto the couch. Brian was obviously feeling better.

Eliana massaged Sterling's downy jawline. His fur hugged her fingers like gloves with fleece lining.

They had something important in common. Two compassionate beings who contributed to Brian's mental stability. Did Eliana really want that burden? She couldn't have anything interfere with her plans. If she and Brian were to become closer, it might be detrimental to him when she left. "Are you going to tell me what happened tonight?"

"It's Shamira."

As Brian explained, a strange sense of anger seared her to the bone. To know that someone treated Shamira that way and that she wouldn't be in that position if it weren't for—

"Stop that." Brian raised his voice to pull Eliana out of her self-reproach. "Don't blame yourself."

"How do you know I'm blaming myself?"

"Because I do it all the time. My best friend died because I fell short on the field."

Sterling left Eliana's lap and rubbed the length his body against Brian's leg, back hunched, tail shaped in a question mark. "Purrrrowe?"

"You're to blame for his death?"

"No." Brian bent over his knees and plunged his forehead into his palms. "Wow…I've never admitted that. I always took the onus, because I didn't die. I should have. I didn't give my life for my country. Neil did. He's the true hero."

Brian held a fist over his mouth when his chin began to quiver. Sterling sprung into his owner's lap and crept into the nook under Brian's chest. "When you go in, you either accomplish the mission, which includes rescuing injured Marines, or you die trying. I tried, but I failed, so I didn't try hard enough. I have to figure out a way to stop blaming myself."

Sterling filled the room with white noise.

Eliana bounded from the couch and swung behind Brian in the recliner. Her hands were like a small child's on his muscular back.

The tension eased. Brian's torso expanded and contracted with each pull and release from his lungs.

"Better?" Eliana's hands fatigued against the solid muscles.

"More than you know." Brian bounced sideways in the chair and held his arms out. "Come here."

"Uhh..." She'd never sat in a man's lap before. No use in giving him the wrong idea. Becoming intimate would make leaving him that much harder. "I'm kind of uncomfortable. I'll go back to the couch."

"Mind if I join you so we're not sitting across the room?" Brian lifted his shoulders and jutted his bottom lip. "No funny business."

Eliana inched onto the cushions and crossed her legs. "Sure. It is your couch, after all." *Just don't get too close.*

"Mind if I ask about your parents?"

"Their names were Seth and Rina Gibbons. My father died young. My mother refused to tell me anything except '*bad people took him away from us.*'" Eliana used her fingers to make quotation marks.

"Do you remember him?"

"Mama was pregnant with me when he died. She kept a picture of him hidden in a drawer." Eliana clicked her fingernails together, a nervous habit she'd developed after moving to the U.S. "She didn't know I looked at it regularly."

"Why did she hide it? Seems like she'd give you the pleasure of knowing what he looked like."

"It doesn't make sense. I was only ten when she died." *To the stars in the sky and beyond...I love you too, mama.*

"What about her?" Brian placed warm hands on Eliana's knees. Their ruggedness and scars paralleled her sorrow.

"A suicide bomber killed her in 2009." It was the first time to divulge her mother's fate since the one and only conversation with her grandparents. "December will be ten years."

Brian's nostrils flared. Sterling rubbed a cheek on his leg. "There's not a word I can say to make you feel better."

The only way Eliana would feel better was to see her mother again. An impossibility.

"Hey, do you have any plans next Saturday?"

"Not that I can think of."

"I uh..." The skin under Brian's five o'clock shadow reddened. "I'm a man of my word and I'm sort of in a predicament. I could use your help."

"With?"

"There's a family wedding. My sisters told me it would be the first Saturday of October months ago. I forgot until Tricia sent a text earlier."

"How many do you have?"

"Three. They're all older than me. I promised Tricia I'd bring a date. I was hoping you'd go with me."

Eliana pulled her fingers into her palms and made tight fists. Another habit she'd developed when she questioned her self-worth. She only recognized it when her fingernails dug into her skin. Like now. "Whose wedding?"

"Some distant cousin. I have a huge family. I don't even know everyone's name. There'll be tons of people there."

How could Eliana agree to meet Brian's family? There would be no leading him on. "I don't do well at social gatherings. I'd probably be boring."

"You wouldn't be boring to me. I promise."

"I don't want your sisters to get the wrong impression." *Let him down slowly, Eliana.* "I mean, you know, so they don't think we're in a serious relationship."

Brian leaned back when Sterling hopped into his lap. "I'll make it clear to them that I'm bringing a friend. If you want to come, that is."

What would it hurt to go to a wedding with Brian? If it would bring him some happiness, Eliana was happy to oblige. He deserved it.

Eliana sat at a round table surrounded by Brian's sisters who gushed about the significance of her presence.

"He's *never* brought a girl around the family," Emily had whispered from the seat behind Eliana after the groom kissed his bride.

"I don't think he's dated since he came back," Celeste divulged in the bathroom as they washed their hands together. "It's been three years!"

Tricia spoke to Eliana in private while the others danced. "He's closest to me. They didn't know about you before tonight." She pointed to her sisters, who jumped with Brian to the beat of a funny rap song from 1989. "A few weeks ago, we talked on the phone. I asked him why he sounded so happy. That's when he told me about you. Thanks for helping him. He's a great guy and deserves someone special after all he's been through."

Brian's sisters already had the wrong idea.

All three flashed perfect teeth in unison when they watched Eliana and Brian in an intimate slow dance. It had started off awkward with a considerable gap between their bodies. Brian's warmth and the ambient lights loosened her nerves. She found herself leaning on his chest. Her insides tickled when he pulled away, lidded eyes affixed to hers. "Thanks for the dance, Beautiful." Eliana retreated when he dipped his head, sure he was aiming for a kiss.

"You handled them well," Brian teased as they waved goodbye from the truck.

His sisters stood side-by-side and watched them leave the parking lot.

"By what I understand, I'm the only one who's had to go through that."

"True-enough." The truck's blinker ticked during a brief pause. "What would you say to a real date?"

The combined odor of musty old seats and dashboard cleaner reminded Eliana of Brian's not too distant hardships. Would he be like this once the newness wore off? The pursuit to regain a relationship with Shamira was hard enough. Did she really want to take on a relationship that might culminate in more disappointment?

But Brian deserved a woman's regard with all he'd been through. After three years, he decided to open up his heart, and he chose her.

Flattering. Scary.

Not only that, but he had also made it back, unlike many service members who fought in the Middle East. Here he was, flesh and blood, right in front of her. Alive. Not another statistic, or a photo on the news, or another sad post on social media memorializing a fallen military hero.

Not in a grave.

How on Earth could she say no?

PART III

Revenge

ELIANA

December 2nd
Eliana's 20th Birthday

"So begins the last month of the semester! Only two weeks left." Professor Ramzi clapped his hands as if he were happier than the students. "Now, I have the privilege to give you the subject of your final."

"I can't wait to be done with this class." Eliana intertwined her fingers through Brian's. They'd officially been dating over a month. He was the best thing that happened to her in a decade. On their first date, she revealed new plans to spend the summer in Israel. He offered to join her.

Irrefutably, the Middle East was not the best travel destination. Tensions were back on the rise between Israel and Palestine. Not to mention everything going on in neighboring countries. But she'd have Brian's companionship and protection. The eagerness to leave grew stronger than ever.

Brian pulled her hand into his chest and kissed her knuckles. "I'll miss this room in a way."

Bad memories from the first three weeks clouded Eliana's feelings. Were it not for the class and all the drama that came with it, Brian would be another face on campus. Tonight, at her birthday dinner, she would introduce him as a friend to her grandparents. Nannie and Pops would know there was more to it than that. With Brian by her side, it would be easier to break the news about the trip.

Jazmin had accepted American culture one hundred percent. "I love this new way of life," Jazmin had said after Thanksgiving dinner in Mississippi. "It's so far from war. I have the blessings of new friends and family. Best of all, there's so much freedom in this country."

Shamira revealed an inclination to reconnect through subtle manifestations. Eye contact and closed-mouth smiles became a regular occurrence. Eliana exaggerated her return gestures, so Shamira knew she remained open to further developments. The most recent came in the form of a wave at the beginning of class.

The one thing that kept Eliana on edge was Hakim. He had left everyone alone. There were no more dirty looks and no bulge from his trench coat. But furtive glances and quiet composure marked inner workings of unfinished business. After all, he had promised that their lives would never be the same.

"There will not be a test." Professor Ramzi interrupted her thoughts. "You're going to write a nice, long essay that'll require some investigating."

A series of laments ricocheted throughout the classroom. Students shifted in their chairs. Sighs, huffs, and mumbled utterances created a somewhat unnerving mood.

"Hear me out. I think you'll find this intriguing. As the conflict between Israel and Palestine has progressed over the decades, one of Palestine's most powerful weapons has been suicide bombers." Professor Ramzi paused in an overt expression of ridicule. "They're referred to as martyrs."

Chills shocked Eliana's body.

"Your essay will focus on the rationales behind these attacks," Professor Ramzi directed. "You are also to describe the effects on Israeli citizens and the government's preventive measures over the past decade."

Students in the classroom hurled insults.

"Terrorists are sick," a female student yelled.

"No, they're not sick, just brainwashed religious fanatics," hollered a male student from the back.

"When they get caught, they should be shot!"

"Their bodies should rot on public display!"

Offenses multiplied despite Professor Ramzi's demand for everyone to hush. They needed a reality check. Eliana made her way down the steps. Shouts abated to murmurs when she approached the podium. "I have something to say."

Professor Ramzi tilted forward in a brief bow. "Take the stand."

Eliana sucked in a breath of dense air. "December is always a difficult month for me. It's about to be the tenth anniversary of my mother's passing." The lecture hall acoustics amplified Eliana's voice. She had everyone's concentration. "I moved to the United States from Israel to live with my paternal grandparents a few days after she died. Shamira and Brian are the only ones in this room who know what I'm going to tell you."

Shamira's eyes glazed over as Eliana continued.

"My mother and I went shopping at an outdoor market in Jerusalem the day before Hanukkah began. We were supposed to celebrate with Shamira and her family." Eliana scanned the rows to make eye contact with each student.

Brian nodded with a smile of reassurance.

Hakim sneered with a crooked upper lip.

Jazmin paled.

"When we left to catch the bus home, one of my bags split. The groceries fell to the ground near the exit." Eliana did a double take at Jazmin, who had become unrecognizable. "I was walking behind my mom, so she didn't see what had happened."

Eliana's voice broke.

Shamira contained sobs by covering her mouth.

"That's when a female suicide bomber detonated a bomb on the bus. My mother died."

Gasps, whispers, and mumbled utterances ping-ponged throughout the room.

The shock was worse than Eliana imagined. Some male students hissed expletives. Female students dabbed their eyes with tissues.

Professor Ramzi placed a hand on Eliana's back in support.

"The terrorist harmed innocent people, but it doesn't mean she was a bad person. There was something wrong with her. I don't know what. I'm thankful to have lived through it for many reasons, one of which is to share this with you today."

Eliana directed her attention to Jazmin, who leaned over the table, shoulders heaving. Her sister had been involved with a militant group. Maybe this was bringing back bad memories from when she died.

"The suicide bomber was never identified, so I don't know her story. Just as someone said, they are sick. Something has gone wrong in their lives. It's usually about revenge. This is no excuse for their actions, but keep it in mind."

Students clapped while Eliana ascended the steps. Brian stood and welcomed her into his arms.

Jazmin swiveled in her chair. Her shoulders slumped heavily.

"Hey, Jaz!" Eliana reached past Brian. "You okay?"

A trumpet-like clap supercharged the room with thunderous sound waves.

Hakim bounded down the steps on the opposite aisle and hijacked the podium. "My turn."

Students rounded their heads, eyes wide to gauge Eliana's reaction.

"My uncle," Hakim hissed through clenched teeth, "was one of the people you call sick."

Eliana pitched a hand into her backpack. The pepper spray had wormed its way to the bottomless pit.

Brian grasped Eliana's wrist. Face tight with calm composure. "Not yet."

Hakim seethed; his glare fixed upon Jazmin. "He submitted to the will of Allah when he detonated a car bomb in Baghdad for the Islamic State. Now my uncle sits at Allah's table in Paradise for his noble act of martyrdom."

Professor Ramzi zipped to Hakim's side. "This is inappropriate. Please go back to your seat."

Hakim whipped an arm around Professor Ramzi's neck. "Shut up!"

A quantity of male students punched to their feet.

"No one move!" Hakim pulled a bulky handgun from his trench coat.

Professor Ramzi squeezed his eyes when the muzzle met his forehead.

Bile crept upward into Eliana's esophagus. Was this turn of events her fault? Would Professor Ramzi have a gun to his brain if she hadn't told her mother's story?

Or did Hakim already have shady plans?

Yes. That's it. He was in the Jewish Studies class to carry out an attack against Israeli students. For that matter, Americans too. There was no other explanation!

"I applaud the Shahida who took your mother's life." Hakim's upper jaw flinched in a fleeting smile.

Brian slid an arm in front of Eliana's torso. Her chair rolled backward when he pushed a hand on the armrest.

The back of Brian's buzzed head obstructed Eliana's view of Hakim.

Jazmin's former state of ashen despondence had been replaced by panic. Her knuckles marbled white against deep olive skin as she clenched the table.

Brian inched backward. "On the floor. Slowly."

Eliana slid from her seat, eye-level with a sea of legs. The odor of dirty shoes compounded her nausea as multiple students followed suit.

"Take this," Brian whispered and pulled a folding knife from his belt. She saw him use the military-issued switchblade to open a package the previous week.

The sharp, buffed steel could slide through steak like butter. Eliana prayed she would not be forced to use it.

With perfect posture, Brain stood up. Every day, without fail, he carried a pistol tucked into his rear waistline, hidden by his leather jacket. She felt the bulky weapon each time they hugged. "Let him go. It's not worth—"

"Sit down." Hakim's barbaric tone trampled all other sounds. "I'm not done."

"I'm coming down." Brian moved sideways to leave the row and held his hands up.

"Stop!"

A click from the podium.

Hakim had cocked the gun.

Brian's boot hung frozen over the edge of the step. "Don't. It's not worth it."

Eliana raised her eyes above the table.

Veins in Professor Ramzi's face bulged.

Hakim spotted Jazmin. "Get your spray."

Jazmin slid a hand into the front pocket of her bag.

"Today, you change your mind." He pointed to Eliana with his head. "Seize her."

Jazmin stood frozen.

"It's your duty as a daughter of Allah." Hakim's voice softened in beguilement.

"I don't want to," Jazmin mumbled.

"You traitor! I'll kill you first if you don't do as I say."

Still in a squat under the table, Eliana slid the knife into a roomy pocket in her sweater.

Jazmin clamped Eliana's wrists behind her back. It would be simple to bust away from the weak grip.

"Let her go." Brian inched back into the row. "This isn't you, Jazmin. Don't listen to him."

Eliana read Brian's eyes. He wanted her to use the knife.

Professor Ramzi grunted.

Hakim's finger twitched on the trigger.

"You." Hakim waved the gun at Shamira. "Stand up."

SHAMIRA

The pepper spray's three-inch canister fit perfectly in her palm. Shamira was going to use it on Hakim. No matter what.

"Do you want to see your teacher's blood on the floor?" Hakim lifted the muzzle from Professor Ramzi's temple. A circular indentation formed on his skin from the pressure.

Shamira pocketed the sweaty bottle, tossed her hair over her shoulder, and stood upright.

"Brian, seize her," Hakim ordered.

Shamira willingly allowed Brian to wrench her arms behind her back. She turned her face away from Hakim and rubbed a fake itch on her shoulder with her jaw. "I have the spray in my pocket."

Brian double-squeezed her arm.

"Bring her here."

Shamira yielded to Brian's lead down the steps.

Perspiration stained Hakim's shirt under the arm that detained the professor.

Spasms from Professor Ramzi's torso synchronized with guttural wheezes.

Brian rotated his body. A barrier between Shamira and Hakim. "Come on, man. You're strangling him. Take me."

Shamira spun her face away to miss the punch. The slug to Brian's cheek sounded like raw steak slapped onto a granite counter.

"Stop interrupting me!" Hakim slung Professor Ramzi to his side and hooked his head like a football receiver running for a touchdown. "Now, you." He prompted Jazmin with a wave of the gun. "Bring her down."

Brian released his hand. Shamira grabbed the spray and repositioned her arm behind her back.

Hakim ordered Jazmin to stand on his other side with Eliana.

Good, she deserves it. Shamira gave herself a mental slap across the face.

What was she thinking? How could she take pleasure in seeing Eliana like that? In a peculiar sense, it gave her satisfaction. It was Eliana's turn to endure a little suffering.

"The rest of you," Hakim addressed the classroom, "I pledge my allegiance to the Islamic State. Watch me as I win a victory for Allah!"

ELIANA

Eliana snapped free from Jazmin's pliant handgrip. Her ears rang when a thunderous shot echoed across the walls. Professor Ramzi lay like a fetus on the floor. No blood in sight.

Brian shoved Hakim backward and rammed his gun-wielding arm against the dull whiteboard.

Hakim fired in the air as he strained to break loose.

Eliana searched for the object hit by the first bullet. Droplets of blood dotted the floor near Brian's boots. A dark crimson circle on his jeans mushroomed.

It was time to emulate her mother's bravery when she fought the suicide bomber.

The knife's textured grip slid against her sweaty palm. She punched the button, just as Brian showed her, and charged.

A hand grabbed her forearm.

"Eliana, no!" Jazmin pried Eliana's fingers open with surprising force. "Let me have it."

Another shot ricocheted. Fiberboard fragments from the ceiling tiles scattered across the floor.

Brian collapsed. Blood saturated his jeans.

Eliana scrambled to Brian's side, whisked her scarf around his leg, and tied a knot before Hakim yanked her up by the hair.

Jazmin crouched like a tiger with the knife ready.

"Good." Hakim snorted a throaty laugh. "Take her out."

Shamira aimed to activate her pepper spray, but Hakim pounded her head with his boot. She hit the floor, out cold.

Jazmin stood upright and raised a foot less than two inches. Her toes brushed the ground. What in Heaven's name?

"You've been through training." Hakim strengthened his hold on Eliana's hair.

Training? The stinging pull numbed Eliana's scalp.

Static concentration shrouded Jazmin's emotionless face. She pinched the smooth blade between her thumb and forefinger. Arm raised in a V-shape perpendicular to the floor, she locked her wrist into place.

The blade suspended beside her ear. Just a twitch of the wrist, and she'd nick her skin.

Brian stirred. "Jazmin," he said and rotated onto his uninjured side. "Don't listen to him."

Jazmin flittered her eyes between Brian and Hakim.

"Eliana!" Jazmin's face hardened.

Brian grabbed his pistol and targeted Jazmin's leg.

But Hakim crushed his arm with his boot.

Jazmin captured Eliana's attention. "Duck!"

Eliana zigzagged to free herself from Hakim when the knife whirled just above her head.

The blade struck Hakim in the eye.

Jazmin sprinted. Slammed him prostrate.

Eliana scrambled to Hakim's gun, still in his hand. Finger on the trigger. Pointed in her direction.

Pop!

A flaming sledgehammer bludgeoned Eliana's shoulder.

Hakim retargeted his aim at Jazmin.

Brian rose to his elbows. "Out of the way!" A fiery flash emitted from the barrel of his pistol.

Hakim's hand ripped in two.

Three football players bulldozed Hakim's thrashing body.

The bullet wound in Eliana's shoulder felt like electric jolts. Cold tiles seemed to raise up, meeting her in the air. She heard her skull crack but felt no pain. Sight and sound faded into nothingness.

SHAMIRA

Shamira's head throbbed.

Students rushed to Eliana and Brian, both unconscious.

Men stripped their shirts and pressed them to Eliana's shoulder.

Eliana. Her friend. The one upon whom she had wished suffering. But not like this.

The Pakistani student who had asked her to the movies three times, always resulting in rejection, held his belt tight around Brian's leg.

Others hovered over Professor Ramzi, who rubbed his bruised throat.

A blur of questions and worried faces deterred Shamira from breaking free of the confusion.

"Are you hurt?"

"Did you get shot?"

"She has a big goose egg."

Students gathered around Jazmin with the same questions. She ignored them and sat cross-legged with her face buried in her hands.

The rest of the class stood in the aisles. Some wept. Some uttered frantic words on the phone.

Police burst through the door with weapons raised.

"Over here!" The football players signaled to the officers. "We have the shooter."

Paramedics wheeled stretchers to Brian and Eliana.

Three crimson-stained shirts lay by Eliana's side. Blood continued to pump from the wound.

"We need an EMT here," an officer yelled as he gripped Hakim's wrist. "His hand is nearly severed."

A stocky, dark-bearded white guy stood with Hakim's trench coat in hand, backpack over his shoulder. He watched the paramedic secure a tourniquet on Hakim's arm.

Brian tried to push off the floor. His eyes slammed shut.

"Don't try to move, sir," the paramedic ordered.

Shamira refocused on Eliana. "Is she going to be okay?"

No answer. It would take a blood transfusion to keep Eliana alive.

ELIANA

Stop.

A bed jiggled Eliana's body like a ride simulator.

The ceiling tiles coasted above her.

"Is she going to be okay?" A familiar voice fired countless questions.

A man returned vague answers.

Sunlight blazed through the cracks of Eliana's eyes.

Now the sky and trees moved above the jerky bed.

"Her eyes are opening!"

Burning needles gouged Eliana's shoulder when she turned to the voice. Shamira jogged by her side.

The bed moved.

Not the ceiling. Not the sky. Not the trees.

Incessant thumps roared from above.

Diesel engines rumbled.

Eliana stretched her neck for a better view of the havoc. Sharp pain shot down her arm.

With no mental capacity to count, Eliana guessed there were two dozen emergency vehicles. A blue helicopter circled the sky. Crowds huddled behind yellow tape. Heads turned all together when Eliana came into sight. Some held phones up to take pictures and videos.

A sudden stop allowed Eliana to ask a question. If she could make her voice work.

"Can I tell her?" Shamira asked the man who made the stupid bed jerk more than necessary.

"Inside."

The bed popped up. Eliana glided backward into a tiny room. Not a room. An ambulance.

Shamira scooted in. "Do you remember anything?"

"No." The man put a mask on Eliana's face. A rush of air cooled her windpipe.

"You've been shot in the shoulder," Shamira said with an airy huff.

Fuzzy images surfaced when Eliana closed her eyes. Mainly a floor. Shoes. Brian's arm pinned by a boot. Swipes of red paint on the tiles by his leg. Or was it blood? "Brian?"

"He's okay." Shamira swayed when the ambulance took off.

Memories of the shooting dappled Eliana's mind. Inexplicable shock set everything into slow motion. The strike of the bullet felt like someone took a sledgehammer to her shoulder. What struck Eliana was Hakim's ability to aim and shoot with only one eye, while the other oozed. It was pure lunacy that drove him to continue. She had wanted to go to Brian, but her body went numb. Then she blacked out.

"How about you?" Eliana tasted metallic blood on her lips.

Shamira winced when she touched the back of her head. "Don't try to talk anymore. They said you lost a lot of blood."

A peculiar smile replaced Shamira's rigid worry. Eliana sensed satisfaction. For what reason? A few dips of the eyelids drowned the thought.

"I'm sorry I waited so long." Shamira swept a tear from the corner of her eye.

"For?"

"To come back to you. I was going to wish you happy birthday after class."

Eliana withheld a happy sob. She was ready for things to be like they were as children. "Remember when we pricked our fingers?"

"After your birthday party."

"Blood sisters forever," Eliana professed in sync with Shamira.

Laughter swung a hammer at Eliana's shoulder.

"That never changed for me." Shamira brought their index fingers together.

"Me neither."

Eliana finally had Shamira back. But there was something odd in her tone that did not sit right.

How would things be with Brian and Jazmin now? Would they take a back seat? Neither deserved it, but Eliana had longed for a relationship with Shamira above all else. The force on her eyes precluded further thought as the ambulance rocked her to sleep.

The beeping woke her again. An unwelcome distraction. Eliana still couldn't open her eyes. Not conscious enough.

Her face didn't hurt anymore.

Strange since the bombing happened two days ago. Or was it longer?

The wounds tormented Eliana the first time she woke up. She had tried to tear off the IV, but they came and gave her a shot.

Is that why her shoulder hurt now? No, that didn't make sense at all.

"Eliana?" The doctor was trying to wake her again. He was so nice, calling her beautiful. Surely, he knew she was a child. She didn't feel like one.

And why were they all speaking English? Where was mama?

Oh right, the bomb on the bus.

"If you hear me, try to squeeze my hand," the doctor said.

She did as instructed.

"That's my girl."

"The sedative is wearing off," a woman said, "but she might fight it. Patients often want to keep sleeping."

Yes, sleep.

Her body ached. She had been in bed for too long.

Eliana forced her eyes open.

"Hey, sleepyhead." Brian stood tall; crutches tucked under his shoulders. "You've been giving the nurses a run for their money."

The warm lights in the hospital room differed significantly from the bright fluorescent bulbs in Jerusalem's hospital. The heartsickness in those waking moments ten years ago was bad, but nothing proportionate to the gunshot wound. "I thought I was…I dreamt it was…How many days have I been here?"

"Two days. You had a few looney spells, so you've been sedated." Brian's crutches rattled against the bed when he sat sideways on the mattress. The skin around his eyes tensed.

"How bad does it hurt?"

Brian shrugged with a dismissive *pfft*. "Tolerable compared to bone-shattering bullets from a machine gun. Just took ibuprofen, so I'll be fine in a few minutes. Wanna try to sit up?"

A simple nod of the head produced stinging spasms from Eliana's neck to her hand.

Sunset-yellow gleams reflected against ice pellets in a cup. Brian hunched over and gathered a spoonful. "Here ya go."

The freezing crystals soothed Eliana's parched mouth. Her stomach growled when the scent of warm food wafted from the doorway. "What time is it?"

"Oh seven hundred."

A cafeteria cart rumbled into the room. "Breakfast?" The nurse tall enough for professional basketball towered over the cart.

Brian gave a thumbs up. "Let's give it a try."

"I'm famished." Eliana lifted the lid and scooped a heap of warm eggs. The dark blue patch surrounding Brian's swollen cheekbone reminded her of the first assault. "That looked and sounded like it hurt."

"Not the first instance I've been slugged."

Eliana visualized the gruesome scene following Hakim's declaration of service to Allah and the IS. She gagged at the sight and smell of biscuits, lumpy gravy, and rubbery bacon.

"That was a bad idea." Brian pushed the table away.

"I want to keep the coffee." Per Eliana's instructions, Brian poured three packets of sugar and enough powered cream to mimic the appearance of egg nog. "How's everyone doing?"

"Good for the most part. Shamira has superficial wounds. The prof's throat is all jacked up. He's wearing a neck brace and can hardly talk. Jazmin managed to walk away with no injuries."

Eliana sipped the coffee, too sweet, but the caffeine took effect. "And, Hakim?"

Brian balled his fists, unintentionally cracking his knuckles. "The SOB will be lucky if he doesn't lose his hand. I failed to protect you from that monster. That's all I wanted." Subtle contractions pulsed from his torso.

"You did protect me." Eliana reached for Brian, ignoring the aches. "I'm alive, right? You fought him. The entire class was spared, thanks to your quick thinking. How many would have been killed or injured if you hadn't stopped him from spraying the room with bullets?"

Brian pulled back. "For a few minutes, I thought I was going to lose you. Blood gushed from your shoulder. Your eyes went blank, just like Neil's."

Eliana began to understand Brian's occasional trancelike moments. Her traumatic ordeal paled in comparison to his.

"That bastard's face is all over the news. I don't get why the media glorifies criminals. It's exactly what they want."

His statement rang true for many. Rather than broadcasting the faces and names of victims more than just a few times, TV producers forced viewers to memorize the name and face of the attacker. In recent years, Eliana had stopped watching the news altogether.

"Everyone wanted to come see you today since they stopped the sedatives." Brian stood without crutches and rubbed his leg. "Your grandparents asked them to wait."

Eliana pushed the remote to elevate the bed further. "Why aren't they here? I want to see Nannie."

"There's someone else you should see first." Brian rubbed a hand along his buzz cut. She'd come to recognize that it was a relaxation massage of sorts. "Your grandparents asked me to prepare you."

The weight of his words confused Eliana. Who warranted priority over her grandparents? "Where are they?"

"At a hotel. They're a little shaken." Brian grabbed his phone from the table and limped around the room at a slow pace. Opaque blue light flooded his face, fingers in action on the screen.

“How can you walk?”

“High tolerance for pain, stubbornness, and nerves.” Brian’s phone chimed a new notification sound. “I’m gonna go get her. Be back in a few.”

Her?

PART IV

The Lie

ELIANA

Eliana pushed buttons until all lights illuminated the room. No one meant more to her than Nannie.

Who was so special that they deserved a surprise introduction?

The door clicked. Brian backed in with wheelchair handles in his grip. The back of a woman's head came into view.

Brian bent over and whispered in the woman's ear.

She nodded.

In a single movement, Brian rotated the wheelchair 180 degrees as if he'd handled one a million times.

Eliana's first visualization, a double amputee. Brown coloration marbled thin hands and arms. Definitely burn scars.

When she looked closer, Eliana thought she was dead. She had bled out on the lecture hall floor in front of everyone. Died and gone to Heaven.

Eliana pinched her arm. Hard. Harder. "Ouch!"

In the wheelchair, elbows resting on spongy armrests, her mother sat motionless.

Either Eliana hallucinated or her mother had risen from the dead.

"Mama?" Eliana choked on a deep sob.

"Yes, my Love." Slightly aged with a few scars and a droopy left brow, her mother's face marked the precursors to a hard cry.

Brian wheeled the chair as close as possible to the bed and affixed the locks.

"How are you here?" Eliana probed Brian for an explanation, but the truth had to come from her mother.

"I came as soon as I heard."

"But I th–ya–you–" Eliana huffed for air. "You di– you died."

Her mother's eyes ping-ponged in all directions of the room. "I did, in a way."

"Wait. What?"

Brian circled the bed and caressed Eliana's back in the same gentle way she did to him during moments of agitation. "Your mom is alive. Isn't that great?"

Eliana didn't know whether to cry for joy or unleash a bucketload of verbal venom.

"I know this is a shock. I didn't want you to be burdened by me." Eliana's mother pointed to her legs. "And I didn't want you to grow up around the violence in Israel."

Eliana tuned out her mother's words as she continued to explain. The individual in the wheelchair was merely a weak replica of Rina Gibbons.

"…I thought it would be easier if—"

"Wait. You faked your death?"

"No, my Love. I asked others to tell you I had passed."

"I don't get your meaning." Eliana's thoughts scrambled to understand. A bitter tang stung her throat. "My grandparents knew you were alive and didn't tell me? They played a part in your lie?"

"According to my wishes. And for your best interest." She set her jaw tight with an authoritative notion.

Eliana felt her toes curl under the covers. She wanted to run from the room, to get away from the confusion, to be alone. But she was stuck. Hooked up to machines, in pain. "How could you do this to me?"

"Please, believe me, my little Eliana, I've suffered every second of every day. Life would not have been the same for you."

"You have suffered? What about me?" Eliana grabbed the bed remote and squeezed the flexible plastic cord. "For years, I've gone home and cried my eyes out after seeing kids with their parents, girls laughing with their moms, complete happy families celebrating the holidays."

Defeated, Rina bowed her head. "There's nothing I can say to make this—"

"You're right, there's nothing you can say!" Eliana threw the remote on the mattress. "I can't believe this. Brian, please tell me I'm still asleep. Or, better, take her out of here."

A nurse rushed in to check Eliana's vitals. Apparently, she set off the alarms.

Brian backed the wheelchair out of the way and leaned down. He whispered near Rina's ear.

Brian should be consoling his girlfriend, not her blubbering mother.

"I'd like to give her something to relax." The nurse flashed a concerned smile and injected medicine into the IV. "Can you come back in a few hours?"

"I've been away from my daughter for ten years." Rina raised her chin and swiped scattered tears. Burn scars mottled her neck. "I'm not leaving her now. Even when visiting hours are…"

Eliana didn't want to hear her mother's proclamation, making herself out to be a good parent. Where was the logic in her mother's plan?

How could Nannie and Pops be in on it too?
It wasn't fair.
The past decade turned out to be one big lie.

RINA

Eliana's hand was as smooth as the day Rina held it at the market. She thought she'd never feel her daughter's touch again. For Eliana's safety, Rina abandoned her. Spared her from the same fate as her parents—victims of war. Eliana had to be free from the violence.

Yet here she was, in a hospital, with a gunshot wound. Why? A terrorist's hatred. The same thing that killed her husband. The same thing that tore her body apart.

Rina stared at the floor where her feet should have been. Perhaps she deserved not to be whole. If only she could turn back time, so many things would be different. Seth would be alive, and they'd all be together in America as a complete family.

"Is there anything I can do for you, Mrs. Gibbons?"

Brian rested sideways on the bed, still holding Eliana's hand long after she'd gone out. How did her daughter get so lucky at such an early age? Yet, luck had nothing to do with it. "My reunion with Eliana would not be the same without you. I can't ask for more than what you've already done."

"My mom and sisters are begging to pick me up. If you don't mind, I'll go for a bit."

"Go to them. Keep in touch."

"Yes, ma'am." Brian carried his squeaky crutches in one arm. "Text me if you need anything."

She needed her daughter's trust. No one could help her gain that.

ELIANA

She crunched the flaky ice pellets between her teeth. Rina Gibbons had offered to spoon-feed the daughter she deserted a decade ago. Eliana refused. She'd gone this long without her mother's help.

"You have every right to be angry." Rina Gibbons glanced at the bathroom and slowly sipped water from a polystyrene foam cup. "I hadn't planned on coming into your life again."

"Why?" Eliana crunched the ice with vigor.

"The world dishes out enough heartache as it is."

"What's worse than losing a parent, much less having both of them dead?" Eliana pushed away a tray of cold, gooey mac-n-cheese.

"My greatest wish was for you to live in America even before you were born. What I did was the only way for you to have a good life." Rina pressed a hand to her breastbone. "Please understand, you would have been stuck caring for me all these years.

Eliana watched as her mother slouched in the wheelchair and massaged the tips of her legs. "Do they hurt?"

"I get ghost pains. Sometimes it feels as if they're still there, burning, on fire." Rina popped a horse pill from her bag and swallowed it in a single gulp. Without water.

"I want to know about my father."

"That's one of the reasons I'm here." Rina pulled a journal from her bag. "I wrote this for you a few months after your father died." She stroked the faded leather jacket and slid it onto the bed. "Please, take it."

"You wrote it for me?" Eliana flipped through pages inscribed in blue ink.

"I did. Look at the inside front cover." Rina's voice trailed with nostalgia. "I've read it multiple times over the years. Seeing you hold it…"

Eliana smoothed the jagged corners and opened the cover. A message in blue ink read,

For Eliana

My Life with Seth. One year, five months, sixteen days.

It has been three months since your father's passing. I cannot believe you will grow up without experiencing his love. This diary is a means for my sweet Eliana to know her father when she becomes a woman.

Eliana flipped through the pages, softened by wear. Her mother's sharp, bubbly script was unmistakable, unlike any other she'd seen. "I grew up not knowing your love. What about the limited memories I have with you?"

"Irreplaceable, I know."

"Why'd you come back?"

"Your grandparents phoned me about the shooting. I had to see you in person to know you were okay. As I was packing, I recognized the necessity to make up for our lost years together. I knew the only way to do that would be to share this with you."

Eliana admired Rina's strength. She held her emotions together and showed no self-pity for her physical disabilities. Her stubs extended an inch past the wheelchair seat. The last time they were together, Eliana had struggled to follow her mother, who scurried through the market in terror.

"I want to read this to you." Her mother swiveled the chair sideways and reached for Eliana's hand. "It will be the perfect way to reconnect."

"Why aren't my grandparents here?"

"Your grandmother didn't want to interfere."

Eliana jerked her hand away. She wanted to read alone, without her mother's presence, but a new bond had to be established. There was no other way to go about it.

"Are you ready?"

With a subtle nod of the head, Eliana handed the journal over.

Rina leaned onto the dulled leather seat and opened to the first page. "Let's begin."

PART V

Through the Eyes of Rina

Israeli Residential Building
April 1998

Rina grabbed the old gas mask and rushed to the stairwell. An air-raid siren warned everyone to take shelter. The enemy had launched a missile to raze the land and shatter lives.

"Why do you always have that?" Her middle-aged neighbor posed the usual question. He stepped aside as Rina pounded down the steps.

With a shake of the head, Rina refused to answer.

"Bring this when the sirens ring." Her dying mother handed over the worn mask she had kept by her bed for decades. *"Evil people want to hurt you. Protect yourself. And your children."*

Rina had granted her mother's death bed wish, but she silently vowed not to inherit the same fears. So far, she had failed.

In the eighteen-story building's basement, Rina crouched in a cold corner of the bomb shelter. Voices and movement echoed across concrete walls as residents shuffled in. The din barely muffled the ascending and descending tones of the siren.

An elderly lady from the top floor, who had no trouble getting around, placed her soft fingers on Rina's shoulder. She had seen far worse in her youth. "It's almost over," she whispered and patted the gas mask. "It's probably another false alarm."

The wise woman was right.

Forty-five minutes later, Rina arrived at the travel agency. A full workday would distract her from the jitters.

"Sirens?" Rina's American boss, Mr. Lively, welcomed her with an understanding smile. He knew Rina well enough. Only air-raids made this punctual employee late.

With a press of the lips to form a forced smile, Rina nodded confirmation.

Weary travelers flooded the office. The Holy Week of Easter for Christians, and Passover for Jews, caused March and April to be the busiest months of the year.

Rina maintained an upbeat spirit all day until Mr. Lively's voice boomed from the front door.

"We're closed!" He clapped his hands to be noticed by all. "Please, come back tomorrow."

The last to leave, Rina trudged from the office. Her feet felt ten pounds heavier than usual. "Only half a day tomorrow," she said to the door, "and then I'm off." She jiggled the stubborn key into the old, jagged lock.

"Excuse me miss, could I bother you?"

Rina fumbled with the key and pretended not to hear the American who had a Southern drawl just like Mr. Lively.

The man stepped closer. "Miss, do you speak English?"

Rina had never pretended that she didn't understand English. The temptation took root, but the man carried a different load than the usual tourist. A large, black camera bag and a folded tripod bulged from one arm. A small suitcase hung from his other hand. "I'm looking for a personal guide."

"I'm sorry sir, but we're closed. Please return in the morning."

The man tilted his head to the side and scratched his unshaven chin. "I'm not here for the holidays."

Rina waited without response.

"I'm working on a documentary." He raised the tripod for evidence. "It focuses on the conflict between Israel and Palestine. I have to find someone to take me to Jewish settlements in the West Bank, Gaza, and other areas where the conflict is at its worst."

Off the hook. "We don't offer that kind of service here. Our business runs strictly for tours, hotel reservations, car rental services, and airline ticketing."

He shoved his fingers through a thick mass of chestnut curls. "Do you know anyone who could assist me? I've done a ton of research and had a few neighborhoods in mind. I got here two days ago and went to some places, but it's more difficult than I expected. Someone with connections who can get me interviews with victims' families would be ideal."

Not off the hook. As the American explained his intentions to cover the history of terror attacks in the past decade, Rina recognized it would be wrong to reject him. He needed help in a big way.

"Let me think it over tonight. Meet me here at noon tomorrow."

"You guys can actually do this?"

"Not the agency. Again, I can't give you a firm answer right now."

His eyebrows raised in question. His mouth twisted in doubt. "Understood. I'll be sitting on the bench over there 'til I see you leave. By the way, my name's Seth Gibbons." He offered his free hand with a drowsy smile.

"Rina Sharett." She returned with a firm shake.

Rina fell backward onto the bed and contemplated her impending two-week vacation. Tomorrow she planned to begin a journey in which she would face her worst fear: travel to some of the most dangerous territories in Israel. She had to do it, not only for the plans she already had in place, but to combat the phobia.

What about this American? Rina weighed the advantages and disadvantages if she were to become involved in such a risky project. She considered the impact on each Israeli she knew who was wounded or victimized by militants.

Citizens of the two countries used to treat each other as equals. They went shopping together, celebrated together, even ate together. There was much harmony. Then, young Palestinians who had grown up in a good environment turned to violence, escalating in the late '80s and early '90s.

Rina forbade herself to become prejudiced. Racism and ill-will would solve nothing. The only thing she knew to do was offer consolation. She desired no vengeance, only change.

The promise Rina made to her mother had to be put on hold while she assisted the American.

This was going to be a dangerous quest.

"Eliana, I can't tell you how hard it was for me to make that choice." Homesick for her cozy recliner, Rina shifted in the confining wheelchair. "I'm sorry to burden you, my sweetness. Would you press the button to call the nurse? I could use a pillow behind my back."

Rina had searched for an excuse to get away from Israel for over a year. She wanted the life in America promised by Seth. To regain that dream required support, but she refused to condemn her daughter to servitude.

"Were you really that scared all the time?" Eliana pressed a button on the remote.

"My job distracted me, so no. Not always. At least, not during the day. I put on a front, careful not to expose my weakness. People shuffled through the doors and saw Rina Sharrett, a woman with the most cheerful expression than anyone in their wearisome travels. Negative emotions didn't surface until I got home. The routine I established helped, but it was ridiculous. First, I went to the shelter at the bottom of the apartment building to ensure accessibility.

"Upstairs, I double-checked my closet for the gas mask mother gave me. We had to learn to use them in school even though there was no likelihood for chemical warfare. I promised myself to stop the obsessive behavior I learned from your grandmother, but at the age of twenty-seven, it was almost too late. I decided to be proactive, so I volunteered with an organization to visit victims of the war."

A plump nurse came into the room with an enigmatic smile. "What'cha need, darling?" She caressed Eliana's head. A loving touch Rina hadn't given since the horrible day of the bombing.

"My mom would like a pillow for her back."

"You got it."

Rina leaned on the armrest as the woman wedged a firm pillow behind her lumbar region. "Thank you. What's your name?"

"Amanda. I'm gonna find something more suitable for you to sit in."

The rented wheelchair provided little comfort in contrast to Rina's mobility scooter at home. "Do you have a reclining chair?"

Amanda pivoted to leave before she answered. "I'll find one for you, one way or another."

Rina pulled the bulky pillow further up her back and opened the journal. "Let's dig back in."

DAY ONE

Rina kept a trash can by her desk all morning. Office colleagues prodded her for an answer about her nerves. "I'm stressed and ready for a break," she lied.

"You can go ahead and pack up," Mr. Lively said at eleven forty-five. A double-tap of his fingers on the desk summoned her to rise. "You sure are prettied up today. Big plans already?"

What did he mean by the phrase, *prettied up*? "Just going to spend time with some friends out of town."

"Well, have a nice time, and don't do anything I wouldn't do!"

"Thanks. I'll see you in two weeks." Rina sprinted from the office to the restroom. Her image in the mirror explained Mr. Lively's comment. She had pulled out her dusty cosmetics case that morning. The eyeliner, mascara, blush, and gloss made her look like someone else. Even worse, she wore her favorite blouse. Way too fancy for work.

What's come over me?

Rina eyed the exit sign and scrubbed a rough, wet paper towel over her lips. It would be easy to go home without being seen. Seth could find someone else. "Put your big girl pants on," she rebuked herself loud enough for everyone in the ladies' room to hear.

With a cheerful façade, Rina traipsed to the bench where they agreed to meet.

But Seth wasn't there.

He had come across as desperate. Maybe he found help elsewhere.

Rina tossed her purse on the bench and plopped down in disappointment. That's when the enormous digital clock with red letters caught her eye.

Twelve fifteen. She was late for their meeting!

The bench's frame rattled when Rina sprang from her sitting position. She scanned the crowd for a sign of Seth. She might catch him if—

"Rina!" Seth pushed through a group of slow-moving travelers who walked shoulder-to-shoulder, blocking everyone who wanted to pass. "Sorry I'm late. Do you remember me?" He pulled a bottle of antacids from his bag and popped two in his mouth.

"Yes, I remember. I've only been here a few minutes myself." Rina tucked her lips in to resist a smile. Excitement swept her to the bones. Why did she feel so happy to see this stranger? "Shall we walk? I have a few questions for you."

Seth eyed the bench with a sleep-deprived longing for rest. Jet lag at its worst. Too bad. Rina didn't want her coworkers, especially her boss, to see her with a man.

"You're in luck," she said and walked without waiting for Seth to follow. "I'm on vacation for two weeks, and I want to help you."

Seth stopped mid-stride. "No kidding?" With a fair, freckled complexion, rose-tinged brownish blond hair, and forest green eyes, he could easily be mistaken for a Scottish man. All he needed was a kilt.

Rina fought the building attraction. "I'm not joking. First, I require assurance that your documentary will not make Palestine out to be a bad country. Have you ever met a Palestinian?"

"I have," Seth said and fell in line with Rina's pace. "I met a woman from Ramallah on a flight once. She shared her story with me. Came to the States in the early '90s before the violence got really bad. The only job her husband could find was as a handyman. They have 4 daughters now. The youngest was born last year. Great family."

"Good. You mustn't go into this with prejudice."

"What exactly *are* we going in to?"

"I know some people who have suffered from this conflict." A sudden hitch in Rina's throat forbade her to speak. She couldn't cry. Not now. Not in front of him. She had to be strong to succeed in this mission. "They will share their stories with you. I just ask that your documentary not portray Palestine as a whole to be evil. It's only the small percentage of radicals who are like that. They give their fellow countrymen a bad name."

"I'll make that clear in both the introduction and the conclusion."

Rina began to ache in every way possible. Her stomach fluttered, back stiffened, feet numbed. She took a deep inhalation, followed by slow exhalation, as demonstrated by a therapist years ago. "This is going to be emotionally challenging, Seth," she said and forced her jaw to slacken. "I know you expect this, but when you're face-to-face with these people, nothing can prepare you."

"Understood." Seth bobbed his head in a confident nod.

As much as Rina dreaded the journey, she had to go through with it. "If you're ready, we can start now. I've already made some phone calls."

⁂

"How did dad handle it when you met the families?" Eliana rolled her feet with exaggerated ankle revolutions.

"As expected." Rina copied Eliana's foot movements with her hands. If only she had feet to stretch and ankles to loosen. "He knew what we were about to do, but he didn't realize the impact it would have on him."

"It doesn't seem right not to make a big deal out of all the suicide bombings and everything else the Palestinians did." Eliana cracked her knuckles exactly like her father. A push with a thumb, one finger at a time. "All they wanted was to kill Israelis."

"Not all Palestinians," Rina corrected her daughter. "Only a small fraction of the population. Many of the terrorists came from other countries. Just like anywhere else on Earth, people make terrible choices. Even here. Think of everything that has been in the news. Children and families killed, school shootings, teenagers gunning down their parents, human trafficking, mass murder. No telling what's to come."

"Nannie and Pops have kept me sheltered, so I don't see much of that stuff." Eliana nibbled her bottom lip. "I have a good friend from Palestine. Her name is Jazmin."

Rina spoke with her mother-in-law on the phone several times a year. Dottie had always assured her that Eliana was safe. "*Not much happens 'round here*," she had often said. Other than the threat of an occasional hurricane, Eliana could not have lived in a more secure environment.

"I'm glad to hear you have a Palestinian friend," Rina said and smoothed out the pages. She just told her daughter another lie. The thought of an association with someone from that country made her insides churn. "I hope it will help you not be prejudiced."

Unlike my thinking right now…

THE WIDOW

Rina popped open the trunk of her 5-speed hatchback. "You can put your belongings here."

"Where are we going?" Seth wedged his bulky black camera bag in a corner and assembled everything else around it like a barrier.

"West Bank." Rina slammed the trunk. "I'll tell you about the widow we're going to see." The transmission moaned with each punch of the clutch and not-so-gentle gear shift. Rina didn't usually treat her car this way.

"Kelila Shalev lives in a small community named Itamar. Her husband, Benjamin, was a city bus driver." Rina merged onto the highway and punched the gas pedal. The speed made her feel strong enough to finish the story. "Two years ago, Mr. Shalev's route had just ended for the night when three men ambushed him. An eyewitness said the bastards came out of nowhere and started firing their guns. Even after he was dead, they continued to shoot in a craze. The coroner found a total of seventeen gunshot wounds."

Seth scribbled notes on a yellow pad. "Why? What did he do to make them so mad?"

"No one knows." The countryside on the short drive to Itamar usually took Rina's breath away when she made the trip. Orange rooftops on white houses contrasted with brown and green knolls. Farms with greenhouses and crops bordered small communities along rolling hills.

Today, the land's warm sentimentality did nothing for Rina. This stranger and his project put her on edge.

A family picnicking on a grassy slope welcomed them at the entrance of the small neighborhood. Eight children waved alongside their parents.

"Do you know them?" Seth waved back.

"Yes. I call upon Mrs. Shalev frequently. I'm sure everyone knows about you by now." Rina felt an urge to propel her car in a full-throttle blast on the rocky dirt road.

Something had gotten to her.

Fearlessness?

No. She was scared to death.

Seth braced his hands on the door and dashboard. "They know I'm coming?"

"I already had plans to see her today, so I called this morning." Rina caressed the steering wheel as an apology to her car and ordered herself to chill out. "They are excited to meet an American. Don't be surprised if you're suddenly surrounded by children."

"I see what you mean," Seth said when they parked in front of a white house with a clay-tiled roof. Children of all ages gathered around Seth before he had the chance to fully step out. They smiled, laughed, and shouted in Hebrew.

"Howdy," one boy exclaimed with a strong accent. "I like rodeo and a cowboy hat!"

"So do I." Seth found the blue antacid bottle in his bag and chewed a couple before gathering his gear.

Rina ordered the children to leave the American alone. "Let's go inside," she said as the crowd dispersed.

"Ladies first." Seth held out his hand, but his stiff posture masked uncertainty.

"I apologize for the erratic driving. Did I make you motion sick?"

"A bit. It's more that I get nervous around new people."

"Don't worry," Rina knocked and opened the door. "Everyone is kind. I wanted to take you here first, as this will be a pleasant experience."

Three middle-aged women greeted them from the living area. The ladies said their usual pleasantries as they hugged and exchanged kisses. Without an introduction, all three approached Seth with open arms as if they had known him for years. They smiled, laughed, and appeared to be the happiest people.

Pink splotches mottled Seth's face when they hugged him, held their hands on his temples, and air-kissed his cheeks. "Thank you. Nice to meet you." He coughed and fiddled with his gear.

Two of the women turned to leave the room. "Shalom, kol tuv," they said and waved.

"Bye," Seth answered.

Rina nudged Seth's elbow. "That means, 'peace, be well.' It's the way we say goodbye in Hebrew."

"Shalom, cool tive," he mimicked. The women raised their voices in laughter at his bad Hebrew and shut the door behind them.

"Seth," Rina said, "I'd like to introduce you to Kelila Shalev."

"Nice to meet you, ma'am." Seth held out his hand.

"Naim meod," Mrs. Shalev offered a fingertip grab and pointed to the couch. "Bevakasha." Her forced smile reminded Rina of the first several months following Mr. Shalev's passing. She would grin at well-wishers, but mourning overpowered strength.

Thick steam wafted from a white tea pot on the coffee table. Mrs. Shalev set a saucer and cup in front of Seth. Deep, vertical creases gathered above the arch of her nose. Fine wrinkles fanned the outer corners of her eyes. Sun exposure tarnished her inherent fair skin. The loose French twist of her dyed blonde hair contrasted with her gray hairline. The forty-two-year-old woman looked older than fifty.

"This is mint tea," Rina said as Mrs. Shalev poured a smooth cascade of hot tea into Seth's cup. "She always has some ready when I visit."

Seth inhaled the minty aroma. "How do I say thank you?"

"Todah," Mrs. Shalev answered with a smile.

"You speak English?"

"No." Mrs. Shalev shook her head.

"She can understand a little." Rina held her cup still while Mrs. Shalev poured.

"Okay," said Seth with a nod. "Well, todah."

"Al lo davar," Mrs. Shalev replied.

"What was that? Hallo divorn?"

Mrs. Shalev's hazel eyes danced as she joined Rina in laughter. She set the teapot on the tray and sat next to him. "Al lo davar." She repeated the words slowly.

"Al lo davar," Seth restated. "That means *you're welcome*?"

"Yes," Mrs. Shalev replied with a smile.

Seth scribbled the vocabulary words in his yellow notebook. "Rina," he said and clicked his pen, "I don't want to stir up Mrs. Shalev's grief on my behalf. The interview isn't necessary."

"Nonsense. She knows you're not here for selfish reasons. I'll speak to her and act as an interpreter." Seth's equipment sat neglected by the front door. "Do you want to record this?"

"If it wouldn't offend her, I'd love to."

Rina turned to Mrs. Shalev and spoke a few words. After a short pause, the widow nodded in approval.

"Yes," Mrs. Shalev told Seth with a slight crook of her mouth. Her shoulders began to shrink. The smile she donned for the previous ten minutes disappeared.

"I'll translate as she speaks," Rina said when Seth pressed the record button.

"Perfect."

The wounded woman began with a melancholic smile.

Kelila and Benjamin grew up in Itamar and played with the same group of children over the years. By their early thirties, everyone was married with children, except for them. As the only single man and woman their age in the area, they began to entertain the thought of getting to know each other better.

Within a short year after their first date, they married. Their son was born eleven months later.

Mr. Shalev sought another career to support the family better than the below-average income he earned on a local farm. One of their mutual childhood friends who lived in Jerusalem worked for the Egged bus company and secured a job for Benjamin. At first, he worked in the office as a dispatcher while he completed the company driving school. On account of his reliable work ethic and proven trustworthiness, he was promoted to a bus driver shortly after training.

When Mr. Shalev threw his wife a surprise party for her fortieth birthday, the couple revealed a surprise of their own. Mrs. Shalev was eight weeks pregnant.

To prepare for the new addition, Mr. Shalev took on additional hours. He worked nights and weekends and even received a bonus. When Mrs. Shalev was seven months pregnant with their baby girl, Egged held a social event for employees and their families. Benjamin loved showing off his glowing wife and their seven-year-old son, who constantly placed his ear on Kelila's ever-growing belly.

The Shalev Family was the highlight of the gathering.

The nightmare occurred the following day.

Kelila dropped her face into her palms. "I pray," she mumbled and rushed from the room.

"Let's give her an hour to rest," Rina said. "I have something to show you."

Eliana had gone into a daze, but she still listened. She responded with head-nods and audible acknowledgments. It was like she saw the events unfold before her.

"Are you all right, my Love?"

"I'm picturing the Egged logo," she said with vacant eyes. "It just came to me as a flashback. When I was on the ground at the market, and the groceries had fallen, I was trying to pick them up. That's when I heard your voice. I raised my head and saw the big green bus."

The Egged logo resembled a big X with a wing on the top right side. It stood out in bright white, crystal-clear on every shiny, forest-green vehicle.

"People started running, and I didn't see you the next time I looked." Eliana gathered her fingers into her palms and balled her fists. "I got up to find you. I saw your body sliding down the steps. You were tangled in black fabric, and I saw other feet push through the cloths. I thought you had fallen down the steps with another person. But you were struggling.

Fighting. There was an eerie scream and then…and…that's where my memory ends."

"I didn't realize you remembered that much, baby." Rina could still feel the fabric from the bomber's tunic. Fancy, high-quality death clothes. From that day forward, Rina never wore black again. Not even shoes.

"Before today, just now, when I told you, I didn't remember."

Half an hour into the reading and Eliana suffered a trauma flashback? Rina hadn't expected that. "How do you feel about it?"

Eliana blinked vacantly as she came out of the daze. "Proud. You tried to stop her."

"And I failed."

"At least you didn't go running like everyone else."

True. She had engaged in her first and last physical fight. "I had to do it. To protect you. My goal was to stop her."

"You did. Not completely, but it was long enough for many people to get out of harm's way."

True again.

"Come on, mama, let's keep reading."

"I'm afraid this is going to be too hard on you, my Love. We just started, and it's already harming you."

"The flashback wasn't bad." Eliana braced her shoulder and shifted sides. "Tell me more."

"Seth and I went for a walk while Mrs. Shalev prayed. While the scenery was romantic, the circumstances were not."

COMFORT

The path behind the house zigzagged up an incline. Sunlight danced in the long grasses that swayed with a mild wind. Rina rubbed the spiky chill bumps from her arms.

"Kelila lost the baby the day after Mr. Shalev died. When the police came to her door at two o'clock in the morning, it didn't register that her husband hadn't come home. She insisted they had the wrong address. When she saw his side of the bed empty and untouched, she accepted the truth."

At the top of a low hill, lush green mountains proclaimed the beauty of the valley. The fresh scent of grasses and foliage heightened Rina's senses. A small, octagonal gazebo big enough for four stood in quaint brilliance. The sunset created a yellow-orange reflection against white-painted wood.

"This is where they got married." Rina stepped into the small space, a few degrees cooler in the shade. "Mrs. Shalev comes here frequently. Sometimes alone. Other times she brings her son for a picnic."

"How's the boy handling it?" Seth ducked his head under the gazebo entrance.

"Like any young boy would. Children sometimes handle these things a little better due to their unawareness. He has flashbacks and good memories with his father. He was more upset about the baby."

The last bit bothered Rina. How could a seven-year-old boy be more upset about the death of an unborn sibling than his father? Did they not have a good relationship? Was there something not right about Benjamin Shalev?

"Let's go back." Rina sidestepped Seth and marched down the path. "She'll be waiting for us by now."

Kelila sat on the couch with her crochet needles and yarn. She wove in hurried rotations, adding to what was going to be a beautiful pastel blanket.

"Beteavon!" She pointed to a table where a tray of sesame crackers, jam, and honey awaited eager appetites.

"Ah, Mrs. Shalev always has something to serve," Rina said.

"Todah." Seth rubbed his palms together. "I'm famished."

"Al lo davar," the widow replied. She graciously replenished Seth's side of the platter as he continued to eat.

Rina folded her napkin and licked the honey from her fingers. "We should get ready to finish the interview."

Minutes later, they sat in the living room. Mrs. Shalev held a tattered handkerchief on her legs.

"I haven't seen her with that in over a year," Rina said. "It was his."

Seth made a time-out signal with his hands. "Let's not go on then. I've got enough."

Mrs. Shalev pointed to the camera and gave a thumbs-up.

"She's okay. It's good for her to talk about it." Rina pushed the button to begin the recording.

The widow spoke with new enthusiasm.

"The day he died," Rina interpreted, "my husband was in a particularly cheerful mood. Before he left in the morning, he kissed my belly and whispered to the baby that he couldn't wait to see her again."

Mrs. Shalev placed a hand on her abdomen.

"He called me a few times throughout the day to check on the three of us. Thankfully, I got our son on the phone. They talked less than a minute, but their last words were, I love you.

"I fell asleep earlier than usual, so I wasn't aware that my husband hadn't come home when I heard knocking on the door in the middle of the night."

The widow eyed the front entry as if she expected Mr. Shalev to walk in.

"At first, I thought Benjamin locked himself out. When I opened the door, I was shocked to see police. The first thought was for my son."

Kelila played with her gold wedding ring and revolved it around her finger. Every few rotations, she stopped to examine the small diamond.

"When I found out Benjamin had been killed by Palestinians, I ran outside and screamed for him. I don't remember much after that except the cramps. They were so strong that it caused me to faint."

The creases between Mrs. Shalev's eyebrows contracted. "I awoke in the hospital with a softer, smaller belly. When I came home, they told me the details of my husband's slaughter. Two bullets remained in his body. Sixteen shells were scattered around him. He was shot in the head so many times that it was shattered beyond recognition. The three murderers also stabbed him several times.

"It rips me to shreds when I think of his mangled body. I grew up with that body. I fell in love with that body. I loved that body. I can see every wrinkle on his face, his birthmarks, even his scars."

Mrs. Shalev grabbed a framed photo from the end table and ran her finger along the edges. Benjamin stood next to an Egged bus in his uniform and pointed to the logo.

"She wants to ask both of us a question," Rina said.

Seth set his writing tablet aside. "I'm going to stop the tape."

Rina forced the waver from her voice and continued to translate. "Close your eyes. Picture the person dearest to you. The one you love the most. The one with whom you have spent much time and know every detail. Try to remember when you last you touched them and looked into their eyes, the final words you said to them, and they said to you."

Kelila probed their eyes for confirmation.

"Now that you see them, now that you recall your final moments with them, imagine that it was the last time you were blessed by their presence. Then, imagine finding out that this horror befell them. Can you picture their slain bodies?"

The muscles under Rina's ribcage convulsed. Her eyes stung.

Seth offered a hand to help Mrs. Shalev stand. He circled his arms around her shoulders and bowed his head. "I'm so sorry."

Kelila leaned into Seth's chest. Sorrowful chuckles preceded soft murmurs.

"Mrs. Shalev said that you are the same build as her husband. Your hug brought her cheer."

A moonless night sky made the drive home on the dark highway feel like space travel. Lights in the distance looked more like stars. Somehow, Seth saw well enough to jot notes in his journal. "Where was Kelila's son?"

"When we walked to the hill, he went to a neighbor's house for the evening." Rina scratched a nonexistent itch on her scalp. "Kelila didn't want him to witness or overhear the conversation."

"I see," Seth said. "I can understand that. I hoped to meet him, but I probably would've done the same thing."

"Actually, you did meet him," Rina said. "He's the one who spoke to you in English."

"I should've known."

"Nannie!" Eliana pressed the speakerphone icon on her cell to answer the call. "Hello?

"Hi, Dollface. How ya feeling?"

"Tired. And my shoulder hurts. Why haven't you come to see me?"

Rina sensed the hurt in her daughter's voice. Saw it in the tremble of her bottom lip. The moisture that glistened in her eyes.

"Pops is madder than a wet rooster right now. Still tryin' to cool his boots after that num nut kid pulled his stunt the other day."

Rina laughed along with Eliana. If there was one skill her mother-in-law mastered, lightening a tense mood was one of them.

"Is that Rina I hear?"

"Hello, Dottie." Rina restrained the tendency to speak like normal in long-winded conversation.

"I can't wait to see you! Listen, as soon as Pops gets his britches out of a knot, we'll make light lightning and get outta this hotel for a visit."

Eliana's expression darkened after the conversation. Rina knew the reason. She had questions for her grandparents.

Why, for one, did they lie to her all these years?

"Ready for me to keep reading?"

"Sure." Eliana rotated her knees in the opposite direction like a barrier. No eye contact. No excitement.

The phone call had reversed the progress they made thus far.

HARM'S WAY

Rina strained to keep her eyes on the road, shrouded on a moonless night. Seth had scribbled two pages full of notes. "There is a hotel five minutes from my apartment building. It will be easiest if you stay somewhere close."

"That's fine, as long as it's not a roach motel." Seth's smile slackened as quickly as it had formed.

"A what?"

"Nothing, sorry. Just trying to make some humor after all that."

Orange flashes upon the concrete synchronized with the click of the blinker. The night was almost over. Seth had experienced a small taste of the turmoil to come. "Rest well and prepare yourself to meet three more families this week. Saturday, we'll take a break. My best friend invited you to join us for Passover lunch at her home on Sunday. Her fiancé is an Israeli Defense Forces soldier. There may be an opportunity to speak with him alone."

"An interview with an IDF soldier would be a great addition."

"Next week is the hard part. Gaza. We'll stay at a hotel Monday through Thursday." Rina hadn't visited with the families in Gaza for over six months. Every time she went in the past, a shadow of fear followed her. She felt like, if she went back, she would find herself in the middle of a violent riot.

"How do you know all these people? How did you plan it out so quickly?"

"I'm part of an organization that supports victims of terrorist attacks. I have befriended many of those assigned to me. Tomorrow I'm going to put letters in the mail so they'll understand your purpose in advance."

In the subsequent days, Rina felt like Seth were a good friend with whom she shared the sad stories.

If only they were fictitious. Not fact.

The first was a family of five who lived northwest of Itamar in the Kedumim settlement. The parents had been married a year when they went to the annual Purim parade. Children danced in the streets in costume, singing, happy with life. Their firstborn son had just fallen asleep in his stroller when tragedy struck.

Sniper fire killed the baby. The shooting was no mistake. A single bullet perfectly found its target in the center of his forehead. His parents conceived three times after they buried him, but the void remained.

A forlorn mother who suffered the loss of her adult son shared more with Seth than Rina had heard in the past. He was seven months from graduating from the Hebrew University of Jerusalem with a degree in Mathematics when he was instantly killed by a bullet fired from a passing vehicle with a vast arsenal. His dream was to be a schoolteacher and baseball coach. He had also bought a ring and proposed to his girlfriend of four years less than a week beforehand.

In the Southern city of Hebron, where the conflict was at its worst, Rina brought Seth to the homes of two families. Their nine-year-old boys were found in an alley three miles from the synagogue where they were last seen playing. They had been bound, blindfolded, and thrown to their knees. Each sustained a single shot to the back of the head.

Seth's reaction had almost been invisible as he listened to the mothers weep through their words. But Rina saw it. A kink in the jaw preceded a subtle red hue that crept up his neck to his forehead. His throat bobbed. Yet, he kept his composure and conveyed strength. Rina's admiration grew by the hour.

On the last day, Rina's car bumped along the streets in the Old City of Jerusalem. She told Seth what happened—this time before they met the family. At a mass Bar Mitzvah, a male suicide bomber took the life of a thirteen-year-old boy who celebrated his entry into spiritual adulthood. Three of his friends were also killed. The boy was an only child and the last male to carry on the family name.

When Rina dropped Seth off at the hotel Friday night, he thanked her in excess. He was right, his documentary would be mediocre without this quest.

Still, doubt remained imprinted on her mind.

Standoffs in Gaza usually ended with verbal blows. With both sides on the brink of violence, catastrophe could strike in an instant.

Come Monday, she would knowingly put this American in harm's way.

The throbbing in Rina's legs did not subside, even after applying her most effective pain relief cream. The obsessive preoccupation that Eliana would never recover from abandonment made it worse. Rina had chosen to send her daughter away, and she took full responsibility for Eliana's resentment.

Amanda propped open the heavy door and shoved a rubber stopper underneath. Rumbles filled the room as she wheeled in a medical reclining chair without effort.

Minutes later, Rina relaxed in the roomy seat, pillows girdling each side so she wouldn't slide. Eliana had watched as Amanda lifted her mother from the wheelchair, set her into the recliner, and made sure she had everything she needed.

"Did you see dad on Saturday?"

"I did not, and I longed to see him. It took five days for him to capture me." Rina pulled the journal from her bag and opened to one of her favorite parts.

"By Saturday evening, I had reminded myself again and again that I barely knew this person. I was so ready for the day to be over. All I wanted was to see him again."

FOCUSED FOILING

Rina put the car in park and massaged the tension from her shoulders. A few minutes early, she hoped to settle down before Seth witnessed the struggle. No such luck.

"Morning," Seth said when he opened the door. "Good to see you again."

"You too. Did you have a nice Saturday?"

"I did quite a bit of work on my script, so I was busy. How 'bout you?"

If he only knew. "It was uneventful, which for me is always good."

Seth whisked the seatbelt into place and arranged his gear on the floorboard. "What are your friends' names?"

Rina pulled her eyes off Seth and shifted into first gear. An accidental pop of the clutch jerked the car to a sudden stop. "Naomi Berkovitz is my best friend. She lives in Jerusalem. Her fiancé's name is Azriel Gorodish."

Seth contorted his face against blazing rays from the sun. "Do you really think Azriel will let me interview him?"

"I'll have to distract Naomi. After lunch, I'll take her into the kitchen to clean. When the two of you are alone, describe the visits from last week. He'll offer an opinion without question. Especially if he drinks."

Naomi's unapproachable demeanor fooled people to think she was not a nice person. Yes, she was blunt, and at times even impolite. Underneath the mask, she was one of the most sensitive people Rina knew.

"Please, come," Naomi held the door wide with an uncharacteristic grin. Perhaps this would be a good reception.

"Naomi," Rina entered with a confident step, "this is Seth Gibbons."

"Oh, who else would be? Seth only!" Naomi mocked in broken English.

"Nice to meet you." Seth reached for a handshake.

"Also for me," she replied and took Seth's hand with a sharp return. A tall, thick-boned woman, many were intimidated by Naomi's presence. "Soon should be here, my future husband, Azriel."

Forty-five minutes later, Azriel's absence had ruined Naomi's good mood.

"Well," she said in an aggravated tone, "not coming, I guess. We go to table. With Israeli food you are familiar, Seth?"

"Some of the families I visited last week cooked for me." Seth pulled a chair and offered it to Rina.

"Naomi loves to cook," Rina jumped in, knowing her friend's snobbery when it came to food. In Naomi's eyes, whatever anyone else made, she made it better. "You're in for a treat."

"Thank you, my friend," Naomi answered and left the room.

"Seth," Rina whispered when he took a seat beside her. He leaned in and put a hand near hers on the table. "In case you haven't noticed, my dear friend has a strong personality. Naomi's true nature is kind. Please don't be offended by her."

"Thanks for the belated heads up." Seth flashed a subtle wink and narrowed the gap between them. "I've dealt with a wide variety of personalities. I can tell she's a good person."

A harsh slam of the front door interrupted the cozy exchange.

"Azriel is here," Rina said. "It is not typical of him to be late. There must be a problem at the border."

Calm shushes muffled Naomi's denigrations. Moments of silence indicated a conclusion to the scolding. For now.

Azriel entered the room in a wrinkled olive-green uniform. His height rivaled that of Naomi, and his bulky form made her look like a twig.

"Sir, I'm Seth Gibbons." Seth stood and offered a hand.

"Azriel Gorodish, nice to meet you." Azriel reciprocated with lengthy pleasantries. "Let us sit." His relaxed mannerisms and melodic accent made him much more amicable than his better half. "Apologies for late arrival. We had a situation at border. I had to stay."

Naomi entered the room with a platter of steaming bowls. "First course, I serve you roasted garlic and spinach soup topped with parmesan."

Seth attempted to mask a sour face. It would change soon enough.

"It's delicious," he said after several bites. "I love it."

Naomi's eyes bulged as she raised her head. "Surprised you are?"

"No. Well, yes," Seth admitted. "I typically don't like cooked spinach, but I've never had it like this before."

Azriel paused mid slurp. A clear dribble stopped just above his cleft chin. "Naomi, where's the wine?"

"Wipe your mouth." Naomi opened two bottles of wine to compliment the multi-course meal.

Rina ate her fill of tangy eggplant salad and matzo dumplings. Fall-off-the-bone lamb chops, sautéed asparagus, and baked rosemary potatoes completed the main course. "I must take a break before dessert," Rina said and touched the button of her jeans. If only she had worn the less fitted pair today.

"Nonsense," Naomi said and began to clear the plates. "Why you make us wait?"

Seth lifted a hand in agreement. "Naomi, I need half an hour before I can consider another bite."

"Fine." Naomi flung both hands in the air, shoulders nearly touching her earlobes, lips stretched in a fine line. Wine always worsened her unpleasant nature.

"I'll clean," Rina said and gathered dishes. She took her time to scour, rinse and dry each dish. Naomi's banter made eavesdropping nearly impossible. The last clean bowl squeaked in the towel when Seth stuck a shoulder through the doorframe. "Rina?"

"Yes?" She turned with her brows raised as if she didn't know what he wanted.

"Azriel's going to let me interview him. He wants to remain anonymous, so I have to do a little setup."

"I'll help." Rina dried the last clean plate and stacked it atop the others.

Naomi's death-stare failed to deter Seth from his mission. Good. She favored people not intimidated by her.

"Let's get the equipment from the car." Rina took Seth's hand and led him away.

Naomi did not wait till they were alone before she began to berate Azriel.

"She's bullheaded when it comes to holiday celebrations," Rina explained when they neared her car. "She likes everything to be quiet, peaceful, and uneventful. I knew it might be a problem to attempt your interview with Azriel today, but it's your only opportunity for something like this."

"No." Seth planted a hand on the hatchback when Rina reached for the lock. "I don't want to cause any problems."

Rina spun to face Seth. "She'll get over it. I will tell her more about the documentary."

"I have another concern. Azriel drank at least four glasses of wine. I don't want the alcohol to hinder his thinking or cause him to say something he normally wouldn't."

"That's not a problem. A bottle of wine is nothing for Az."

Naomi yapped on the phone from her bedroom. Probably complaining to her mother as usual.

"Is not happy about this," Azriel yelled, not loud enough for his fiancée to hear.

With the blackout curtains closed and lights off, the bright light shining behind Azriel's head revealed only his silhouette. The interview began.

"Please state your rank and occupation," Seth instructed.

"I am second lieutenant in Israeli Defense Forces Army." Azriel's hard stare matched his rocklike posture. "I work at security checkpoint in a

Palestinian city. Northern West Bank."

"How long have you been in the Army, and what other positions have you held?" Seth spouted a string of questions he had prepared ahead of time.

"Five years active duty. First, my involvement was low-intensity warfare operations. After a year, I entered sikul memukad."

"Could you please elaborate on the latter?"

"Sikul memukad means focused foiling." Azriel expressed himself with his hands as he continued. "We use this targeted killing method to destroy Jihad organizations and their leaders. When exact location of target is discovered, direct hit at site follows."

"What were some of your experiences with these operations?"

"I was involved in several successful missions, but now I like to refer to one in particular." Azriel's eyes glistened in the shadows. He studied the floor, wordless. "It is the mission that led me to change occupation in Army. We were successful in killing target, a Qassam rocket and bomb maker, so the mission was victory. What affected me is…" For the first time, Azriel hung his head. His shoulders dropped from their upright position.

"Ten civilians were killed. Women. Children. I saw picture on TV of a fifteen-year-old Palestinian girl. On a stretcher, dead. She looked peaceful, almost like sleeping. Except bruises on face, she was fine. She looked…" Azriel's Adam's apple bulged, half visible in the camera's angle. "She looked beautiful. Made me sad to think I helped kill that girl. What if I have a daughter? I could not think to lose her that way."

Azriel leaned over and propped his elbows on his knees.

"I can edit that out," Seth said.

"Please don't. IDF have emotions like anyone else. Some people think we're robots. Not true. We just do our job. It's the duty we swore."

Seth nodded in approval. "Are you against focused foiling operations?"

"Not at all." The reflection of light over his green beret created an ethereal halo. "Sikul memukad is necessary to stop terror attacks on Israelis. I know civilian casualties are part of war. Can't be avoided. I just don't want to be responsible." Azriel leaned back in his chair and steepled his fingers. "In reality, targeted killings decrease civilian fatalities, both Palestinian and Israeli citizens. By using this method of self-defense, knowing exactly where to aim, Israel avoids going into Palestinian territory for all-out military invasion.

"This technique also weakens groups who perform and support attacks in Israeli territory. It will get worse in coming years if we're not diligent." Azriel's eyes contracted. Voice vindictive. "Suicide mission groups and leaders must constantly be on the run to avoid direct attack. Makes it difficult to communicate with collaborators. Most important thing to know, these operations are not performed out of revenge. Sure, we make mistakes and sometimes kill innocents. Palestinians do the same to Israelis. It's a sad consequence of all wars in history."

Seth stopped the video recorder. “Perfect,” he said. “This is going to be a key component in my documentary.”

Rina pulled the curtains aside. Late afternoon soon flooded the room with sharp rays.

“Chocolate cream torte, anyone?”

They all turned around at once. The image of Naomi in the doorway with a relaxed expression was enough to satiate Rina’s sweet tooth.

“Let’s eat!”

Seth devoured two pieces of the creamy confection. That alone won him some points. He had much to prove before Naomi would accept him completely.

Shooting pains coiled around Rina’s legs. Or at least what remained of them. Right now, it felt like they were whole, from hip to toe.

After almost a decade, reality still hadn’t registered. Rina fought off a young woman who wore an explosive device. When the blast sent her body parts into the air, she survived. Before the blackout, Rina saw her severed legs next to the suicide bomber’s head on the concrete. Intact.

An older nurse came to check Eliana’s vitals. “She’s doin’ good, mama.” Silvery wisps sprouted from her loose bun. “I brought you cold sandwiches from our fridge. In case you’re hungry.”

Rina inspected the cellophane-wrapped deli sandwich. Hunger pangs set in. “Thank you.”

“You’re welcome.” The nurse scrutinized Rina’s position in the seat. “Can I get you better situated?”

With two thick pillows next to each arm and one propped under the ends of her legs, Rina felt cozier than she had since her departure from Israel two days ago. “That’s better.” Rina leaned back, thankful to concentrate on her daughter again. But tears gathered at the corners of Eliana’s eyes. “What is it, my Love?”

Deep amber waves spread across Eliana’s shoulders like the reeds of a soft, straw broom. As a girl, she did the same thing upon an impending emotional reaction. Dim lights accented her ruddy complexion, just as perfect as the last time Rina had seen her.

“Don’t feel sorry for me.”

“I can’t help it. Seeing you so dependent on others…” Eliana’s voice broke before she finished. “You were never like that.”

“I’m as strong now as when I was whole. Just not as mobile.” Rina pulled the flap of the sandwich wrapper. Food was always a welcome distraction. A pale slice of meat, mushy cheese, and limp lettuce on a croissant did not entice her to eat. She wanted hummus and pita bread. Maybe Chuck and

Dottie would bring breakfast in the morning.

"Why was Aunt Naomi so rude?" Eliana stuffed a corner of the flaky bread into her mouth and licked her fingers.

"She didn't mean to be. It was just her demeanor. I never met her family, but that's probably how they were at home. She softened up after Shamira was born."

"What happened after you left?"

"We walked to a nearby cemetery and had a deep discussion about your father's beliefs. You can read about that as well as a surprise diversion to a historical site another time."

"Which historical site?"

"The Mount of Olives."

"I want to hear about it."

"There's not enough time, my Love. It's a long part of the journal." Rina had cherished the events of the afternoon with Seth when they bonded on a deeper level. "Before the night ended, I prepared him for our trip to Gaza. I wasn't so sure he could handle it."

GAZA

Sharp sunrays refracted through each crack and ding in the windshield. Opalescent speckles on the dashboard reminded Rina of colorful conversations with Seth the day before. After their discussions and excursion, there was something deeper to their relationship. Only willpower could be her driving force over the next few days. This was no time for romance.

Seth emerged from the hotel with a flip phone pressed between his ear and shoulder. Rina popped the latch to open the trunk and met Seth in the back.

Seth engaged in gentle conversation. "Love you too. I will. Don't worry, Rina's keeping me safe." He cocked a sideways grin. "Bye, mom." He flipped the phone shut and stuffed it in his back pocket.

Seth's reassurance was utterly false. They were about to enter hostile territory.

The short ride to Gaza offered Seth a glimpse of the land's undeniable beauty. Pockets of lush greenery contrasted from the bleak landscape at the dusty border. "This is a hard place to be. Different from the West Bank and other towns we visited."

"I should be able to handle it after last week, right?"

Rina recalled Seth's sensitivity to the other families. "It's more intense here. Our hotel is on the beach. The Mediterranean Sea is always a reprieve after I visit the families."

"Works for me. I love the water." Seth pulled his passport from a small bag and handed it to the border agent by the window. "Who are we seeing this week?"

When Rina first heard the factual stories, she equated them with a movie drama. As she came to know the people, denial flew out the door. "There are three families in the Gush Katif bloc in the Southern Gaza Strip. First, I'll introduce you to the daughter of an elderly couple murdered in their home in the Kfar Darom kibbutz. They were celebrating the first day of Hanukkah when a Palestinian crashed through the door and began firing. They left behind five children, nine grandchildren, and five great-grandchildren."

Seth's nostrils flared. "Unbelievable."

"I'm afraid it doesn't get any better." Rina gauged how much more she should tell Seth. Or if she should even introduce him to everyone as planned. He needed to meet each family to learn legitimate facts about Gaza, but could he handle it?

"Who's next?"

Another hard one. Only a forthright answer would be fair. "In Rafah, near the border between Gaza and Egypt, we'll meet the ex-husband of a woman also killed in her home. They had divorced just a few weeks prior.

"Bad timing." Seth flipped through the pages of his passport as he listened. "How did it transpire?"

"A Palestinian disguised as an IDF soldier entered her home, shot her daughter, then raped and strangled the woman." Rina shivered. "The daughter survived, but she witnessed everything."

"How old is the girl?"

"She was eight when it happened."

Seth turned his head to the window. The ginger scruff on his jawline rose and fell with sharp undulations.

"Are you alright?"

"You know I have a hard time when children are involved."

"I do. I'll never get used to it." The remaining stories would explode in intensity. No sense in upsetting Seth so much at once. "I'll tell you the rest later."

"No, I want to get it over with."

Rina surveyed the decrepit car in front of them. What if the driver had a car bomb? What about the other heaps of metal on the dusty road?

"Two families in the north live in Sderot, which is just outside of Gaza. It's one of the places where violence is severe as a consequence of rocket attacks. There I will introduce you to a couple who had their first child at a young age. Only seven years old, he was playing in the street with several other neighborhood children when a Qassam rocket was fired from Gaza. Only their child was killed, but some of the other children suffered severe injuries, including lost limbs."

Seth broke out in a slew of whispered profanities. "I don't get it. Why would these imbeciles fire at children?"

"Most of the time, I believe they don't see the target....nor do they care."

Seth propped an elbow on the door and massaged his forehead. "Sorry."

"No apology needed. Your anger is just."

"Let's get this over with. Tell me what's next."

"Thursday, we'll drop in on a widow whose husband was also killed by a missile. They had a grown son who left home to study at Tel Aviv University.

After his father died, he came back only for a brief period. The woman has no other family." Rina came to a slow stop by the hotel. "Friday, we'll visit a widower who lives in Gush Katif. I won't tell you his story now. It's the worst."

"Probably a good idea."

⁂

"I felt as much sadness as your father during the first four days in Gaza, but in a different way." Rina envisioned the moments Seth had hugged each person before they left. "With each face-to-face account, he grew more frustrated."

Eliana winced as she shifted positions. Weary creases pulled at the corners of red-webbed eyes. Progress. "Did my dad cry?"

Rina tore her mind from the bitter memory, only to see sorrow wash over her daughter's face. "He never shed a tear in my presence, but he separated himself when we returned to the hotel each day."

"What did he do?"

"He went straight from the car to the beach where he took a solitary hike along a rocky jetty. In my room, I could only see a minuscule version of his figure from the balcony." Rina pictured Seth's return along the boulders. Forced to jump from rock to rock, the workout alone was enough to take his mind off the days' turmoil.

"Did you spend time together besides that? Like, in the mornings?"

"Oh yes, every waking hour together. After Seth's evening hike, we ate dinner at the kosher restaurant next door. I joined him on the balcony of his room to watch the spectacle of colors as the sun parted ways for the night." Rina recalled each sunset, the most striking of which included distant thunderheads that lit the sky with needlelike lightning bolts.

"Sounds romantic." Eliana's slender lips lengthened as a touch of pink brightened her pallid complexion.

"It was, but we finished the days working on the documentary. Tight hugs before bed supplied the happy balance we both yearned for. Except for the final night. That one was rough."

SYMPATHY

Rina sat cross-legged in the thin-padded hotel chair and rotated her body for a spinal adjustment. They had been working on the documentary for over an hour. As much as she enjoyed Seth's company, she needed to go. Otherwise, she'd ask for a back rub or a kiss or even something inappropriate if she let her mind wander much more.

"I'll miss this," Seth said and slapped his laptop shut.

"As will I." In the past, Rina had traveled alone and slipped under crisp sheets at night, listening to a din of mixed voices that kept her awake for hours. This trip turned out to be the best ever. "Seth, it's time to tell you the story of the man we're going to see tomorrow."

"The worst for last, right?" Seth edged onto the hard chair and interlaced his fingers.

"It's horrific. Two years ago, a man named Elijah Zahavi lost his entire family."

Seth heaved a prolonged sigh.

Rina leaned against the creaky desk next to Seth. Maybe it wasn't such a good idea for him to join her tomorrow. "You know, I think you have plenty of material. You've heard enough."

"No. I have to finish this." Seth's tone deepened as if he were scolding himself for self-doubt.

Rina hesitated to cause this unsuspecting American more sadness, but she had to keep her word. The world needed to know the worst stories. "His forty-year-old wife had just picked up their six-year-old daughter from school, as well as their three boys, ages eight, ten and fourteen. Their two-month-old daughter slept in the infant seat in the third row of their SUV."

Seth's knuckles whitened as he clenched his fingers.

"When they were two blocks from home, a crazed Palestinian dressed in women's clothing ran to their vehicle. He pointed a machine gun at the car and fired until the ammunition ran out. The brute even opened all doors and shot them one by one with a pistol to make sure none survived—including the baby."

Seth shoved the chair backward. "A woman? He dressed as a woman?"

"Yes. To hide weapons underneath the loose clothing."

Seth bunched his hands in fists and paced by the sliding glass door. "Then what?"

"Later on," Rina continued despite Seth's agitation, "when the man was captured by the IDF after a brief chase, he admitted that he attacked the vehicle because of the three boys. In his perverse mind, he won a victory by eliminating what eventually could have been three IDF soldiers or parents of more Israeli children."

Blue veins protruded against Seth's reddening forehead and temples, revealing venomous abomination. "I'm gonna get some air." He opened the balcony door and egressed into the darkness.

Rina retreated to the bathroom to process her thoughts. A nudge of regret nipped at her heels. In an intense eleven days, Seth had to swallow and digest what she came to know in two years.

He was right. They had to finish this.

Stretched flat on the bed, Seth lay with both hands clasped behind his head. "Sorry 'bout that."

"About what?"

"I shouldn't get so mad." The bed shifted under Seth's weight when he sprung upward in a rocking motion.

Rina hesitated before she extended a hand to caress Seth's back in reassurance. "Don't be embarrassed around me."

Seth's sudden embrace caught Rina off guard. She found refuge in the warmth of his arms and welcomed the uncharted passion from his caresses. The newness of their intimacy intensified as Seth threaded his fingers through Rina's hands.

"All of this must be hard for you to tell me," he said and pulled back. "Especially, Mr. Zahavi."

"It's hard." Rina struggled to find her voice.

Seth guided her hands around his torso and enfolded Rina into his chest. Had she become another object of his sympathy?

He had offered affection to the families, but it lasted seconds.

This was more than a fleeting gesture. Rina felt care, intimacy, even a sense of love. Whatever Seth meant, Rina dismissed it as nothing more than compassion.

Soon, he would be gone, and she would be a faded memory.

"Does it make you uncomfortable to hear about your parents' romance?"

Eliana thumbed her phone, revealing a picture of Brian on her lock screen. "As long as it's rated G, or PG-13 at the worst, I like it."

"No worries there, my Love. We kept it clean."

THE WIDOWER

Rina dug her toes into grainy sand with each step along the beach. Friday morning's sunrise stroll along the shoreline proved bitter-sweet. Rina's work for Seth would draw to a close in a few hours. At home, thoughts of him would consume every minute. It was going to be a lonely, depressing weekend.

First, they had to endure the cumbersome company of Elijah Zahavi, the only person she dreaded to see.

"Seth," Rina interrupted his enthrallment of the sky, "this is the most difficult case I have dealt with. Out of everyone you met in the past two weeks, this man will surely be the one you find most grim."

"Am I naïve to think that I'm prepared for this one?"

"It's impossible to prepare for it." Rina strained her voice to be heard over the noisy oscillations of the surf. "A good thing you'll experience is the community where he resides. It's called Neve Dekalim."

Neve Dekalim was an oasis amidst the forces of enmity between two homelands. Ivory homes with clay-tiled rooftops boasted ordinary beauty. Lavish greenery, flowering plants, and palm trees lined the streets.

Rina inhaled the Mediterranean Sea's aquatic aromas. Mr. Zahavi's yard flourished with colorful blooms. "Must be a volunteer," she mumbled.

"This is nice…almost exotic." Seth threw the tattered camera bag over his shoulder and slammed the hatchback.

Rina pocketed her keys and watched Seth grab his gear from the trunk, a ritual she had witnessed almost every day over the past two weeks. This would be the last. "Get ready for a change in scenery. Throughout his depression, Mr. Zahavi has not taken care of himself or his home."

A pleasant chime sounded in place of Mr. Zahavi's old buzzer. Firm footsteps approached in contrast to the slow shuffle Rina commonly heard. A swift swing of the door revealed a refreshed version of the widower.

"Rina!" He laughed with outstretched arms. A thick mass of groomed black hair ended in a well-shaped, newly buzzed neckline. Another unusual trait. She had always thought about bringing clippers for his shaggy mop.

Rina welcomed Mr. Zahavi's warm squeeze and began standard greetings in Hebrew when he interrupted. "Please," he implored as he glanced at Seth, "let's speak English so we can all understand each other."

Mr. Zahavi's British accent acquired from school differed from Seth's American way of speaking. Rina loved the sound of both.

"Rina posted a letter last week to notify me that you would accompany her to Gaza. Welcome to my home." Mr. Zahavi patted Seth's back.

"I'm extremely grateful for this opportunity, sir," Seth said. He followed Mr. Zahavi through the front door and questioned Rina with an extended lift of the brows.

"You look great, Mr. Zahavi." Rina shrugged in response to Seth's curious expression.

"Yes, I have much to tell you." A mellow breeze journeyed with copper sunrays through open windows. "Shall we enjoy the afternoon sun on the patio?"

"Mr. Zahavi, I'm—"

"Oh, stop with this Mr. Zahavi business," he jested. "Call me Elijah so I don't sound so old. I'm only forty-five."

A new home, a new appearance, and a new sense of humor? "This is a nice surprise, Elijah."

Elijah sat on a painted wood chair with an ankle crossed over the opposite knee. "I feel better than I have in ages. I presume Rina informed you about my family."

"She did." Seth's growing locks bounced across his forehead. "I'm so sorry for your loss. I can't im—"

"No, no." Elijah waved his hand to stop Seth's condolences. "Don't be sorry. I'm no longer searching for pity. For two years, it was all I craved, especially when I felt like my family died on my account."

Rina interrupted Elijah's unmistakable self-rebuke. "Anyone in your situation needs a listening ear."

Elijah grazed his fingers along his jawline, lost in a distant memory as Rina had seen many times. "There's something I never told you."

As long as it's not a graphic detail, Mr. Zahavi. Rina's tolerance for violent details had fizzled out.

"I was supposed to be with them that day. I had returned early from a business trip, and our children didn't expect to see me till the following day. I thought it would be fun to go with my wife to pick them up." He tapped his knuckles on the thick armrest as if it would open up and give him more words. "I got sick right before it was time to leave. I still could have gone, but my sweet wife insisted I stay home to rest. She said the surprise would be just as good when the kids saw me standing by the door, ready for hugs."

For the first time, Elijah talked about the day it happened. Something about Seth's presence incited people to open up.

"Perhaps, if I had been a little tougher, my wife wouldn't have convinced me to stay home. I would have gone and acted as their shield. Their defense."

Seth pressed the pads of his fingers together to form a temple. "Do you feel responsible?"

Elijah nodded. "If I had gone with her, I would have died protecting them. They might still be alive. Enjoying good health. Thriving. Making a difference in the world.

"The radiant lady seated by your side brought much relief when she called upon me." Elijah cupped Rina's knuckles with his palm. His fingernails were bitten back to the nail plate. "Somehow, she knew exactly when to come. Her visits were always at my lowest points."

Rina scrunched a sideways smile. "I should have come more often." But she didn't, because the result was a depression that took several days to get over. Sometimes a week.

"Your selfless support lifted me up in times when all I wanted was to join my family in eternal sleep."

"Why are you so happy now?" Rina retracted from Elijah's grip.

"The simple answer? I recalled a conversation with my late wife. Little Raziela was a happy individual. Many were impacted by her warmth." Elijah smiled and shook his head. The memory of his wife irradiated through his eyes.

"I must take you to our time in America, where I worked as a professor at a university in New Orleans for two years. Raziela became depressed in the first month we moved there. She wanted to go back home."

Rina settled onto the cushions of the wicker chair, eager to know more. Elijah had never spoken more than a few words about Mrs. Zahavi.

"We went on an outing to a nearby plantation with colleagues and their families." Elijah pressed his lips together and raised a corner of his mouth. "My Raziela befriended a colleague's fiancée. They spoke at length that day and swapped telephone numbers. Within that small period, she began to emerge from her depression."

Rina glanced at Seth without turning her head. "Why?"

"She became a Christian."

Rina shifted in the rigid, wicker chair. At last, the first moments of edginess with Mr. Zahavi materialized. They had been much sooner in past visits.

"Naturally, my Raziela wished for me to convert, which I had no intention of doing. All that mattered, as she and the children began to go to church, was that my wife was happy again. Happier than I'd ever seen her.

"Two years later, she was cruelly stripped of life." Elijah raised both hands in the air, eyes upward. "*God*, I said aloud on the night of the funeral, *how could you do this to her? To the kids? To me?* Bitterness cast a heavy burden on my entire existence. Rina, the last time you came, you saved me. I had planned to slit my wrists after you left, but you said to think of Raziela watching me from Paradise. I recalled the little seeds she planted in my mind. I knew what she would have wanted me to do. So, I did. My salvation changed my life even more than hers."

Rina's pulse raced. She had saved Elijah from suicide! But how could a mere change in faith transform someone so profoundly? The idea was deep but shallow. If it made him happy, that's all that mattered.

Elijah's rough palms covered Rina's hands. "My ambition is to share this knowledge with loved ones. This includes you."

Hope for a short, simple conversation with Elijah vanished. She really wished they hadn't come.

Sharp hunger pangs drew Rina away from the journal. "I could eat a horse right now. That's what your father used to say."

"Here." Eliana unwrapped the soft cellophane from Rina's sandwich. "Maybe take the lettuce off, and it'll be edible."

"Thank you, my Love." Rina suppressed a gag when she pulled out the wilted leaf.

"Not that I have a problem with what Elijah said, but he sounds odd."

"Just wait till I finish his story! I thought he was weird since the first day I met him." The droopy croissant alone was all Rina could manage to eat.

"What did he say next?"

"The most bizarre tale I had ever heard."

ELIJAH'S FABLE

Elijah hunched over his knees, head held high. "Now, I wish to address the national crisis. Our fellow countrymen—"

"Wait," Seth interrupted, "can I record this part of the conversation?"

"Of course."

Gold reflections on the Mediterranean captured Rina in an enchantment. The swelling surf promised change and hope for the dissolution of violence...a dream destroyed by the camcorder's pitchy beep.

Elijah raised his chin, ready for a speech. "Our fellow country-men suffer severely." He scrunched peppered eyebrows and perused neighboring homes. "Israel is under attack by an evil enemy. One who has been after God's people for thousands of years."

Jagged edges of the wicker chair pricked Rina's skin. The red indentations emulated her aversion as Elijah continued.

"The most glorious creature to come from the hand of God turned against his Creator. I speak of Lucifer, God's most beloved angel." Elijah's voice deepened as he indulged in a lengthy story.

Now Rina understood. Consumed by despair, Mr. Zahavi had entered a pseudo reality to escape. He was crazy, not happy! But Seth's reaction baffled her. He pressed his lips downward. A somber nod denoted familiarity with Elijah's account.

"The devil became God's enemy," Elijah continued and scrutinized the canvas of clouds. "Like a ravenous beast, Satan charges full speed to demolish his prey."

His prey? Rina locked her gaze downward, unwilling to show interest in Elijah's long-winded fable.

"Who are his prey, you may ask." Elijah nodded at Rina as if he'd read her mind. "We are many. Those who claim to be Christians. Those who are a part of the Jewish race. He searches the world and seeks to destroy us. Just think of the persecuted who fall under these categories over thousands of years. Even in the last century!"

Elijah stared into the lens and paused. His demeanor softened. "The enemy of God will not be triumphant. Our nation will always be preserved. May you find comfort through these words as the war rages on."

A hallowed stillness followed the conclusion of Elijah's exhortation.

"That's it." Elijah stood and pointed to the camera. "You'll run out of tape if you don't shut it off!" He laughed as his audience stood agape, unable to move or think. Most likely for different reasons.

"Thank you, sir." Seth stood to shake Elijah's hand.

The men turned to Rina. Late afternoon sun beams behind them formed an aura around their bodies. A pair of superior beings with wisdom to impart? More like folly.

"Excuse me," Rina said and left without acknowledgment.

A plush leather sofa in the living area offered warmth amidst the cold gush of emotions that rattled Rina's mind. Unintelligible chatter from the balcony strengthened doubt. The men found common ground. She wanted to share in their excitement, but none of it made sense.

The sky cast missiles of rain upon the car as they headed north. Intense concentration on the dangerous drive gave Rina an opportunity to drown her thoughts and wash them away with the precipitation. Modi'in welcomed them with pristine weather conditions and an occasion to talk before the final goodbyes.

"What did you think of our visit with Elijah today?" Seth's deep, raspy tone melted Rina's mistrust.

"I'm shocked." Rina deliberated furthering the conversation. Seth had understood Elijah's odd fabrication. She didn't. "I can't come to terms with the strange things he said. If it even does exist, what does the war between God and Satan have to do with *our* war?"

Seth turned to face Rina, back resting against the window. He squeezed his eyes shut in contemplation. "It's better explained on a personal level. Everyone has inner battles. Elijah's snare is guilt. He feels responsible for his family's massacre. His weakness threatens to pull him away from his newfound faith. As humans, we try to do what's right, but temptation is powerful. We are all influenced in different ways. It's all about the choices we make."

Rina pushed on her legs to keep her knees from bouncing. "How is that relevant to the documentary?"

Seth cracked his knuckles one-by-one. "When we fight personal weaknesses, our choices lead us to win or lose. If we succeed, great. If we fail, it's okay. All things can eventually become good if we handle it right."

"How so?"

"Elijah is a shining example. Out of all the people we interviewed, his story is the worst. Yet he's the only one who conquered his demons. People will see that you can overcome the worst of circumstances. It'll be the perfect conclusion to the documentary and make the message all the more powerful."

"And his story about the war between God and Satan?"

"That's way over the heads of the general populace. I'll filter most of that out, but not every word."

Weary from conversations too bizarre for Rina's liking, she had to stop before it drove her crazy. Seth's explanations made sense, but how much of Elijah's footage would he use? Viewers were sure to consider the man delusional. Then the documentary would be a farce. All she hoped to achieve by helping Seth would be lost. At worst, counterproductive.

The American national anthem, a song Rina heard only when watching the Olympics every two years, chimed in a bell tone throughout the hospital room. Eliana's phone buzzed on the table.

"That's Brian." Eliana hissed through clenched teeth as she reached a hand to answer. The song left an exquisite echo when it ended.

"I'm calling the nurse." Rina used the strength of her arms to grab the bedside remote. "You need medicine."

"No," Eliana pressed a hand to her wounded shoulder. "It'll just make me go to sleep."

Rina punched the thick, plastic button to summon assistance. "We've been reading almost five hours. Don't you want a break?"

"Even if I did, I—" Eliana stopped short when the door handle clicked.

Amanda pushed through the door with a hand on her hip. "You ladies hangin' in there?"

"Yes, sorry," Eliana giggled in fake dismissal. "I didn't mean to call you."

"You're due for meds, sweetie." Amanda turned to leave. "I'll be right back."

I could use some myself. Rina gripped her overstuffed sling-bag and dug for the plastic bottle at the bottom. To no avail. Too much in the way.

"I'm going to refuse the medicine." Eliana lifted her phone and tapped a finger on the screen.

Rina wanted to take the more potent medicine for her phantom leg pains. The pill she took earlier only dulled the agonizing sensations. It wasn't time yet to sleep, though. Eliana needed to hear more, so she'd live with the torture. Sweet memories of Seth would kill it.

"No, not really." Eliana covered a hand over the receiver as she spoke.

Muffled words gave Rina an indication that something was wrong.

"…kind of mad right now…You know how I've always blamed…"

The meaning of the indistinguishable utterances became clear.

"Now that I know…all these years…" Eliana squeezed her free hand into a tight fist. Each knuckle stood out like a rounded mountaintop.

Rina prodded deeper into her bag. She would take the meds after all.

"I don't know that I can…let's talk after she leaves."

After she leaves…

Rina found the pill bottle and swallowed two with the icy water Amanda brought in a large insulated mug.

"Mama?" Eliana tapped the power button and allowed her phone to slide down the thermal blanket. "What happened next? I mean, obviously, he didn't go home."

"Our courtship began." It was the right moment to plunge into the best part of the journal. In the end, heartbreak and disappointment would prevail. A factor Rina did not think of when she decided to share the story with Eliana.

No stopping now. The journey had to go on.

WELCOME COMPANY

Threads of Elijah's tale wove in and out of Rina's consciousness, leaving a blanket of doubt in his recovery. Yet, Seth understood the story to a certain degree. The uncertainty did not subdue her hope to see him again.

"I'm not ready to leave you." Seth slammed the hatchback with delicate force. "Could you stand a little more time with this weary American boy in need of your company?"

Rina's sizzling thoughts dared her to expose her innermost desires. The slide of his manly fingers through hers provoked an equally expressive response. "Are you sure you want more time with this weary Israeli girl in need of your company?"

"Really?" Seth leaned a hip against the back of the car and tugged Rina closer. The crisscross wrinkles on his forehead slackened. "You need my company?"

He had been in her life for two weeks. Did she need Seth? Maybe.

Did she want to develop more with him? Best not.

Soon he would be gone, and she'd never see him again.

"I'll take you squeezing my hand as a *yes*."

Cold tingles pulsed through Rina's fingers. "Sorry." She released the inadvertent clench and shook her hand.

"Rina," Seth said after a few seconds of cozy tranquility, "you still have two days of vacation. I'd like to spoil you a little. You've done a lot for me. I'd like to repay you."

"You don't owe me a thing."

"I don't agree with that at all." The distant, dark sky flashed with lightning. The storm had followed them from the south. A sudden breeze whipped Rina's hair into her face. Seth tucked the strands behind her ears. His fingers traced the lobes and stopped where the soft flesh met her jaw.

Rina suppressed subtle pants.

"Come with me to dinner tomorrow evening?" The earthy scent of an imminent downpour hastened their farewells.

Cold, weighty drops thumped against the car and ricocheted from Rina's scalp. No time for a delayed answer. "Yes, I'll go with you."

"See ya at 7."

⁂

"Dad was pretty bold!" Eliana wiped her cell phone screen and scanned through photos of Brian. "I mean, it's not like you had given him any clues that you were that into him. Or did you?"

Rina recalled instances when Seth had caught her staring at him. She had never averted her gaze nor disguised where her thoughts were. "He was a natural at reading people. He knew."

"Well, if you wrote something that I would find gross, please skip over it. No one wants to hear about their parents making out."

⁂

Firm leather seats in a fancy limousine matched the firm worry in Rina's gut. Rigid with embarrassment, she planted her heels into the thin carpet and searched for the seatbelt. "I feel famous."

Seth slid onto the shiny leather couch. "You will be someday. After all, you're going to be in the documentary."

A group of kids on the street waved in obvious admiration as the limo bumped into motion. "They've likely never seen one of these in person." Rina returned the wave as they jumped up and down with crooked smiles. She held an interest in nothing apart from Seth during the smooth ride. Only when the limo came to a stop did she care to look outside.

Built into the structure of a stone shopping center, a windmill with a broad base dominated the surrounds. Four sails dwarfed palm trees that aspired to reach the same height as the dominant wheel. "Come on," Seth said and opened the door before the chauffeur arrived. "Ever been to Keyara?"

"No." Rina scooched out of the low-lying vehicle. "I've always wanted to go to this restaurant."

"Good evening, Mr. Gibbons," the refined host said in an eloquent tone.

"Did you reserve the table in a quiet location, per my request?" Seth carried himself with a poise Rina hadn't witnessed. Rather than informal business mannerisms, eyes set sternly on the documentary, he sported regal sophistication.

The hostess curtsied with a short bend of the knees. "Yes, sir. Please, follow me."

"Want some wine?" Seth flipped through the drink menu when they took their places in a secluded corner.

Rina unfolded the starched napkin and spread it across her lap. "Sure. In a hurry to order it?"

"Actually, I am." Seth's lengthy bangs whisked with each flip of a page. "It's been a rough couple weeks."

The sun's glare set the rims of the empty wine glasses aglow. This was a special night, so she would drink alcohol for the second time ever.

"We'll be here a while," Seth said to the bushy-browed waiter. "Your best bottle of local red wine and a meat and cheese tray to start off with."

Rina marveled at Seth's decisiveness. He had no questions for the man. Only polite requests. She admired his ability to make such simple decisions typically overcomplicated by many.

"Tell me something about you," Seth said as he repositioned the silverware to meet his left-handed needs.

"What would you like to know?" Rina tilted her head to deepen the question.

"Whatever comes to mind. Do you have any hobbies, do you have any pets, what is your family like, do you travel?"

"My life is plain. No excitement. Only work. My single hobby is reading. Does that even count?"

"Many consider reading to be a hobby."

"Then that's mine. I usually read a novel or two per week, depending on how busy I am with work. Fascinating, right?"

"I believe reading can make the ordinary evolve into the extraordinary."

"Even those who read science fiction? That's all I read."

"That alone intrigues me. What else you got?"

"I have a cat, and I've never been outside Israel, except for Gaza. That's it. Your turn."

The waiter appeared without a sound. Gentle ripples of deep burgundy wine settled into the lower half of Rina's goblet.

"So far, we have one thing in common: cats. I grew up with them. In my eyes, a home isn't a home without one." Seth lifted his glass over the table. "Let's make a toast. We met two weeks ago today."

The ring of crystal filled the silent exchange of emotion.

After the first sip, Seth engaged in a strange tasting ritual. His sounds of approval intensified with each new swallow. "Who would've known an Israeli wine would be so good?"

Rina inhaled the woody scent from her glass. "Grapes have been cultivated in this part of the world for thousands of years."

"You're right." Seth retained the next sip longer than others with a satisfied nod.

The dark blend coated Rina's taste buds with hints of black cherries and spice. "You like wine and cats. What else?"

"I love photography, play a little piano, and travel a whole lot. Until this trip, my favorite foreign country was Switzerland."

A giant figure with a white coat and chef's hat placed a wooden platter on the table.

"Thank you, chef," Seth said and rubbed his palms together.

"My pleasure." The herculean man explained the assortment of gamey meats and exotic cheeses. "Enjoy."

Seth clicked the tongs and designed an appealing presentation on Rina's plate. "How about your family?"

Whiffs of garlic and spices from the salami gave rise to a low grumble in Rina's stomach. Her parents had never indulged in such extravagance. Her sister didn't live long enough to have a chance. All three of her family members died young—father at twenty-five, a sister at fourteen, mother at thirty-nine. Why did she deserve this kind of treatment any more than they? "You met my family."

"Who?"

"Naomi. She's my family."

"Sorry to hear that." Seth offered silent condolences with a sympathetic curve of the lips.

"Now that you're bored and sad, please tell me something good." Rina copied Seth's wine swirl and subsequent inhalation. "As a reporter, your past must be full of excitement."

Seth gave an ardent account of his early adulthood. Two years at the University of Southern Mississippi, one year at Rice in Houston, and a semester at Tulane sent him on a quest to reassess his future. He traveled the country, took hundreds of photographs, and kept detailed journals.

"That's what led me to decide on journalism." Seth paused to enjoy the neglected food on his plate.

"Do you still write journals?"

"Yep. Ever since I began my travels throughout the States," he said and washed the bite down with a gulp of wine. "It became an obsession."

"I also keep journals, almost obsessively." Rina pictured a collection of pages filled with reflections on her travels with Seth.

Seth raised his glass for a toast. "To common ground."

"To common ground," Rina restated when the chime quelled.

"The next two years, I attended a journalism institute in New York where I became involved in a group that focused on the news media's role in war and peace. This is where I discovered my passion for independent filmmaking, specifically regarding Middle Eastern conflicts. I knew I couldn't participate in mass media with all the biased views." Seth gulped a copious swig of wine. "Enough about that mess."

"Your education and explorations have made you wise," Rina said in admiration.

"Ha!" Seth choked on the wine and guzzled his water to subdue the coughs. "Try audacious. Your turn to talk."

Rina scoured her mind for excitement in her lackluster life. No story of her own could rival Seth's adventures. "All I have for you is a story from someone else's viewpoint."

"Good, now I can devour what's on my plate." Seth cast a sideways smile before stuffing a bite in his mouth.

"When I was just over a year old, I loved to play peek-a-boo with my parents. My mother said it was overwhelming at times, because I was always in their faces to play. One morning, my mother noticed that I was uninterested in the game. She showed me all my favorite toys, to which I showed no interest. When I didn't respond to her hugs, she knew there was something seriously wrong. My eyes became glassy, I labored to breathe, and I lost consciousness. When the paramedics arrived, she yelled at them. Less than ten minutes had passed since she telephoned, but to her, it felt like months.

"It was a living nightmare as she watched her limp baby be handled like a rag doll by strangers. They exchanged no words with her at first. At that point, it was a matter of saving my life. While they worked on me, she called my father at work with the words, '*Meet me at the hospital.*' The paramedics had me on a stretcher ready to go."

Seth stared open-mouthed as if he didn't know the outcome.

"I lived." Rina teased with two fingers place over her carotid artery.

"You tell a good story," Seth said with a shake of the head. "I was in the moment."

Rina savored Seth's attentiveness as she resumed. "Once we were in the ambulance, they asked my mother a million questions. She named everything we did, everywhere we went, and everything we ate in the previous twenty-four hours. At the hospital, she insisted to stay by my side. The staff said her presence would hinder their stabilization efforts, so she complied and waited on a bench in the hallway.

"When my father arrived, he found her unresponsive. He had to squat down and shout her name to bring her out of shock. After forty-five minutes, the doctors were finally able to stabilize me. They discovered deficient levels of insulin in my body and diagnosed me with Type 1 diabetes."

"Wait a minute." Seth raised a finger. "You're telling me that when you were a year old, you almost died from diabetes?"

"Yes. I told you the story just like my mother explained it to anyone who would listen."

Seth's gaze wandered to Rina's neckline and rechanneled posthaste. "What was life like after that?"

"Hard." Rina's brows conjoined to form a frown. "I got insulin injections every day. My mother had to keep hard candy or something similar for hypoglycemia attacks. I remember once all she could find were sugar packets.

I had to eat three before I stabilized. Over the years, the doctor said I had a small prospect of outgrowing diabetes. I was one of the rare cases who did."

"That's fortunate," Seth said. "My mother is fifty-two, and she still suffers from it."

Rina considered the benefit of another common ground, but it was nothing to celebrate. "How bad is it?"

"So serious that she could easily die. Dad and I typically aren't prone to worry. Mom's illness is the exception. When I was home, dad and I, as a team, urged her every day to be ready to treat an episode. I felt guilty when I left for college. It's all up to him now. He said mom is in God's hands, not ours." Seth wagged his head. "I still have a hard time with it."

As dinner continued, Rina surrendered her entire existence to Seth. Their stories coalesced to form a connection that could not be passed off as coincidence. Hungry souls packed the restaurant, but an invisible veil obscured their surroundings. The man with copper hair and eyes the color of a mossy reef fascinated Rina with each passing second.

"What are we seeing?" Rina stepped onto the street outside the symphony theatre.

Seth handed Rina a ticket. "Beethoven's 5th. I've been wanting to hear it live for years."

Four rows from the stage, Rina fixated on the expressions of the musicians as they practiced notes, turned pages, and arranged articles in the small stage portion belonging to each of them. In a single movement, they suspended preparations as the conductor took the stage. Upon hearing the opening four notes, Rina recognized the classic tune.

In dynamic movements, the conductor led the musicians as he oscillated his arms. The vehement whipping caused his full head of white hair to convulse. He bent his knees up and down, clenched his fists, gritted his teeth, and scrunched his face as the vigorous music unfolded.

The heads of the musicians danced briskly as they directed their instruments to keep tempo with the conductor. In the string section, a sea of bows jumped up and down in sync. Cellists swayed their upper torsos as they struck the thick strings. Double bassists thrust their bodies back and forth behind their massive instruments.

A minute into the song, the arrangement decelerated to a serene melody. Rina's emotions soared from highs to lows with the radical shifts in tempo. Each section of the orchestra petitioned for her observations. Commanding horns outweighed all other instruments at times; the violinists countered with their own directive. All the while, drums and cymbals roared in the background.

Rina stuffed crumpled tissues in her purse when the final notes concluded and stood with the rest of the audience who thundered with applause.

Seth clapped with enthusiasm. "Powerful, huh?"

People rushed the aisles, but Rina could not move. "I had no idea music could do that to me."

The crescent moon traversed the sky's breadth as hours passed. They strolled narrow streets in the Rechavia neighborhood where European charm, fountains, and sculptures flaunted resplendence. Villas flourished with greenery and floral designs. Rows of trees proclaimed impeccable symmetry. Massive crepe myrtles, quaint squares, and elegant garden apartments inspired a dream to reside in the community.

"Can you believe it's after one?" Seth said when they found their way back to the limo.

Rina plunged onto the couch and kicked off her heels. "Yes and no." She fought the urge to break down as his imminent departure became a fact she had to face.

"Want to have lunch today?" Seth said as they neared her apartment building.

The breaks' gentle screech signaled the conclusion of the most romantic night of Rina's life. "What's the point? You're leaving soon. In my twenty-seven years, no one has treated me the way you do. It will hurt me when you go home."

Seth skimmed Rina's shoulders with his fingers. "In my thirty-one years, no one has connected with me the way you do. Let's take advantage of the time we have."

"That would make it even worse after you leave."

Seth dipped his head and pressed their interlaced hands to his chest. "Amen," he whispered after a short silence.

Prayer? Seth found a way to offer strength and guidance. It confirmed the goodness Rina loved about him. *Love?* Rina scrambled to understand her thoughts.

"It's going to be okay," Seth said and ran his fingers along her jawline. "I believe our relationship will continue after I leave. I'm sure of it."

Rina wanted to leap into Seth's arms, but she could not fall further for someone who resided across the world. "I must go to bed if I'm going to be up for lunch."

"You pick the place," Seth said and opened the door. "Let's go to one of your favorite restaurants."

Blisters on Rina's feet shouted for relief when she stepped from the limo. Seth swept her up and carried her to the building. The white noise of his breath and the bounce of his stride sent her into a hasty doze.

All events of the night mobbed Rina's mind and body in a single instant. Savory food, full-bodied wine, physical exertion, elation, joy, sorrow, love…Rina jerked in part from the inconceivable thought, in part from the edge of slumber.

"Want me to take you up?" The unrestrained passion in Seth's gaze spoke silent promises of the care she yearned for.

Yes, take me up, put me to bed, kiss me goodnight.

"Just to the elevator." Rina looped her arms around his shoulders to lessen the burden of her weight.

"Only comfortable shoes from here on out," Seth said as he backed into the apartment building door. "You're beautiful, no matter what you wear."

Beautiful.

"Here we are," he said without strain when they reached the elevator.

The ding of the bell did not compel him to release her. His expression exhaled a fusion of lust and respect.

The elevator doors bumped closed.

One foot at a time, Rina stepped from his grip. The cold tile floor numbed the aches enough to enjoy a final hug. Shivers raced through her body as Seth ran fingers across her scalp, down her earlobes, and along her jaw. Rina spread her hands along his firm upper back and glided in tempo with his rhythm.

With his body close, Seth leaned over to call the elevator. The doors popped open, impatient to receive the intended occupant. "See you at noon?"

"Agreed," Rina said as she backed against the wall for support. "Thank you for tonight. For everything."

"You're welcome."

After the doors closed, Rina discharged an uninhibited groan. The intensity of her romantic feelings for Seth quadrupled. After his departure, she was sure to live in misery.

"Dad was so romantic. Brian should be here to get some ideas!" Eliana attempted a stretch and stifled a nasally whimper when her shoulder muscles lengthened.

Rina grasped the plastic bed frame and inched forward to reach the remote.

"Was dad the first person to call you beautiful?"

"Yes. He was. First and last."

"Brian, too. He calls me beautiful all the time."

Amanda rushed through the door and squirted foamy hand sanitizer from the wall dispenser. "What'cha need baby doll?"

Eliana's chalky complexion bore a mark of exhaustion and pain. "Can you give my daughter some medicine? She needs to rest, but she's in too much pain."

"I can see that. I'll be right back."

"Tell me more before she gives me the meds." Eliana released the weight of her head upon the firm pillow.

"To counter what you said earlier, your father wasn't inherently romantic. He tried, and that night he succeeded. After he left me at the elevator, I staggered to my bedroom and cocooned under my downy duvet. My mind traversed alternating terrains between dream and reality. I awoke to my cat, Mr. Big—I'll tell you about him soon—who yowled until I got out of bed. I thought something was wrong with him until I looked at the clock. The electronic green numbers told me I had slept till eleven! I went straight to Mr. Big's bowl and filled it."

"What made you give him that name?" Eliana's eyes followed Amanda as she injected liquid medicine into the IV. Her puffy eyes drooped within seconds.

"Oh, the anticipation, my sweet daughter." Rina liberated a quiet yawn. "You'll find out."

Crisp sheets and two woven thermal blankets were sure to keep her baby warm in the frigid room. Amanda pulled the coverings up to Eliana's neck. "Want some covers, Miss Rina?"

"Please." Rina forced her eyes to remain open long enough to watch Eliana drift into sleep.

Amanda reclined the chair and draped the layers over Rina's body. "Sleep tight," Amanda said with a sympathetic survey of Rina's lower half.

Rina blinked to thank her. Amanda's somber smile was the same type of look she constantly received from strangers.

Maybe I shouldn't be offended when people look at me that way. After all, those who did externalized compassion and concern. Still, Rina did not want to be someone who received pity from others. She just wanted to be recognized as a normal person like she used to before everything was taken from her by a monster. First her husband, then her legs…then her daughter, by her own disastrous decision. She nodded off in recollection of Seth's speech about the choices we make.

"I'm tired of this same breakfast." Eliana poked at chunky eggs that sprung back into place. She bit into a strawberry, apparently sour since she spit it out and replaced the lid.

The Star-Spangled Banner blared from Eliana's phone. Rina bowed her head to study the journal and pretended not to listen to her daughter's conversation. The happiness in Eliana's voice made everything worth the anguish Rina had suffered over the years. And Eliana, for that matter. She was happy here in America.

"Mama?" Eliana held the phone to her chest. "Brian wants to know what you want for breakfast. Let me guess. Pita bread and hummus?"

"You still remember my favorite morning meal." Rina envied Eliana's delight as she finished the conversation.

"Can I read some of the story now?" Eliana pointed to the journal. "Out loud?"

Rina flipped to the middle of the book where they had left off. "Here, it was meant for you to read anyway."

Eliana spread her palm across the pages as if she wanted to feel the emotions in the words. "Shall I begin?"

Rina hadn't prepared to hear Eliana read the story, penned in her early status as a widow with an unborn child growing in the womb. She'd have to fight from breaking down. "I'm ready if you are."

"When we saw each other Sunday," Eliana began, "I asked Seth if we could act as friends for the day. It reminded me of our trip to Gaza, and I missed his unconcealed passion from the night before.

"I was selfish to expect Seth to let go of his romantic feelings. So, as we walked through Anabe Park, I initiated the affection. He reciprocated with tight squeezes of my hand, sighs of relief, and overt pleasure. We sat on the grass, observing the idiosyncrasies of passers-by. I found myself wrapped in his arms. He seized my heart with little effort. In those few hours, I didn't care what our circumstances were. I was his, and he was mine."

Rina pressed her eyelids shut. The moments appeared as clearly as the day they took place. With no requirement to look at the pages, she relived the memories with the love of her life as never before.

DECISIONS

Rina rolled to a slow stop at the hotel. Early twilight shadows obscured Seth's expression.

"I'm trying to decide what to do." Seth leaned against the head rest and looked vacantly at the ceiling. "My flight back to the States is two weeks from today, but I have all I need for the documentary. Now I have to concentrate on my script."

Rina bit her lip and fiddled with the zipper on her purse. She needed him a little longer before a sad return to her solitary life.

What if Seth were to take a vacation? He could use a breather before diving back into his work.

"I'm not ready to go," Seth said in a husky undertone. "I'm not ready to leave this country. I'm not ready to leave you."

"I'd like you to stay longer if you can."

"What would I do? You go back to work tomorrow."

"I know. It doesn't make sense for you to stay, does it?" Rina racked her mind for ideas. "I'll try to convince my boss to let me be a travel guide this week and show you around." What a silly thought.

"I don't see that as a possibility," Seth chuckled. "By what you've said, you're the best agent in the office." Quiet tension began to reverse the harmony of the day. "Let me think about it tonight."

"You must have been sick!" Eliana slammed the journal shut. "Oops, sorry, didn't mean to do that."

"I had to flip my pillow a few times that night. It was soaked with tears. I couldn't imagine Seth leaving so soon, especially after the romantic weekend events." Rina forced a laugh as she remembered what a mess she had been that night. "In the previous two weeks, I received more consideration and kindness from him than any other person in my life. I couldn't fathom that something so special would be so temporary.

"Everyone at work questioned my puffy eyes. My excuse was exhaustion, but no one believed me. Especially my boss who recognized something was amiss. I resisted the temptation to call Seth. His voice would have calmed me. But what if he had made the decision to leave? I would've heard it in his tone."

"Morning, ladies!" A nurse with deep dimples flashed a pristine smile in the doorway. "I'm Angelique. My parents are from the Côte d'Ivoire in Africa, hence the French name. You can call me Angie. I'll do my best to get you out of here today."

Rina watched the middle-aged woman tend to Eliana. Most of the actions Rina could not physically perform. "Thank you for taking care of my daughter."

"I could say, it's my job, but really it's what I love to do. Take care of people." Angie's dimples deepened so much that the pits disappeared into her skin. "Why do I keep talking about myself? You ladies are what's important. How ya feeling, honey?"

Eliana gently prodded her shoulder. "Only a little sore."

"Perfect. I'll let the doctor know." Angie waltzed out the door.

"I need to sit up." The bed hummed as Eliana compressed the incline button. "Did you call him?"

With a reach of the arm, Rina requested the journal. "No, thankfully, I held out." She fanned through the pages as she had done dozens of times. "After work, the crying recommenced. I accepted the fact that I was about to see Seth for the last time. The tears, huffing, and puffing didn't stop until I pulled myself together in the shower. I hid the agony so we could enjoy our final hours together.

Rina parked outside the hotel. A modicum of hope for another week with Seth lingered. He tapped on the driver's window and pointed to the lock. A gust whipped the door open, knocking Seth backward.

Could that have been a sign? That he was supposed to stay here? Or an omen of the bad news to come?

"How was your first day back at work?" Seth jumped to his feet and brushed off his jeans.

"Crazy. Are you okay?" Snug arms lassoed Rina's tense shoulders. He was doing far better than her.

"Yeah." Seth laced his fingers through Rina's, but the gesture offered no sign of the near future. "Do you want to walk to the Indian restaurant down the street?"

Throughout the evening, the sole topic Seth wanted to address was Rina's first day back at work. When she tried to change the subject, he asked questions about destinations in Israel. The attempt to skirt the issue concerning his looming departure was apparent.

He would leave the next day.

After a brief, but succulent meal, Rina prepared herself for the news she did not want to hear. They strolled without a word to the hotel—a bad sign.

But when they came to a stop in front of Rina's car, Seth smiled with a toothy grin.

"Breathe." Seth pushed strings of wind-tangled hair from her face.

"What?"

"You're holding your breath." Seth cradled Rina's shoulders in his palms and kneaded the length of her arms.

"Can you please tell me what your decision is? I think I already know." Rina inhaled deeply to release the tightness in her lungs.

"About that." Seth dropped his hands, leaving Rina's skin frigid as a rare April cold front moved in. "I came here for one purpose and one purpose only. My focus must remain on the documentary."

Rina nodded in understanding.

"My script is due June first, which gives me a little over a month. It's quiet at the hotel. I don't get phone calls or any other interruptions. I worked all day and got much more accomplished than I would have in two days back home."

Oh, thank goodness I didn't call. Rina swallowed a hard gulp as the thought lingered.

"I feel it's in my best interest to stay here for the uninterrupted time. I will, however, require a few hours away from it every day." Seth studied the sky as if contemplating a significant plan. "Maybe around dinner. I think that'd be perfect."

"Do you plan on spending those hours alone, or would you like some company?"

"Do I really need to answer that question?"

Rina dropped her forehead against Seth's chest and slipped into his embrace. "No."

NO ASSURANCE

"That totally makes sense." Eliana shifted into a cross-legged position on the bed. "To be closed up in a hotel without distractions? Good thing you didn't call him."

"I patted myself on the back for the self-discipline." Rina longed to sit in snug positions like Eliana, who pulled her bent knees into her upper trunk.

"When we said our goodbyes, your father and I agreed to have dinner together every evening. During long hours at the office, all I thought of were my moments with Seth. I tuned out all of the sadness of the first two weeks and concentrated on our personal time. Each afternoon, as I watched the sun travel across the horizon through my office window, anticipation took over my ability to concentrate on work."

"I'll bet." Eliana cradled the elbow under her injured shoulder and edged off the bed. "Brian should be here soon with breakfast."

Rina dreamt of a heap of creamy hummus on warm pita bread. "How bad does your shoulder hurt?"

"It comes and goes." Eliana sat in a padded chair by the window. "Did you and dad have dinner every night that week?"

"Oh yes, but our visits were short—two hours, three at the most."

"You must have been ready for the weekend."

"I had two surprises for your father when I picked him up Friday. First, I took him to my place for a home-cooked meal. We were both so relaxed that we fell asleep. I woke up the next morning in my bed. Your father slept on the couch with Mr. Big."

"Finally, I get to hear about your cat!"

"Mr. Big was a whopper of a black cat I adopted from a shelter. As ominous as he appeared, he was the epitome of what anyone could want in a feline friend. Your father was so silly with him, and Mr. Big loved it."

Eliana's sweet chuckle sounded the same apart from a slightly deeper tone. "What was the second surprise?"

"Mr. Lively gave me another week off. I explained the documentary's purpose, and he felt Seth should get a taste of Israel's good side."

Bright morning sun illuminated Eliana's face. Rina studied her daughter's features. She had more freckles, most likely from sun exposure. Her hair had darkened to a deep auburn. Gone, the naïve innocence of a small child, replaced by facets of womanhood. Only twenty, with all she'd been through, Eliana had matured beyond her years.

"What did you and dad do that week?"

"Your father had shared his Christian faith with me after the Passover meal at Naomi's, so I made an itinerary to show him sights from the Bible. I'll skip those pages for now and let you read them alone."

"Did you include any racy details?"

"Absolutely not! Your gentlemanly father remained respectful, so there was nothing to write." Rina huffed a sarcastic sigh. "Besides, do you really think I would include it since I wrote this for you?"

"I guess that's a no-brainer." Eliana scooted back onto the bed. "There's Brian," she said after the classic 5 tap—2 tap knock pattern sounded from the door. "Come in!"

With a white paper bag in one hand and a brown bag in the other, Brian entered with their breakfast.

"Mrs. Gibbons," he said with a lively smile, "I got this from a Turkish restaurant nearby."

The aroma of fresh-baked bread reached Rina's nose before Brian finished speaking.

"I had to knock on the back door since they were closed. I told them a white lie." Brian kissed Eliana's head. "I said it was for a friend from Turkey who's in the hospital. That's why they let me in."

"Close enough." Rina lifted a sealed plastic container from the bag and popped the lid off. The nutty hummus smelled no different than her homemade recipe. "Thank you, Brian."

Eliana had already sunk her teeth into a fluffy white biscuit with golden-fried chicken in the middle. The last time she'd seen Eliana eat was the morning of the bombing. Cocoa Krispies.

Brian beamed, aware of his accomplishment. Two women, famished, relishing breakfast. "Did you ladies sleep well?"

Nasally mother-daughter laughter filled the room.

"I take that as a no?"

The first to swallow a bite, Rina enlightened Brian. "We've been busy."

Eliana crumpled the fast-food bag and chugged the rest of her chocolate milk. "You missed out on a lot after leaving us. Mama, do you mind if Brian hears the rest?"

"Of course not, my Love."

"The rest of what?" Brian scooted onto the bed, where Eliana made him a spot.

"My parents' love story." Eliana took Brian's outstretched hand. "I'll give you a quick summary of what has happened so far."

Rina eased the lid over the white container, now half-empty. No longer warm, the remaining pita bread nestled into the thin, grease-stained paper. Brian had missed most of the story. What remained was bittersweet. He would be the shoulder Eliana needed to lean on for the frightening details at the end.

That part of the journal had not been touched since the day Rina penned the worst and final day with Seth.

"Okay mama, we're ready." Eliana and Brian gave Rina their full regard.

"On the weekend, Seth and I hardly left my apartment. We didn't want to miss a second of our time together, so we stayed up all night Saturday, only drifting off a few times."

Visualizations of their final hours engulfed Rina like never before. "Your father had become more important than any other person in just four weeks! And he was leaving. There was no assurance we would see each other again."

COMMITTMENT

The walk through the airport felt like hours. Seth slumped his arm over Rina's shoulders, but she didn't complain about the backache. His posture continued its descent as they neared the gate. The noisy crowd grated at Rina's ears. There would be no quiet, intimate goodbyes.

"Come here." Seth pulled Rina into a partially hidden nook near the gate. The tripod dropped to the floor with a clank. The camera bag landed atop and rolled like a forsaken car on a cliff.

"Be careful!" Rina leaned against the wall. A chill replicated the feeling that would linger after Seth's departure.

"Over the last few days," Seth mumbled and caressed the curve of Rina's nose, "I've been hearing the voice of my mother. She always told me not to waste my time on '*the ladies*,' as she put it."

Seth slid a finger along Rina's collarbone and pulled her closer. His body heat enveloped her like the first warm front of Spring—a taste of deliverance from frigid winter months. Only now, as soon as he left, Rina would be in the cold again.

"Mom told me to value being alone, but that when I find the woman meant for me, not to let her go. I'm not wasting my time right now. You're the one mom always talked about. But here I am," Seth's voice broke, "and I have to let go of the woman I love."

Rina demanded herself to breathe through a series of huffs.

Seth leaned in for what Rina had longed for since the night he carried her to the elevator. "May I?"

The manly rasp in Seth's voice unearthed a carnal appetite. Rina met his lips with fever and exploration. His supple brushes reignited spent flames.

"Good thing we didn't do that before." Seth dug his fingers into Rina's back. "I don't know whether I could've controlled myself."

"I know I couldn't have." Another round of gentle presses from Seth's lips thrust Rina further into their newfound realm of intimacy.

A voice erupted over the intercom. First-class passengers herded to the boarding area. "What do we do now?"

"We make a commitment to finding some way to see each other again." Sanguine lines formed in the ivory whites of Seth's eyes. "Soon."

"I'm going to feel so alone without you here." Rina thought of her independent nature before she fell in love with Seth. Now she depended on him for happiness.

All hopes for a sudden change of mind fled from her irrational reasoning. It would be selfish to ask him to stay. Impossible.

Another call for passengers trumpeted. Only a few stragglers waited to board.

Seth placed Rina's hands over his breastbone. "I'm making another commitment to you. I'm yours, and only yours. I want you to know that."

"I pledge my faithfulness to you." The last call to board blared. Rina found herself compacted into Seth's arms.

Seth bent down to pick up his tripod and bag. "This is the hardest thing I've ever had to do."

Rina wanted to tell Seth she loved him. She could only express it with, "Bye."

"See ya soon, Lady Love."

"What?' Eliana huddled closer to Brian on the rigid hospital bed. "I thought he stayed. I mean, I know he died in Israel, even though you wouldn't tell me how.

Rina sucked in a deep breath. Her chest expanded, then contracted as she debated the right answer. "Eliana, a mother cannot tell her young child that her father was murdered. It was for the protection of your own soul. You would have been different growing up had you known more details. It would be a morbid circumstance to dwell on every day. I didn't want that for you."

Rina reached to smooth snags of hair from Eliana's face. Cartilage at the bottom of her stubs seesawed as she drove her weight forward.

"Here." Brian edged off the bed with a slight flinch. He needed meds too. "I'll push you closer."

The recliner vibrated against the floor as Brian closed the few inches that had hindered Rina from touching her daughter. "Thank you."

"You're welcome."

Eliana leaned forward. Her long lashes fluttered when the tangles budged.

"Thanks, mama." Eliana leaned into Brian and slid her fingers through his. "Thank you, Brian," she whispered.

Brian responded with a shrug as if the undertaking were a triviality. "What happened after he left, Mrs. Gibbons?"

"I was a mess. My heart had been torn in two, the other half in a distant galaxy. Then, I got a package. Seth sent a letter with a framed photograph we had asked someone to take of us on vacation. Moving forward, we wrote every day. No matter what was going on, no matter how bad the weather, no matter how busy we were, we put a letter in the mail. Seth and I continued to get to know each other most profoundly through our correspondence.

"After a month of coaxing, my boss allowed me to take unpaid time off. He wasn't happy, but he graciously held my position so I would have a job when I got back. Two months had passed when I reunited with your father on June 24th. I dropped everything when I saw him waiting for me with a bouquet of red roses."

Rina laughed as she recalled the look on Seth's face. "I nearly knocked him down."

AMERICA

Rina nuzzled her nose into Seth's neck, spellbound by his masculine scent. She could not fathom separation from him again, but the hard fact remained. She would return to Israel in four weeks. He would not.

"I can't believe you're here," Seth whispered in Rina's ear without loosening his grip.

"Me too." Rina let go and absorbed Seth's loving gaze. In her mind, she had relived the moment of their kiss time after time, thirsting for the day to feel it again.

"I missed you so much," Seth said, his eyes serious, stern.

Rina held her face close to his and closed her eyes, intoxicated by his presence. "I missed you more." Rina got the kiss she had been waiting for. Long, passionate, and even more special since they were not parting company. Well, not for a month.

"Come on, let's go home."

"When your father said those words, I knew America would be my home one day." Rina cringed as the hurt and disappointment compounded. "I was wrong."

"You're alive. There's still a chance." Eliana cocked her head, proving her point.

Rina's sole wish was to live in America. With Eliana. They belonged there together. "Is it tangible, though?"

Brian leaned forward. "There are a number of ways to go about it. I have a sister who is a paralegal at an immigration law firm. I'll get some info for you. I believe it's pretty expensive."

The cost didn't matter thanks to the proceeds Rina still received from the documentary.

"Mama, what did you and dad do first?"

"For a few days, we stayed close to home where it was quiet with few distractions. Your grandmother and I bonded quickly. We cooked and shared secret recipes. She showed me at least a hundred photographs and narrated the stories behind them. Then, your father showed me some sights. We went on tours of Civil War-era antebellum homes and plantations, a Cajun country tour, and an overnight stay in New Orleans.

"We came back home just in time for the morning church services where your grandfather still teaches. At the country club, we had brunch. It was one of the most touching, embarrassing, and heartbreaking circumstances.

Rina slid a juicy strawberry through chocolate syrup and stuffed her mouth. Her plate resembled an abstract painting of pink and brown smudges speckled with dots from the seeds.

With a tap of a spoon on his glass, Seth's father stood at the head of the table and nodded to a waiter who began to pour champagne.

"I'd like to say a few words," Chuck Gibbons began. "Today, we're celebrating a special blessing the Lord has provided us. It is the presence of this beautiful lady sitting next to my son here. Dottie and I have come to understand the reason Seth developed such strong feelings for Rina during his stay in Israel. He told us everything before she came, and just by that, we knew she was something special."

Rina swallowed the partially chewed strawberry. Small, prickly seeds lodged in her trachea. An uncontrollable coughing fit obscured Chuck's speech. Rina reached for her water glass and wolfed down the contents.

"We love you, too, sweetheart." Chuck took the limelight off Rina as she regained control.

The seeds were gone, but the scratchiness remained in her throat. "Thank you. I'm better now," she rasped.

With his crooked smile, Seth began a round of applause. A gesture to ease Rina's humiliation.

Chuck returned to his heartfelt speech. "Rina, you are family. We love you and will gladly do whatever it takes, including the Heimlich maneuver, to make you happy with us. We'll miss you when you leave."

Murmurs of agreement from the table surrounded Rina with verification that everyone held the same opinion.

"Folks, we still have two weeks left with her, so let's enjoy every minute we can." He held up a flute of fizzling, gold champagne. "Cheers to Rina!"

"Thank you." Rina raised her glass in all directions. The carbonation stung her raw throat, but the love in Seth's eyes crushed the discomfort.

Each family member visited with Rina and made it a point to give her a hug. "They're wonderful," Rina said as she followed Seth out of the luxurious building and squeezed his arm. "I wish I had a family like that."

"Didn't you hear what dad said?" Seth wrapped his free hand around Rina's waist. "You're a part of our fam—"

"Hey!" A woman's voice interrupted the declaration.

Seth removed his hand from Rina's body and froze.

"Is that you Seth?"

Rina turned first. A woman of elfin charm stood with her hands out in surprise. Apple-red curls surrounded a pale, skinny face. Her curt, nonchalant glance at Rina flaunted jealousy.

Seth initiated a slow spin. "Nicole, what are you doing here?"

Dressed in black slacks and a white button-down shirt, she planted her bony hands on cadaverous hips. "Working. You?" She glanced back and forth between Seth and Rina.

"You know my parents are members."

Rina clasped her hands and smiled.

"Uh, Rina, this is Nicole." Seth stood stiff, arms crossed. "Nicole, this is Rina…a friend from Israel. She helped me with the documentary."

Friend? Rina felt her veins surge with fiery anger.

Nicole offered her hand. "Nice to meet you."

Rina accepted with a firm grip. "Likewise."

Seth glanced at Nicole, then down to the ground. "We'd better get going."

"Alright. I understand." Nicole approached Seth and gave him a tight hug. She had feelings for him. "I've missed you. Call me soon. I'd love to go to dinner again."

Go to dinner? Again?

"Bye, ma'am, nice meetin' you." Nicole walked in the opposite direction with a glimpse over her shoulder. Her wink at Seth said it all.

"Who is she?" Rina stepped close to Seth with clenched fists. "And why did you tell her that I'm your friend?"

"Please, please don't cry," Seth said and cradled Rina's face with his palms.

Be strong. Don't let him see the tears fall. Rina withdrew from Seth's touch and marched in an aimless direction.

"Wait! Rina, where're you going?"

"I don't know."

"I want to explain myself."

Rina stopped and faced Seth. Less than a foot away, she locked eyes with him. "Did you go to dinner with her?"

"Yes, but…"

"When?"

"A month and a half ago."

"I thought that we…" Rina hung her head just in time to conceal a teardrop. "Can we please go back to your house?"

"Whatever you want, but would you at least hear me out?"

"No." To justify his actions would make Rina angrier. "Not now."

COMPLICATED FUTURE

Eliana elbowed Brian.

"What was that for?"

"Don't you ever do something like that to me!"

"Like what?"

Fully aware of Eliana's intent and Brian's sly retort, Rina restrained a chuckle.

"Hurt me like my dad hurt my mom."

Brian placed a hand on Eliana's knee. "I'll do my best, baby, but that's just part of human relationships."

Rina flipped the journal shut. "Exactly. I had to remind myself that no one is perfect."

"So, you didn't you leave?"

"On the ride home, I pretended like he wasn't there. I had endured the passings of my father, sister, and mother, yet I never felt so heartbroken. All that time, I thought we were together, as a couple, as more than friends. But in front of this alluring young lady, he acted as if we were just buddies."

The skin of Brian's neck rolled when he shifted his head back. "Was she a true redhead?"

"No. Her eyebrows were so blond you could scarcely see them."

"Glad to hear it." Brian smiled. "I've always liked every redhead I met. I would *not* have liked her."

Eliana smacked Brian's arm. "I never knew you had a thing for redheads."

"Well, duh!" Brian ran his fingers through Eliana's hair. "It's a darker shade on the spectrum. Still, you're a freckle-faced ginger."

"Oh well that doesn't make me sound too pretty."

"If you only knew. There's a reason I call you beautiful."

"Yeah well…so mom, did dad beg for forgiveness?"

"It took all my strength not to leave. When I got back to my room, I walked straight to the phone to call Naomi."

⁂

The line rang ten times before Rina punched the 'off' button on the receiver. Naomi was the only person she could talk to right now.

A gentle thump on the door caused Rina's stomach to twist in a tighter knot. She was nowhere near ready to see Seth.

"Rina, it's Dottie."

Was Dottie mad that Rina refused to talk to her son? Would she want to be defensive of him or reprimand Rina for not giving him the right to explain?

"Listen, hun." Dottie's gentle tone answered Rina's doubts. "I haven't whooped my son in twenty years, but I gave him a mighty strong verbal spankin' after he told us what he did to you."

Rina inspected the rutted lines of the sandy wooden door as Dottie continued.

"If I were you, I'd be mad too. By all rights, I'd be out the door by now. You're a strong gal since you're still here."

With a hand on the cold knob, Rina contemplated allowing Dottie in.

"You must really love my son."

Air rushed into Rina's face when she jerked the door open. Dottie enveloped her with loving arms. Tender caresses helped Rina settle uncontrollable sobs.

"I feel so stupid," Rina said, unable to pull away.

"Stupid for what?"

"Because I'm blubbering like this."

Dottie tried to back up, but Rina did not let go. "Come on now, darlin.' Let me see your sweet face."

Rina loosened her grip. When she came face to face with Dottie, she did not expect to see her crying as well.

"You're like the baby girl I never had." Dottie noticed the packed suitcase by the closet. "Hun, I know you're hurt. Shoot, it hurts me just picturing your face when Seth introduced you as his friend. Makes me downright mad." Dottie planted a hand on her hip. "I oughta go back down there and…Well, never mind."

Rina failed to refrain a chuckle.

"Anyway, it's none of my business. I just wanted to come give you a hug and tell you I love you."

She loves me? Rina smiled, honored that she'd been taken in so quickly by Seth's family.

"He's a mess, ya know. I've never seen him so upset. He knows he screwed up. Big time."

"Thanks for the talk." Rina held her hand against the door as she nudged it closed. She had to prepare to face Seth.

⁂

"I'm not surprised Nannie acted like that." Eliana rested on the pillow. "She always stands up for me when Pops scolds me." Eliana pushed a button on the remote. A loud buzz quashed the quiet in the room.

"Feeling sleepy?"

"Yeah, but I want you to keep going."

Brian stood to stretch. "I'll get a chair."

"No." Eliana reached for his hand. "Does your leg hurt?"

"Not really. It's my back could use a break."

Eliana bowed her head.

"I'm not going anywhere. I wouldn't miss what's next."

Rina settled into a new position as Brian pushed a bulky, padded chair next to the recliner.

"An hour later, a light knock startled me from a doze. When I opened the door, Seth stood with hunched shoulders and a regretful expression. Seeing him in anguish, I wanted to hug him immediately, but I maintained my guard."

Seth's pink, puffy eyelids revealed he had endured a number of tear fests. "Will you please talk to me?"

Rina broke her study of Seth's pitiful state. "Sure."

"Do you want me to come in, or should we go somewhere?"

"You decide."

"Let's go outside. It's not hot, and there's a breeze. We could both use some air." Rina ignored the hand Seth offered and wrapped her arms around her torso.

The swinging bench on the wrap-around porch creaked when Rina edged onto the seat. Seth squinted at the swaying grasses in the distance. After a deep sigh, he eased into an iron chair next to the bench. "I want to start off by apologizing. The last thing I want is to hurt you."

Rina blinked fleeting glances as Seth continued. She couldn't manage to make eye contact for more than two seconds.

"I have no excuse for what I did. It was wrong of me to act like you were nothing more than a friend in front of that girl. Gosh, I…" Seth punched a fist into his palm. "I'm such an ass!"

Rina stopped short from agreeing with Seth.

"I want to clarify the story with that girl…"

"Nicole."

"Uh, yeah. I don't want to say her name. It makes me mad at myself all over again. She was a girlfriend in my senior year of high school. We talked about getting married and having kids. It was silly, young love. Our goal was to go to the same college, but we couldn't agree upon one. I wanted to stay close to home; she wanted to go to California—far from her family. Two weeks before prom, we had a fallout and broke up.

"After high school, we never saw each other again until last February. We ran into each other at the mall and had dinner at a nearby restaurant. As we caught up, I could tell she was a different person from the girl I knew in high school."

Rina leaned on the worn backrest. The knot in her throat slackened.

"I had no intention of seeing her again, but when she asked to exchange phone numbers, I did so just to be polite. She called me a few weeks in a row and constantly complained about her problems. I could tell she was lonely and wanted company, so I considered an invitation to dinner. As friends only. When I asked her, she took it as if we were going on a date."

As Rina listened, a strange feeling overcame her. She felt defensive for Seth since Nicole was trying to push a relationship on him. "How could you not consider it a date? After all, you were a man taking a woman for dinner."

"I believe my exact words to her were, '*If you'd like, we could go to dinner so you can have a friend to talk to*,' or something cheesy like that. I should've known she'd misunderstand my intentions." Seth huffed and ran both hands through his hair, making a mess of it as he scrubbed vigorously. "Two weeks before I left for Israel, we went on the so-called date. When I dropped her off, she threw herself at me. I tried to let her down easy, so I gave her the excuse that I'd be leaving soon and didn't want to get into a relationship."

Rina stifled a laugh at the sight of Seth's hair that stood on end, similar to Einstein's wild mane. "How did she take it?"

"She tried to convince me it would work." Seth bent over and rested his elbows on his knees. "She wouldn't leave it alone. A picture of the typical, complicated woman in pure form."

Rina allowed a semi-grin after Seth's eyes lit up with lighthearted humor.

"Anyway, I promised to call after I got back, but I forgot. Then, the unthinkable happened. I ran into her at the post office when I sent the package with our picture."

"Did she throw herself at you like before?" An intense feeling of possessiveness struck Rina as she pictured Nicole in Seth's arms.

"In a way. It was just a tight hug," Seth said as he massaged his stubble. "She was in a rush, and I didn't ask why. That night she called, asked a million questions, asked me why I hadn't called her yet, and asked to see me. The only reason I said yes was that I wanted to tell her about you in person."

Seth rolled his eyes. "And it wasn't dinner! She said that to make you jealous. I was ready to get her off my back, so I asked her to meet me at a café in the mall one late afternoon."

"Mm, hum. Whatever and whenever it was, you didn't tell her that you belonged to someone else."

"I couldn't get a word in. There was this huge drama going on in her family. She cried a few times, and I didn't want to hurt her more. After that, I ignored her calls. Finally, she got the hint. Today was the first time I saw her since then."

Rina clicked her fingernails on the armrest as thoughts began to process. It started to make sense. "The reason you said I'm your friend is that you didn't want to hurt her feelings?"

"Yes, but I didn't consider the fact that I was hurting the one I love in the process. I should've introduced you as my girlfriend."

"Seth, in less than a minute, you went from telling me that I'm a part of your family, to telling a woman from your past that I'm just a friend. I haven't had a family for almost ten years now, except Naomi adopting me as a sister."

"I saw you packed your suitcase." Seth slipped from the chair and bent at Rina's knees. "Please, I beg you not to leave."

Rina closed her eyes and pictured a taxi in the driveway of the Gibbons' beautiful home.

"That wasn't me earlier. It was an inconsiderate coward." Seth took Rina's hand and kissed her knuckles. "Please. I love you. Don't go."

Rina's eyes felt like she stood inches from a burning fire. "I don't ever want to feel this way again."

"You won't. Never again. And I called that woman to tell her she met the love of my life."

"You did what? Why?"

"I wanted her to know."

"That wasn't necessary."

"Oh yes, it was." Seth pressed his lips to Rina's knuckles. "I want everyone to know who you are."

"And just who am I?"

Seth's eye gaze drifted to the fields of swaying grasses. The fixation deepened. "You're the woman I want to marry."

Rina allowed her head to fall forward.

"Come here." Seth sat next to Rina, enveloped her body, and pulled her onto his lap.

"Do you forgive me, Rina?"

Breathless, Rina could only nod and whimper in Seth's neck. Caressed and kissed by a man who genuinely loved her, a complicated future posed a serious question. Did she really want to leave her home country for good?

Rina traced circles around the giant diamond on her ring finger. "As much as it hurt, the fight only brought us closer. He revealed his intentions, and in my soul, I felt the same. I wanted to be with him forever."

Eliana's hair fell past her temples when she lowered her head. Tears dropped one by one onto the velour blanket.

"My Love, what's wrong?"

Brian limped to Eliana's side.

"You and dad." Eliana leaned into Brian's chest when he clasped his arm around her side. "You wanted to grow old and be with each other until the day you died."

Too many times, Rina had stumbled over the thought. "I didn't get the long life I wanted with your father, but we'll be together for eternity in Heaven. This is what brings me comfort."

Eliana swept a palm over her cheeks. "Still, it's such a long time for you to live without him."

PRIME TIME

Rina swallowed the last sip of smooth, fresh-squeezed orange juice. Hand-held American flags and other Independence Day decorations lay on the bench in the breakfast room. How many guests at the big party tonight would notice them?

Seth had purposely taken her to dinner at the country club the night before. He planned to shower Rina with affection in front of Nicole. To his dismay, his ex-girlfriend had the night off. His gesture made Rina toss out all trivial doubts that still lingered.

"Your mother's breakfasts are so filling." Rina resisted the urge to undo the top button of her jeans. "I don't think I'll be able to eat again until dinner!"

Seth tilted his head and chugged the last of his orange juice. "Enjoy it. I don't think you'll find fluffy pancakes like hers when you go home. Not to mention Uncle Joe's homemade sausage and the farm eggs from Aunt Becky."

Rina picked at her cuticles. "I don't ever want to go home."

"You really don't want to go back?" Seth's chair scraped against the hard tile floor. He extended his arms, a summon for her to sit on his lap.

"If I had the choice, I'd stay." Rina curled up on Seth's legs. "I feel safe with you, your family, and in this country. I know it's not perfect. There's plenty of danger. Still, it's a haven compared to Israel, where it's hard not to fear for your life every time you step out the door."

"There's a means for you to stay."

Rina reflected on Seth's statement. He could only be referring to one thing. "I can't in good conscience leave things like they are."

"What if I paid for some kind of service that would pack all your belongings and ship them here?"

A significant expense.

"I can't leave Mr. Big behind."

"I can send someone to get him. He gets to ride first class. I don't care how much it costs."

Persuasion at its finest. But rationality prevailed. Decisions fueled by emotion led to mistakes. It had to be done right. "I didn't say goodbye to Naomi, and my boss is holding my job for me."

Seth pulled Rina up and threaded his hands through her hair. "We'll figure it out, Lady Love."

⁂

Eliana's laugh startled Rina. "You're not looking at the journal. How many times have you read it?"

"Too many to name." Rina had memorized every word. The reading sessions always took place on the couch, her favorite place to snuggle with Seth. "Your grandparents threw a big party for July 4th. A hundred friends and family members gathered around all sides of the house." Rina recalled the food served at the celebration—honey barbeque chicken, smoked brisket, homemade sausage, crawfish, beans, gumbo, corn on the cob, slaw, potato salad, and fried okra. "Your father took me to a private place and asked me to marry him. I'll let you read that part on your own." Rina flipped through the pages.

"I'm craving pizza." Eliana licked her lips and gulped water from her mug.

Brian slid a thumb over his phone screen and tapped four numbers to unlock it. "I've got the apps for all the big chains. Tell me which one you like."

Rina skipped past many pages. The reading had drawn out too long. Minor details would have to wait.

"Mama, were you surprised when he asked?" Eliana stood to stretch. No grimace from pain. Only a slight undulation of the jaw.

"Surprised, yes. Seth bought a ring the day we made up." Rina wanted to go into detail about the proposal. Dottie and Chuck were in on it. They even planned a small firework show after the proposal. "When he asked, he said wedding plans were already underway—if I said yes. We got married two days later."

Brian stood behind Eliana to catch her from a potential fall. "Dizzy?"

"Kind of." Eliana followed Brian's guidance onto the bed. "Was it a big wedding, mama?"

Another thing for Eliana read later. "No. I'd say 40 guests."

"Where did you honeymoon?"

"Anna Maria Island on Florida's east coast. We spent most of the time lounging on the beach, kicking through powdery sand, and floating in the clear-blue water long after sunset. I started to worry about sharks once twilight passed."

Brian's phone rang out in a thunderous guitar riff. He juggled the phone to stop the music. "Pizza's here. Be right back."

"On the day I left, my gut flurried with biting butterflies. Your father gave me some fantastic news on the way to the airport. He received word that the documentary would be aired on primetime TV on August 12th!"

"How? Wouldn't it normally take months, or a year or longer to get a spot like that?"

"Yes, but thanks to his connections, he secured a slot that had been cancelled."

Brian shouldered through the door with two pizza boxes stacked in his arms. Scents reminiscent of a bakery, zesty tomato sauce, salty cheese, and herbs filled the room.

Rina could already taste the pizza.

Brian distributed flimsy paper plates while Rina filled him in.

"That's really cool. I'd like to have connections like that." Brian opened both boxes in front of Eliana so she could choose from the variety.

Rina pulled a slice topped with colorful vegetables and meats. The stringy cheese adhered to other pieces, causing a mess. "Sorry."

"No worries, Rina."

As they stuffed their mouths with hot, doughy pizza, Rina recalled the lengthy departure from Seth at the airport. For five weeks, she would be incomplete, separated from him by thousands of miles. Fear struck her core when they shared parting kisses. What if they never saw each other again? Should she stay in America, as Seth suggested? There was too much to lose. If something were to go wrong, it would be her fault without a doubt.

Rina's foreboding thoughts predicted the doom to come. Here she was. A widow. A double amputee with a grown daughter who had almost been shot to death.

"If I were to read you the rest of this journal, it would take at least another 12 hours." Rina handed her empty plate to Brian, who had assumed trash duty. "I'm going to give it to you to finish later."

"I'd offer to speed read," Brian said, "but that wouldn't do justice to the story."

Eliana plucked tangles from her forehead. It would take three rounds of conditioning treatment to tame the unruly mane. "I'm ready to get out of here. I wish the nurse would come back already. This reminds me of the day I woke up in the hospital after the bombing."

Remorse clutched Rina's insides as she witnessed hollow darkness distort Eliana's expression. Delicate curves bunched across her forehead. They told a tale of worries, laughter, and anguish. "Eliana, I don't know what the rest of our time together will be like. I want to tell you about your father's final day in person. Not reading it from the journal."

"Why?" Eliana leaned sideways onto Brian when he took a seat on the bed, now strewn with a mess of bundled sheets and blankets.

"I owe it to you. You deserve to know." Rina leafed through the frayed pages. After today, she would never reread the journal. "It's going to be hard to hear, my Love."

"I'm not a child anymore. I can handle it."

You may be an adult, but you don't know the brutality your father suffered.

BLAME

Mr. Big nudged Rina with his cold nose. She stretched under the downy duvet and felt for Seth. "You can't be hungry, big boy. Surely papa already fed you." An imaginary smell of foul, wet cat food sent Rina running for the bathroom.

She had been back in Israel five and a half months. Much longer than she wanted. Mr. Lively requested she stay at the agency six months upon her return from America. He'd done so much for her that she couldn't say no. After Seth arrived, he agreed.

"It'll be a good excuse to get mom and dad to see the Holy Land," Seth had said the night he returned to Israel.

Dottie and Chuck came for the month of December and left on New Year's Day. Now, almost two months later, Rina was sick every morning. She washed up and went to the kitchen to study her wall calendar. *How is it already 1999?* Not that she had marked a day, but she remembered the approximate time of her last cycle.

"Morning, Lady Love." Seth snuggled against Rina from behind and rested his hands on her belly.

Rina turned to see Seth's green eyes aglow from the bright morning sun that blazed through the window. He was more happy than usual. "How did you know?"

"How did I know what?"

"That I'm pregnant." Rina found herself swept up in Seth's arms. "Are you surprised?"

"I guess I shouldn't be. We haven't been careful."

"Your father made a fuss over the whole thing." Rina had agonized over thoughts of her mother and grandmother's history of multiple miscarriages.

"We prayed that the family curse would not affect me. We were supposed to leave for America in three weeks, but we decided to stay in Israel until after you were born."

Eliana fidgeted with the blanket. "Wait. Wouldn't it have been better for me to be born here? An American citizen?"

"We talked about that, trust me. It wasn't your nationality that worried us. Once we agreed to stay, Seth came up with an idea that I feel cost his life."

If I had just stayed in America, as Seth suggested, he wouldn't have put himself in that position in the first place. "In a way, I still blame myself."

"I'm going to bring a copy of the documentary to Mrs. Shalev," Seth revealed after a visit to Naomi and Azriel. Rina had surprised her friends with news of her pregnancy. Naomi, in turn, declared she, too, was expecting. "In fact, I want to bring a copy to every family we interviewed."

"Seth, it's too dangerous." Rina massaged her abdomen, stuffed from Naomi's feast. "I want to see Mrs. Shalev, but can't you mail the rest?"

"I could." Seth jerked the car to a stop to avoid hitting an elderly woman who'd apparently lost her way on the street. "I think it will be more personal to bring the copies in person—a small token of my appreciation. Plus, I'll bring DVD players in case some don't have one. It'll only take a matter of two days."

"I had a profound respect for your father's intentions." Rina pressed on her lower belly just as she had in multitude throughout pregnancy. "He desired to reach out to others, and I completely supported him. Rather than completing the task in two days, Seth decided to call upon one family per day. That way, he could stay to watch the documentary and have enough time to talk with them afterward."

Eliana shared a curious glance with Brian. "Did you go with him?"

"I did. We went in the same order. Mrs. Shalev came first and the one more moved than all others. Elijah was the only person we hadn't seen two weeks later. That's when my future changed forever."

"Seth, I have a bad feeling." Rina had noticed a dilapidated car on their trail from her apartment. Sure, it could be a coincidence. Someone on her street, maybe from her own building, planned a trip Gaza that day as well. Seth's erratic driving caused Rina to believe he had suspicions too. "Do you think the documentary fell into the wrong hands?"

"What do you mean, Lady Love?" Seth slowed to a stop as they approached the border checkpoint. It was particularly busy today.

They'd be in line at least forty-five minutes.

"Some may consider it offensive." Rina crossed her arms to hide the shakes.

Seth gripped the steering wheel. His eyes darted from each side mirror to the rearview mirror.

"Anyone on Earth could've seen it after the primetime broadcast. I'd already be targeted by now."

"But, Seth," Rina unbuckled and corkscrewed in her seat to spot the followers, "not many people here watch American TV. After handing out copies in this area over the past week, the DVD could easily have been lent, borrowed, or stolen. Many have seen it by now."

"Why are you so worried all of a sudden?"

"I need to get out." Countless vehicles rumbled. Exhaust polluted the air.

Seth shoved his door open. Dust kicked up under his feet as he rushed to Rina on the pot-holed road.

"I shouldn't have let you come." Seth's hands found their way to Rina's shoulders. The building tension eased with his gentle massage.

"I'm too hard-headed to let you stop me."

A deep exhale was the only response Seth could offer to her attempted humor. "We're being followed."

"I know."

"Why would someone give away the DVD?" Eliana reached for Brian's hand.

Rina and Seth had discussed the possibilities. "We suspected it was something innocent. Most likely an interviewee shared it with friends or family. One person is all it took to react. They probably followed us after one of the previous visits and just waited for an opportunity to catch us."

"Mama, did you find the car? Was it in line?"

"It was. Just two behind us. That's why I didn't see it from my seat."

PURSUIT

"Get back in."

Rina obeyed Seth's command. The driver and passenger in the car had wanted to be noticed.

The grungy, older man behind the wheel had scowled and pushed an elbow in the youngster's chest. The teenager protested the offense until he caught sight of Rina and Seth.

He snickered and elbowed the man in response. Were they really following them? Gofers for extremists? Or were they members of the community who laughed because Seth stood out like a sore thumb with his pale complexion and auburn hair?

It didn't matter one way or another. Rina and Seth needed to get away from the men.

Rina twisted in her seat after they passed the checkpoint. When the IDF border police motioned for the men to stop, the car plowed past them, almost hitting an officer. Gunshots echoed.

Seth punched the gas. "Get down!" his voice cracked as he shouted the command repeatedly.

Rina doubled over and flattened against her thighs. Her belly had only hardened by then with no signs of showing. "It's the IDF shooting at the other car!"

Seth sailed around a corner. "If they're not stopped, *we* will be shot at!"

"Let me drive. I know my car and these roads better than you." An irrational request. Any headway would be lost if they stopped.

A dog sauntered into the street, unaware it was about to be roadkill.

Seth ground his teeth and screeched to a halt. "Why the hell did I…? You're more important than a damned dog!" Frozen in place by fear, the canine crouched in front of the car. Seth pounded the horn and stepped on the gas. The wheels bumped into action on the pavement.

The dog dashed to a short alley in the nick of time.

Seth shifted from third gear into fifth. The transmission roared.

Rina spread her hands across her lower abdomen. An ineffective shield. “I don’t see them. I think they’re gone.”

“They’re not.” Seth soared up an incline.

Buildings marked by graffiti, artistically painted faces, and Arabic lettering were like a crowd cheering them on. Or booing them. ‘I Love Gaza,’ one illustration proclaimed in English with large eyes dripping blood.

Suddenly, the junky car flanked them from an alley. Windows down, the grisly driver aligned with Rina. His young sidekick laughed. It was like a game to them.

Or so Rina thought until the teenager aimed a pistol at her head. Black-marble eyes narrowed like seeds sprouting with a determination to kill.

Rina hooked the steering wheel and crashed into the other car. The gun flew from their pursuer’s window and bounced on the pavement.

Seth grabbed the wheel and slammed the gas pedal, taking the lead. “What are you thinking?”

The car fishtailed like a pendulum. Rina braced her hands against the dashboard. “He pointed a gun at me!”

“What?” Somehow, Seth managed a proud smile.

But the abettors rammed them from behind.

Seth forced another notch of speed. The transmission howled. “Tell me where to go.”

Rina barked orders.

Seth slammed around corners.

Buildings rushed past. Pedestrians stood with mouths agape.

Accelerations jerked Rina to and fro like a seesaw. “This is hurting the baby!” The taste of pungent burning rubber scathed Rina’s tongue.

Seth wrapped his bottom lip over the top. “Your life matters more.”

He was right. They couldn’t stop just to save their unborn child’s life. Its survival depended on Rina’s survival.

“How far behind are they?”

“Close. Three car lengths.” The stench of smoke engulfed the car. Rina covered her nose with the top of her shirt and pulled a deep breath. “My car can't handle this. She's going to break down!”

“I can’t shake ‘em, damn it!” Seth ground the clutch. The car shot forward, proving more capable than Rina thought.

They careened through streets, a missile on course for its target. Residents opened windows to watch. People on foot recoiled. A crotchety old man shouted, face gnarled in anger, chin dotted with spittle.

Seth and Rina were unaware of it all. Only escape mattered.

Pungent gasoline fumes reached Rina’s nose. The strange sweetness of the odor dizzied her mind like the early beginnings of sleep. She continued to give directions, en route to Elijah’s neighborhood—a bad idea. They wouldn't make it to his house anyway.

"We're running out of gas." Seth punched the dashboard. The car swerved out of control and hopped a curb.

A light pole was directly in front of them.

Seth threw the steering wheel left and clocked 180 in the other direction. His forearms crisscrossed before his hands returned to the 9 and 3. They'd missed a collision by inches.

The car sputtered.

Their pursuers crushed the distance.

Seth snapped the steering wheel back and forth. Gasoline swished in the tank. His measures to avoid the light pole had slung Rina's body against the door. She pressed a palm to her head. A dizzy spell cast her to the brink of unconsciousness.

No way would she give in and let the henchmen win without a battle. She had to at least try to protect the baby. She squeezed her eyes. Inhaled raunchy air. Gathered her wits. "If you fight the big man, I can fight the teenager."

"You're not going to fight. You're going to run."

Gas fumes gave the engine a final boost of power.

Rina spotted a run-down petrol station. "Over there!"

Seth turned the steering wheel hard.

Rina's forehead cracked against the window.

The car lurched to a stop inches from the gas pump.

"Go inside!" Seth stretched over her lap and tugged the door handle.

Shrill sirens wailed.

Rina hopped out of the car, but the pursuers had been forced to stop.

Police wrenched the boy from the car and shoved him prostrate on the hot, tar-stained concrete.

"Why aren't they…" Rina sucked staggered breaths, "… looking for us?"

The pudgy older man lay less than a foot from his accomplice. He probed Seth with a hateful sneer and thrashed to fight the police. But he smiled, almost nodded, as if he hadn't lost.

"They didn't see the chase."

A military hummer roared into sight. Armed IDF soldiers pounded from the vehicle, assault rifles raised.

But Rina sensed the hunt was not over. People had been angered by the documentary. Yes-men for a radical agenda waited to retaliate. To get revenge. Where were they? Could they be watching, even now?

Rina stared at the pages, still lost in the scene. The terrifying moments were as real as the day it happened. She hadn't read it since she wrote the journal over nineteen years ago when her belly grew day by day with the baby inside her.

Brian slid the journal from her grip. "You're shaking."

Eliana hunched over. The sharp curve of her spine convulsed. Sniffles coincided with deep inhalations. "I have to get out of this place." She tapped a button on the remote.

No words could alleviate Eliana's distress. She had just heard a harrowing story in which her parents were nearly killed. To know the details of her father's murder, even the fragment Rina had included in the journal, would devastate Eliana. The pages would have to be ripped out.

The door cracked open a few inches. Voices engaged in conversation on the other side.

"Check her vitals one more time," a male voice said. Further instructions, muffled by shrill door creaks, rolled from the doctor's tongue in choppy undertones. "…prescribe something for anxiety…"

A beefy woman rounded the door. Arm muscles bulged under her scrubs. "The doctor has ordered your release," she announced without an introduction. She hustled through the room. Drafts trailed each step. A bitter fragrance slew all cheerfulness that had remained. Not that anyone felt happy right now.

The nurse left as quickly as she had entered.

Brian propped the door open and fanned the room with a flimsy magazine.

"When are you going back?" Eliana's face hung limp, inexpressive.

Rina had booked the return flight for January first. What if Eliana didn't want her to stay that long? It may take her daughter longer to forgive, if at all. "I haven't decided yet."

"I'm going with you."

Brian flung the magazine on the chair. "That's a bad idea."

"My Love." Rina pushed her hands on the armrests to stand, forgetting the impossibility of it. Brian caught her before she landed. It wasn't the first time this happened. Only when Rina sensed danger did she forget her status as a cripple.

"Mama!" Eliana scurried from the bed, cupping her shoulder with the opposite hand.

Brian repositioned Rina in the recliner.

Eliana hovered over his shoulder.

"I–I'm sss–so sorry." She swallowed hard and withheld a sudden yelp. "I'm not hurt." A lie.

The burly nurse barged into the room, unaware of the unfolding drama. "If you two'll step outside the doors, I'll get Eliana dressed."

"My mom can stay."

Rina kept her eyes low to allow Eliana privacy.

"Do you have prosthetics?" The woman cast a glance at Rina's lower half.

"No disrespect intended, but things would be easier. Not just for you."

With the arm sling in place, Eliana pulled away. "Do you talk to everyone like this? Besides, what do you know?"

"My brother's a retired Navy medic. Took care of injured Marines in Iraq. He was in the wrong place at the wrong time." She crossed the room and swiveled the wheelchair. "Double-amputee, just like your mom here. Dang lucky to be alive. He's lived with me since the day he came home. Mind if I transfer you, ma'am?"

Rina stretched an arm over the woman's upper back, now appreciative of her character. She delivered Rina to the rigid wheelchair with remarkable strength and care. "Thank you."

"Call this doctor. He's the best in town." She scribbled a name on the hospital release papers and handed the stack to Eliana. "Good luck!"

The prosthetic legs Rina got six years ago never felt right. Extensive therapy became cumbersome. She had no aspirations to live a normal life anyway. Now, she had cause to believe in a future with Eliana.

"You ladies ready?" Brian stood in the doorway. A noisy set of keys dangled from his fingers.

Rina exchanged glances with her daughter. They headed out the door, a new relationship in the works after so many years. One thing she knew for sure, Eliana wanted to be together. Rina had to convince her that Israel was not where they needed to be.

Mr. Big was the best cat Rina had known, yet today she met the most loveable cat ever. Sterling rubbed his jaws and forehead on her limbs. Rumbly purrs and throaty vocalizations left a sweet tenderness in her heart. His presence nourished a hunger for attention.

Eliana savored warm saffron rice and chicken-kabobs, still eating long after everyone else finished. The Mediterranean takeout food flooded Brian's apartment with scents of spice, grilled meats, garlic, and fresh bread. The ambrosial aftertaste left Rina satisfied with her cultural cuisine.

"I'm ready to hear more." Eliana lounged on the sofa near Brian's recliner, which he graciously relinquished to Rina for as long as she needed.

More snug than her own recliner at home, Rina would have no trouble sleeping on the overstuffed chair. But the inner disquiet set in. The moments leading up to Seth's death were too intense for Eliana. Why did she write them to begin with? "I'm pretty tired."

"Come here, boy. Let's give our guest a break." Brian scooped Sterling under the belly. "I think we should all rest. Especially you two with the little sleep you've had."

A full belly, sleeping pills, and Brian's cozy apartment brought Rina to a lethargic state. She plunged into slumber with ease.

Orange beams from a streetlamp slipped through cracks in the curtains. Brian lay on the floor, bundled in a camouflage sleeping bag. Soft snores comingled with loud purrs. Sterling lay where Rina's legs should have been. Eliana was nowhere in sight. Brian told them both to take his bed tonight, but Rina had requested the recliner. '*Whatever it takes for you to be comfortable, ma'am,*' he had said.

Brian, the epitome of a Southern gentleman, just like Seth. Although the Marines gave him quite a different character. He was exactly what Eliana needed.

Her daughter had grown up an orphan with grandparents she hardly knew at first. Rina had confidence in Chuck and Dottie. She was sure Eliana would be better off in the long run.

But would Eliana forgive her?

A vision captured Rina. It happened frequently over the years. Random, without warning, she saw Seth's body on the floor. She had relived the final hour with him in excess and felt more guilt-ridden each time.

If only she had followed his lead.

NOTHING TO GAIN

"We should go talk to them." Seth replaced the fuel dispenser on the gas pump with force. Apprehended by the IDF, the men who had chased them were no longer on the scene.

"I think we should leave." Rina glided shaky fingers over dark-raspberry bruises on her right arm. The misshapen splotches deepened as minutes passed. "I don't trust anyone here."

Seth didn't argue. "You need to be checked out. Where's the nearest hospital?"

"Not too far." Rina's body ached. She would be diagnosed with whiplash and lacerations to the head at worst. "I don't think I have any broken bones. You?"

The only injury Seth sustained was self-inflicted. His eyebrows snapped together when he opened and closed his swollen right hand. He'd punched the dashboard hard, but not enough for a fracture. "Nah."

"We can take care of our injuries on our own. Elijah lives five minutes from here."

"If there's someone else following us right now, we'll put him at risk." Seth circled the mangled car. "I say we leave, cross the border, and get back home."

Seth turned the ignition key. The engine sputtered. A black puff of smoke heaved from the muffler. No luck.

Rina grieved for her car. She named it Charlotte when she left the dealership a decade ago. The torturous moments of the chase far outweighed the years of dependability Charlotte had given Rina.

"We have to walk to Elijah's house."

Rina trudged three miles in flip flops. Blisters stung her toes.

The joy in Elijah's eyes vanished when he saw Rina. She fell onto the downy couch and kicked her shoes to the floor.

Hints of anger tore at Elijah's expression as Seth explained the circumstances. "I have a friend in the IDF," he said and popped out his flip phone. "He'll know what to do."

Seth traced Rina's profile, careful not to touch the raw wounds. He explored her eyes like never before. "I thought I'd never be able to tell you again how much I love you. I felt for sure we were going down one way or another, by a wreck, or a gunshot, or an all-out fight."

"I should have listened when you said not to come." Rina's hair stuck to her temples, still moist from the sweltering heat. Weather reports had predicted the hottest day of the year. "And you should have listened when I said to mail DVDs."

"I'm so sorry." Seth held Rina's fingers to his lips, prolonging the kiss on her ring. "I promise never to put you in danger again."

Rina relaxed on a plush cushion. With Seth's hand on her belly, centimeters from their baby, it was one of the happiest times with her soul mate. "We're having a girl. I can feel it."

Seth's mouth lifted in a subdued grin, eyes dazed with a red web of events crisscrossing over time. "I like the name Eliana. It means *God has answered.* Mom wanted that name for a daughter. What do you think?"

"I love it." If the life inside her womb survived, Eliana would indeed be an answer to prayer. "I'm ready to leave Israel. If the baby is meant to live, she'll make it whether we're here or there."

"My parents would be thrilled to be at the hospital when Eliana is born. We'll leave next week," Seth said and pressed his lips to Rina's navel.

A slam of the front door ripped the sweet exchange in two.

Elijah stormed into the room. "Hide! They're here!"

Seth's pupils narrowed to pinholes.

Rina leaped from the couch.

"Come on!" Elijah ushered them into a dark room.

A large closet stuffed with Raziela Zahavi's wardrobe provided an effective place to hide. Elijah bulldozed a mass of clothing aside. Hangers pitched to and fro, clinking as they collided. "Go now! Both of you!"

"Wait!" Seth gripped Rina's shoulders. "They're here for me. They'll search until they find me."

Crashes from the door reverberated through the house. Elijah pushed through endless hanging clothes. "In the back," he said in a calm, stern voice.

Seth leaned into Rina's body. "Do not come out until I tell you it's okay. Do you understand?"

Rina kissed her husband and squeezed his hand. "Be careful." She stumbled over a stack of purses and hustled to the furthest corner.

"Don't make a sound," he whispered and wrapped the clothing around her.

Seth retreated through the pathway the men had formed to Rina's safe spot, his breath the last thing she heard before the door shut. The light went out. Absolute darkness, one of her greatest fears became her greatest ally. A shield from the enemy.

What would Seth do to defend himself? Kitchen knives would work. Seth and Elijah were strong enough to fight.

Hope for victory grew stronger as seconds passed.

Dust drifted from the fabrics, untouched since Mrs. Zahavi's death over two years ago. Sleeves trapped and shrouded her arms. Silk, polyester, denim, every textile imaginable.

Like an insulated room, the wardrobe dampened the sounds of a scuffle. Two voices engaged in a shouting match.

Devoid of fresh air, Rina's haven engulfed her in fear. She sucked in stagnant oxygen. Fine particles of dust entered her airway. Musty spores wafted in the confines. Pungent camphor mothballs stung her nasal cavities.

Bashes and rumbles crushed the silence. The voices were gone, no one yelled, no one spoke. Did they gag Elijah and Seth? Footsteps shuffled on the floors. They arrived in the bathroom. One room over.

Arabic rattled from their tongues. Rina understood.

"She's here?" The authoritative voice snapped the question.

Doors smashed against walls. They hunted in every room.

Rina stepped back. Her blistered heels scraped the baseboard.

"Yes! I swear!" A puny, juvenile voice answered. "They came in together."

Elijah spoke. Angry yet calm. "I don't know how you didn't see her leave," he said in Arabic, his voice near. "The ambulance, they came to get her. She's pregnant and bled badly."

The dominant voice thundered rebukes. They had entered the room. "Have you gone blind?"

Rina slid to the floor and pressed her knees into her chest. Fur itched her nose. Soft leather brushed her shoulders.

The closet door swung open.

"I took the bicycle to use a Bezeq phone," the young voice ranted excuses. Hangers crashed in his wild search. "How else would I call you?" The boy shoved past fabrics to reach the back. Soon he would reach Rina, only a few more steps, and he'd be there.

But Elijah had the perfect story. The kid who followed them from the petrol station, the undetected snake, left just long enough to use a payphone. In the meantime, an ambulance came and went.

Rina sunk lower. If she didn't die at the hands of the enemy, death by asphyxiation would be certain. Odors of animal hide clutched her insides. Gags advanced and retreated, threatening to expose her.

Willpower over fear. Rina had to triumph. For Eliana.

"Stupid idiot," the older voice boomed. "You should have broken into the neighbor's house."

A head slap snapped like the crack of a whip on a racehorse. The boy yelped.

Then, just like that. He was gone.

The door crashed to a close. Walls vibrated from the force.

Vertigo mushroomed with each fraction of a second. Rina had to get up. But what if this was a trick? What if someone were in the closet, more silent than she?

Rina pointed her face up for a breath of stuffy air. The shallow puff merely teased her lungs. She had no choice but to move, but the clothes pushed her shoulders. Warned her not to go further. She didn't listen.

A musty odor reminded Rina of the homeless man who begged for money every day outside her building.

A subtle exhale by the door, softer than a baby's sigh, alerted her.

Someone was there.

Light blinded Rina. The pull-chain seesawed like a pendulum.

A small figure stood still. She blinked hard, again and again, to clear the blur.

Then, she saw him. Fourteen, fifteen, maybe. Scrawny. A worn, oversized shirt hung on his torso.

His sinister smile and beady eyes marked a feeling of satisfaction. He had caught her. And he was ready to boast to his boss. He grabbed the door handle and dragged a deep breath, ready to yell.

"Wait! Please!" Rina pleaded in Arabic. "I can't die. My baby." She pointed to her belly.

The kid cocked his head back. "You die. Baby dies," he mocked in Hebrew.

"How do you know my language?" She mouthed, her voice quieter than a whisper. The only chance she had now was to distract the kid. "You can use that, you know."

He faltered. The cockiness vanished.

"You have a future." Rina raised her hands Heavenward. "This isn't it. Don't ruin your life!"

"What do you know" he rebuked in Arabic, "about my future?"

"You're young." The pull-chain settled to a stop in front of his face. "You can be successful. I'm sure of it since you already know two languages fluently. Any others?"

He nodded. Pride ushered over his gaunt features. "I watch videos on the Internet," he said in clear English. "It's easy to find lessons."

His boss, whoever he was, called from another room. "Yosef!"

"Yosef," Rina spoke in English, "you're so smart if you can learn on your own like that!"

"Yosef!!"

Frazzled hair fell in the teen's face. He backed out of the door, eyes darted to and fro. There was one decision to make. Turn Rina in and follow the same path he already traversed. Or use his intelligence for better purposes.

"You'll gain nothing by telling him I'm here," Rina pleaded in the gentlest of tones. "By walking away now, you will always know that you saved two people from murder. Please, Yosef, let me and the baby live."

Yosef propped his arm on the door frame. Hints of every type of emotion flitted across his face like a flip photo book. The boy was scarred. By what, Rina did not know, but she did know that it was not too late for him.

The voice snarled from the hallway. Cursed and belittled the kid. When the man called him *useless*, Yosef locked eyes with Rina. "My uncle insists I am good for nothing," he said in Hebrew. "I shall prove him wrong."

Yosef retreated from the closet. But he stopped. An upward flick of his lips said thank you in nuance. "Coming," he barked in interjection of his uncle's continued insults. He closed the door in a way that would not be heard even by someone in the same room.

Rina took in enough oxygen to lessen the dizziness and scrammed back into her corner, sinking further into Mrs. Zahavi's clothing.

Yosef and his uncle argued in the room.

"You let her get away, stupid!"

"I apologize," Yosef said, sounding more adult-like. No sense in challenging his angry uncle.

"Go get the car ready, foolish boy."

They stomped from the room. The uncle shouted obscenities, this time directed at Seth and Elijah. Where were they?

Half a dozen booms blasted Rina's eardrums; something fell, or somebody fell.

Rina choked on a sob. Her husband or Elijah had just been shot.

Not Seth. Please, not Seth!

Another round of gunfire. Another thud.

They had both been shot by Yosef's uncle.

Footsteps rushed from the house. A car door slammed. Tires howled.

Seth said not to leave the closet until he came to get her. But how could he? She had to save him. To stop the bleeding. To keep him alive.

Rina muscled through the clothes, pushed her shoulders forward, tripped over shoes, and shawls, and other items that littered the floor. Light beamed from the bottom of the door. Fresh oxygen cooled her nostrils in the bedroom.

But Rina held her breath when she entered the spacious living area. Furniture had been turned upside down. Cobwebs and dust bunnies stretched across sofa legs. Clay décor lay shattered on the tile floor.

Not until Rina rounded the corner did she see Seth's feet, sideways, one atop the other, lifeless. She advanced slowly out of fear, then quickly to help if her husband were still alive.

He wasn't. There was too much blood.

She refused to look at his face. What if he'd been shot in the head? What if his eyes were open, drained of life?

It's not how she wanted to remember him.

Rina stumbled to the bedroom, snatched the top sheet from the bed, and willed herself to return. With eyes focused on the floor, she trudged to Seth's side. Maintaining an indirect view, she dangled the linen and allowed it to fall over the length of her husband's corpse.

A shallow cough echoed from the balcony. Rina hustled over spiky clay pieces, shattered glass, and strewn furnishings.

Elijah lay rigid on the concrete. He had tried to flee and escaped death. For now, anyway.

Rina scurried to his side. Between the collar bone and shoulder, scarlet red blood seeped from his white cotton shirt. A dark patch formed a perfect circle on his khaki shorts. Wrists bound behind his back, mouth loosely gagged, he grunted.

Why couldn't Seth be the survivor? Horrible thought. The flimsy knot behind Elijah's head budged easily. Rina pressed the thin linen to his shoulder. His wrists had been bound with an electrical cord.

"Hold still," she said to Elijah, who struggled to free his arms.

"I told him to stay here with me," he gasped. "He got loose and ran to the kitchen for a knife."

Rina untangled the thick plastic cord from Elijah's wrists. Black skin mottled to blue, then light purple. He tried to reach for his leg, but his limbs failed him. Rina scurried to the kitchen for a towel, eyes diverted from her husband's covered body.

An IDF soldier pounded through the door. He ran to Elijah's side. It had to be the friend he telephoned before the attackers arrived.

Sirens wailed, car doors slammed, boots pounded on the floor, voices ranted.

Rina fell to her knees. She knew what was happening, yet she couldn't accept the actuality that Seth was gone. She had heard the gunshots and seen his body surrounded by a dark red pool of blood.

Her worst fear had transpired. She held the fateful status as a war victim. An expectant mother whose child would never meet her father.

Dreams of living in America with her family shattered.

Nothing in life remained other than the sole purpose of protecting her daughter. Eliana would live in a state of uncertainty, tucked under her mother's wing.

Sterling launched Rina from the memory. His soft vibrations voided the stillness that normally frightened her more than the flashback. She needed to go to the bathroom. How? Awaken Brian, then what? Ask him to carry her to the toilet, and then have Eliana hold her upright?

Precisely what she did not want for her daughter! Why didn't she think of that before? Dottie had tried to convince Rina to go to the hotel with them after dinner. She personally knew a caregiver from Canada who had experience with amputees. Yet, Rina couldn't see through the thicket. She wanted to be with Eliana, whatever the cost.

What a fool.

Rina lifted Sterling from her lap and felt for her phone. She contemplated calling Dottie. Four fifty-four in the morning. A text would have to do for now.

Rina screamed silent curses while she waited for Camille. The caregiver arrived forty minutes after the text to Dottie.

Brian and Eliana had insisted to help, but Rina promised herself not to be a burden to her daughter. Not even once.

"She needs to go to the bathroom," Brian said when Camille bustled through the door. "Now."

"I know." Camille pulled a box of latex gloves from her bag. "Put these in there."

Camille approached Rina in calm reassurance without introductions. "I'm going to pick you up, ma'am."

By the time they finished, Rina felt more at ease with Camille than anyone in years. "Thank you."

"My pleasure, Miss Rina."

Thanks to the journal, Rina had made significant progress with Eliana. With a hope to be a regular part of her daughter's life, Rina would discover a way to live in America. Perhaps she could even get a job or go to school.

The biggest problem was Eliana's infatuation with Israel, stronger now than ever. Why? Superficial knowledge of her father triggered a need to make a deeper connection.

"*When are you going back? I'm going with you.*" Eliana had made the statement more than once. Did she mean to move there?

Little Eliana was an adult now. If she made the decision to relocate, it was hers to make. But Rina would risk it all to convince her not to leave. Even if it meant sharing every detail about the day her father died. She'd understand better what she was facing. If Eliana still decided to go, Rina would wipe her hands clean.

But reality overpowered logic.

By coming to America, Rina had taken Eliana to an emotional point of no return. The self-centered choice was sure to result in disaster.

PART VI

Closure

ELIANA

New Year's Eve 2019
Helena, Mississippi

Icy gusts numbed Eliana's cheeks. Nannie and Pops put on a huge spectacle to celebrate the turn of the decade, but she felt hollow. Even with Brian and Rina by her side. Only her father's presence would fill the void.

Fireworks rocketed and swirled in the black night sky. Halos surrounded the multi-faceted bursts of light, only to be extinguished by the high winds.

Rina Gibbons wept during the finale. Nearly twenty years ago, the love of her life proposed in the same place, under a similar display.

Yet somehow, Eliana sensed her mother's emotions came from bad memories. Rina had plugged her ears and leaned forward. Distorted her features into a mass of tight mounds that plunged into deep ravines. Did the pops remind her of the gunshots she heard from the closet? Or did she think of the bombing?

The flashes of light created angular shadows along Brian's whiskered jawline. His eyes darted from the spectacle to Rina Gibbons, then landed on Eliana. He pressed his lips inward to offer a strained smile.

Eliana glided a palm on his back. "You're tense."

"This should be a romantic night for us," he sighed and kissed her knuckles.

"It's not too late."

Ten minutes after one, they stood outside the door of her room. Eliana snuggled against his firm chest. His warmth snuck into her body, flushing her with heat. An hour prior, when everyone had shouted 'Happy New Year,' Brian pulled her into another room for their first real kiss. Until December, simple pecks were all he'd offered, out of respect, just like her father. Hearing her parents' story together at the hospital did something to them, and the lip-locking sessions developed into multiple deep pecks.

Brian chose the perfect occasion for their first passionate encounter.

Eliana had shivered uncontrollably under the crisp winter sky most of the night. Now she burned under the cashmere turtleneck. She unlatched the door handle and tore away from Brian. "Goodnight."

With a pout, Brian hung his head. "Happy New Year, Beautiful."

Rina slept soundlessly. Eliana scooted into bed, but she lay cold without Brian's touch.

Stuffed full of Nannie's egg and sausage breakfast tacos, Eliana wanted to plummet back into bed, throw the duvet over her body, and return to a heavy slumber.

"We have a surprise for you, Dollface," her grandma said as she gathered empty plates from the table.

Brian smiled like he formerly knew of the surprise. As a matter of fact, everyone did.

"Rina," Pops said in a serious manner, "are they ready?"

Without waiting for an answer, Rina walked into the next room with the use of a cane. She'd had her old prosthetics shipped from Israel. The new ones would be ready in a month.

Eliana had heard the brass door chime before she came downstairs for breakfast. Not an uncommon occurrence for her grandparents to welcome visitors. They had been frequent since her mother's arrival. Why didn't she think to ask who came this morning?

The back door to the wrap-around porch shuddered open from the living room. Mama spoke in Hebrew with high inflections that marked happiness in her voice.

Footsteps echoed on the oak flooring.

"My Love," Rina said from the doorway, "I want to introduce you to some special friends."

For a decade, Eliana sought her grandparents' permission or encouragement when she questioned whether something was in her best interest. Even as an adult, she needed their assurance. She did not yet hold enough trust in the mother who'd hurt her more than anyone.

Nannie nodded. "Go on, hun. They're waitin.'"

A petite woman, face bronzed and deeply wrinkled, stood in the den. A man with coarse, gray hair and bulbous features smiled with friendly eyes.

Elijah Zahavi had hardly aged in a decade.

"Do you remember me? I visited you in the hospital."

"You were the last person to see…my father alive." Eliana had found the pages ripped from her mother's journal. The crumpled details of dad's death had been tossed in Brian's bathroom trash.

Fine lines cratered from the corners of his eyes. "Yes, dear," Elijah said in straightforward acknowledgment. "I was. Please believe me, I wish I had been killed in his place." He turned to the woman and rested his arm around her shoulders. "I'd like to introduce you to my wife, Kelila."

Kelila's throat bobbed. "I met your papa two times," she said in a thick accent.

Eliana searched her mind for mention of this woman. The name sounded familiar. Then she remembered. "Mrs. Shalev?"

The woman beamed in satisfaction. "Mrs. Zahavi now."

"Kelila met you when you were a baby," her mother said.

"You don't know us," Elijah began, "but—"

"I do know you," Eliana interrupted. "From mama's journal."

"Mr. and Mrs. Zahavi traveled a long way for a special purpose," her mother's voice trailed in a deep sigh. "I asked them to be here when you saw your father's documentary."

Nannie's face splotched with red freckles. She's the one who forbade Eliana to watch dad's videos. "*It's not worth the emotional pain,*" her grandmother always said. "*You'll be better off waitin' to meet him in Heaven.*"

It was something Eliana had come to agree with and accept. "Should I watch it, Nannie?"

"You're an adult, hun. That's for you to decide."

Eliana thought she favored her father in photos, but not as much as when she saw him on TV. Same eyes, hair, face shape, even the small forehead. The only characteristic she didn't inherit was his milk-white skin tone. She had her mother's olive skin, but still, her father's inherent freckles and green eyes dominated all else.

His mannerisms were just like that of her mother. Had they really connected so quickly as to mirror their behavior patterns and habits? Or had Rina become like him over the years? Eliana would never know.

Kelila Zahavi's story came first in the documentary. She sat on the floor next to Eliana and gaped at the television. Elijah settled on the other side of his wife and squeezed her hand.

Eliana felt her mother's presence before she approached. Brian helped Rina take a seat in the closest chair. A widow of nearly nineteen years, she watched her husband on TV without expression. Neither happy nor sad. Only intense concentration.

Mama was so young in the video. She shone as if in her prime, even when she explained the tragic stories. Did dad really make her so happy that no one could ever replace him? Not even her own daughter? Would she have left her husband to ensure his welfare? According to the journal, she thought of it many times. She felt responsible for his fate. If she hadn't agreed to be his guide, he would still be alive and well.

Or would he? Pops always said that God chose everyone's departure according to his perfect timing. Eliana never liked that. Both parents deceased—or so she thought—what sense did that make? Nannie responded to Eliana's doubt by telling her that's the only way she could be in the United States, the safest country on Earth. An unquestionable point, but Eliana had always wanted her life with mama and Shamira in Israel.

Shamira hadn't spoken to Eliana since their moments in the ambulance. No visit at the hospital. No phone call. No nothing.

Eliana's instincts about Jazmin, who had disappeared, were correct all along. She demonstrated in front of everyone that she had been trained to inflict harm.

Deep percussion boomed with the closing credits. Eliana had missed almost everything.

But she reached a conclusion.

All this time, she had needed closure. Someone from the past, like her mother or Shamira, could not give that to her. A trip to Israel with random destinations would accomplish next to nothing.

With Rina's journal, Eliana knew exactly where to go in her homeland. And Palestine. Even Gaza. She would go to the same places as her father…except Neve Dekalim. The neighborhood had been destroyed long ago.

Her mother would forbid the journey. But she relinquished her parental rights years ago.

Nannie and Pops would try to persuade her not to go.

Brian as well.

Wasted breaths.

Only the end of the world would stop her.

BRIAN

February 2020
Over the Atlantic

For the first time in years, Brian hearkened back to the Color Code of Awareness, a system to gauge situational perception of potential threats. With five colors, white being the least aware in a relaxed mental state, and black being worst in panic mode, Brian tried to decide where he was. He would never sink to black.

Right now, somewhere between yellow and orange sounded about right. Somewhat relaxed, but aware of potential threats.

The weird-looking guy in first-class set off all sorts of red flags. His knees bounced incessantly. He stretched his fingers in and out, in and out, in and out. A few lines of snow dust would explain that. But what about the large glasses for the blind? He made his way about the cabin without a cane or a guide.

Brian first saw the dude at the airport in Nashville. Everywhere they went, he lingered close behind. Olive complexion. Chin-length hair, orangish-blond with dark roots. Thick, black beard. Ridiculous.

No one else had noticed the dweeb when they made their way through departures. Eliana wandered ahead, faster than everyone. Shamira lagged behind, all smiles and eager to catch up. Brian pushed Rina in the wheelchair. Half an hour lumbering through the airport in her new prosthetics, and she was done.

Now, mid-air, the guy seemed familiar.

Brian had never worn the burgundy t-shirt his mom gave him for Christmas. He had needed it for the trip. Maybe he'd get access to certain places wearing it with the bold proclamation, '*MARINES The Few The Proud*' in yellow letters with the USMC logo stretched across his chest. It proved to be an advantage. Flight attendants had no problem with him circling the aisles like a running track.

The rounds curtailed the jitters and gave Brian an opportunity to assess threats.

The carrot top, every time, immediately averted his glance. The only person Brian hadn't made eye contact with was a girl, possibly late teens, with a baseball cap, a football jersey, and long black hair that covered the sides of her face. She always had her head down, immersed in a book, playing games on her phone, or asleep. Brian would not rule her out until he saw her face.

In the dark cabin, with hardly a noise besides the engine's incessant roar, Brian headed back to his seat. Shamira, who had been sacked-out the first three laps, was gone. He hadn't trusted her when she started coming around. Something was off.

The first-class curtain rippled. Brian looked in time to see Shamira slip through sideways.

Brian advanced. Two inches of visibility between the drapes would more than suffice.

Bingo!

Her hip bumped the weirdo when she walked past him. Totally intentional. He followed her to the front lavatory area, where they huddled in hushed conversation.

Whatever he was up to, so was Shamira.

Code Orange. Brian identified the potential threat.

RINA

Eliana was the only one in the group who kept her cool. She tried to be strong for everyone. With her head in a dense thicket, lost in dreams of Israel, she shrugged off Rina's warnings about the unfolding events in Asia.

On New Year's Day, Eliana had announced she would skip the Spring semester and leave for Israel in a month. Brian volunteered to go with her. "*I don't need your protection, if that's what you're trying to do,*" Eliana had said in response. The smart man Brian is, he answered with, "*I know you don't. I just want to see the country. Always have.*"

Rina exchanged glances with him. They knew how to handle Eliana. "*Of course, you know I'm going too, my Love. What if we wait till summer? That way, we have time to prepare. I can get in touch with some people to visit,*" Rina had said with a smile as if the trip were a logical thing to do.

Eliana rejected the idea. "*What if there's a big world event, and we can't go? I don't want to take the risk.*" The next ten minutes she spent posting her plans across social media platforms. Shamira texted within an hour and asked to go on the trip. Rina encouraged Eliana to consider the request. Perhaps it would bring them close again.

Eliana's premonition of a 'big world event' materialized in the form of a pandemic, but that didn't stop her. The plans remained written in stone.

"Can I switch seats with you for a bit?" Brian had been walking the aisles for half an hour.

"You don't want to be next to Eliana?"

Shamira exited the curtain from first-class. Brian stared her down.

"You go ahead. Better to sit here in case I need to go for another lap or two."

Rina had sensed Brian's paranoia at the airport. He panted at times as he pushed the wheelchair, veering in slight curves on the smooth tile floor. Something distracted him even on the plane. The cabin walks had helped him calm down.

Without Brian, three women alone would be in jeopardy on such a dangerous trip. Rina tried to set aside her feeling that something terrible was bound to happen. Would she be naïve to ignore it?

Good thing Brian asked to sit on the end. He sprung to his feet when Shamira returned from her bathroom break.

Why did he take her arm like that?

SHAMIRA

"Ouch!" Shamira jerked away from Brian. "What are you doing?"

Brian's nostrils flared. "To the back," he ordered and grabbed her arm like a father taking his child to be disciplined.

"Let go of me!" Shamira's arm tingled.

Flight attendants gaped when they entered the area used to prepare food and drinks. Brian took a water cup from a tray and led Shamira to a corner.

"Drink."

With another yank, Shamira broke free. "I'm not thirsty." She pushed the cup away. Tepid water splashed on her hand. "What are you doing?"

"What are *you* doing, Shamira?"

"I was going to take a nap."

Brian's strong hands covered Shamira's shoulders. He bent down, face-to-face. "What's your motive for coming on the trip?"

Shamira wriggled to free her shoulders from Brian's grip. She peered past him. Both women in their crisp suits glanced sideways.

"Is everything okay?" The middle eastern woman with full lips and frizzy hair addressed Shamira.

Shamira reassured the woman with a simple nod. She wouldn't ask to be rescued. Everything had to appear normal, but Brian was ruining it.

"Who's the guy in first class?"

Shamira gulped hard. "None of your business!"

Brian gritted his teeth. "The hell it isn't!"

How could Brian know her plans? Had he become a detective? Or was his PTSD, which she thought was a load of BS, to blame? "I don't know why you're asking me questions like this. I'm with my friend to have some fun on vacation. Besides, I'm allowed to flirt with strangers if I want. Maybe you should go take some medicine or get a drink to calm down."

"Watch your step. I'm on to you." He backed away—only enough for her to squeeze past.

With Brian out of sight, Shamira returned to the aisle and brushed Jazzy's arm with a soft stroke of the finger. She had concealed herself well. The all-American attire suited her perfectly.

Shamira's plan was on the brink of success.

But Brian became a problem. She refused to let him ruin her chance to even the score.

ELIANA

Everyone was so damned worried. The trip would have been better solo. Now she was forced to play the role of a parent. A pillow for her travel companions to rest their heads.

Brian's PTSD returned, worse than she had witnessed before. With each lap around the cabin, the physical signs manifested. He acted like nothing was wrong, but Eliana knew how to read him.

Rina attempted to dismiss it. Just like her old self. The classic hand wringing, knuckle-whitening, fingertips turning red from the pressure. It was just like the day of the bombing.

Shamira strained to be friendly and interact. Eliana still held hope that things would return to the way they were long ago. A trip to Israel could help reestablish the forgotten bond.

But Shamira's new style did not sit right. The tight bob was cute, sort of. Leah's bad bleach job resulted in an overall dull, copper tone. The dark eye makeup looked like a mask.

Did she have something to hide?

Eliana would not allow her travel partners to bring her down. She intended to have fun on this trip, even if it meant abandoning the group.

Mama would have to deal with her fears on her own. Or, Brian could stay with her. Shamira might open up if it were just the two of them.

To be alone was best.

If not, Eliana would continue to be that person everyone leaned on. At the airport, she'd excuse herself to go to the bathroom, disappear, and send an apology text to everyone. *Sorry, I have to do this on my own.* That way, they wouldn't think she had been kidnapped or gotten lost.

Shamira eased into her seat across the aisle, posture stiffened, face flush. On the verge of tears. She smiled at a sudden thought.

Eliana caught her in an eye grip and waved. "All good?"

Shamira gave a thumbs up.

Her smile was so fake.
Did she really still harbor that much resentment? Whatever.
Eliana was done with all of them. Even Brian for now.

BRIAN

Out of two options, one decision would have to be made.

Do things the right way.

Or do things the smart way.

Dangerous people were on the plane. The Air Marshall needed to know. Would he find some kind of background on the guy in first-class? Did Air Marshalls even do that? What if he had no record, just like Hakim?

If Brian were to take matters into his own hands, he'd get better results. Every person on this flight was in jeopardy.

What had his father done thirteen years ago? He had been a smart man, but also a man of honor. Someone who followed the rules. Always. Did he do things the right way on the day of his kidnapping? Brian would never know.

Everyone slept. Even Shamira. Directly across the aisle. Backpack tucked by her side. Brian had to find some hard evidence. Impossible without waking her.

A dull reflection by Shamira's hip caught Brian's eye. Her tablet had slid crosswise when she slipped into dreamland. Brian surveyed the cabin, dark besides one overhead light. In a swift motion, he snatched the device and sailed to the back.

Brian slid the lavatory bolt into place.

Airheaded Shamira didn't set a lock on the tablet. Brian scanned each page of the home screen littered with multicolored icons to no end.

The door handle rattled. "Occupied!" Brian flushed the vacuum toilet system. Unpolluted water pulled from the bowl into what would be a nasty tank. The blue stuff softened the stench of sticky urine on the floor.

Brian returned to the screen. Time to dig deeper. He scanned the internet history. Just a bunch of travel info on places to stay in Istanbul. Why? What about Israel?

Next step in the search, My Documents.

And there it was.

Her itinerary shouldn't be any different, seeing that they were all traveling together.

But her trip stopped at the Istanbul airport. No connecting flight. She had no intention of proceeding to Israel after the layover. "Lying little…"

Brian tugged the door open. A platinum blond flight attendant stared him down. Don't want to get on her bad side. Just the opposite. He'd use her to his advantage. Shouldn't be hard. "Hello, ma'am," he said with a flirtatious smile.

What a crappy thought.

"Can I get you anything, sir?"

Brian lifted his shoulders and studied her name badge. "No thanks, Tiffany."

Tiffany deflected a glance at his chest and turned to a water tray with clear cups. Droplets lined the plastic rims of each.

"Water?"

"Nah, I'm good." For whatever reason, he had piqued Tiffany's interest.

Brian lay the tablet just as he'd found it and embarked on another trip around the cabin.

Shamira's friend had crashed hard. His mouth hung open. A disgusting string of drool hung from his jaw. Without a smidgeon of doubt, Brian concluded that the dude's final destination was Istanbul. He and Shamira had an action plan. Hopefully, nothing big, like a hijacking. That would be hard to stop.

No, they planned something at the airport. Kidnap Eliana? Then do what with her? How would they pull it off with no weapons? Unless…someone was going to meet them there.

None of it made sense.

Brian's windpipe slammed shut.

Heart palpitations punched every inch of his body.

Sweat beads tumbled down his temples. The hairs on his arms stiffened as chills took over.

Damn, not an attack.

Brian dragged his feet forward. Something helped him walk. Or someone. It didn't matter. He was going to die.

Grainy sand crunched between Brian's teeth. Stung his eyes.

The firefight was over. And so was Neil's life.

The tourniquet positioned over Brian's trousers made it hard to move. He tried to pull himself to Neil's body. All he wanted was to say goodbye.

Dizziness knocked him sideways.

A rush of memories followed the blackout. Dirty baseballs. Split wood after a hard hit into the outfield. Dad applauding the homerun. A proud smile was the only distinguishable feature of his father's blurred face.

White teeth, corners of the mouth turned upward.
A Casevac copter landed somewhere.
The corpsman was there to keep him alive.
Big mistake.
Total darkness enveloped him in bitter torment.

"Sir?"

Cool air flushed Brian's respiratory tract.

"I think he's coming out of it."

The floor revolved like a spinning top.

"Go tell the captain."

An oxygen machine hissed. Brian sucked in deeply through his nostrils.

He sat on the floor near the cockpit. Tiffany knelt and held the mask to his face.

The door inched open.

"…wearing a Marines shirt…"

A deep male voice mumbled noises of understanding as the woman continued to speak.

"He probably did twenty laps around the cabin. I think it's PTSD."

Shiny black dress shoes shuffled through the door. "Get him some water."

Brian said as little as possible. The captain and flight crew did all they could to bring out of panic mode. It had worked.

Partially.

He hadn't had a full-blown attack in over a year. Not even the classroom shooting brought him down so deep.

Right now, he was trapped. Thousands of feet in the air. No possibility of escape.

What if everything were all in his head? Shamira? Was she really up to something? Or just nervous? Maybe she hadn't saved a copy of the second leg of the flight on her tablet.

And the weird dude? Was he really a random person who caught Shamira's liking?

Brian had to face a strong possibility. He'd had a series of small panic attacks, from their arrival at the airport until the bad one.

"I'm fine now, thanks."

Tiffany had offered help more than once. "You don't want me to walk you to your seat?"

"Nah." Brian spun from the crew. With his eyes to the floor, he hustled from first-class and plopped into his seat.

"Hey." Eliana stretched over her mother. "You're all wet!"

"Oh, that…" Brian pulled the cold shirt from his torso. "I ran into the lady with the water tray."

Brian leaned back, exhausted. It was time to let go of the suspicions. If not, he'd have another meltdown.

Still. Shamira and the oddball triggered red flags.

Brian's mind drifted, as did his thoughts. His role wasn't to protect Eliana. Or anyone else for that matter. He needed to act and think like an average person. Have a normal life. Marry, have kids, a house. Get a puppy to keep Sterling company. Turn depression into wisdom, weakness into strength. Brian's future would become a memorial to honor the loved ones he lost. First and foremost, his father.

"I'm done," he mouthed, audible only to him. He let his head fall to the side. A pinch in his neck would lead to a bad crick after he woke up.

Something across the aisle clunked. Brian glanced sideways at Shamira. She was messing with an object in her backpack. A weapon?

"Damn it all to hell." A splash of cold water in the face might bring him to his senses.

SHAMIRA

Within minutes everyone would think she was sick. She'd run to the bathroom with the false impression of urgency. With the door locked, she'd cough and gag. Flush the toilet. Repeat. The makeup foundation, way too light for her skin tone, would give her a sickly complexion. A thin coating of nude lipstick would mask her lip color. Smudged dots of pink lip liner on the outline of her eyes would perfect the masquerade.

Arms wrapped around her waist, Shamira moaned. Not that it really hurt. She doubled over and hissed in fake agony.

"Shamira!" Rina reached over, unable to stretch far enough. She rattled a slew of words in Hebrew, instructing Shamira to go to the lavatory.

Shamira pretended not to understand. After all, she'd left Israel over ten years ago.

"To the bathroom! Hurry!"

So easy. Shamira flung the backpack around one arm.

Rina shook Eliana to wake her from sleep induced by motion-sickness medicine.

Shamira continued with the act. The poor girl in a rush to find a place to vomit. Eyes clenched. Staggered breaths from the intense pain. Heads bobbed in the cabin. Passengers' eyes widened. Murmurs and whispers amplified.

Both doors displayed the red *Occupied* sign. Shamira tugged at each one to let the occupants know that someone needed in.

A flight attendant showed up with a vomit bag, too small to hold the contents of someone's stomach.

Both doors opened at once. A girl, probably twelve. And Brian. He didn't recognize the charade.

"Hey," he said, hands in pockets. "I just wanted to apologize for what I did—"

"I'm sick!" She rushed past him. No apologies would be accepted today.

Inside, she made the sounds. Flushed. Turned the faucet on, then off. Made more sounds. Her throat stung from the dramatic pressure on her vocal cords.

Time for a break.

She fished for the makeup at the bottom of her bag.

First problem: the foundation's citrus scent. How could she get away with smelling like lemon and oranges? Would anyone notice? A thin coat of the stupid makeup would have to do.

"Shamira?" Eliana's groggy voice preceded a gentle knock. "Can I come in?"

"No!" She engaged in another fake vomiting episode. The plasticky taste of cheap lipstick leached through her lips.

Brian spoke with someone outside the door. "How long before we land?"

"Only thirty minutes. Everyone needs to return to their seats."

"She's sick. Don't you hear her?"

Shamira rubbed a loose cotton swab under her eyes, smudging the lipliner just enough. A few drops of Visine. Done.

One more gagging cough. A blast from the faucets. And ready.

Hunched over, Shamira slid the lock with uneasy movements. Eyes cast down, she staggered past the flight attendant, Brian, and Eliana. At her seat, she opened the vomit bag. Her insides reeled. Not from sickness. From excitement. From the descent of the plane. The funny drop feeling with each downward drift.

Her plan was working. Soon, Rina would be sorry for her stupid decision ten years ago. Eliana had rushed her mother to leave on that dreaded day. But the bombing wasn't her fault.

They were in the wrong place at the wrong time.

Rina's lie is what sent everyone packing. Eliana had to live with strangers in a foreign country. Shamira moved across the world with a family who alienated her. When her uncle started doing bad stuff, they ignored Shamira's cries for help. Her parents dismissed the accusations as lies to gain attention.

No more excitement and happiness on this trip. Shamira's revenge plans were already making everyone miserable.

Part VII

Schemes

BRIAN

A stamp reading "Good-for-Nothing Bastard" would be suitable on his forehead. Shamira dry-heaved into the bag as the plane taxied on the dark runway. Some plugged their ears. Others balled a fist over their mouth to subdue gagging sensations. It was all Brian could do to hide his own disgust. Not in Shamira. In himself. Had the threats disconcerted her so much that it made her sick?

"I can't stay on this plane." Off balance, Shamira sunk into the seat.

Eliana hovered over Shamira with an unreadable expression. "The flight to Tel Aviv is only two and a half hours. You'd be better off to tough it out."

Shamira stood with more determination. "No, I can't."

Brian recalled Shamira's itinerary that had no indication of a connecting flight. He pulled his ticket from the backpack. Right there in plain letters, it showed the departure from Nashville, connecting flights at Orlando and Istanbul, the final destination Tel Aviv. Shamira's stopped right where they were.

So, the question was, did she have a separate ticket? She did book hers separately. But what's in Istanbul?

Get a grip. Brian mustered some humility. Drove the suspicions aside. Back to Code Yellow.

"Here, lean on me." He slid an arm behind Shamira's back to help her stand.

"If you get off, you'll miss the flight and be here all alone." Eliana crossed her arms.

"I'll stay with her." Rina appealed with her eyes.

Shamira propped a hand on the seat to pick up her backpack. "I can stay by myself."

Eliana faced Brian head-on, clearly annoyed. "There's probably a flight that leaves in the morning."

Tiffany whispered with a hand to her lower jaw for Brian and Eliana to hear. "My advice, let her rest at a hotel tonight. Book a flight home ASAP. That virus from China is getting really bad."

Smart idea.

The captain's voice echoed throughout the cabin. Overhead lights flickered twice.

Some passengers arose and removed carry-ons from the overhead bins. Those continuing to Tel Aviv sat still, eyes hungry for the final leg of the journey.

"We can't leave her here by herself." With the lights on, Brian realized just how sick Shamira was. Pale complexion, no color to her lips, eyelids pink. Really pink. Unnatural in a way.

Shamira looked in another direction. "Whatever you guys want to do. I just have to get off. Now." Her diaphragm convulsed. She reopened the vomit bag. Thankfully, no results. Brian could handle it. He'd seen worse. Others who gagged at the sight and sound? Not so much.

"Please clear the aisle." Tiffany had lost the caring tone of voice.

Eliana huffed. "Let's go."

SHAMIRA

"I got a suite," Shamira whispered into the receiver. She had told the group she needed to call her parents. Not! They hadn't returned any of her phone calls since she left Chile.

A darkened area of the hotel lobby gave her privacy. Sort of.

Others from the same flight followed them to the hotel.

An older woman in first class had been hacking out her lungs for the past six hours and complained of feeling dizzy. The flight crew wanted her to be checked out by paramedics, but the ornery woman said, "No, I just need a cigarette."

A newly wedded couple decided to turn around and go back to the United States. "I don't want to catch that bug," the bride whined in a deep twang.

"Let's go home and drink some Coronas," the obnoxious husband laughed.

Whatever. Shamira had to continue the sick act. On the way to the hotel, she had the taxi stop twice to dry heave outside the door. Brian had rubbed her back each time. His hand felt dirty, horrible. She told him to leave her alone, but he stayed. She really had him fooled.

"Room 232. I'll text you when we're inside." She glanced at the people who had so faithfully fallen into her trap. They cared for her so much as to alter their travel plans so she wouldn't be alone in a big city.

Shamira tuned out the voice on the line to watch the others. Eliana leaned against the wall next to the elevator and studied her fingernails. Rina rummaged through her oversized bag.

Brian typed on his phone, probably in search of the flight they'd take the next morning. "We'll find something," he had said en route to the hotel. "We'll fly together, even if it means waiting an extra day."

Brian caught her observances. His head remained in a dip, but he eyed her with more than a passing glance. A tinny ringtone resounded from his phone.

But who would be calling him?

The voice on Shamira's line commanded her to listen. "Get the details. I need to tell my contact ASAP."

Shamira began to speak, but the *end call* bleep stopped her short. Arms wrapped around her torso, she lumbered to the elevator. Rina and Eliana looked worried. Were they the only human beings on Earth who loved her? No one else would invite her on a trip, let alone show such compassion.

"Here's something for motion sickness." Eliana offered the box of medicine that had put her to sleep on the plane. "If I'd known you would get so sick, I would have given it to you before we left."

Eliana pushed the button to summon the elevator.

"Thanks." Shamira pocketed a pill soon to be flushed down the toilet. "I asked for a rollaway bed. The concierge said it will be there in ten minutes."

Brian rejoined the group and scooped up everyone's baggage.

In the suite, Shamira made a beeline for the bathroom to send the text.

We're in.

Ten minutes passed. Then twenty. What was taking so long? Everyone tried to tell her to take a shower or lie down to sleep. She retreated to the bathroom, turned the shower nozzle full blast, and splashed with her hand. The warm water felt good. What if she were to get in? Just five minutes?

She started to undress. All the way down to her undergarments. Then the phone buzzed.

Time for action.

Shamira thrust her legs into the jeans, bouncing as the humidity in the bathroom turned her skin clammy. The top hem of the denim bumped over the new cuts on her legs. She had made five perfect lines on each thigh before leaving for the airport yesterday. The stinging sensation felt good.

Wait five minutes.

Hurry the hell up! You should be ready.

Thirty seconds later, she pressed the letters on her screen.

Ready

Rina was the first to see Shamira come through the door, unshowered. Then Brian. He finished typing a message on his phone and slid it into his pocket.

A forceful knock diverted their scrutiny.

"I'll get it," Brian said and opened the door. "Who are you?"

"I have the rollaway bed," a stocky man said. Of course, Shamira knew exactly who he was. How did he come up with such a perfect accent? "Where would you like it?"

Brian waved him in with a sideways glance to the hallway, then to Shamira. Was he on to her again?

"Your color is returning," Brian said as the accomplice rolled in the bed, folded like a half sandwich. "Did the bath help?"

Yes, a bath. Not a shower. That's why her hair wasn't wet. "Sure."

Two clicks echoed from the doorway.

Brian's back went rigid. He knew the sound.

Everyone turned in unison. Her disguised friends stood with handguns raised, pointed at Brian and the ladies.

Another click. The guy who brought the bed joined the gun-wielding aggressors.

"Here, Jazzy." Shamira pranced to Jazmin and grabbed the pistol. "I want to hold it."

ELIANA

Shamira exposed her true nature in unmistakable colors.

But Jazmin had fooled Eliana beyond belief. She'd had doubts from the beginning.

What an excellent actress *Jazzy* turned out to be.

"How could you? Both of you? And why? What's the big deal?"

Brian moved in front of her. Just like the day of the shooting. Her twentieth birthday.

Eliana needed to stand up and be a big girl now.

"What did I do so horribly wrong that you want to kill me?" Unafraid, Eliana elbowed past Brian.

Shamira shushed her. "I'm not mad at you. We are blood sisters, after all."

A silly term they had used as naïve little girls. It still meant something to Eliana.

"My vengeance is directed at your sweet mama. She's the one who ruined everyone's lives."

Rina pressed a palm into her chest. "You're right. Let them go. Take me."

The person with blind glasses and orange hair told them to shut up. "Everyone sit down. Jazmin, tie them up. Get their phones." He waved his gun at the beefy rollaway bed guy. "Stand guard outside the door."

One by one, Jazmin tied their wrists with thick rope from her bag. She made such expert knots.

Yes, of course, she was a trained terrorist.

"How does it feel?" On the cusp of hyperventilation, Eliana taunted Jazmin. "You really got me. What did I do to you? Oh right, your sister. She was brainwashed. Now you are."

"Thanks to me," the weirdo said, his plan in action. He strutted to the bathroom. "Ready for a big surprise? I'll be back."

Eliana had never been violent. Right now, she was ready to punch the lights out of Shamira and Jazmin, then kick their guy friend between the legs.

The screens on their cell phones cracked when Jazmin hammered them with the pistol grip.

"Hey!" Brian's voice boomed. "Point the muzzle away!"

Jazmin rotated the gun. Red crests of shame branched across her face.

"Here I am!" The formerly blonde Hakim left the bathroom, laughing. He had shaved the beard, cut his hair to the dark roots, and exposed his empty eye socket.

BRIAN

Brian would have to stay in Code Orange, although it would be a mental strain. He had identified the threat, but now was not the time to act.

His gut hadn't failed him after all. With three tours in Afghanistan in heavy combat operations, he had learned to recognize threats. Locals approached with an innocent façade, only for the act to be a setup. His squad had succeeded in identifying each of them. The team accomplished the mission each time. Kill the enemy.

Now, he had to take out a new enemy. The one who wanted to murder them. Possibly torture them first.

A double-tap on the door distracted Hakim from minutes of incessant chiding about his hatred for America, Israel, and all their allies. "Ah, there it is. What I've been waiting for."

The person who came inside the room wasn't who Hakim expected. Brian knew some Arabic from his experiences teaching the Afghan military and police. Hakim spat words. The other guy—ragged, unshaven, but remarkably fit—spoke with authority. "Abdullah was needed somewhere else. I'm here in his place."

"Why wasn't I informed?" Hakim barged to the bathroom where he'd left his phone. "Where is it?" He tore through the room on a frenzied search.

Jazmin helped. "There, on the floor." She pointed to the space between the nightstand and bed.

"Pick it up!" The thin floor shuddered with each footstep. "Give it to me!" He vacillated between Arabic and English. "You're almost as stupid as the Americans."

Jazmin dipped her head in submission.

Hakim fiddled with the phone that was clearly out of juice. "It was at one hundred percent two minutes ago!" He punched the power button with no results.

The young military trainees in Afghanistan loved to spout cuss words.

They had no idea what they were getting themselves into, ready to fight the Taliban for their country. Nonetheless, that's how Brian had learned how to cuss in Arabic.

Profanity rushed from Hakim's lips like a train on a long journey, rambling as the miles go on and on and on. Finally, he threw the phone against the wall and smashed it with his foot. He sneered at his hostages. "No matter. I'm not going to need it anyway." He snatched a bulky duffle bag from the shaggy visitor, who then pivoted to leave.

"Do it right this time," the man said over his shoulder. "No excuses."

"The mission will be accomplished." A mild slam of the door reinforced his words. Hakim slowly opened the zipper, one notch at a time, each preparing to reveal the contents.

Brian guessed it had something to do with explosives.

SHAMIRA

"Wait, what are you doing?" The gun had become burdensome in Shamira's hands. They had been to the shooting range. Lots of times. Too many to count. She knew how to use it.

But right now, a serious doubt crept upon her.

Had she done the right thing? "I thought this was supposed to be a joke?"

"What?" Eliana ensnared Shamira with a fiery scowl. "This is funny to you?"

"Actually, yes."

"You like seeing us tied up, about to be victims of manslaughter?"

"Quiet!" Hakim raised a vest for all to see. "Many will die tomorrow when these six kilograms of explosives blow them up."

Jazmin lifted her chin and held her hands to the side. "Insha Allah."

Hakim boasted of his glorious plans to become a martyr.

After each claim, Jazmin followed with, "Insha Allah." *If God is willing*. A term used in excitement and hope for a future event.

"This isn't what we came here for!" Within minutes, Shamira had lost all confidence in herself. "I just wanted to scare them…to make Eliana and Rina recognize what they did to me!"

"Now you've accomplished your mission." Hakim nodded at Jazmin.

The gun grip grazed Shamira's palm when Jazmin jerked it from her hand.

Jazmin tossed the weapon on the bed. With a long piece of rope, she grabbed Shamira's wrists to immobilize her.

"I thought we were friends?" Shamira wrestled to break free.

"Just like Eliana thought *you* were *her* friend. Now the tables are turned." Jazmin pushed Shamira to the floor next to the other hostages. "Now keep your mouth shut!"

Eliana huffed with a fleeting shake of the head. "I thought you were my friend too, Jazmin."

Jazmin curled her lips through her teeth.

A semblance of regret cut her frigid demeanor like a red-hot sword immersed in cold water.

Eliana's statement had hurt Jazmin.

RINA

"Please, let them go." Rina wanted to stand. To make a move. To take the focus off the girls.

The shackles of disability infuriated her.

Hakim snickered. "Poor crippled lady. She wants to be the hero."

Jazmin laughed with Hakim.

"At last, I can prove to my family that I am worthy," he said and admired the explosive vest.

Rina swore to stop this man. A smart fool with a ruined soul. "Worthy of what?"

"To be accepted by the family again. Did you hear the story of my uncle?"

No one had mentioned a word about Hakim. Rina only knew he was the shooter on Eliana's birthday.

"I'll take your silence to mean no. The same day my uncle blew himself up in Iraq, I was supposed to as well." Hakim wedged his arms through the vest. Pleased with the fit, he sat it on the pillow in full view.

"I was recruited for a camp that trains children to become jihadists. We were to sacrifice our lives to kill infidels. As you can see, I'm still here." Hakim laughed in sarcasm. "A child jihadi, only fifteen years old, assigned to a suicide mission on the same day as my uncle. When I heard his bomb explode, it scared me. I ran and hid in a dark alley."

Hakim ran his fingers along the length of the pistol on the bed.

Rina gnawed the inside of her cheeks. Time to do some manipulating. "You were only a boy. They trained you to be a killer. Did they also remove the natural vulnerability and innocence every child possesses?"

"They tried."

"How?" As long as Rina kept talking, the more time she had to come up with a plan.

Brian sat motionless, silent. A plot brewed beneath the composed masquerade.

"They showed us things to drive fear from our psyche. The worst was a kidnapped woman's decapitation. They made us pick up the head."

Rina pictured the suicide bomber's decapitated head on the pavement. It had remained intact when the blast ripped it from her body.... just like Rina's severed legs. *How did I survive that? Who acted so quickly to save me?* Rina had asked that question hundreds of times. The doctors told her it was a miracle. Somehow, the arteries naturally receded into her legs. Her muscles pressed against them enough to weaken the blood flow.

"My family is rich." Hakim snatched the gun from the bed. "When I went home, I lied at first. I said that the detonator malfunctioned. It wasn't hard for them to find someone to test it. I disgraced them, so they sent me away with no intention to bring me back home."

"They disowned you?"

"Yes, after my father beat me for a month. What I'm going to do tomorrow will be a greater accomplishment compared to my first mission."

There had to be some way to make Hakim recognize that he had chosen the wrong path. If his family had such corrupt thinking, Hakim was better off without them.

"What about the honor to your country? If you do this, you'll just be another name on the list of those who make Iraqis out to be bad people."

Hakim tossed the weapon to Jazmin.

Brian flinched.

"This is for my country. For the Republican Guard troops killed by Americans. For Saddam Hussein, the greatest leader of all times."

"Please, Hakim," Rina said and bowed her head in phony deference, "you don't have to do this. Honor your country in an act of nobility, not revenge. It's not too late to serve your country in another way. What about the Iraqi Police?"

Jazmin cocked the gun.

"Keep it pointed at the crippled lady," Hakim seethed. "If one more word comes from her mouth, pull the trigger. Kill the rest of them too. Except for your former friend. She's going with me tomorrow."

"N—" The pistol grip cracked against Rina's skull, stopping her short.

Jazmin gritted her teeth. Rage...and something else...flared. "Did you hear what he said? I have to kill you if you say another word!"

But he's going to blow up my baby. Just like a suicide bomber blew me up!

Everything happening in this room was her fault.

The casualties tomorrow would be her fault.

She should have died alongside the suicide bomber on the bus. Their heads should have landed together—two women, equally culpable for the slaying of innocent souls.

PART VIII

Friends and Foes

BRIAN

It's just a bunch of propaganda.

Listening to Hakim's suicide statement brought it all home.

Brian welcomed the memories of war. No panic. Nothing to make him falter.

Now it empowered him. No more allowing the past to tear him down.

Focus on the objective: Kill the enemy.

Over there…in combat…you have to be 100% at all times. That often included static hours in a mud compound, 130-degree heat bearing down on you, flies buzzing all over the place, landing on your face and mouth as you try to sleep. Biding time till the late afternoon cool down and recommencement of battle. Then there were the convoys. Cooped up in a mine-resistant, ambush-protected truck for days. The vehicle's high-pitched creaks and deep groans were like white noise to some. Others it grated at their ears. Brian belonged to the latter group.

The jarring experiences prepared him for this juncture. All he could do was sit there. Still. Nowhere to go. And listen to a psycho rant in self-glorification, grating at Brian's ears. Hakim's family would watch the video, filmed by Jazmin, and proclaim pride once the mission had been accomplished.

Not on Brian's watch. Especially not with Eliana in tow.

"Put it on social media and video websites after the deed is done." Hakim clapped twice in celebration. A premature victory.

His plan. An attack worse than the 2016 suicide bombers at Istanbul's old Atatürk Airport. Take a taxi to departures, get out, walk to a crowded area as far as security would let him. Then, *boom*! Cripple the Turks' fancy new airport, open a little over a year ago.

One villain determined to take the lives of many.

Brian would do everything in his power to pull the plug.

"Do you want to go for a last meal?" Jazmin plugged her phone into the charger and pointed at the detainees. "They're tied well. Check the knots if you want."

"Not hungry." Hakim trailed his fingers along each dynamite stick on the suicide vest. If he didn't be careful, the sociopath would blow them all up. Brian said jack-nothing. There's no reasoning with a deranged crackpot.

"But there's a fast-food hamburger place. Your favorite." Jazmin picked up the submachine gun Hakim had been holding. "You know I can handle this."

Why did she speak in English? To scare everyone? She and Hakim's conversations were primarily in Arabic.

Hakim's desert-tan tactical military boots clunked on the creaky floor. He opened the door and summoned his accomplice. "I'm going to eat. Keep an eye out." He pointed to Jazmin. "You know how weak women are. If anyone tries to leave, shoot him."

The dumpy puppet responded with a thick nod. His scowl landed on Brian. No fear in his eyes. No caution.

Some of Brian's buddies got pretty bulky as Marines. Jay, for example, worked out every day like he was preparing for the Ironman World Champs. Part of what kept him sane. People feared him. No one with a brain dared to challenge Jay.

Brian, on the other hand, had remained lean. Did that make him less capable? No. The muscle-mass was there. He had an advantage in that no one suspected him as a person who could do some serious damage. Like Stocky.

Hakim said, shoot *him*. Did Hakim expect Brian to orchestrate an escape?

With a roll of the eyes and slump of the shoulders, Brian gave the false impression of defeat.

The only one who would be defeated was Hakim. He thought he was invincible with his suicide vest, military getup, and elaborate plans. As Hakim and Stocky walked out the door, Brian initiated his planning.

Until the ladies started to bicker.

Shamira slammed Jazmin with a slew of insults.

Eliana chastised Shamira.

Rina raised her voice to quiet the girls.

Jazmin commanded them to stop arguing. No luck on that one.

The high and low intonations made the room sound like a flock of cackling chickens.

"Hush!" Brian's voice doused the heated commotion.

"Thank you, soldier," Jazmin spoke to Brian in Arabic.

"How did you know I speak your language?" Brian addressed Jazmin in English. "And I'm not a soldier. I'm a Marine."

"I saw you listening to us, Marine. You understood everything we said." Jazmin set the gun on the table. "Now tell me what to do to stop this man.

I'm on your side."

Shamira's body stiffened. "Liar!"

Jazmin pulled a thin black scarf from her bag and pushed Shamira to the floor. In one quick move, she roped the fabric through Shamira's teeth and yanked it into a tight knot behind her head.

Impressive. Unexpected. What kind of stuff was this girl in to?

"I'm tired of listening to you whine!" Jazmin's insult ripped through the room in a furious hiss. "You, my foe, are the liar. How could you be so stupid? Deceiving someone who cares for you, so full of selfish resentment that you seek revenge by dreaming up a plot to frighten her. All she wanted was your friendship."

Brian had witnessed some bizarre situations in his twenty-eight years. This was at the top of the list. "If you really want to stop him, we need to get to work now."

JAZMIN

"We *must* stop him!" An unprecedented sense of power drove Jazmin to act with confidence. Now, in the most critical chapter of her life, she had to stay strong.

Over the past month, she managed to make Hakim and Shamira believe she was on their side.

Jazmin had seen Hakim's mutilated eye way too many times. The patch annoyed him. He hated the way the strap constricted his head.

But that wasn't the sole motive Hakim exposed his disfigurement. He wanted Jazmin to be plagued by the reminder of what she had done. To know that paybacks would be hell if she didn't cooperate.

Jazmin chastised herself every day. She should have aimed for his heart or jugular region, but that would have killed him, and she vowed never to take someone's life. Unlike her sister. She could have aimed somewhere else besides his eye to impair him. Eliana had been too close to his groin. The risk was out of the question. In the moment, all that mattered was saving her friend. Jazmin stopped Hakim enough to slow him down, but he kept fighting. He came so close to killing someone that day, but Brian's quick thinking saved Eliana.

The doctors and surgeons ensured a quick recovery for Hakim. They wanted to see him in prison. Unfortunately, someone paid a considerable sum to bail him out of jail, something no one expected. Who could afford a million dollars? His family, apparently, but they had disowned him. Jazmin had tried to prod him for an answer. Certain things, he wouldn't tell her. She guessed a terrorist organization had funded him, but didn't they have other culprits who don't require such a huge sum?

Before Jazmin had a chance to learn the news of Hakim's release, he sent his beefy friend Warren to fetch her after class. With a gun pushed against her ribs, she followed Warren's lead to the parking lot, where Hakim waited in the back of a minivan.

Hakim exposed the place where his eye used to be. Raw, red, ugly, sewn together, she couldn't understand how they did it, but somehow, he survived, and here he was, alive and well, ready to kill her with the same type of knife she used to maim him.

An alternative came into play.

A forced opportunity to join the fanatic.

He brandished a piece of bright white printer paper with her mother's address typed in large letters. "*My friends follow her everywhere*," he had said. "*Join me, and she lives*."

She had no other choice. Jazmin agreed to abide by Hakim's wishes. He and his friends tried to indoctrinate her with radical Islamic beliefs. She listened and understood where they were coming from, but she would never be fooled like her sister.

Jazmin played along, wore the black attire and head veil with only a small opening for her eyes. Oh yes, that's the way women should dress. She concurred with the dress code, masking her own lie. Suspicious stares didn't bother her. She had to save her family.

Then, she found out she was going to have to face Eliana in Hakim's elaborate plan. He insisted that her participation was the only way to redeem herself. Not until later did she find out his plot was a terror attack that would result in mass bloodshed.

That she would not do. Not like her sister.

Jazmin had one month to plot with zero freedom. Hakim's sidekicks followed her everywhere. She had to sneak around like a child. On a day when Hakim's drug addict friend had been assigned to babysit, she left class from an inconspicuous side door and found an employee phone.

With no one there, the timing was right.

Jazmin dialed her uncle's number, memorized as he had insisted. "*If you're ever in trouble, call me first*," he commanded before her departure for the U.S. She spelled out every detail, from beginning to end. Her sole request, "*Please don't let them hurt my mother*."

Hakim put his plan into operation, but submissive little Jazmin played her own trickeries. So far, everything was going the way Hakim wanted. Except for the person who delivered the vest. An unexpected variation she hoped would cause problems. He had no way of calling his cohorts to confirm the validity.

No phone meant no phone numbers.

Jazmin had enjoyed watching Hakim's search. His struggle to make it work was even better. The Galaxy Xcover 4 came with a removable battery. Jazmin brought an extra battery, completely drained, and switched them out in the bathroom where Hakim had left the phone. Disabling it was simple.

"How can you trust her?" Eliana snapped at Brian. "What if this is part of Hakim's plan?"

Brian lifted his shoulders in an exaggerated shrug. "You have every right to doubt her intentions."

"I'm not asking you to trust me." Jazmin had to find a way to make Eliana see that she was not on Hakim's side. "I don't expect you to believe what I say. All I want to do right now is stop that man from killing dozens of people!"

"Eliana," Brian expelled a deep huff, "I have to believe Jazmin. My gut tells me she's not one of the bad guys."

Brian put a plan in action without an acknowledgment. "He left five minutes ago. Jazmin, I need to be able to free myself from the knot. Good job on that, by the way. I didn't take you for that kind of girl." Brian pressed his elbows out—a demonstration that he was going nowhere.

That kind of girl.... someone strong? Well, he should think it since she took Hakim's eye out with near-perfect knife-throwing skills. Jazmin wanted to feel happy and proud. Her uncle had taught her his most inescapable method to tie wrists years ago. Along with the knife skills. Now, she felt stupid. "I didn't think to bring something to free you."

Shamira tried to talk through the gag, now soaked with saliva.

"She might have something useful to say," Brian said with an approving nod.

Eliana turned away.

All Jazmin wanted was to do was help. How was she to follow Brian's instructions if Eliana didn't like them?

"Listen, Beautiful," Brian softened his voice. "You trust me, right?"

A slow blink of the eyes affirmed Brian's statement. Eliana trusted him more than anyone in the room.

"I've been in hostile situations with worse people during my deployments." Brian's body movements became jerky as he continued to speak. "Firefights with Taliban insurgents are brutal. Trying to distinguish Afghan citizens from the enemy when they're hundreds of meters away, it's mentally taxing. The Taliban are masters at blending in."

A shadow of amazement in Eliana's eyes escalated to near shock as Brian continued to speak.

"Me and my guys, we never got it wrong. We never killed a civilian." Brian rolled his shoulders, posture straightened in confidence. "Shamira is harmless."

"Immature and selfish," Jazmin chimed in, "but foolish above all."

Shamira's hair entangled in the knot made for a painful release. But she could talk now.

"Hakim's razor," Shamira grunted and rolled her jaw.

"Good thinking. There's an unused disposable razor in my backpack and a lighter in my pocket."

Jazmin grabbed the razor and knelt on the floor next to Brian. He stood straight on his knees and shook his body to allow the lighter to shift to its lowest position.

Eliana's nostrils flared. "I haven't even done something like that to him!"

Brian laughed from his nose; lips pressed tight. "You never tried, beautiful."

In one quick motion, Jazmin snatched the lighter without causing a scene. She concentrated on Brian's instructions. Removing the blades would be easy.

In the bathroom, she raced to follow Brian's instructions. First, she had to melt the plastic on the sides of the blades. "*Don't melt it so much that the plastic drips*," he had instructed. Thick, hot liquid stung her finger. A stench like burnt turpentine defiled the air.

With the tweezers from her bag, she pulled out the first blade.

One would be enough.

What if she needed to protect herself somehow? What if she were tied up or Hakim turned on her?

SLAM!

The walls rattled.

Hakim cursed.

"Where are you, woman?"

"In the bathroom!" She blew into the air, hopeful the stench of hydrochloric acid with would dissipate.

"What's that smell?"

Jazmin flushed the toilet. What else could she do?

"What are you doing in there?" Hakim pounded on the door.

"I have cramps!" She turned on the water to drown out the noise of the lighter flicks. In less than a minute, she'd have the second blade free to use if she needed it.

"You were supposed to be watching them!"

Jazmin continued despite Hakim's fit of rage on the other side of the door.

The blade slipped out with an overeager pull of the tweezers and landed deep on the center of her palm.

Blood droplets ascended from the slit in her skin. Jazmin wanted to scream, for fear, for the burn, for pure fury over the stupid accident! The single blade for Brian would have been sufficient.

She snatched a towel from the counter, white and slightly damp, covered with small shavings from Hakim's beard. At least it stopped blood flow. But the speckles of hair, she could feel them, and they made the stinging sensation worse. She thrust her hand under the running water and cried out.

BANG BANG BANG!

"What's going on?"

Jazmin fought the urge to spout insults at Hakim.

The deep wound was bad enough to require cleaning. A small bottle of neon-blue mouthwash sat next to Hakim's used razor. The alcohol content would be enough to disinfect the cut, and the wintergreen scent to ease her spirits. But the mouthwash was a bad idea. *Stupid girl!!* The hanging skin stung like jellyfish tentacles. Her body trembled as she flushed the solvent under a blast of frigid water.

She found a fresh washcloth and covered the gash. The pressure alleviated the pain, but she couldn't let Hakim see the wound, he was smart, he'd want to know what she was doing and for what reason. There was no way to associate cramps and the removal of a razor blade.

Her scarf lay on the floor in the bedroom. She could use that to keep the cloth in place.

No, Hakim would watch her pick it up. Not possible to make that work.

BAM BAM BAM!

"Get out, woman!"

Jazmin flushed the toilet with her foot and began to wipe down the bloody sink, but dizziness crept upon her like a vapor cloud. There was nothing else she could do other than hope Hakim would assume Jazmin dealt with her monthly cycle. A natural explanation for the residual blood and mess in the trash can.

He'd get grossed out by that. A distraction and further deviation to his plan.

She just had to make it out of the bathroom and get the blade to Brian without Hakim witnessing the exchange.

PART IX

Always Faithful, Always Forward

BRIAN

Something had gone wrong. Brian explained the simple method of blade removal three times. Jazmin said she understood. It should have taken her less than a minute.

Hakim got in her face. He ranted in Arabic about stupid women not doing their job because they're just women. She apologized and said she was going to check that the ties hadn't loosened.

"She doesn't look good." Eliana bumped elbows with Brian.

"She's just nervous." Brian played an act. No sense in worrying Eliana.

Rina mumbled something to Shamira. A cloak of authority in her expression revealed her intentions. She meant to keep Shamira in line.

Jazmin stepped behind each of them and tugged at the rope where she had tied their wrists.

Brian held his thumb and forefinger open. Still warm from her touch, the sharp blade gave him further assurance that he would be able to break free.

Jazmin trudged to the bed, face blanched, a bloody washcloth tied over her palm.

Bad place for a cut.

Her head hit the pillow hard. Brian feared she might not wake.

There was a lot Brian loved about the Corps, but a lot he hated too. He'd come to forget the bad stuff, mostly. He longed for the feeling when you know in the pit of your gut that something intense is about to go down. The firefights had calmed him after hours of complete boredom in the hellish heat of the day. Why?

He operated better under pressure.

Now he was ready to unleash everything that had been building up since he stepped foot on American soil over three years ago.

Why did they medically discharge him? Just because of an injury?

There was something the Corps could have him doing all these years. He'd have gone with a happy heart wherever they called him to duty.

All of that was past. Brian had to remain in the present.

All night, Hakim fidgeted with his phone, paced the suite, and struggled to clear a dry cough.

Brian pretended to sleep. He pinched the blade between his fingers, slowly sawing the scratchy sisal twine, strand by strand. He kept his eyes closed with a sliver of visibility. Hakim needed to think Brian slept. Sure, he was tired, but it was nothing like the desert. Going from compound to compound, clearing each one out as heat worse than a blow dryer pushed you to finish. At the end of the day, all he wanted to do was sleep when they got to the last dumpy living space.

Then came the flies…assassin bugs that won't leave you be.

Hakim was worse than a hundred of those flies.

Before the break of dawn, the assassin bug burst from the bathroom, where an intense snorting session had transpired. Brian wondered how many lines Hakim had done. In a maniacal rage, he boasted his impending good deed. Bliss and hysteria packed into a mortar. Ready to launch a lethal shell.

Brian fought the urge to tell Hakim what a fool he was. His plan would fall short. No one was going to die today. Except for Hakim if he went so far as to blow himself up.

The ladies jumped from their sleeping positions, disoriented, eyes puffy. Not Jazmin. She lay still. Until Hakim shook the bed.

Jazmin arose elbows first with the sleeved pulled over her wounded hand.

"Get her up." Hakim pointed his finger like a missile at Eliana. "Time for us to go." He reached for Jazmin's elbow.

With a subtle jerk, Jazmin pulled away and lumbered to Eliana. Her bandaged hand dipped from her sleeve. The once bright white washcloth now took on the effect of tie-dye, red the predominant color. How had she pressed the blade deep enough to hit an artery? And how was she standing in front of him on two feet?

"I'm not going with you," Eliana turned her back.

Click. Hakim released the safety on his Glock 17.

Rina squinted. The muzzle pressed into her temple.

Eliana screamed. "Fine! I'll go!"

Two options presented in Brian's mind. On the tactical level, he'd stop the enemy now. Launch to his feet like a catapult and make a beeline. Would he be quick enough to stop Hakim from shooting Rina? No.

On the strategic level, he'd wait it out. Brian knew how Hakim operated. He had done the same thing in December. Held the gun to Professor Ramzi's noggin until he got what he wanted.

At this point, there would be no shooting as long as everyone obeyed his orders.

Dealing with a psycho like this, Brian had no room for poor decisions.

The timing had to be right if he were to stop Hakim's plot.

Jazmin staggered to the bed.

"Useless woman," Hakim shouted in Arabic, "I should have known you would fail."

Brian remained quiet and composed. No point in wasting energy. Jazmin slumped sideways onto the pillow, legs dangling from the side of the bed. Not a good sign.

Stocky entered the room at Hakim's demand. With his .45 pressed to Rina's temple, he waited for instructions from Hakim, who grabbed Jazmin's phone.

"Give me your number," Hakim punched the screen as Stocky mumbled the digits. He flashed the phone in front of Eliana's face. "Tell me what you see."

Eliana squinted to read. "It's a text message. It says, *Do it.*"

"If you're a smart girl, you will follow every instruction I give you." Hakim pulled Eliana forward to face her mother. "With one hand, Warren is going to keep the gun pointed at your mother's head. With the other hand, he will hold his phone. If he sees the text you just read, he will pull the trigger. Try to get away. Try something sneaky. I'll have my finger ready to send the message if you make one wrong move."

Hakim snatched a folding knife from his pocket and sliced through the ropes.

Eliana massaged her wrists and flashed a grim expression.

Brian gave the faintest of nods.

De inimico non loquaris, sed cogites. The words of the captain who led the platoon on their mission had begun his battle speech in Latin. "*Don't wish ill on your enemy, plan it. Like a game of chess, you have to stay four or five moves ahead. The safest way is to make our own way.*"

The plan would come at the right time. For now, Brian had to bottle up emotions. Keep himself in line. Push back the old feelings of rage. Acting out right now would get him nowhere.

"Poor soldier boy," Hakim said with a hoarse grunt. "He had a meltdown on the plane, and now he's worthless. Don't count on him to save you."

"I'm not a soldier. I'm a Marine." Brian stifled hot embers that smoldered beneath his skin. He wanted to get up and fight. Now. But he couldn't take down two guys with loaded guns ready to fire.

Or maybe he *could* take them down. Why shouldn't he try? It would feel awesome to bulldoze them in one fell swoop.

A warm glob of saliva landed on Brian's forehead. The worst insult from a Middle Eastern.

Hakim wiped his mouth. "From everyone exterminated by the American military."

Arteries pulsed in Brian's neck, ready to burst. He curled his fingers in a tight fist, fighting the urge to attack Hakim on the spot.

Nerves always kept Brian sharp, unbeknownst to his captor. Spikes of adrenaline made Brian more powerful. Hakim's antics helped him prepare for the bigger fight.

Hakim jerked Eliana by the arm. "Say bye-bye to your girlfriend."

Eliana stumbled in front of Brian, nearly knocking him down. Her demeanor wrote pages of impending doom. She had come to accept that she was going to die today. She obviously didn't know her boyfriend well enough. Didn't know what he was capable of.

His bad. He never opened up to her completely.

"I love you, Beautiful." Brian hadn't said it to her before. It would not be the last time.

The tension in Eliana's face softened. She grinned with a trace of conviction.

Good. Eliana hadn't given up. Brian would need her to be sharp for his plan to work.

ELIANA

Guilt. Blame. Anger. Eliana was done with them all.

She was about to die.

Unless Brian could save her.

How was he so calm? How could he smile? Hadn't he cut the rope? Was he in panic mode? Why didn't he stop Hakim?

Hakim. He buttoned the suicide vest and circled a finger around the red detonator. Strapped to the front of the dark green camouflage material, ten red tubes, marked TNT, foretold destruction. Five more tubes on the killer's back heralded his fate. Carefully placed wires led to the little black box with a little bitty red button. That scared her more than anything. The bomb could accidentally go off with the slightest wrong movement.

Brian looked at Eliana the same way he did when he had a spell. They'd been less frequent, usually a short thirty seconds. The shooting hadn't even stirred him. But yesterday's flight did.

He had sensed all along that something was amiss.

"I-I l-love you." Eliana stuttered the words. The nerves had dried her mouth, sent her stomach into a flying whirlwind, and controlled her movements like a marionette. Stiff, sporadic, robotic.

"I know, Beautiful." All seriousness in his eyes gave her hope that he had a plan. And that his plan would work. "Don't give up on me.

BRIAN

Everyone was saying their goodbyes.

Rina wailed.

Shamira cried like a toddler.

Eliana repeated, "mama, I'm sorry," non-stop.

In unison, Hakim and Stocky told them all to shut up.

Jazmin slept. The rise and fall of her chest nearly nonexistent.

An oversized black puffer jacket covered the explosive vest well. Hakim slid his semi-automatic handgun into the deep front pockets. The noisy quilted overcoat swished with Hakim's jerky movements, muffling the women's whimpers.

Another trip to the bathroom for a final snorting session, this one lengthier than the last, concluded Hakim's pre-martyrdom agenda. The coward didn't have to guts to do the job in a clear state of mind.

"Time to go, Eliana!" He dug his fingers into her arm. "Let's go kill."

Eliana stumbled to keep up with Hakim, head twitched, eyes darting back and forth from Brian to her mother.

The door slammed, Rina screamed her daughter's name, blurted utterances in Hebrew, succumbed to shaking fits.

Stocky ordered her to be silent.

Brian allowed the rope to slide from his wrists. Slowly.

Rina continued in Hebrew. Lengthy sentences directed to no one.

Stocky pointed at Jazmin's scarf on the floor. "If you don't shut up," he snapped, "I'll gag you."

Code Red. Go time.

Attaboy, pick up the scarf. Brian prepared for a slugfest.

"But, my baby girl!" Rina moaned the words.

Stocky squatted.

Brian charged.

Rina fell backward and smashed her hard, prosthetic feet into Stocky's face. She shrieked in pain.

The gun clunked to the ground. Stocky reached for it, but Brian had him in a blood choke. Stocky passed out within seconds.

Brian tied Stocky's ankles and wrists together, he was going nowhere fast.

Rina's rope budged easily to the blade. Brian rushed to Jazmin.

The bleeding had stopped, but her ashy complexion and shallow breaths concerned him. "Probably the onset of shock."

"Go get Eliana! We'll take care of Jazmin." Rina pushed Brian to the door. "Go!"

Brian slung the backpack over his shoulders. "Call an ambulance, but not the police." Brian pointed to Stocky. "When the paramedics ask, say you'll only tell the police. By the time they get there, Hakim will no longer be an issue."

"Put pillows under her legs!" Rina commanded Shamira.

The door slammed. Brian dug the balls of his feet in the woven carpet and sprinted. He found the stairwell and bounded down every other step.

They had only left a few minutes ago. Probably not via the stairs given Hakim's altered state of mind. He wouldn't be thinking straight.

Brian landed firmly on the concrete at the bottom of the stairwell and pushed through the door. Dense fog dulled the morning sun's glare, but there was enough visibility to see Hakim shove Eliana into a taxi a hundred fifty meters away. Brian could be there in fifteen seconds. He darted on the slick pavement, soundless.

Four or five moves ahead, like a game of chess. The captain's advice reechoed, bringing Brian to a full stop. He wasn't close enough to get to the taxi before they left. He didn't want Hakim to know he was on his tail.

Just before Hakim turned, Brian ducked behind a construction barrel. Had Hakim seen him? Brian could not afford to look.

There was no slam of a car door. No wheels driving away. Only the shrill caw of swooping seagulls.

The back door popped open. A heavy-set woman in plain clothes, early thirties, gripped a bulky trash bag. She eyed Brian, then the street. Back and forth like a black cat cuckoo clock.

"Ssshhhh." Brian subdued the communication to a dull whisper. He pressed his palms together, fingers pointed up. Maybe silly, but it did the trick. She tossed the bag into a trash bin and returned to her duties inside the hotel.

"To the airport!" Hakim's voice was distant. "Departures!"

Wheels squealed. Now, Brian could do nothing for Eliana other than stay on their track.

Taxis rushed by. Travelers rushed to the airport like army ants.

Brian whistled through his fingers at a moped driver in front of the hotel. "Come here."

Black puffs billowed from the exhaust as the scrawny driver scurried forward.

Brian snatched bills from his backpack. Two hundred dollars. Much more than the little motorcycle's value. Much less than the value of the lives Hakim wanted to destroy. He waved ten, crisp green bills in plain sight.

The pip-squeak, nineteen at most, flashed a set of hellacious crooked teeth. He tossed the helmet to Brian and grabbed the money. Likely going to the nearest drug dealer.

The moped puttered. Brian pushed it to its limits, remembering the story of Rina & Seth's chase in Gaza. The car had been nearly destroyed, yet Seth managed to make it go faster than Rina thought capable.

Admirable.

Odors seeped into the air like fumes at a gas station. Saltwater from the sea, tolerable. Rotting trash from dumpsters, not a big deal. Abominable alleyways reeking of fresh sewage, intolerable. Socks, dirty feet. Where the hell had that come from? Brian squeezed the worn rubber throttle and accelerated.

A sea of yellow taxis packed the roadway. Brian approached each one carefully. Rank cigarette smoke coiling from open windows evoked memories of sitting in the desert for hours, waiting for action.

The crowd at the airport was just as Hakim anticipated. Packed.

What the crackpot didn't expect was heavy security. In his doped-up condition, he figured everyone would be distracted by the incredibly contagious Coronavirus. He said the Turks were foolish. The police wouldn't be worried about terrorists. Wrong.

Brian ditched the moped and scoured the line of taxis. Eliana's head pitched from one at the front of the line. She stood erect, waiting for Hakim to exit. Brian ducked behind a black SUV with tinted windows. The large vehicle gave him the advantage to spy without being noticed.

If the drugs hadn't impaired Hakim, he'd see the high presence of security and abort.

Eliana scoured the crowd, in search of something. Possibly a way to escape. No, she wouldn't do that to her mother. Hakim held the phone out for Eliana to see in plain view. She could easily knock the phone from Hakim's hand. Or someone else could.

That's it. Brian had to disguise himself. Punch his way through the crowd, force the phone from Hakim's hand and pull his arms behind his back. The crowd would break up. He'd yell at Eliana to run, and the others would follow suit. Brian would immobilize Hakim, and security would rush in to do their job.

It could work.

If not, he was willing to put himself on the line. For Eliana. For Neil's memory. For dad. For every innocent person in the periphery. He had to move forward, even if it meant he'd die trying.

Brian pulled the zippers on his backpack and snatched a green USMC hoodie. That, with his sunglasses, would have to do the trick.

Here goes nothing. And everything.

"Hang tight, son."

The voice came from nowhere. Like one of the Taliban ghost soldiers. There one minute, gone the next. You never knew where they were at.

Someone wanted to stop the mission. But Brian was under no one's orders.

ELIANA

On the first day of school, when Eliana arrived on campus, she had it all wrong. She was supposed to be there. In America.

Mama had done what she needed to ensure a better future for her daughter. Life in a country where things were much more stable than anywhere.

Even if that meant never seeing her again.

Eliana had been so wrapped up in self-condemnation that she couldn't see the bigger picture. If only she had stayed where she belonged.

Alas, here she was in the circumstance her mother had feared. Mama's sacrifice had been fruitless.

Everyone has a way of self-sacrifice and heroism. Some more visible than others. No matter. If it's done for the right purposes, without self in mind, that's what makes the difference.

What had Eliana done? What kind of difference did she make in her twenty years?

Nothing significant. And now she was about to die.

Eliana walked next to Hakim as if they were together. He secured the phone in his left hand, lanky arm swinging to and fro. The other hand rested inside his front coat pocket. He had told her of a plan to shoot people before detonating the bomb.

Hakim relegated Eliana the task of choosing the targets.

If she didn't, he'd send Warren the message.

"We're going to that crowd over there." He pointed with the phone. "Decide who you want to kill."

Who she wanted to kill? No one.

She didn't even want to kill Hakim.

Where was Brian? Still tied up? He had the razor blade. Could he have defeated muscular Warren? Brian was taller than him but lean. Maybe not as strong. His skills as a Marine made him much more powerful. They'd been to the gym together many times. She saw him in action.

Brian could save her. Everyone else at the airport too.

Eliana couldn't die now. She had to tell her mother she understood.

Mama had done the right thing by letting her go.

BRIAN

"We've got the situation under control, thanks to you."

Brian glanced over his shoulder. He had seen the man in first class. Older. Blue eyes contrasted against rosacea-blemished cheeks. They had made eye contact with each passing lap around the cabin. "We?"

"We, the CIA."

Hakim had been released from jail and didn't make an appearance at his hearing. He was a wanted man.

"I've been on his tail since the first time you called Jayson." The man arched a mischievous brow. "I'm Officer Cabrera."

Brian remained fixed on Eliana and Hakim.

Eliana surveyed a group of teen girls. She shook her head.

Hakim snarled and pointed to the phone.

"Wait, you're Jay's dad?"

"Yes, sir. Thanks for calling him from the hotel. We had a plan in place to follow Hakim, but there was a misunderstanding with the captain." Officer Cabrera scrubbed a palm over his whiskers. "We lost Hakim's track."

"What did my call have to do with it?" Dumb question. He chatted with Jay for a few minutes by the elevators when Shamira made her phone call. Brian had explained the circumstances on the plane. The panic attack. Details of his flashback. Shamira's act.

Jay just listened. And smoked.

"Had you not given Jay the hotel location, our contact would not have stopped the transfer of the real explosive belt. The one he's wearing now is a fake."

Brian wanted to run to Eliana. The fake suicide vest would do jack-nothing. He pushed off the pavement, only to have Jay's dad grab his elbow.

"Wait, son," Officer Cabrera said with forced restraint, "he still has a weapon in his front pocket. Do you know what it is?"

"It's a .45."

"I've got five officers over there now."

Brian scanned the crowd. The CIA did a great job of blending in. "I can't just stand here and watch."

"I know." Officer Cabrera stood parallel to Brian and pulled the mic from his ear. "I believe you can come up with a better plan than my men."

"Why?"

"It's been three years since you guys came back. Jayson still talks about you. He says you were the best in the company. You led them to secure locations when everyone was sure they were pinned down inside a compound. You're the one who found most of the booby traps and IEDs." Officer Cabrera rocked on his heels. "Son, you ought to remember your successes in battle. Like the day you ran out onto a muddy field to grab a wounded Marine. There was fire coming from two compounds, and you did what you were trained to do. Remember that?"

It was the day before Neil died. Brian's instincts had kicked in when he saw one of the guys collapse. He snapped to and ran into open terrain.

Brian didn't know how he pulled that off without getting shot. It didn't matter either. He knew there was a chance he would die from the beginning. He had prepared for it, engraved in his mind that he wasn't going back home. The fear of dying had waned.

Eliana pointed to a group of elderly tourists who wore disposable face masks.

"I know what happened on the day you were wounded."

Brian's TMJ fused his teeth shut in stressful situations. He rolled his jaws to slacken the tension. Jay's dad faced him now.

"You have to stop blaming yourself. If someone's going to die, they're going to die. Fate isn't in your hands." Jay's dad lowered his head in a heavy nod. "It doesn't depend on you."

Maybe Brian didn't really need to be there. Eliana's life didn't depend on him. The CIA officers were closer than he and more skilled in this kind of situation. What if he ruined their efforts by coming up with a plan of his own?

"I know you lost your dad—"

"Sir, with all due respect, I don't care to discuss that." Brian hated the feel of tears on his face and the resultant burn in his eyes. None of that mess today. "What's your point in all this?"

"I could never replace your father, but I'm coming to you like a son." Officer Cabrera paused to assess Hakim's movements. "You blame yourself for things that aren't your fault, and you're not thinking about your accomplishments. You still have the same skill and know-how as your days in combat. It's time to use it. I'm looking for some out-of-the-box thinking. I don't want that monster killing anyone today."

Years ago, a veteran in a counseling session had told Brian to stop being selfish in his thinking. "*Stop saying 'I' so much. This isn't about you. Stop feeling sorry for yourself.*" Others in the group told the guy to shut up. An argument ensued. Brian rejected what he said, but now it made sense.

"This isn't my job." Brian observed the CIA operatives. They wore plain clothes and stood still. Sunglasses blocked their occasional glances at Hakim. "I believe in your guys. There's not much I can do."

"You're one of the most courageous human beings I know. More than them." Officer Cabrera jutted a thumb over his shoulder. "This is the most significant moment in your life to put that courage in action."

"Why? Remember, fate doesn't rest on me."

Brian whipped the hood over his head and walked away with a sinking feeling in his gut. He refused to interfere with government operations. This was not the time or place for redemption from past failures.

ELIANA

Security herded travelers into groups.

Everyone had to be checked for fever.

This was going to make things even worse. Masses of civilians chattered, yelled, joked, coughed, grunted, all making their own verbal utterances. The death toll was going to rise drastically. It would be one of the worst suicide bombings in a long time.

"This is perfect," Hakim whispered and coughed into Eliana's face. He reeked of onions from his last meal. "We may not need to use the gun."

Eliana fell into a daydream. She slapped the phone from Hakim's hand, reached into his pocket to retrieve the pistol, and clawed his eyes to temporarily subdue him. Before he could push the detonator, she rammed the gun in his open mouth. *Splat!* His brain and blood sprayed from the back of his head.

Disgusting.

The dream ended. Eliana inspected the positioning of the gun in Hakim's pocket. The idea, realistic but impossible.

"Don't get any ideas, little Israeli girl." Hakim had read her mind.

BRIAN

How could he leave Eliana? He was right there. The CIA had asked for his intervention. Contrary to Officer Cabrera's belief, his guys had the airport situation under control.

They did not, however, have the hotel situation under control. New mission: go get Rina. Let her know what's going on.

Exhaust fumes permeated the air. Dark oil marks streaked the pavement where taxis waited for their next passenger. Brian grasped the handle on the closest one and popped in. "Take me to the nearest hotel."

The driver whipped the steering wheel hard. The taxi sprang forward, leaving the other vehicles behind.

But what if the operatives were unsuccessful? What if Jay's dad was right?

Could Brian really outsmart everyone? He'd done it before.

Brian rotated on the worn seat and looked out the greasy window.

Hakim had Eliana by the hair. People eyeballed them. Mouths agape.

Police didn't seem to notice. There were two standing right there. They had to be deaf. Or blind. Or dumb. Or all three.

I'm an ass for leaving her.

"Stop!" Brian yanked the door handle. Gray concrete rushed underfoot. Tires skidded. The car slowed. Brian braced himself.

The taxi driver squawked protestations in Turkish.

Brian jetted from the door and jogged to keep up with momentum.

He still had a part to play in this. A special purpose. That's how his mom had put it when she threw her arms around his neck for a final hug. He was about to ship out for his first deployment. She'd stopped bawling long enough to give him reassurance—something he never valued until today. "*I hate saying goodbye, but you have a special purpose everywhere you go. God is sending you on this mission for a reason. Remember that, always.*"

Jay's dad helped Brian recognize the critical part he had played. He brought a wounded buddy to safety in an inconceivable situation. He may have eliminated other casualties by finding the IED's and booby traps.

The bigger picture involved successes *and* failures. Brian had to move on, put hardships in the past, and leave them there.

Time to tackle the mission head-on.

Hakim's fake explosive vest was harmless, but he had the prospect of killing a considerable amount of people with his hand weapon.

Including Eliana. Brian's girlfriend. The only person he'd been able to open up to in years.

Brian zigzagged around concrete pillars. With a better view, he held his position.

A clean-cut man tapped Hakim on the back.

Hakim released Eliana's arm and spun.

The two men spoke as if they knew each other.

Brian searched for Officer Cabrera....same location as before. He spoke into his mic.

The operatives held a finger over their ear.

Hakim's face said it all. This guy was someone who helped organize the operation.

With a modicum of hesitation, Hakim pressed the detonator.

Eliana ducked. A worthless move if a bomb had exploded next to her.

It didn't.

Hakim pressed the Send button on the phone.

Eliana's face twisted; shoulders heaved with the assumption her mother had just been shot.

Brian wanted to tell her Rina was alive. Unless Hakim's collaborators had returned to the hotel room and held them hostage, again. If they had untied Stocky, the ladies were dead.

Hakim's partner showed him a green duffle bag.

They smiled. Nodded simultaneously. Damned puppets.

The CIA had managed to foil the suicide bombing, but the rebels had made back up plans.

With everyone grouped together, two assassins with assault rifles had the capability to do serious damage.

Brian had to figure out a way to stop them from spraying the crowd with bullets. He'd have to wedge through the bodies unnoticed by Hakim. A near impossibility given his 6-foot three-inch stature.

There had to be another solution.

Brian expected zero casualties. Except for himself if necessary.

That's it.

ELIANA

She wanted to fall down on all fours and cry like a baby.

Mama was gone.

Jazmin and Shamira as well.

If Brian hadn't escaped, he too had been shot by now.

The vest didn't work. In a way, Eliana wished it had so she could be with all of them.

It wasn't too late for that. Eliana knew what was in the bag.

Now that Hakim had nothing to threaten her with, she could scream. Tell everyone to run. Yell at the police, "*They have guns!*"

Eliana inhaled a lengthy breath. Time to test the strength of her vocal cords.

BRIAN

Time for Condition Red. No holds barred.

Officer Cabrera's plea for help would not be in vain. If he knew Brian had the ability to devise a solution out of thin air, Jay must have told him a lot.

Brian snaked into a dark, dirty corner.

With the backpack over his chest, he snatched pieces of twine from the front pocket where he'd stashed them before leaving the hotel room.

He had always been resourceful. Find and keep things that might be of use later. More often than not, stuff got chunked.

Not today.

Time to improvise.

A backpack with protruding explosive wires would be easy to replicate. The twine didn't resemble wire up-close. No biggie.

With bad memories of the attack four years ago, people would not think twice when he stepped into the open with Hakim's Beretta. Now set to three-round bursts.

Brian opened the zipper 45 degrees. Left hand ready to grab the powerful machine pistol.

With the attention of the Turkish Police focused on Brian, the CIA officers would run in and take down the real terrorists.

Good day to be alive, sir.

Good day to die.

Brian sprinted to the opposite side of the street.

Adrenaline forced his heart to pump what felt like two hundred beats per minute. Endorphins would soften the blows.

"I have a bomb!" He roared like a shepherd chasing a beast from his flock of sheep.

Brian pulled the gun from his backpack. Fired rounds into the air.

The crowd scurried like ants rushing from a crushed pile of soil.

Panic ensued.
Brian prepared to take gunfire from the police.
With any luck, they'd shoot him in the head to make it quick.

ELIANA

Eliana tried to duck, but Hakim jerked her arm.

All she could see through the mayhem was a madman with a big gun who shot in the air. Not at people.

Hakim shouted at the other guy, both confused, both angry and both grabbing machine guns from the bag. They were going to be more effective than the psycho across the way who had yet to hit anyone.

Except most of the crowd had vanished.

A handful of men stood nearby. Some taxi drivers remained, waving people into the cars, and peeling out to get away from the chaos.

Eliana inhaled deeply and screamed until she had no air left in her lungs. She dropped to the ground, tucked her knees into her chest, and waited for Hakim to shoot.

But the weapons clattered on the pavement.

Hakim's forehead slapped onto the concrete. Hard. He thrashed to break free from a hero who cuffed him.

The other guy tried to get up and run. Police outmuscled him. Beat him.

Did they get the other lunatic?

One of the bystanders helped Eliana to her feet. She fingered the webs of hair from her face.

That's when she saw Brian on the ground.

"What were you thinking?" Eliana leaned over Brian, lifeless on a stretcher. No response.

Two Americans and a Turkish officer engaged in a lively conversation. Oddly, in his craze Brian had not been shot by the police.

Eliana had never seen him have a panic attack like that before.

The younger American approached. "Eliana." A man capable of steamrolling two professional wrestlers at once held his hand out. "I'm Jay."

Eliana retained pressure on the ice pack positioned on Brian's head where someone had knocked him out. She recognized the man's face from a framed picture on Brian's wall. Three combat Marines held an American flag. Desert and mud buildings their backdrop.

"Not to be rude, but what are you doing here?" Eliana accepted Jay's handshake.

"Getting some training from my old man." Jay pointed to the other American.

Eliana turned to make eye contact with Jay's father who joined the introductory discussion.

"I knew he could pull something out of that stubborn head," the aged man said. White and gray hairs pinstriped his dark mustache. "Never expected him to do what he did. He was willing to die today."

Eliana had no idea why Brian's friend and his dad were here or how they had become involved. "Why didn't they kill him?" She pointed to the police who kept the crowds at bay.

"I told them ahead of time that he was with us. Good thing I did." The man reached his hand out. "Officer Cabrera, CIA."

Brian grunted. Mumbled curses slipped from pale lips.

"Hey man," Jay said in a sober tone.

Brian cracked his eyelids.

"Semper Gumby, bro."

"What the…?" Brian tried to use an elbow to sit up sideways and plopped back down, eyes closed posthaste.

"Your boyfriend is a bona fide hero, Eliana." Officer Cabrera straightened his spine, revealing his tall stature. "Your encouragement over the past several months contributed to his newfound strength."

So that's where I made a difference.

"You can say that again," Jay chimed in. "Our conversations have been much different. It's like the anxiety is gone. I don't know what you did, but I've never heard him so happy."

"What the hell?" Brian rubbed his eyes.

"Good to see you too, man." Jay clasped Brian's hand. "Oorah!"

"Errr." Brian sniffed and snorted as he came to his senses.

The two Marines voiced utterances back and forth. Not words. Some kind of Marine code. They understood what the sounds meant.

"Your mom is okay." Officer Cabrera put an arm around Eliana's shoulder. "Shamira has been taken into custody. She's looking at imprisonment. Same as Jazmin, but she's getting IV fluids at the hospital overnight."

"No! Jazmin helped us. She wasn't really on Hakim's side. It was all an act. We wouldn't be here if it weren't for her!"

Officer Cabrera nodded. "Your mom told my guys everything. The girls will be charged, but they have three people to testify on their behalf. Jail time may be minimal."

"Hey, beautiful," Brian coughed the words.

Eliana rested her cheek on Brian's collarbone.

Her mother called out in a voice similar to the day of the bombing. "Eliana!" Rina limped in her new prosthetic legs.

The tears came without warning. Moments ago, she thought her mother had been murdered, and that their next reunion would be in Heaven. But here they were, alive. There was so much to be said, but that would have to come later.

For now, Eliana could only think one thing.

How stupid she was to drag everyone on her escapade. They almost died. Two women in the beginnings of their adulthood were going to prison. All thanks to the quest for her true place in life. It was sitting in front of her all along.

America, the place mama wanted her to be.

PART X

Forgiveness

ELIANA

May 2020
Nannie & Pops' House

Eliana sipped fresh-squeezed orange juice, savoring the sweetness of Nannie's signature beverage. Chopped mint leaves from the garden drifted amongst glassy ice cubes. She held a new appreciation for the concoction. COVID-19 had wiped out her sense of smell and taste for fifty-two long days.

When she reunited with her mother and Jazmin in Istanbul, Eliana had come up with the idea for a group respite at the ranch in Mississippi. Brian, Rina and even Jazmin planned to join her. Pops asked them to wait two weeks in case they had been exposed to the virus.

Good thing.

According to Jazmin, Hakim's girlfriend had returned from a vacation to northern Italy the day before he left. She complained of feeling ill, but Hakim didn't care. They spent one night together. Long enough to spread the virus. Hakim coughed in Eliana's face more than once at the airport. No doubt the germs came from him.

The night of their return to the U.S., Eliana's temperature spiked out of nowhere. Severe gastrointestinal problems kept her in the bathroom overnight. Day two, she felt like cotton balls had been stuffed into her lungs. No matter how hard she coughed, it wouldn't come out. When her breaths began to sound like crinkly tissue paper on Valentine's Day, Brian insisted she go to the hospital.

Mama had tried to warn Eliana about the virus before the trip. "*Stop being so scared of life*," she had chastised her mother.

Contracting the novel Coronavirus of 2019 was a just punishment for her arrogance. She got what she deserved…and then some.

The whole experience felt otherworldly. Being in ICU, sleeping twenty hours per day, waking only to the fluctuating symptoms of the virus. Once, she felt sure she had appendicitis. Horrible aches, worse than the flu, jolted her from sleep on several occasions. Scariest of all was the shortness of breath. She lay in bed too many times, convinced someone had put a stack of bricks on her upper body.

The thought sent Eliana into a coughing fit. Or was it a piece of mint that got stuck in her throat?

Pops, Brian, and Jazmin jumped to their feet.

Eliana's head spun as she brooded over the days that blurred together into weeks. She remembered little of the time when respiratory failure and sepsis nearly killed her. Ting, the nationalized nurse from China who lost three family members to the novel virus, had cared for her like sister. And on the day Eliana knew she was going to die, Ting pulled up a live chat so everyone could tell her goodbye.

All the family in Mississippi gathered for the farewell video. Brian and Jazmin were there. Everyone held hands and sang "Amazing Grace." It was Pops' prayer on forgiveness that got Eliana through that day. And the next. And the one after that.

Four weeks later, Eliana left the hospital after three negative COVID-19 tests. She spent two weeks isolated in a hotel, 100% symptom free, then two more weeks at Brian's apartment. Recovery was ongoing, but Eliana finally felt comfortable enough to go home.

Just in time for Mother's Day.

"Y'all just give her a minute," Nannie said to Rina and Brian who collaborated to help. "She'll come out of it on her own."

Eliana's grandmother knew her better than anyone.

"I'm fine," Eliana lied. The scratchy tickle made her eyes water. "A piece of mint got stuck in my throat."

Jazmin chugged the OJ as if she had been in the desert for days. "This is heavenly." Thanks to Jay's dad, she made it back to the States without consequence. A bit of questioning by the authorities, and she was free.

Shamira did not fare as well. Deportment back to Chile. Prolonged time in a mental institution. Revenge motivation and naivety got her into a heap of trouble. She had conspired with a terrorist, held people captive with a weapon, and was considered a threat to society.

Nannie piled a third serving of breakfast on Jazmin's plate. "Thank you," Jazmin said and drove her fork into a sausage link.

"We're going to have to get her a personal trainer if you don't stop that," Pops said to Nannie with a downward tilt of the lips. The corners of his eyes lifted as everyone laughed.

Brian closed a fist into his chest to flex his bicep. "I can show you some moves before I leave tomorrow."

Rina dipped her last bits of pancake in syrup. "Did you decide what you're going to do?"

"Yes and no." Brian cracked his knuckles, a habit he developed after the concussion. "I want to support our country in some way. Still fight terrorists but from home. Maybe DOD or FBI. Gotta finish my degree first. What about you, Rina?"

Nannie and Rina exchanged glances with knowing smiles and mutual silent questioning.

"May as well tell her," Pops chimed in.

Eliana hated surprises, even when they were good. She would rather be in on the secret from the beginning. "Tell me what?"

Rina smiled like a young bride on the verge of a revelation to her family that she had eloped and married her boyfriend in Las Vegas. Happy. Worried. Uncertain. "I met with an immigration attorney. If you would sponsor me, I can apply for a green card and stay. I could work and make a life for myself here."

"I need some water." There would be no denying her mother's request. Eliana bolted from her chair and opened the refrigerator door harder than intended. Glass jars clanked against each other and skidded into new positions. "What about Israel? You don't want to go back?"

"I have no reason to go back, and I have every reason to stay." Rina rubbed her hands on her pants and bit her bottom lip.

"That's right." Nannie retrieved a glass from the cabinet and handed it to Eliana. "It makes no sense for your mother to go back to a place where she has no one other than a few friends. In this small room, she has a family that loves her. It's more than she's had in a long time, Dollface."

"Yeah but, what if I decide to go there someday?" Eliana scooped ice into the glass and filled it to the top with water. "For a visit? Or a college transfer?"

"Why in the hell would you do that?" Pops slapped a flat palm on the counter. "What about the rising tension with Iran? They hate Americans and want to destroy Israel! Then there's North Korea. Not to mention that damned virus. You want to get it again?"

Pops rarely got mad. He never cussed. And he usually only used the word hell when referring to the actual place.

"Chuck!" Nannie waved a forefinger in the air and made a clicking sound. "Do I need to send you to bed for a nap?"

Everyone burst out in laughter except Pops.

"What? I'm just saying it like it is." Pops crossed his arms and turned before leaving the room. "After all that's happened, you're still talking about living in the Middle East. You're going to send me to my grave."

"You stop that duck fit!" Nannie grabbed a fly swatter and chased after her soul mate. She knew how to handle him.

"My Love," Rina said and pointed to the chair Nannie had occupied. "Come sit down next to me."

Eliana slid onto the smooth wood seat.

"I want you to listen to me. We've been through a lot. Both of us." Rina scooped her hair to the side and rolled her shoulders. "I'm going to support you in whatever decisions you make for yourself, even if I don't like them. I ask the same of you."

"I didn't say that I dislike your decision to live in America."

"It's a great idea." Brian squeezed Eliana's leg. "Start all over again, new home, new career. Who knows, you may even meet someone."

Rina hid a grin behind tresses that had fallen over her cheeks. "No. Seth was my one, true love."

"Mama, of course he was. No one could ever replace him." Eliana pushed her mother's hair behind her ears. "See? You're smiling! What if there's someone else out there for you?"

"Yeah," Brian pumped his head, "someone to grow old with."

"Maybe," Rina said with a lazy shrug. "Jazmin, we've been ignoring you. Will you go home after all this is over?"

Jazmin had put on a few pounds thanks to Nannie's cooking. She had always eaten like a horse, but she never gained weight. She no longer looked like a middle-schooler.

"No. I want to stay." Jazmin rubbed her belly and bent forward. "I think I ate too much."

Brian grabbed the trash can and held it in front of her.

"I don't need to vomit." Her knowledge of the English language had improved so much that she spoke with more eloquence than an average citizen. "I feel nauseated, but not from too much food. It's the secret I hide. It's time to tell you."

"Me?" Brian glanced at Eliana with a shoulder shrug.

Jazmin's expression slackened. "All of you."

This was the moment Eliana had been waiting for since the day she met Jazmin. The answer to her perpetual suspicions was about to unravel.

"This is hard." Jazmin wrung her hands, fingers whitening with each twist and turn.

Eliana flicked her thumbs against her fingernails. Each click synchronized with the fluctuation of emotions that threatened to destabilize her soundness of mind. "Is it necessary to tell us?" What was she thinking? Jazmin needed to spill it out! But what if the knowledge would ruin the harmony they had? "I mean, does it involve us?"

"Let her talk, Dollface." Nannie stood in the doorway with Pops' hands resting on her shoulders.

"On that day in class, when you told the story about how your mom died in the suicide bombing," Jazmin blinked with a quick side-glance at Eliana, "I nearly fainted. I knew many details about that attack as well as others. You know they never discovered who did it?"

"Yes, I said that in class." Eliana assessed her mother's reaction after hearing that her lie had been shared with a room full of students. She had prepared an explanation that, so far, she hadn't used. *Actually, my mom is alive! The hospital got her confused with another patient who died.* She hoped never to have to tell the lie.

"A Jihad organization claimed responsibility," Jazmin continued, "but they refused to boast the identity of their martyr other than using the word Shahida."

"Family and friends did not come forward." Rina locked eyes with Jazmin. "Her DNA did not match any records."

Eliana had hoped for a meatier revelation. "What does this have to do with you?"

"Everything." Jazmin stared at the doorway.

"Well? What is it?" Eliana's pulse quickened. Nagging, chill-like tingles in her body made her feel like crashing through the window and running until the feeling subsided.

"The day of the bombing," Jazmin said to Rina, "is the same day my big sister went missing. Her name was Ismat."

Rina rested her elbows on the upper prosthetic portion of her legs and pressed her forehead into her palms.

Eliana recalled her first dinner with Jazmin. She spoke of a deceased sister who had become involved with radical Muslims.

"A month after the bombing, a letter with Ismat's handwriting on the envelope arrived in the mail." Jazmin closed her eyes and resumed in a lower pitch. "I was so relieved until I read, '*Beloved Amourra*,' at the top of the paper. It's the pet-name my father gave me, and she hated it. The rest of the letter was bizarre until the final sentence. '*For your safety,*' she wrote, '*don't tell anyone your sister is a Shahida.*' Centered at the bottom, in all caps, Ismat concluded with, '*IN HONOR OF FATHER*,' and the date."

Eliana opened her mouth to speak, but no words formed. How could she voice the millions of thoughts running through her mind? "You think your sister is responsible for blowing up my mom."

"I know it for a fact. Ismat signed the letter on the first anniversary of our father's death...the same day of the bombing." Jazmin's hair dangled in her face like a veil. Teardrops bounced off her arms. "I knew I could die or go to prison for what I did with Hakim. I did it to make up for what my sister did to your family."

Farm dogs barked outside, filling what would be a heavy silence. The house cat waltzed into the room with a chirpy meow and jumped into Brian's lap. Rina unclasped the prosthetics and rubbed her legs.

"How did your dad die?" Pops pulled a chair for Nannie. "If you don't mind my asking."

"IDF soldiers killed him."

Each head popped upright in unison.

"It was during a period of severe hostility, and they mistook him for an extremist." Jazmin released a sharp exhale. "This is the reason for her revenge."

Brian cracked his knuckles. "I joined the Marines to get revenge for my dad."

Yet another detail Eliana wanted to know. She refused to ask Brian questions regarding his painful past. His timing was what mattered.

"Al-Qaida captured him in Afghanistan in '03. I was 11. We never knew if he was dead or alive. They found his remains in '09. I joined the Marine Corps Junior ROTC in 12th grade, signed up for delayed entry, and went to boot camp three days after high school graduation."

Pops placed a hand on Brian's back. "Son, revenge or not, you're a hero to us all."

"I don't know. I went in with the same motivation as Ismat—kill people to get vengeance for my dad's death." Brian shrugged with a jutted lip. "Nothin' heroic about that."

"The difference between you and my sister," Jazmin clarified, "is that she shed the blood of innocent people. You honorably fought the enemy."

Nannie slapped a palm to her forehead. "My word, I just realized somethin' y'all. Five out of the six of us had someone we love murdered by terrorists. Even more head-scratching, the three of you young'uns all had your father wrongfully killed!"

A more fitting conclusion could not have ended the whirlwind of a conversation on a better note. Or so Eliana thought.

"Not only that," Brian suggested, "three of us blame ourselves for circumstances that were completely beyond our control. I, for one, relinquish that self-indictment."

Rina had been silent throughout the huge revelations until now. "You're exactly right, Brian. If I ever had a hero, it's you. The guilt stays in the past. Nothing I did caused or could have prevented my husband's death."

Eliana felt their eyes. They wanted to hear her story of self-forgiveness. She had made many mistakes over the past year, all fueled by shame and selfishness. But what's a mistake if you don't learn from it?

"I've hated myself for years. You didn't die," Eliana said without eye contact, "but, you were burned, crippled, and our lives were torn apart with it. All because I wanted a stupid rugelach before bed!"

Sniffles, whimpers, and snorts jumped from one person to the next.

"You know it's not your fault, my Love." Rina clasped Eliana's arm. With mottled skin in brown and pink shades, only a few patches of her original coloring remained. "Everyone in this room will tell you the same thing."

"But, they didn't see how I hurried you to the bus!"

Rina seesawed on her legs until she faced her daughter. "My little Eli, do you not remember how I rushed through the market? I pulled you, dragged you at times, so scared that something bad was about to occur. I led us to that stop, and I thank God every day that your bag broke."

The truth of her mother's words sank in. Eliana was not the only one in a hurry that day.

"I thank God he let my daughter-in-law live," Pops said and squeezed Nannie's shoulders.

"Amen to that." Nannie kissed the cross on her necklace. "Thank you, Lord, for making all this happen so we could be here today, workin' out our issues."

Brian took Eliana's free hand and reached for Rina's. "How about it, Beautiful? After all you've heard in the past ten minutes, do you still blame yourself?"

"I'm working on it."

Pops gathered his keys from the counter. "I think it's time to wrap it up. I'm going to town to get some barbecue for dinner tonight. We're going to have a hankering for some good, hearty nourishment before long."

"Don't you dare go without a mask!" Nannie pointed to a box on the counter. "Grab one of them new ones we got in the mail today. Oh, and some gloves too!"

Brian helped Rina reposition her prosthetics, even though she didn't require assistance. Eliana could see she liked it. Her mother definitely needed a man.

As for Eliana, she didn't know what she needed other than to get over her misery. It was like a fight against colossal waves that sucked her into an ocean of self-condemnation.

Late August 2020
Nashville, Tennessee

Eliana felt Brian's truck come to a stop.

"Wake up, sleepyhead! We're here."

The pleasurable, annoying reflex from Brian's fingers on her ribs made Eliana jump from sleep. She squirmed to break free from the nudges. "Stop it! I give! I'm up."

Eliana navigated the campus, admiring its beauty as never before. Her best friend walked by her side, held her hand, and appeared just as content as she felt.

One year ago, they had both been in different places in their lives.

The new decade had launched the world into a series of unprecedented events. History books would be rewritten with several chapters dedicated to the year 2020.

Each survivor would have a story to tell. When it came down to the nitty-gritty, Eliana's emphasis to anyone who cared to listen would focus on choices.

"Wanna have kids?" Brian flashed a wink.

Eliana shuffled back a few paces. Her smile went stiff. "What?"

Brian drew close to meet Eliana face-to-face. "You know, in the future."

"You may be nearing thirty, but I'm not even drinking age." Eliana pushed a finger on Brian's torso to make him back up. "No way I'm having kids in the near future."

"That's not what I said, Beautiful."

Creepy crawlies tingled from Eliana's neck to tailbone. Did Brian just propose? If so, it was a peculiar way to do it. Although, she had learned from both Brian and Jay that Marines express themselves in the strangest of ways. She didn't know how to take certain things. Playing along was always the answer.

"How can you be a CIA counter-terrorist agent, and I be an international journalist when we have tots totting around in demand of our attention?" *Crap, I just accepted his proposal!* The real thing with ring presentation had better be damned good. And a long time from now.

"Point taken."

"Did I say that out loud?"

"What?" Brian pulled Eliana into a lush area with flowers, greenery, and low-hanging trees. "That you want to be with me, pursuing our careers, but that the serious stuff has to wait?"

His face was too close to answer.

"You're going to have to be patient with me." Eliana stepped back for a few inches of space. "I need to gain some perspective. Live a little."

"You mean, like date other guys?" Brian tossed his hands to the sides. "That's cool. I understand."

"No!" Eliana grabbed Brian as forcefully as he pulled her into the bushes and kissed his lips against a tight embrace. "Why would I want to date other guys when I have the one who is perfect for me?"

Brian shook his head with a *pssht* sound. "I'm not perfect for anyone."

"Oh stop it!" Eliana slapped Brian's arm. "All I'm trying to say, is that it may be several years before I'm ready for the big stuff. What if I'm not ready to have kids till you're in your forties?" *Great. The marriage talk is official. He may as well propose and get it over with.*

"As long as I'm alive, and as long as we're together, it doesn't matter. I'll wait till I'm fifty if that's what it takes."

Eliana dove back into Brian's chest. She felt a lump in his pocket. One possibly shaped as a box. Containing a piece of jewelry.

"Come to the point, First Sergeant."

From that day on, Eliana would wear Brian's ring with honor. She would reflect on 2020 as a year of change, growth, and self-forgiveness. No more looking back on the past. No fretting about the future. There was only one way to live.

One day at a time.

THE END

Want More?

If you're not ready for the story to end, you're in luck.

Bonus material follows the acknowledgments!

First, I would like to ask a favor. If you enjoyed *Charge of the Beast*, would you please leave a rating on Amazon? No need to make it long or detailed—unless you want! The main thing is to share your honest opinion. This benefits me, as reviews are hard to come by for an independent author. You, the reader, have the power to make or break this book.

If you have the time to leave a review, visit my author page on Amazon and click the link for *Charge of the Beast*. Even a simple star rating is of great value. This helps better my rank and push my book to the top of the search results! www.amazon.com/author/rosalieking

Thank you for spending time with me!

Rosalie King
www.rosalieking.com

ACKNOWLEDGMENTS

Mom and Dad, I owe everything to you. Without your training in my childhood and continuous support in my adulthood, I would not be who I am today. Thank you.

About Brian Draeger. Brian is an accurate portrayal of a scarred war hero. Countless hours of research in various forms—including written articles, books, documentaries, helmet cam, interviews, and more—led to the creation of this character who, in effect, is authentic.

I would like to thank the following United States Marine Corps combat veterans for your counsel:

- Sergeant Addison Stevens: Operation Iraqi Freedom 2008
  Thank you for the conversations, insight, encouragement, and reassurance that Brian is the real deal. My prayers for you continue.
- Major Christopher Westhoff: Operation Iraqi Freedom 2006-2007, 2008-2009
  Thank you for answering all my questions, your assistance with Brian's flashback, knife-throwing instruction, and enlightening me on a personality befitting a Marine.
  Please buy Major Westhoff's memoir, *A Captain At War: Stories of an American Advisor In Fallujah, Iraq*. Available on Amazon.
- Sergeant Otis Ford: Vietnam 1966-1968
  Thank you for sharing your story about the burden you carry. You had every right to go on R&R.
- Colonel W. Griffin: Vietnam 1964-1970
  You jumped on a grenade and lived to tell about it. Thank you for offering your extensive knowledge of PTSD.

My gratitude to Kathy and LeRoy Neel for sharing personal details about their son, Phillip, who gave his life in service to our nation. Mortally wounded, First Lieutenant Phillip Neel continued to give orders and ensured his team's safety. Phil, your legacy lives on in the hearts of many.

The stories about victims of the Israeli-Palestinian Conflict are based on true events. I would like to thank the two ladies, Hila from Israel, and Hiba from Palestine, who opened their souls to share their individual experiences. My chance encounters with Hila (at a wedding) and Hiba (on an airplane) enabled me to present both sides of the conflict from a civilian standpoint.

Many thanks to my faithful editor, Sharla Barfoot. My novels would not be the same without your invaluable input. Jessica, thank you for sitting down with me to share the photos and stories of your travels in Israel.

I would like to give a shout-out to my brother, Corporal D.C. Freeman of the United States Marine Corps. On behalf of the family, we are so proud of you and thankful for your service!

"Now to Him who is able to keep you from stumbling, and to make you stand in the presence of His glory blameless with great joy, to the only God our Savior, through Jesus Christ our Lord, be glory, majesty, dominion and authority, before all time and now and forever. Amen."

Jude 24-25

BONUS CONTENT

Authors must make tough decisions during the editing process. One of the most difficult is choosing portions of the narrative that must be removed. Oftentimes, these scenes slow the book down or do not play an important role in the overall story arc.

I have chosen to offer some deleted scenes and chapters as bonus content. Most of this unedited material was written between 6-10 years ago before I had advanced in the craft of writing. If just one person enjoys these chapters, my goal has been accomplished!

ISMAT
THE SUICIDE BOMBER

Ismat's chapter was one of the hardest to delete. While I desired to present it as a part of the novel, I could not find the right place for her story.

The original narrative took place in the early 2000s when fighting in the Israeli-Palestinian Conflict was severe. After extensive research, I was able to recreate a character with the mindset of a female suicide bomber in that time period. I studied material about women who were successful in the mission, others who were too overcome by fear to continue, and others who were caught and imprisoned.

Albeit fictitious, what you are about to read is a true representation of a Palestinian Shahida in the first decade of the 21st century.

November 2009
Gaza, Palestine

Ismat al-Hourani lay curled in a fetal position on the balcony of her family's apartment in the Gaza Strip. The cold concrete held no empathy for her skeletal frame.

Eyes clinched; all she could see was the smile of her father. He was the center of attention in the family and had a strong bond with each member. Ismat and her sister relished his ways of showing love, one of which was the ritual of tucking his two girls in at bedtime. When Ismat was in her early teen years, she insisted she was too old for it anymore. Her father, on the other hand, said she would always be his little girl. As long as she was still under his roof, he wanted to see her off to bed every night. She came to cherish that time again, even more than when she was a small child.

Ismat knew she was more important to him than her sister. The best thing Jazmin got out of him was a nickname: "Amourra, because you are like the moon," her father said at the time. Ismat didn't think it was so special. It made her sister so happy, she decided to use that name from then on.

His outward displays of affection toward Ismat were more overt than those he demonstrated to Amourra. He even took Ismat on special excursions, which made her feel more cherished than anyone else. For her eighteenth birthday, he had planned an evening out, just the two of them. She was secretly aware of the surprise plans he had for her, but all she cared about was the undivided attention he would pay her.

That evening never came to pass.

Tears streamed, soaking Ismat's cheeks and neck. "Damned IDF," she struggled to whisper. "He did nothing wrong. Just an innocent bystander. Why, why?"

She sat up and grasped the iron rail. Her eyes burned from the tears as she gazed down from the second floor of the apartment building. Her mind gave way to a vision of a body lying on the ground. It was the girl from the building across the street. A teenaged drug addict. In a craze, she threw herself from the balcony to her death. She was on the first floor when she jumped, yet it was the way her head hit the curb that killed her. That was two months ago. Blood still stained the concrete.

What if that were me? No, she wouldn't do something so absurd. She was better than that. She had dignity.

As much as it hurt, she could not help but think of another gruesome scene: how her father's final moments of life must have been after being gunned down by the Israeli Defense Forces.

Each night before that dreadful day, he came home and told the family about the Palestinian militants who, in the vicinity of his pharmacy, had been shooting at Jewish settlements. He cursed them for putting the lives of so many people in danger. "They're Israelis, we're Palestinians. So what? We just need to enjoy life and stop this nonsensible war!" He ranted.

So many times, he thought of closing the store in fear for his life, but he remained open. Most of his customers were regulars who he had come to know personally. With no other pharmacy nearby, if he were to close the store, they would have had to travel twenty minutes to get their vital medications.

Fear would not force him to shut them out. So, he opened the doors every day.

The morning he died, he felt comfortable about going to work. Tranquility in the area for two days gave him a sense of relief. A sense of hope that both sides agreed. A hope for peace.

The IDF were apprehensive, though. They knew the opposition had not yet come to an end and expected violence to recommence at any moment. They were on the lookout for anyone who appeared suspect.

That day they made a horrific mistake. Ismat's father was ten minutes late opening the store, and as he ran in hopes that no one was waiting, he heard the first shots in days.

This time, he was the target.

A jumpy Israeli soldier determined Ismat's father was a rebel running toward them in attack.

Ismat tried to push the visualizations of her dying father out of her mind, but the effort was futile. All she could imagine were his gasps for breath as blood filled his mouth and gushed out the side. She could see him lying on the pavement, a crimson pool encircling his body. Eyes wide as his final breath escaped.

What was he thinking during those moments? Of me? Our evening we were supposed to spend together?

To make life even worse, Ismat's mother became obsessed with the idea of finding a man to take his place both as a husband and as a father. Within eight months, she married a man she thought to be the perfect replacement.

Friends, neighbors, even family members who viewed her action as a crime spouted venom. By the way they carried themselves around her and avoided eye contact, her mother sensed their contempt.

"I don't care what they think," her mother asserted. "I want what's best for all of us. You'll get used to it."

Ismat's new father was worse than any other she knew of. Mother favored him over Ismat and Amourra, even though he was brutal toward each of them. With all of the yelling and bruises, mother never gave in. She did not want to lose another husband.

Would she rather have lost her mistreated daughters instead? What if he killed them during one of his rages?

Amourra, just nine at the time, was the first to be victimized by this brute. Their mother left for medical testing which took up most of the day on a Saturday. She left them in the hands of the man who, just like so many of her friends' fathers, was disinterested. He closed himself off and stared at the TV. Not even a commercial break compelled him to check on his stepdaughters.

"What a joke," Ismat said to Amourra. "We don't need him to watch over us. Come on, let's go hide his wallet and keys. It will be so funny when he tries to find them later." Ismat had more malicious ideas in mind. Those would come another day.

Amourra didn't follow Ismat's influence. She thought she was too good for that. Her behavior was just a front. Ismat knew she would turn out to be a bad apple. The only resemblance she would have with the moon is coldness in her core.

Late in the evening, Amourra became hungry for something more than the snacks she got throughout the day. When her incessant grumbling tore at their new father's nerves, he pounded the power off on the remote control, threw it on the coffee table, and bolted from the couch.

He spat curse words while searching for his wallet and keys. Ismat retreated to the bathroom to hide her enjoyment. She flattened her hand over her mouth to quiet the laughter, but the subsequent sounds sent her out of control. A few splashes of cold water on the face helped. It was time to go out and take the blame. She would get the wallet and keys, hold them right in front of his face, and smile. When she came out of the bathroom, though, she changed her mind at the image of a snarling wolf.

He hurled a curse at both of them, then stormed off to his bedroom. "Come on," he growled with a wad of cash in hand.

I'll have to find his stash later, Ismat thought.

The girls followed him. Neither spoke a word, still frightened by his outburst of rage.

The menu at a nearby restaurant offered nothing to Amourra's desire. Her twisted expressions and huffed complaints annoyed Ismat.

Their stepfather ignored her.

Without asking anyone's preferences, he mumbled a few selections to the waiter. Ismat and her sister had no choice. No freedom. They would either eat or be hungry.

Amourra chose to be hungry. She turned her nose up at the plate set in front of her and shook her head. "I am not eating that!"

Their stepfather's fork clanked on the table and bounced to the floor at the force of his throw. He slapped Amourra upside the head so hard she nearly fell out of her chair. Ismat could still picture her in shock, catching herself with the palm of her hand on the table in order not to fall.

Obedience followed. Without a word, she cleaned her plate.

In a way, Ismat was proud of her sister's humble response. If she had been the victim, his fork would have found its way into his neck.

When Ismat told her mother what happened, she blew it off. "You're exaggerating," she said. "Look, I don't see any marks."

That was the first of many incidences of both verbal and physical abuse. Their mother received the worst of it, yet through it all, she remained more devoted to this man than her own daughters.

Throughout the following months, Ismat isolated herself from everyone. The only person she spoke more than just a few words to was Amourra whom she had more compassion for after the restaurant. She became Amourra's protector since their mother didn't care.

Now, it was one month before the first anniversary of her father's death.

Stories of other casualties suffered by innocent Palestinians in the West Bank and Gaza filled Ismat with hatred for the Israelis. With each incident she heard of, her fury ballooned. The news reports about the death of children angered her the most. She dwelled on her suffering and knew there were other people who suffered in the same way.

Her pulse ran laps throughout her body as thoughts of what had transpired during the last year swarmed through her mind. She had the right to be angry about the war, about her father's death, and about her life.

She pushed off the cold balcony floor and focused on the blood-stained curb. Wrath turned to sorrow. She hated everything about her life and wanted nothing more to do with it.

"What if I jump?" Her voice shook.

I could take myself out right now and be with my father.

But she was only two floors up. Survival would mean a few broken bones. Confinement in a mental institution.

"No," she said out loud. "There can be no possibility of survival."

She smeared the last of the tears from her cheeks. Her feet shot into the concrete like arrowheads. Her legs, like the spiny shafts of the arrow, directed her heels in place. A firm grip of the rail turned her knuckles white. Fury prevailed, but her girlish frame did not threaten the night air.

"I'll avenge my father's death," she hissed through clenched teeth. "I'll do it for him. For him and for all Palestinians."

Yes, I will sacrifice myself in honor of my father and in service to my community.

The next morning, Ismat pushed herself out of bed early. For the first time in months, she headed to the kitchen for breakfast. As they did every morning, her mother and Amourra sat at the tiny table attached to the kitchen wall. When Ismat walked in, she took a piece of bread, dipped it first in olive oil, then in the za'atar dish filled with herbs, sesame seeds and salt.

"Is this a joke?" Amourra said. "You're really going to eat that?"

Ismat said nothing. She didn't miss eating breakfast, but she knew she needed to be strong for her new mission. And why not try to enjoy food? Before long, she wouldn't be there to eat anyway.

"It's been months since you've eaten breakfast," her mother said as Ismat chewed. "Have you decided to start taking care of yourself now?"

Ismat shrugged her shoulders and took another bite before leaving the room. If only they had known the motive for her sudden boost in morale. If only they were able to read her thoughts, they would discover that she was headed out the door to plan an end to her life.

This plan derived from an incident nine months prior. Not too long after she returned to school following her father's death, one of her classmates asked how she was coping. She thought it strange, as she did not know this person. He never spoke to anyone besides the teachers. He always kept to himself. No one had dared to ask about her father. She did not speak of the tragedy, and she pretended not to notice the glances and whispers of those around her. This young man, with no pretenses, approached as if they were childhood friends.

"Who are you to ask me that?" she had responded. "I don't need a psychiatrist. Mind your own business." It was the only answer she could come up with. A dense fog in her soul suppressed the truth.

"I know it's hard to express yourself," her classmate asserted. "You are lost in a maze of anger from which you cannot escape. Your father didn't deserve to die like this."

His coarse tone pulled her into his world of words. Wrath peeked through the vanishing fog.

"You feel powerless because you want justice," he continued, "and you know nothing will be done about it."

His pause requested an answer.

The words froze upon Ismat's tongue.

"Am I not correct?"

She raised her head halfway. The expression in his eyes spelled revenge.

"Do not allow his death to be taken for granted. Reclaim his honor." He tore a penned page from his notebook. "Call this number and give them my name, Ahmad."

He placed the note on her desk and turned to the teacher who rapped on the desk in demand of their attention.

Ismat understood Ahmad's message. She knew what he wanted her to do.

After class, she crumpled the note. When she neared the trash can, something stopped her from disposing of it. She shoved the wad in her jean pocket and threw it in the back of her drawer at home.

Now she was ready for redemption. She would even the score.

The public pay phone on an empty street provided ample room for the first step in her new mission: to kill the enemy. With the torn paper in her trembling hands, she scoured her surroundings to see who might be watching.

Only a few kids played two blocks away.

Her dry mouth beckoned moisture.

Pull yourself together. You must do this.

Ismat rolled her head to ease the tension from her neck and took a deep breath. The receiver chilled her ear. Her fingers locked with the punch of each number.

Determination propelled her every uncertain move.

She stood upright, head held high, and waited for an answer. After five rings, she began to pull the receiver away from her ear, somewhat disappointed. Somewhat relieved.

Then, she heard a male voice.

"Who is it?" His tone was deep. Intimidating.

Ismat gulped.

"Who is it?" This time he snapped.

"Your number was given to me by Ahmad. I am ready to do my duty." Surprised by her assertive tone, her confidence began to build.

Squeaking filled Ismat's ear. Muffled voices ranted in the background

"How do you know Ahmad? What is your location?"

As Ismat explained her whereabouts, the man shushed someone in the background.

"Stand at the side of the street with your head down," he commanded. "In ten minutes, someone will be there. When the car pulls to the curb, keep your eyes closed."

A clank rapped at Ismat's ear. The connection was gone.

Her heart pounded. Surging breaths filled her lungs.

It hit her that this was really happening. She could run away now if she wanted to get out of it, but this was not her desire. Ahmad was right, and she had to move forward.

Not knowing what to expect, Ismat did as the man told her. Every time she heard a car approach, she squeezed her eyes. Her shoulders tensed and her stomach fluttered. At last, a vehicle came to a screeching halt in front of her. When the door flew open, a man yelled, "Keep your head down and your eyes closed!"

Feet stomped. A grasp and push of her shoulders sent her tumbling into the vehicle.

The unintentional peek she stole made her the object of aggression.

"Eyes closed! Eyes closed!" Two voices yelled in unison.

A cloth whipped around her head and eyes, restraining any possibility of further glances. It was tight, yet she knew she must not complain. She must show no weakness.

The car sped and swerved around corners. Her body rocked on the seat with nowhere to go. Side-to-side. Lashing like an angry ocean squall.

Then, the storm stilled.

The driver slowed down. No one said a word.

Tight, creaking leather hinted at movement in the front passenger seat.

A lighter flicked.

A strong odor of smoke ensued.

When the window of the driver seat rolled down, the noise and feel of the wind brought Ismat to calm waters. The silence that made her uncomfortable just a few moments beforehand washed away.

After what seemed half an hour of travel in the car, she became tired and felt like relaxing in the seat. She knew, however, that she needed to maintain good posture. Poise out of respect for those with whom she entrusted her life would play a part in her outward character.

Strength. Submission. Full compliance. These would demonstrate her resolution to adhere to whatever she would be instructed to do.

A bumpy road punched her upright just as she succumbed to the ache. Moments later, they came to a stop. Everyone jumped out and left Ismat in the comfort of solitude. Silence was not her friend now. She held her breath to decipher the hushed conversation outside the car. She flared her nose as she struggled for adequate breaths in the unventilated confines.

Approaching shoes crunched in the dirt and rocks.

Shoulders up and back rigid, she waited. The door opened, but she did not move.

"You may get out." This voice was different from the one she heard on the phone and the one who pulled her into the car. "I will lead you indoors," he said and placed her hand on his shoulder. "Don't even try look through the bottom of the blindfold. Even when we take you inside and unmask you, do not look around the room."

A strong odor of dirt offended her nose. Her ankles swayed as she trudged over large rocks before an easy ascent upon smooth steps. They entered some kind of building or residence. As she heard the shoes of her guide clicking on the floor and the resulting echo, Ismat sensed she was in a vast, open area. A soft flow of water, possibly from a fountain, could be heard from a distance. The odor of chlorine contrasted with the scent of Bukhoor incense.

Although she could not see, what she heard, felt, and smelled put her at ease. She sensed that she was in a safe place. Maybe even a lavish home. At last they turned a corner into what she assumed was a room.

"When I take the cloth from your eyes, look straight ahead," Ismat's guide said.

The release of pressure from her head and face brought about a sensation of freedom. The air could have been a caress of silk around her eyes.

Legs and feet back backed away. When she raised her head, Ahmad sat in a chair about ten feet away. A dim light gleamed from the ceiling in the windowless room.

Ahmad leaned his elbows on his knees with his arms stretched out in a triangle. His serious expression made her wonder if he was disappointed that she waited so long. After a moment, he half-smiled and nodded in approval. "I thought you weren't going to call. I am pleased you have made this choice."

A red glow stared at her from a video camera which sat on a tripod next to Ahmad. Blinding light pierced her eyes.

"Tell me, why are you here? What do you expect from this meeting?" Ahmad's voice was steady and made her feel at ease. He looked manlier than the last time she saw him, more like an adult. His composure made him seem experienced and mature.

Ismat began, "I want to avenge my father's death as well as the deaths of all the innocent people who have died at the hands of the IDF."

While this was true, it was not the only reason for this act she wished to fulfill. If she told them she felt worthless and wanted nothing to do with life, they would have dismissed her. They would have thought her motive was not to serve her fellow Palestinians and Allah, but to commit suicide due to her misery.

They would be correct.

"I want to train to be a Shahida," Ismat said with confidence. To be a successful female martyr would be her greatest accomplishment. "This self-sacrifice I will do in the name of Allah. If you allow me to do this deed, there is just one thing I ask. The one-year anniversary of my father's death is in three weeks and six days. I would like to carry out the mission on that day."

Shuffling movements sounded from the corner behind her. Ahmad looked in that direction as someone drew near.

A tall, well-dressed man stood in front of Ismat. "Young lady, do you understand the gravity of this deed?" It was the man who answered the phone. His voice was even deeper in person. "Your martyrdom will kill and wound innocent Israelis. Does this not bother you?"

"Sir," she said without pause, "I only wish to serve my people no matter what the outcome may be. Besides, after all our suffering at the hands of the

IDF, vengeance is just."

"If you want to carry this out so soon," the man said through a cough, "you will have to spend many hours in training. You will have to watch recordings of martyrs who have been victorious in fulfilling this privilege. You will have to gain knowledge of the explosive vest and how to use it.

"I want you to understand that it is expensive for us to do this. We use the best materials to ensure the vests will not turn out defective." The man was exceptionally articulate in the way he spoke. She could tell he was an educated man. His appearance was extraordinary. He had the poise and confidence of a king.

"Our organization is private," he went on, looking down at Ismat with raised eyebrows. "When our martyrs perform this honorable feat, no one knows who they are or where they came from. Their families are not aware of what happened and often report their loved ones as missing. They receive no reward. Please understand, this is for their protection from the IDF."

"Whatever it takes, I will cooperate. I'm ready to move forward."

The man nodded. "You are resolute. You have no uncertainty in your eyes. Very different from the other recruits."

No uncertainty, Ismat assured herself. "I promise you will be pleased."

"Good." At that, the man nonchalantly left the room.

Ahmad stood. "I must blindfold you again." Rather than strapping the cloth around her head, Ahmad draped and tied it only enough to keep it from falling. "Please, keep your head down and eyes closed as before."

During the walk to the vehicle, Ismat was even more tenacious. She was confident that she would be provided with the right training and materials to be successful as a Shahida.

When they reached the car, Ahmad helped her in. She only heard the driver's door close, so Ismat assumed the other people were already in their seats.

As they drove away, Ahmad consoled her, "You can relax, it's just the two of us now."

Ismat's mind was mentally exhausted. After drifting off for what seemed only a few seconds, she felt the car come to a stop. Ahmad exited, then opened her door and removed the blindfold. They were at the same place on the street where she made the phone call that morning.

"I'll pick you up here at 10 a.m. tomorrow," Ahmad said when they returned to Ismat's street. "Make up some excuse to your mother, such as community service. Get plenty of rest tonight. Tomorrow we begin your training."

A lifeless statuette, Ismat watched the trail of exhaust from Ahmad's car until it was out of sight. How many cars like that would her martyrdom throw into flames, leaving only a charred memory of what existed before? How many people would suffer the same fate?

Over the next few weeks, Ismat immersed herself in Ahmad's indoctrination. Defense and liberation of Palestine was the central focus of the rationales and principles behind suicide missions. Shahidas were one of the most powerful weapons, because they appeared unsuspicious. Their loose clothing allowed plentiful room for an explosive belt and concealed any evidence of a bulge from their abdominal area. Through this strategic war tactic, Ismat became convinced that she would be a useful tool in defending the land and homes of Palestine. Her desire was to spread horror into the hearts of her country's oppressors.

Above all, Ismat came to recognize the importance of fulfilling her spiritual duty as a martyr. She felt it a privilege to perform this heroic act for Allah and anticipated the rewards she would receive in paradise. She looked forward to meeting the prophet Muhammad and to sitting in a place of honor at Allah's table for eternity. More than anything, she longed for a new life in the presence of her father.

After three weeks, Amourra approached one night before bed. "Ismat, what's going on with you? You've been acting weird lately."

"How?" Ismat shrugged to fake ignorance.

"You're always studying the Qur'an. What's with these daily confessions and prayers you say in front of everybody." She huffed and held her hand toward Ismat. "And I'm not used to seeing you in these clothes. You used to dress normal in jeans and t-shirts. Now all you wear are abayas and hijabs."

"You see it as a bad thing?"

"I don't know." Her sister cocked her hip and crossed her arms. "Maybe it's good. Is it helping you deal with father's death?"

"Sure." What a perfect explanation, Ismat thought. She knew Amourra wasn't convinced.

"What about the phone calls? One minute you're on the phone, the next you're out the door."

"I'm training for a large-scale community service project. You'll find out more soon."

During the final days leading up to her mission, she watched hours of video recordings containing final statements of suicide bombers who accomplished their operation. The videos, by far, were the most effective tool in her training. The martyrs' determination, personal motives, and poise intrigued her. They all seemed joyful and eager to fulfill their final endeavor in life.

The night before her martyrdom, Ismat did not return home after Ahmad took her back to their usual meeting place. She could not bear seeing Amourra and her mother again. It would have been too difficult to leave in the morning. She returned to the telephone booth where she began her final journey in life and curled up on the floor. Her knees were in the perfect place to rest her forehead. Sleep was not on her mind, but somehow it took her. She dreamt about the paths she memorized from the training map. To enter Israel, there were trails, fields, and other unwatched areas she was to follow rather than risking a border check point. She studied the map so many times that she could see it with closed eyes.

As the soft sounds of the city waking to a new day began to reverberate, Ismat awoke. Today, she would not be blindfolded as she had so many times during the previous four weeks. There were no more secret locations.

Paradise awaited a new member of royalty. In only a few hours, she would be in the embrace of her father in the Garden of Eden. As much as she anticipated this, she had her sister and mother in mind.

By now they're worried about me, she thought as she observed people walking on the street. They probably didn't sleep last night.

Before long, they would be out to look for her.

Or they'd call the police. The worst thing that could happen.

Ismat knew her mother wouldn't take that route yet. She didn't need any more public embarrassment than she already endured. For a few days she would hold out hope.

Worthless hope.

Ismat sat on the curb with her knees pulled into her chest. The confidence and poise she felt over the past weeks disappeared. A twinge of doubt entered her mind.

"Don't do this to yourself, there's no turning back now," she scolded herself.

Just then Ahmad pulled up. The clothes she bought for her special day hung on the hook in the back seat. The excitement she sought just a few moments earlier rushed in.

Every day since she purchased her new garments, she constantly admired and caressed them. She could not wait to feel the soft, flowing material of the abaya around her body. Exquisite black embroidery encircled the neckline and the ends of the sleeves. Detailed white embroidery adorned the matching hijab head covering. Never had she owned or worn such fine garments. She was sure to be the most beautiful Shahida in all of history.

Ahmad opened the door and put one leg out.

"You finally get to wear it," he said as he looked sideways at the rear seat. "You ready?"

Ismat donned an enthusiastic smile. Yes, she was ready.

"I'll let you dress in the back." Ahmad opened the door behind the driver's seat and waited for her to get in. "The belt is inside. It is packed with eleven pounds of explosives."

Ismat felt the extra weight before she even put the belt on.

"Be careful with it," Ahmad stressed. "Remember everything from our run-throughs. Let me know if you have any trouble."

He pressed the door closed and stepped away with his back turned toward the car while she prepared herself.

A few minutes later she rolled down the window, fully dressed in her Shahida attire. "How do I look?"

Ahmad's face brightened. "Like a heroine." His voice soothed her nerves. "So mature. Such a lady."

During the short ride, Ahmad opened up. "Ismat, I've come to respect you," he said in a soft voice. "I care for you. Like a sister."

"I feel the same." Ismat paused. "I forgot to thank you for planting this idea in my mind. If it weren't for you, this honor never would have come to me. Today, horror will fill the eyes of our enemy as they see the carnage on TV. I hope at least twenty people die!"

"I know you will be a success," Ahmad affirmed. "Your devotion to Allah inspires me. Every day you speak of your enjoyment to serve him in such a way. It's made an impact on my own faith."

Ismat turned her thoughts to Ahmad's words. She knew this was the most faithful and loving deed she could do for Allah during her lifetime.

"Your absence will cause me sadness," Ahmad continued, "but that does not overrule what you are doing for the Palestinians. Your motives are clear. You care for your fellow citizens and want to sacrifice yourself for their own well-being. The Israeli's will discover what it means to be an enemy of Palestine."

When they arrived at the site of the first trail, a long moment of silence stopped Ismat from parting ways.

Ahmad exhaled a deep huff, then turned around.

Ismat held an envelope in her right hand.

"What's that?"

"I know my family won't be informed," she began, "and I'm struggling with it a little. I wrote a short letter to my sister. My hopes are that you will do me a favor, in secret, by putting it in the mail for me.

"If you want," she pleaded, "wait a month or so until the bombing is not spoken of so frequently by the media. I promise, she won't tell anyone."

"That is a lot to ask of me," he answered. "I could suffer gravely if my leader were to discover this disobedient act."

"I know, but please do this for me. It's a favor for a martyr, and I will make sure you receive rewards for it when you arrive in paradise."

"I'll do it," he promised. "Not because of eternal reward, but because I care for you. I trust you."

"Thank you." Ismat held the envelope out. "It's already addressed and stamped."

When Ismat handed it to him, he caught her arm before she could pull away. He cradled her hand between his palms. "Go in peace." Ahmad's voice was thick with emotion. "Insha'Allah. May it be Allah's will."

"Insha'Allah," Ismat answered in a soft tone.

Ismat al-Hourani thumbed the delicate embroidery on the neckline of her abaya cloak. A silk head covering caressed her cheeks when she stepped from the car. Fine garments made her feel like the martyr she was to become, packed with an eleven-pound explosive belt.

"The most beautiful Shahida. A true heroine." Ahmad, encourager and friend, exalted her as she prepared to do the duty. "Be careful with the belt. Remember everything from our run-throughs?"

Sweat bonded the weapon to her skin. Many who saw her that day would not notice it from her abdomen, hidden by the loose robe. "I remember. I will be successful.

Ahmad shoved unsteady fingers through his veil of black curls. "Your absence will cause me sadness, but that does not overrule what you are doing. You care for your fellow citizens and want to sacrifice yourself for their own well-being. Go in peace."

"Insha'Allah." Ismat turned and left Ahmad without a goodbye. The trail to cross into Israel was difficult to follow. At times, landmarks were all she had to rely on as she backtracked to find the lost path.

At last, she spotted the vehicle that was supposed to be waiting for her. The shiny, white sedan had dark tinted windows, so she could not see inside. Her shoes crunched on fine rocks as she advanced from behind. The window rolled down halfway.

Ismat spoke the code word, "Insha'Allah." Chills flurried along her spine at the sound of a thump from all sides of the vehicle. The doors unlocked.

"Insha'Allah," a male voice said in return.

She entered the confines of the sedan. The new car scent bespoke immediate delivery from the manufacturer. The heavy door yielded to her tug.

Wheel rotations screeched the vehicle into action. "We'll arrive at the target in an hour," the driver said. "Palestinians will shoot their guns in the air today because of the victory you will achieve."

With steady breaths, Ismat mentally prepared to carry out the mission.

"You're doing great," the man said, disrupting the silence.

Good, it brought Ismat back to the greater purpose.

"Such composure can only be esteemed." A flash of eyes in the rearview mirror encouraged her more than his words. "You will bring great honor to yourself. Rewards in paradise will be immeasurable."

During the remainder of the ride, Ismat envisioned her father waiting with outstretched arms upon her arrival in the Garden of Eden. She then pictured her stepfather and was relieved that she would never have to see him again.

After turning through several streets, Ismat knew they had reached

Jerusalem. She looked out the window at the street sign.

"Jaffa Road." Her heart pounded.

"That's right. We're only a few blocks from the market. You memorized the map well."

The street became crowded, causing their forward progress up Jaffa Road to slow.

"I'll turn right onto Agrippas Street and drive down a short way. When I pull over, get out and walk back toward Jaffa. You'll see the market entrance on the other side."

Ismat lengthened her spine as she prepared to take the first few steps on Israeli ground. Pops along her vertebrae provided momentary physical relief. Possibly the final comfort she would feel in life. The weight of the explosive belt strained her lower back. Sweat dampened her clothes.

As soon as they turned onto Agrippas, Ismat gripped the door handle and pressed on the window. Before the car came to a stop, the door surrendered to her force. No goodbye greetings came to mind. Just the mission.

She moved toward the target in a rush, taking great strides.

"There it is," she murmured as she neared the outdoor market. She slowed her pace. Stilled the heaves in her chest. Dressed in such attire, suspicion prevailed amidst the crowd of Jews.

As she followed the pedestrian crossing, she began to look around. She had never been outside of Gaza and did not imagine that the Israeli's would look so similar to those she saw in her everyday life. She thought they would have a different appearance and demeanor, but they were no different than many people she knew at home.

Stop looking at them. Just walk.

Ismat felt sick when she arrived at the entrance to the market. People were all around, coming and going. Some strolled leisurely. Some were in a hurry. Others sold goods.

I can't do this.

Glancing from side to side, Ismat went through the entryway and pretended to shop.

Thoughts of the surrounding crowd flooded her mind. These people were minding their own business, living life, and doing no crime.

A laughing woman made faces at her baby boy who sat in his stroller.

An elderly couple held hands while they meandered through the crowd.

A little boy pleaded with his mother to buy figs.

Why should they die right now?

These people were not the ones responsible for her father's death. They weren't hurting the Palestinians or taking over their land.

Just shopping.

I'm leaving. This isn't right.

Ismat began to turn away from the vegetable vendor.

Just then, she saw an Israeli Defense Forces soldier standing nearby.

Look at that gun. What if it was the one that killed my father?

Her determination returned. She knew she had to proceed and win this victory for her father.

"I'm ready," she said loud enough for the person next to her to hear. Their stare pierced her peripheral vision.

People herded like a flock of goats when the roar of a bus engine announced their ride home. Perfect timing.

But a girl the same age as Amourra joined the crowd. Same height and petite frame. Not her. I can't kill her.

The girl fell to her knees. The handles of her bags had snapped. Loose produce bounced when it fell to the concrete. Potatoes rolled from the deflated plastic bag.

Far enough to survive the blast, Ismat felt sure the girl would be safe.

Wide eyes from numerous faces followed her sprint to the bus. She shoved past people in line. Elbowed a woman at the bottom of the steps.

The stranger said something in a gentle tone.

Ismat did not look. She did not need to feel sorry for another person.

Her dress had twisted, wrapping her body like a blanket. Unable to wedge her fingers through the top buttons to reach the detonator, anger raged. She used all the might she contained in her small body to push people out of the way.

The gentle-spoken woman made eye contact. Fear transformed her beautiful face. Amber speckles of her irises alight with rays of the sun, she pleaded without words.

But Ismat felt no pity for her.

The woman's benign nature disappeared. Replaced by stern strength as she allowed her shopping bags to plummet to the floor.

Milk and oil containers busted against the force of the step's sharp edge. Splatters reached Ismat's lips. The final tastes of life.

She was sure of it. Until the woman tugged her hijab and thrust her to the floor. The fight was fast, intense, and frustrating…until the woman grasped her from behind and locked her arms into an unyielding chain.

Perfect. The detonator was within inches.

A teardrop rolled down her cheek, and she took the final step to carry out her mission.

Looking to the sky, she groaned, "Glory to Allah! Glory to my father!"

POST-SUICIDE BOMBING

Many changes were made to the plot over the years. Originally, Rina died in the attack.

The following chapters take place in the days subsequent to the bombing.

ELIANA

The call of Eliana's name beckoned her from sleep. Visions of shadows and fire tugged her back into dream.

"Eliana."

"Mama?" The nightmare left her mind. Her eyes did not budge.

"Eliana, can you hear me?"

Fiery pain burned her face. A metallic taste offended her tongue. Blurry images appeared as she ordered her eyes to open. An unfamiliar room greeted her with cold confusion. She lay stretched out on a rigid bed covered by an eggshell white blanket.

A woman sat on the bed next to Eliana's legs. Shallow creases indented the skin above her nose. "Are you awake?"

"Who are you? Where am I?"

"I'm Sarina Blum from the Christian organization your mother used to donate to. You're in the hospital."

Images erupted: fire, smoke, concrete, darkness. "What happened to mama? Where…" The throbbing on her cheek cut her short.

Sarina pushed a deep swallow down her throat. "The Lord took your mother home to Heaven yesterday. She is with your father now."

Rain pounded the window sideways. Water droplets distorted gloomy clouds. The pieces came together as she listened to Sarina explain what had happened. She fought to control the quiver of her chin as she remembered her rush to catch the bus.

"It's a miracle you're alive. You have only minor scrapes and bruises."

A few scrapes and bruises? A slight twist of the head seized the muscles in her neck.

"Eliana, your mother is a hero. Dozens of civilians on the street, sidewalk and entry of the market would have died or suffered major injuries if she hadn't fought the suicide bomber."

The lives of others didn't matter. She would be at Aunt Naomi's, with Shamira, were it not for her selfish desire to eat a rugelach before bed.

"The only family you have left is in America. They've been contacted and anticipate your arrival. We arranged everything with the authorities to expedite your passport. Our organization is going to pay for your plane ticket, as your mother has always been generous to us." The thunk of Sarina's boots on the floor overpowered the droning downpour. Each step echoed on the hard floor.

Eliana pulled her hand away from Sarina's gentle grasp. She didn't deserve kindness from anyone. "We have family here. I can go to my aunt's home."

"Your mother has a sister?"

"She's not my real aunt."

"Are you blood related?"

"No, but they're our family."

"I'm sorry. The only—"

"I know I could stay with them!" Erratic tears of anger stung the wounds on Eliana's cheeks.

Sarina leaned on the edge of the bed. A woodsy scent weaved calm through the crevices of scattered emotions.

"It has to be a blood relative. There are foster homes here in Israel, but life with your grandparents in America would be much more beneficial for your future."

Eliana did not know much about her father's parents. Grandma Dottie and Grandpa Chuck sent letters and Christmas gifts every year. Her mother received a monthly envelope and spoke with them weekly on Sundays. Her smile during conversations with them was unique from any other. "Could I go there for just a little while, then come back to live with my aunt?" Eliana hoped that some way, somehow, she could be with Shamira.

"I can't personally guarantee that. It will be up to your grandparents to decide whether that happens."

Eliana bent over. This had to be a continuation of the nightmare. "I have to get up." Her chest heavy, she flinched at the touch of Sarina's hand and shoved it away. "Mama's not dead. I have to go see her!"

"Eliana, please." Plastic cords interfered with Sarina's attempt to subdue Eliana.

"I need to take this off." Eliana tugged clear tubes. Her hand throbbed as blood penetrated the tape.

Sarina took a hold of her shoulders. "Stop Eliana!"

Fury stirred. She wanted to run. "No. I have to go see mama."

Sarina stomped to the other side of the bed where nothing blocked her. The force of her restraint overpowered Eliana. "You must stop. If they see you like this—"

The door flew open. A nurse rushed in.

"I'm sorry," Sarina addressed the nurse. "I accidentally sat on the cords. They pulled the IV. That's why she's upset."

Why did Sarina lie to the nurse? What would happen if she knew about the struggle?

The nurse flatted Eliana's arm on the bed. "I'll fix it."

Tears plopped onto the pillow while Eliana endured the pain inflicted by the tape and needle. The nurse raised her eyebrow at Sarina as she stood to leave. "Make sure that doesn't come off again."

"Eliana," Sarina said after the door clicked shut, "as long as you're stable for the next day or two, the doctors will discharge you. If you don't want to be in this hospital, you can't do that again. Eat, go to the bathroom, and prove that you can function without medical care."

Eliana abandoned hysteria and delivered her emotions to reason. Sarina's caress across her head offered a sensation opposite the force she used to restrain Eliana from her outburst. She didn't push away this time.

"I'll come back tomorrow."

A stranger's reflection stared at Eliana from the mirror in the bathroom. The bruise on the right side of her face resembled sweet date palms often served after dinner by her mother. Splotches of crusty blood dotted her scalp, ears, and neck. There was no way to escape the hospital, so she surrendered to the cold bed. A faint knock plucked her from the beginnings of sleep.

"Eliana?" A man's voice spoke through the crack in the door. "Are you asleep?"

"No."

Waves of salt and pepper hair framed the man's broad face. A heavy smile contrasted from the gloom of his red-rimmed eyes. "My name is Elijah Zahavi. Your mother was a close friend of mine. I also knew your father for a short period of time."

The bed buzzed as Eliana pushed the button to raise it to a sitting position. "A close friend?"

"Yes." Elijah's shoulders bounced as he nodded. "Your grandparents gave me permission to pay you a visit today."

"You know my grandparents?"

"Not personally, but they know who I am. Sarina helped me get in touch with them after… Eh, after…" Elijah's moistening eyes reflected the fluorescent light.

"Were you and mama together? I mean, in love?"

"Oh, no!" Elijah's cheeks rounded when he laughed. "All I can tell you for now is that we were close friends, and when your father was here, he helped me in great ways. Now I want to do the same by helping you." Elijah caressed Eliana's lower arm in reassurance. Another gesture she didn't deserve.

"When the time is right, we'll talk. Don't forget about me." Elijah reached for the button to lower the bed. "I wish you luck on your voyage, dear. Go back to your rest now."

Eliana studied his features as he pulled the blanket to her shoulders. If she weren't to forget about him, she needed something by which to remember him. Sturdy build, sculpted cheekbones, dimpled chin, crooked nose.

The doctor pressed his cold stethoscope onto Eliana's chest for the fifth time. "You're fine." He shoved his bottom lip out and turned to Sarina. "There's no reason for her to be here. I'm going to release her today."

Sarina pulled some clothes from a paper bag and handed them to Eliana. "They're from my daughter's closet. She's also ten. Same size as you." While they waited for the release papers, she jotted down a bullet list for Eliana to follow. "Once we leave, I'll take you home so you can pack. I want to caution you. It will be painful. Things will be just as you and your mama left them two days ago."

Eliana visualized breakfast before they left for the market. She had gobbled two bowls of Cocoa Crispies, while her mother delighted in her usual colorful plate of pita bread, hummus, Kalamata olives, tahini, and feta cheese. Before they left, her mother gave the dishes a quick scour and left them to dry on a clean towel.

SHAMIRA'S HANUKKAH NIGHTMARE

Scents of the days' feast tickled Shamira's nose. She pushed off the flannel sheets and willed her body out of bed. Excitement made for a night of restless sleep, but it did not matter. Eliana would arrive in a few hours, and they were sure to be spoiled.

Clanking silverware invited Shamira to breakfast. It was only six o'clock, and a pile of dishes had already taken residence in the kitchen sink. What trouble her mother went to for this day. It turned out perfect every year.

"Hanukkah Sameach!" her mother said. A kiss landed on her forehead.

"Happy Hanukkah to you too, mama." Shamira confidently looked her mother in the eyes. "Remember, Eliana likes for her Aunt Naomi to speak English when she's here. You should practice with me before they get here."

She dismissively waved her hand. "Oh, fine. If insist! The big deal I don't understand it."

"Even though Eliana won't say it, the big deal is that you spent time with her papa. She wants to hear the way you talked to him."

"True, could be this." Her mother paused and gazed at the opposite end of the table.

"That's where he sat, isn't it mama?"

Before the tears could fall, her mother wiped them away as quickly as they formed. "Yes. Come now, we eat. I made special soofganiyot doughnuts for special girl of today. Freshly fried and filled with chocolate cream."

"Yes!" Shamira shoved the pastry in her mouth. Only chocolate rugelach from Marzipan's could top her mother's soofganiyot. "Do you think Aunt Rina will let me spend the night?"

"Why wouldn't she? You do every year."

Apart from her parents, no one meant more to Shamira than Eliana. She was more than a friend. She was a sister. She felt sorry for Eliana since her father died before she was even born. Shamira hoped her papa filled in some of that void.

Eleven o'clock arrived, and Shamira expected Aunt Rina and Eli at any minute.

Minutes rolled by, but they didn't show up.

Her mother said it was not a big deal. "Maybe they woke up late. I know what it is. Rina didn't finish frying the cheese latkes in time."

By noon, however, mama began to wonder as well. "I give them a call."

Shamira followed her mother to the front hall and watched.

"It's ringing," her mother whispered after punching the light-up buttons on the receiver.

Shamira leaned in to listen. The ringing did not stop.

Her mother forced a smile when she hung up. "There, see. On their way now. I'm sure. Soon will be here."

Shamira took comfort in her mother's embrace and kiss on the forehead.

Another hour passed. The gong of the grandfather clock at one was the signal to begin the first course. Now, food did not matter to anyone.

Shamira followed in silence as her mother padded over to the phone. She didn't smile this time after she punched the numbers and waited.

Shamira counted twenty rings.

"Mama, I want to see them. Why aren't they here?"

"Come," her mother said. "Go to room and rest a while. I send your father to look for them."

"I don't want to go to my room." Hot tears spilled onto her cheeks. "I want to wait here."

"I know. You're upset, though. Go relax."

Shamira did not soften the sobs as she stomped toward her room. The thought of slamming the door brought momentary satisfaction. She would be in trouble, and a sleepover with Eliana would be out of the question.

I know they'll be here soon, she thought. She left the door open enough to hear their arrival.

Her eyes burned. Her mind drifted into a fog. Her mother was right. She needed rest.

A slam of the front door propelled Shamira from slumber. Her father's footsteps rushed through the front of the apartment. A muffled cry told Shamira something was really wrong.

"Where's Shamira?"

"Az, what's wrong?"

"Where's Shamira?" This time, his tone became impatient.

Shamira heard only silence for a few seconds. Light steps approached her room. Her cracked door closed. No words could be heard. Not even a whisper.

Down the hall, she heard her parents' door close, then the click of the television. Only muffled words and voices resounded.

Shamira approached her door. The wiggly knob yielded a few inches of visibility down the hallway. Her eyes rounded the corner of the doorframe when she stumbled backwards at the sound of a shrill scream.

Shamira left the confines of her room and approached her parent's door. Her mother struggled to subdue her cries while her father shushed her.

Now, Shamira could make out some of the words from the television.

"…will take months to repair…those who witnessed yesterday's attack describe the mayhem that broke out after the blast…"

A blast? What blast?

Shamira pounded on the door. "Mama? Papa?"

Feet shuffled. The TV silenced. Her father opened the door only wide enough to squeeze through. "Shamira." Her father's eyelids were pink and swollen, his hair disheveled, his voice rough. "I need you to go back to your room."

"Papa, what's happening? What's wrong with mama?"

"She'll be okay. Don't worry."

Shamira did not relent to the gentle press of his hands on her upper back. She had questions. "What attack were they talking about on the TV?"

"Shamira!" His eyes widened. "No more questions. Just go to your room, now!"

She conceded at the force of his command.

Shamira stumbled to her door. "But, Eliana and Auntie Ri. Did you find them?"

He scrunched his eyebrows, shook his head, and padded away.

Shamira lay on her bed and sobbed until sleep overcame her emotions.

Something on wheels barreled through the apartment.

"Papa? Mama?" Shamira rubbed at her crusty eyes.

The flapping of her mother's house shoes set off in the direction of her parent's room.

Rumbling wheels closed in. The late afternoon sun blinded Shamira when her father opened the door.

His face was flushed, and his hairline beaded with sweat. In his right hand, an oversized suitcase on wheels leaned behind him. "Shamira, pack this with everything you can. Stuff it full."

"Where are we going?" Her voice trembled.

"This is the last question you will ask. Is that clear?" The uncharacteristic, angry tone in her father's voice provoked fear.

"Yes." She breathed in and out heavily, tears flowing. "Yes, sir."

"I will give you an answer, then we're done talking." He gave Shamira a sharp eye.

The gathering saliva and drowning tears interfered with her ability to breathe.

Her father drove his hands through his hair and stared at the floor. After several slow, deep breaths, he briefly made eye contact. "We're going to Chile to see your uncle, and we're never coming back. Ever."

ELIANA PREPARES TO LEAVE ISRAEL

The unintentional slam of the front door spawned a sharp echo throughout the apartment in the seventeen-story condominium tower. Floral, earthy scents of her mother's essential oils nurtured Eliana's soul with sweet remembrance as she suffered her absence. "I need to call Shamira. We were supposed to go there for Hanukkah. I wonder if they know what happened?"

"Everyone knows by now. It's on the news around the world."

Shamira alone could make Eliana feel better right now. After eleven rings, though, hope for relief diminished. She envisioned a dewdrop of blood on their pinkies from a needle prick. "Sisters for life, our blood is one," they had promised in unison after Eliana's tenth birthday party. They pressed the beads on their pinkies together, forging a commitment never to be broken. "

Sarina put her arm around Eliana's shoulder and guided her down the hallway. "Let's try back in a little while. For now, let's pack. Bring a few clothes. You can always buy more. I want you to focus on the irreplaceable things you don't want to leave behind. Look in your mother's room for some of her special belongings and jewelry. Get a few of her small clothing items that have her scent on them. We'll place them in plastic bags so that they'll never get worn, dirty or ruined. You'll be able to pull them out every so often to smell them. Be sure to bring pictures and your mother's Bible."

Half an hour later, Sarina gathered the suitcases near the door. It was time to go.

"I need to call Shamira again." Eliana paced. Unanswered rings mocked Eliana's agitation. Pressure swelled behind her eyes.

"Here." Sarina pulled her phone from her bag. "Type in their names and phone number. I'll try as hard as I can to reach them."

Eliana walked through her home one last time. She recalled the final moment with her mother in each room and promised herself never to forget it from her memory.

With Sarina's bullet list in hand Eliana followed Sarina through the airport. The lights created a mirror on the windows against dark skies. Her reflection stared her down as did the gawks of others, curious about her beat up face.

"I have to leave you here." Sarina stopped before the security checkpoint. "An airline employee will be waiting for you once you get through this line."

A din of voices and foreign languages welcomed Eliana to a commotion she would have to endure for at least forty-five minutes.

"Eliana," Sarina whispered tête-à-tête, "rely on God during your times of grief and despair. Only through him will you find relief."

ELIANA'S JOURNEY

In the original manuscript, Eliana found her mother's journal while packing at the apartment. She read most of it during the flight from Israel to America.

These are scenes during the trip when Eliana takes a break from reading. While the plot changed to make Rina survive the bombing, Eliana would have experienced these emotions with the belief that her mother passed. This plays a major part in who Eliana becomes as an adult.

DEPARTURE

"Flight 91, Tel Aviv to Newark, now boarding. First class customers, please bring your boarding passes to the gate."

Eliana popped the last puffy piece of cheddar popcorn into her mouth and licked the salty cream glaze from her fingers. A room full of people scattered the waiting area. The obstacle course of bags, stretched out legs, and shoes threatened her first-class boarding privileges as she made the trek through the crowd. Odors, coughing, sneezing, and sweaty faces drove Eliana to hasten. "Here!" She shoved her ticket to the flight attendant.

A swarm of passengers flooded the aisles before Eliana had a chance to sit. She tried to ignore the inquisitive stares of those who hushed their gasps before it was too late. Some questioned their travel partners aloud without realizing Eliana listened.

"Poor thing, I wonder what happened?"

"Maybe she was in a car accident."

"What a horrible thing to happen at Christmastime."

Eliana pressed her forehead against the cold window as the roaring engine nudged the plane in reverse. The jet bridge disappeared from sight. Eliana fixed her eyes on the flight attendant who demonstrated safety instructions from a prerecorded voice. The volume of the engine competed with the hiss of the changing cabin pressure. Eliana's stomach fluttered as they rounded the corner for takeoff. She wanted to feel excited, but her thoughts returned to the loss of her mother. The reason she was in this position was nothing to be excited about. As the aircraft charged the runway, heart-piercing thoughts ambushed her soul.

ARRIVAL

"Good morning passengers, this is your captain speaking. We'll be arriving in Newark in approximately twenty minutes. The local time is four twenty-five a.m. Weather forecast calls for partly cloudy skies with a high of fifty-five degrees Fahrenheit, then falling to thirty-nine this evening. I hope you've enjoyed your flight. Please fly with us again."

Eliana extended her head sideways to unbind a fiery intruder from her neck. A lash of heat whipped into an inextinguishable spasm.

"Are you okay?" An unfamiliar female voice whispered from the seat next to her.

All Eliana could see without turning her head was a sweatshirt with NYU. Tight black curls dangled from the shoulders of a petite frame. "My neck." Hot tears plunged down her cheeks.

"Hold on," the stranger said and disappeared. Zippers zoomed across the aisle. A vigorous rip of thick paper heralded a boisterous crackle of peeling plastic. "Here," the girl said and pulled Eliana's hair back. "I always keep these with me."

A soft, sticky material girdled Eliana's neck. As the girl smoothed it out, cool relief smothered the fire.

"Now this. My neck pillow is all yours."

The velvety pillow reminded Eliana of a bean bag as it hugged the contour of her neck. Soothing heat fused with the chill to relax the muscles. "Thanks."

A college-aged woman with thick, round glasses angled herself in the chair next to Eliana. Disfigured skin from a severe burn tarnished her left cheek. "Better?"

Eliana nodded.

"Keep the pillow," she said. "After my car accident, I keep them everywhere. I have two or three waiting for me at home today."

The foam balls of the neck pillow bristled as Eliana adjusted her neck.

"My name's Camille. What's yours?"

"Eliana."

"Nice to meet you Eliana." Camille extended a disfigured hand for a shake. "Where are you going?"

"Mississippi. To live with my grandparents."

Camille lifted a hand to the webbed skin on her cheek. "Did something happen to your parents?"

Eliana felt no emotion as she formed her thoughts to words. "My papa died before I was born. Mama was killed by a suicide bomber three days ago."

"Oh my gosh." Camille blinked away tears. "You mean the bombing in Jerusalem?"

Eliana nodded.

"I saw that on the news!"

"Yeah, she was on the bus. I was still at the entrance of the market. That's why I'm alive."

"I'm so sorry, I shouldn't have asked. It's just that I was in a car accident when I was a girl and I thought you might need someone to talk to."

"What happened?"

"Drunk driver." Camille's chin quivered as the corners of her mouth turned downward. "My parents died. That was almost ten years ago."

"I'm sorry."

"My condolences are all yours, Eliana."

As the wheels of the plane bounced on the runway and brakes screeched, Eliana realized she hadn't accepted the truth. Shock faded. Salty streams bit at her wounded flesh.

NIGHTMARE

"Excuse me, Darling."

Eliana pulled herself from the story. A flight attendant smiled at her.

"I'm sorry to distract you," the woman said. "Do you have a meal preference for lunch?"

Eliana nodded. "What do you have?"

Recalling each aspect of her parents' story, Eliana's mind darted while she nibbled on a cheeseburger and picked at her bowl of fruit. After the food settled, Eliana's eyes complied before she made a conscious decision to sleep.

Grassy sand dunes dot a shoreline. A waveless ocean sweeps the dead beach with melancholy. On a distant dune, Eliana spots the figure of a woman. She hurries forward only to find the person further than she envisioned. Eliana continues to scurry up and down each hill, until finally, two sand dunes away her mother appears. She stands rigid with her back toward Eliana.

"Mama!" Eliana screams out of breath as she runs. "Mama!"

When she reaches the bottom of the sandy hill, her mother turns to face Eliana. She sobs with a baby in her arms. Spattered blood stains her white dress. A lifeless arm dangles from the baby's body. Blood drips from the fingertips.

A rabid gust resuscitates the ocean. Her mother's hair flares like flames in the wind. "Eliana," her mother's voice reverberates throughout the sky, "you're still a baby. You're too young to understand these things."

Rina covers the baby's head with a flapping cloth and turns away.

Waking up with a jerk, Eliana found herself crying in her sleep.

She quickly stood up and nearly tripped as she rushed from the seat toward the bathroom. It was the first time she had been inside an airplane lavatory. Once she entered, it felt eerie inside, just as the first time she entered the aircraft in Tel Aviv. The sound of the engines clouded her thinking. She closed the seat cover, sat down, hugged the journal, bent over it, and wept bitterly.

It was at this point that her state of shock began to fade.

She had never heard herself cry in such a way before. It was very audible, and she could not control it. The tears and emotion poured out.

As she grasped the journal, she rocked in short, swift movements.

"Mama's gone," she mumbled to herself with teary eyes as wide as the sun. "No mother. No father."

She looked up. "What did I do wrong, God, to deserve this? What did my mother do? What did my father do?"

She wanted to understand but couldn't.

A knock at the door interrupted her thoughts.

"Just a minute." She spoke as loud as she could through her sobbing.

When she opened the door, the flight attendant was waiting for her with a concerned expression on her face. "Are you okay? I heard you crying."

The woman's compassion caused Eliana to break down once again.

"No, not really." The stream of tears flowing from her eyes caused her wounds to sting.

"My name is Bethany. I'll stay with you for a while." She took Eliana's hand and led her to the area where the flight attendants sat.

Without thinking, Eliana followed Bethany as the energy in her body depleted during her breakdown.

"Please let me know what I can do for you," Bethany tenderly said. "If you want to talk, I'll listen to you. If you need silence, but someone to be close to you, I can do that, too."

"I'm so tired," Eliana whispered as the flow of tears slowly let up. "I just had a bad dream, though, so I'm afraid to go back to sleep."

"Why don't you lay your head in my lap and stretch your feet out. I'll be right here with you while you sleep."

"Okay." Bethany's nurturing manner reminded Eliana of her mother. She felt comfort as she rested her head on the woman's softly perfumed clothing. The body heat from her legs penetrated through her skirt, which brought about a sense of warmth on Eliana's cheek.

When Eliana awoke to the sound of the fasten seatbelt signal, she felt Bethany caressing her hair.

"I'm sorry to do this, but I have to prepare for arrival," she said while gently squeezing Eliana's shoulder. "When we arrive at the airport, I'm going to escort you to your next flight, so please wait for me. Come, follow me back to your seat now."

Eliana was too groggy to say anything back to the kind woman.

After the plane landed, she got up from her seat in haste as soon as they arrived at the terminal. When she exited the jet bridge, Eliana took a seat and waited for Bethany.

She thought about her dream and what it meant.

Was the baby supposed to be me? Was I supposed to die rather than my mother?

NEW FAMILY, NEW HOME

Please enjoy these scenes of young Eliana's first days in the United States. The writing is quite elementary!

GRANDPARENTS

Eliana prepared herself for the worst as she exited the baggage claim area in Mississippi. Grandma Dottie and Grandpa Chuck were always nice on the phone, but how would they be in person? Would they like her, or be mad that she had to live with them since she had nowhere else to go?

"Look." The male flight attendant who held her suitcases signaled to a group of people who waited for their loved ones. "There's a sign with your name on it."

A tall, slender man with white hair and rosy cheeks waved an outspread hand. The corners of his lips rose and transformed the shape of his eyes into crescents.

Eliana willed her feet forward and met him halfway. "Grandpa Chuck?"

"That's me, sweetheart." Grandpa Chuck took the suitcases from the flight attendant and wished him a Merry Christmas. "Your grandma is excited to meet you, Eliana. She's waiting for us in the car."

Eliana savored the crisp air as she walked on American ground for the first time. Grandpa Chuck set the suitcases down by the trunk of a white Cadillac parked in a handicap parking space. "Here we are. Let's meet your grandma now." Grandpa Chuck reached a long arm to open the back-passenger door. "She's here, mama."

Hugging the journal, Eliana waited as a hefty woman expressed a happy squeal when she lumbered from the car. "Oh Eliana! Come here, Dollface."

"Hi Grandma Dottie." Eliana walked into open arms and immediately sensed the love that awaited. Her soft chest and large, warm arms gave Eliana a sense of comfort she hadn't felt since the final embrace she shared with her mother at the market.

"Merry Christmas, my sweet grandchild," Grandma Dottie said in a thick southern accent as she pulled away and looked into Eliana's eyes. "You're the best gift of all today."

"Thanks." The drying scabs on Eliana's face strained with each word and expression.

"Let's get on home darlin'." Grandma Dottie enveloped Eliana's shoulder and led her to the front passenger seat. "I want to doctor up your little face. The wounds look like they hurt!"

Eliana slid onto the warmed leather seats of the luxury sedan. Her grandmother gently patted her from the back seat.

"Buckle up. We don't want anything else happnin' to ya. You've been through enough as it is."

"It'll take us about half an hour to get home," Grandpa Chuck said as they pulled away from the airport. "Would you like to listen to some music?" He turned on the radio and flipped through a few stations. "I'll let you take control."

Eliana pressed the seek button a few times to be polite. Music held little appeal as she observed the landscape of America. When they passed the state line from Alabama to Mississippi, a blue sign read, Mississippi Welcomes You. Eliana's stomach leapt as she thought about going to her father's home.

Half an hour later, Grandpa Chuck exited the freeway in Helena. After traveling for five minutes on a country road, they turned onto a private path with a white picket fence on either side. "See that big ol' antebellum home?" Grandma Dottie pointed to a low-lying hill. A white house with four columns, a triangular roof, and a wraparound porch towered over the landscape. "That's ours. Do ya like it, Hun?"

Unable to muster up words in her amazement, Eliana nodded. Even more amazing was the tall Christmas tree in the front entryway. Shiny ornaments reflected the light from outside until Grandma Dottie flipped a switch on the wall. Hundreds of multicolored lights turned the ornaments into a kaleidoscope of colors.

Grandpa Chuck wheeled the suitcases in and shut out the cold with a kick to the door. "What do you think of that big tree, sweetheart?"

Eliana inhaled the fresh scent of pine she'd experienced only once in her life. "It reminds me of the time mama took me to a Christmas market in Tel Aviv. We only had a little ceramic tree for the dining table at home."

Grandma Dottie pointed to a small, decorative tree on a windowsill. "If you ask me, the size of the tree isn't what matters. Your dad was always partial to big trees, though."

My dad. Eliana had always called him her father. Never dad. It felt right. Personal. Familiar.

"Well, young lady, let's go pick out a room," Grandpa Chuck said and held his hand toward the spiral staircase. "You have four to choose from."

Dozens of frames covered the wall of the staircase. Eliana recognized her father in a few of them. In the middle and higher than the rest of the frames hung a larger version of the wedding photo in mother's room.

Grandma Dottie had prepared every bedroom for Eliana to choose from, but she had only one room in mind. "Which one did mama stay in when she came here?"

Grandpa Chuck pointed to her left. "You're standing right in front of it."

"Is that the same bed she slept on?" Eliana fanned her hand across a downy duvet comforter.

"It is." Grandma Dottie's delicate voice soothed Eliana as her heart began to ache. "Those are the same pillows she used." Grandma Dottie patted the bedding with smooth, plump hands. "It's the same blanket, the same sheets. These rooms are hardly used, so we haven't had to get new ones."

Eliana grasped a feather pillow covered with a white, lace-adorned pillowcase. She stared at it and smelled it, almost as if she could catch her mother's scent.

Then she broke down.

Wrapped between her arms and legs, nothing could make Eliana feel closer to her mother than the pillow on which she once lay her head. Grandma Dottie's gentle touch on her back soothed the involuntary huffs from her lungs.

"Darlin', in the past few days, you've been through more heartache than I have in my entire lifetime." The tips of Grandma Dottie's fingernails slid along Eliana's scalp as she continued her calming touches.

Eliana's eyes stung from tears and exhaustion. "Thank you for letting me live with you."

Grandma Dottie groaned and laughed at the same time. "Thank you for comin' to live with us."

Grandpa Chuck set the suitcases at the end of the bed. "The room is all yours. Welcome home, sweetheart."

Knots of tightness formed in Eliana's throat as Grandpa Chuck leaned in for a hug. Not only did the love from her grandparents bring her comfort, but the fact that her mother stayed in the same room made her feel at home almost immediately. "Thanks."

"I'll leave you alone with your grandma now. See you at dinner."

"Now, I wanna sterilize the sores on your precious face, then I want you to get all cleaned up. We're gonna have our Christmas dinner in a couple hours. You're in for a real treat!"

CHRISTMAS

On the mahogany dining table, Eliana beheld a spread of unfamiliar American food for Christmas dinner. Her stomach gurgled as she took in the aroma of carved turkey, steaming ham, and buttery mashed potatoes. Grandma Dottie explained the other dishes, visually less appetizing, such as cornbread dressing and cheesy green bean casserole with crumbled bacon and crispy breadcrumbs on top. The candied yams reminded Eliana of her mother's candied carrots except for the flavor of the sweet potatoes. The brown sugar and honey syrup tasted the same as if it were a shared recipe.

"Well," her grandfather said after he swallowed his last bite, "it's seven o'clock, which is a little late to open presents! Let's go to the living room and get started."

"Presents?" Eliana took Grandma Dottie's outstretched hand and followed her to the tree.

"Of course, Dollface. We're not gonna let you go without opening some gifts.

Three tiny gift bags stuffed with tissue paper lay underneath the Christmas tree.

Grandpa Chuck sat cross-legged on a gigantic rug next to the tree and handed Eliana the first two bags. "Have at it!"

Underneath soft folds of tissue paper, a two-hundred-dollar gift card to a shopping mall verified Sarina's suggestion that she would be able to buy more clothes in America. "Thank you."

"You're welcome. I'll let you, your grandma and cousins go have fun with that."

The next bag jingled as Eliana rummaged through the glittered tissue paper. A candy-cane shaped ornament held a sign with bells on either side and her name inscribed in the middle.

"Hang it on the tree," Grandma Dottie said and pointed to an open area. "I saved this space for you."

Pokey pine needles brushed Eliana's hand and she placed the loop around a branch.

"Now give her the last bag, papa."

Eliana took the bag and found a small can inside with a picture of a cat on the label and the words Sliced beef in gravy. "What is this?".

"Well," Grandma Dottie began as Grandpa Chuck walked out of the room, "it's somethin' you're gonna need for your next present."

When Grandpa Chuck came back in, he held a small, white kitten in his hands. It had one blue eye, one green eye, and a pink nose.

"This is for you, sweetheart."

A gust of cold air-dried Eliana's throat when she inhaled with an open mouth. She reached for the kitten when Grandpa Chuck handed it over. "It's so soft."

Grandma Dottie's chest bounced as she giggled. "Yes, she is, and she's all yours. Cats are one of the best therapies for a broken heart."

"That's right," Grandpa Chuck said and tickled the kitten's cheek with one finger. "While your grandma and I will always be here for you, there's nothing like a cat to keep you from feeling alone in times such as these."

Eliana brought the sleepy kitten's face close to hers. Its squinting eyes and soft purr brought tenderness to Eliana's heart.

Grandma Dottie hugged Eliana sideways. "You're not the only new one to this house."

"Thank you for my gifts. All of them. Especially her." Eliana lifted the purring kitten to her cheek.

"You're welcome. We love you, hun. It's been a dream of ours to meet you some day. I'm just sorry—" Grandma Dottie's eyes glistened as she choked on her words. She folded into Grandpa Chuck' arm when he reached for her.

A new rush of pain struck Eliana as she saw her grandmother's suffering. She wasn't the only one who grieved her mother.

"I promised myself I wouldn't cry. Come here."

Eliana joined her grandparents in their embrace. The kitten's purr lulled the ache in her heart as she relished the closeness of her new family. After Grandma Dottie and Grandpa Chuck left, Eliana gathered the kitten and lay sideways on the bed. The petite feline stretched out on its side, curled up by Eliana's shoulder and looked right into her eyes. Eliana lost herself in the kitten's sweet purr as she pet it, rubbed underneath its chin, neck, and cheeks, and played with its oversized ears.

NO CONTACT

Eliana gasped and jumped up. "Auntie Nao! Shamira!" She scrambled up from the bed.

Leaving the journal and the kitten behind, Eliana quickly left her room.

"Three doors down to the left," she whispered as she started to cry. I can't believe I forgot to call them, Eliana thought.

When Eliana reached her grandparent's room, she lightly tapped on the door. After a few minutes, she knocked harder. The door opened.

"Eliana." Her grandmother stepped out, clearly groggy from sleeping. "You alright darlin'? Why're you crying?"

"My Aunt Naomi and Shamira. I don't think they know what happened. I…I need to call them."

Her grandmother took her hand. "Alright, Dollface, let's go downstairs."

Eliana explained how she tried to reach them before leaving, and how they were supposed to go to their house for Hanukkah, but never showed up.

"Let's see." Her grandmother sighed when they reached the phone. "It should be about 5 in the mornin' there. That's awful early, Hun."

"It's okay." Eliana took a few deep breaths as she stopped crying. "That's even better. They'll definitely be home."

"We'll give it a try."

Eliana dictated the phone number to her grandmother after she dialed the country code. "Here you go, it's ringing,"' she said and handed the phone to Eliana.

Eliana listened to the ring over and over again. "Ten rings and there's still no answer." She looked at her grandmother and began to tear up as her chin quivered. After five more rings, Eliana handed the phone back.

"I'm so sorry Hun." Eliana's grandmother stretched out her arms for a hug. "We can try again in the mornin.'"

"Okay. I'm sorry for waking you up," Eliana said and rested on her grandmother's soft chest. "They were expecting us, and they're probably worried."

"I'll do my best to help you get in touch with 'em soon." Her grandmother let go and walked over to the refrigerator. "Let's drink some hot cocoa, then go back to bed."

Eliana had hot cocoa made from powdered chocolate mix before, but the way her grandmother made it was completely new. She whipped the ingredients up from scratch in just a few moments, and before long Eliana had the best cup of hot chocolate ever.

Once she was back in her room, Eliana was relaxed and ready for a good, hard sleep. What kept her from succumbing to it, though, was her concern for Aunt Naomi and Shamira. The mystery behind their disappearance wore her spirits away.

What if something happened to them, too? Or, maybe they already know what happened, but why wouldn't they answer the phone?

She searched her soul for an answer.

After lying flat on her back on the floor and staring at the ceiling for twenty minutes, Eliana finally decided to let it go for the time being. Carefully laying her mother's journal on the nightstand, she slipped under the soft sheets and duvet comforter, and placed the kitten by her side. She reached over, turned off the lamp, felt the kitten crawl up and lay against her neck in the space between her shoulder and ear, then fell asleep to the sound of purring.

SLEEP

When Eliana awoke from her dreams, darkness still filled the room.

Not yet daylight. She stretched, feeling the warm kitten still nestled by her neck. Although she felt like she had plenty of sleep, it was dark outside. She looked over at the digital alarm clock.

6:07, I've only gotten five hours of sleep? Eliana's stomach growled.

"I'm going downstairs to eat, see you in a while." She kissed her friend on the belly and left the room.

When Eliana arrived in the kitchen, both of her grandparents were dressed as if ready for the events of the day to begin.

"Well, hello sleepyhead," her grandfather teased. "We were about to come wake you up so you could eat with us. You must be starving."

Eliana was confused. "It's so early. What time do you wake up in the morning?"

Eliana's grandparents laughed.

"Why, it's dinner time, Dollface." Her grandmother walked toward her for a hug. "It's after six o'clock in the evening.'"

"What?" Eliana felt disoriented.

"You slept over seventeen hours!" Her grandmother's laughing eyes caused Eliana to smile.

"I guess I was pretty tired," Eliana said through a yawn.

After reading about her mother's experiences with her grandparents, Eliana relished the time with them at dinner and throughout the evening. While her grandmother cleaned up in the kitchen, she and her grandfather spent some time alone in the living room.

"Grandfather," she began.

"Hold on a sec," he interrupted. "Calling me grandfather is so formal. Why don't you call me something like grandpa, pa, granddad, Grandpa Chuck, or something else?"

"Um, alright," she said. "Grandpa Chuck. Is that okay?"

He nodded. "Much better. "Now, you were saying?"

"How is grandmother's, I mean, Grandma Dottie's diabetes? Mama wrote in her journal that she has Type 1 diabetes."

Grandpa Chuck stared in the direction of the kitchen. "Your grandma has a pretty severe case of it. I have to stay on her all the time, make sure she takes her medications, tests her blood and so on. She's very forgetful.

"After your father died," Grandpa Chuck said as he focused on Eliana, "she turned to food for comfort and gained a lot of weight. So much so that she developed Type 2 diabetes as well. That makes things even worse."

"Oh." Eliana played with her fingernails. "Is she going to be okay?"

"As long as the Lord wills her to be alive, she will most certainly be fine. Don't you worry about her."

"Can I do something to help? Can I remind her of things? I know my fath- I mean, my dad used to help you a lot."

Grandpa Chuck seemed to go into a daze. "Yes," he said. "He did. I'm used to doing it on my own now, though. Even so, I would indeed love your help. I'll start off by teaching you what to look out for in case she starts getting sick and needs help."

For the next twenty minutes, Eliana's grandfather explained the disease, how she could help, what she should look out for, and so on.

Grandma Dottie entered the room after finishing up in the kitchen. "What're you two up to in here?"

"Oh, we're just talking about you," Grandpa Chuck jokingly replied.

This concludes the bonus chapters from
Eliana's transition into her new life.

RINA AND SETH IN AMERICA

The following chapters about Rina and Seth's time in America will be enjoyable to romance fans.

The first scene follows the breakfast conversation when Seth and Rina discussed her potential move to Israel. As much as I wanted to include the proposal in the novel, it lacked relevance for the overall narrative arc.

RINA

That evening, Rina delighted in the feast. She had never tasted anything like what was served: honey barbeque chicken, smoked brisket, homemade sausage, beans, gumbo, slaw, potato salad, fried okra, and corn on the cob.

While they ate, a local bluegrass band played on a small stage. There must have been a crowd of about one hundred people. Seth taught Rina how to two-step, which was the most country dancing he knew how to do. After a few minutes, she was better at it than he was.

"You're wearing' me out girl," Seth said after the fifth song ended. "Come on, I want to show you something."

Seth took Rina's hand and led her up to the top of the hill behind the house, where they could see the sun sinking into the horizon. Looking at her sideways, he said, "Do you remember the gazebo on the top of the hill where Mrs. Shalev was married?"

"Of course," she replied. "How could I ever forget?"

Seth led Rina to an area on the ranch she had never seen. On it stood a charming white gazebo. Rina beamed when she saw it. She was without words.

"I didn't show you this yet for a reason." Seth grinned as he led her into the structure.

Rina heard what Seth said, but was distracted while she looked at the intricate woodwork. "This is so divine," she whispered as Seth sat her down on a white, wooden chair which matched the gazebo.

"Not more than you are," Seth said and sat down next to her. "Rina. I must confess something to you." He took Rina's left hand and clasped both of his hands around it.

"A year ago, six months ago, even three months ago when we first met, I never would've thought it possible to come to truly know and love someone in just three months." He played with Rina's fingers, pressing on each one, and sliding his fingers along them. "My idea was always to be with the woman

I love for two or more years, then get married after going through all the ups and downs."

Rina's eyes widened. She looked at him, intently listening to every word he had to say.

"I think we have a different situation though. We went through ups and downs while I was there in Israel. Then the other day, that was a real trial." Seth shook his head and puffed. "The time we've known each other has been so short, but I believe that we're supposed to be together. Do you?"

Unable to say a word, Rina nodded.

"I've prayed about this and have had endless discussions with both my mother and father—before you were here, and in the last week as well. I already knew what I wanted to do, and what you told me this morning at breakfast made everything even more real. So, I believe that what I am about to do is the right thing and the right time."

Rina thought she knew what was about to happen. She had a feeling but wasn't sure about it.

Seth stood up from his chair, pulled a small, black velvet box from his pocket, and knelt in front of her on one knee. At first, he bowed his head toward the floor and squeezed his eyes shut. Then, he opened the box, which held a simple engagement ring with a gold band and a half carat princess cut diamond.

"Rina," he began, "I have no doubt that you are the woman God created for me. I want to do this now so that we can get you back over here as soon as possible. I want you away from the danger. I want you here, at home, with me. You belong here.

"I love you, and along with the reasons I just mentioned, I'm hoping you will say yes. Will you be my wife? Will you marry me?"

Rina's hands trembled. She almost couldn't believe the words she just heard. It was something she was not expecting, but at the same token, they were words she hoped she would hear.

"Yes." She held her left hand out as Seth removed the ring from the box. "Yes, I will."

The ring fit perfectly.

Seth and Rina embraced and swayed back and forth for a few seconds.

Just then, they heard clapping. As they turned around, Rina saw her future mother and father-in-law standing in the distance applauding them.

"Did," Rina stuttered, "did they know you were going to do this tonight?" She waved and smiled at them as they turned around and walked back to the party.

"Um hum." Seth held her hand and looked at the ring. "They completely approve. Like me, they don't have a doubt in their mind. Now…" Seth's face became serious. "We have to do this soon. The sooner we do, the sooner we can get your visa and you can come back home."

"Okay." Rina's palms became moist as she and Seth continued to hold hands. "Well, how soon?"

"This Friday, the sixth."

"Wow! How are we going to do that?"

Seth looped Rina's arms around his back. "My parents and I have secretly been talking about it and had some tentative plans in case your answer was yes."

"What?" Rina's mouth dropped. "They really were in on this."

"Yep, and they're excited about it. So, we have two choices. We can get married in the church, or we can have our ceremony right here where we're standing. You and mom are going out tomorrow to find a dress and anything else you'll need for our big day."

Just as twilight fell, the fireworks show began. The newly engaged couple sat on the steps of the gazebo to watch the display of lights. Their hands were clasped tightly, and every so often they would both look down at the diamond, which reflected all of the colors from the fireworks.

Once the spectacle was over, they walked back toward the party with their arms tightly wrapped around each other's waist. When they arrived, everyone began to clap. The news had spread. After the well-wishers approached to congratulate them, the crowd quickly died down. Seth and Rina were once again alone.

As they sat in some chairs near the stage where they had been dancing earlier, Seth faced his bride-to-be. "Do you have any doubts in your mind about this? I want to make sure that this is really what you want. You'll be leaving Naomi, your job, your homeland."

"Yes, this is a dream come true. To be away from the danger and with the man I love in such an unforgettable place. I'll miss Naomi, but she would not want me to stay for the sake of our friendship. She would want this for me."

SHOPPING WITH DOTTIE

Rina felt as if she were about to embark on a great adventure when she stepped into the bridal boutique with Dottie. Rather than wedding gowns, all she could make out on the crowded racks was a sea of white fluffy foam.

If she wanted to be picky, it could take hours to find the perfect dress to wear for Seth on their wedding day.

"Oh, mighty me!" Dottie said as they inched forward. "Which way you wanna go?"

Rina exhaled through pursed lips and scanned all directions of the store. "I don't want to wear something like that," she said and pointed to a headless mannequin wearing a ball gown with a poufy skirt.

"Alrighty, well that's a start. Come on this way."

Rina followed Dottie to the left side of the store, which housed at least two hundred gowns.

"I don't need anything fancy. What do you think Seth will like?"

Dottie's shoulders bounced. "That boy's so in love with you," she chuckled, "he wouldn't care what you wear. Shoot, you could walk down the aisle in a bright yellow dress tomorrow, and he'd be thoroughly satisfied."

Rina shook her head. "No yellow dresses for me."

"I sure am happy for you both," Dottie said as she began to flip through the hangers. "You excited? Nervous?"

"A little of both. When I met Seth four months ago, I never imagined I was staring my future husband in the face. Or that I'd be married to him in such a short amount of time."

"I bet." Dottie paused and looked at Rina out the corner of her eye. "You okay with it?"

"Oh, yes, of course." Rina pulled an ostrich-feather dress from the rack. "Look at this! I'd only wear it as a joke."

Dottie clapped her hands, leaned over, and laughed. "I like your sense of humor, darlin'."

"I don't have any doubts, mom," she said and continued to flip through the array of dresses. "I just hope we're not jumping ahead of ourselves and doing this too quickly."

"Well, you know he's the one, right?"

"I do know. For sure."

"And you two have quite a special set of circumstances, don't ya think?"

"Absolutely."

"Soul mates need to be together…not thousands of miles apart." Dottie grimaced at a dreadful gown. "Ugh! Who in the world…?"

Rina slid her palm along the sleeve of a subtle, long-sleeved dress. The sparkle of her engagement ring caught her eye. Rainbow glitters danced throughout the diamond as she titled her wrist back and forth. She had never owned a diamond or any other piece of fine jewelry.

"I wanna let you in on a little somethin', sweet pea."

Rina donned half a smile and faced her future mother-in-law.

"Chuck and I are goin' on strong after thirty-nine years o' marriage."

"Wow," Rina silently mouthed.

"Wanna know how long we knew each other before we got married?"

"Do tell." Rina folded her arms and softly gazed at Dottie.

"Three weeks."

"Three weeks?"

"Yes, ma'am. Ya heard me right."

"Why so fast?"

"I was workin' as a nurse at the local hospital. That boy came in with a big 'ol gash on his forehead. He and some o' his college buddies were playing baseball. Chuck was at the plate and hit the ball so dog gone hard that the bat split! The top half flew straight up into the air, then dove at Chuck. Almost like it was tryin' to get even with him."

Dottie put her hand on her hip and shook her head. "If that splintered wood had landed just an inch further down his forehead, he could'a lost his eye. Imagine that, would ya'?"

"He'd be just as handsome."

"Ain't that the truth. Anyway, that boy came into the hospital with a bloody t-shirt held across the right side of his face. 'Course I saw the play clothes he was wearing', and he was laughin' with his buddies, so I made him wait."

Rina snickered.

"When I was stitchin' him up later, he wouldn't stop lookin' into my eyes. Made me downright edgy. 'Would you stop staring' at me?' I finally said to him. He blew me off. 'Don't flatter yourself,' he told me, 'I'm lookin' at the ceiling to distract myself from the pain.'

"I knew he was lying', so I didn't say anything back. Then he tried to be all cutesy with me. 'Do you want me to stare at you?' he said. I looked back and forth between his eyes and the stitches as I continued on. His dang eyes, they were so blue. And they were lookin' all over my face. Such a distraction.

"Well, after I put the needle aside and was dabbing' peroxide on his wound, he said, 'I'm not going to be able to leave this hospital until I know I'll be seeing you again.'"

Dottie huffed and tried to conceal a smile. No success.

"'You can stick around as long as you want,' I said when he sat up, 'then watch me leave when my shift is up.'

"'Can I walk you home?' he said and grinned, still starin' at me with those doggone gorgeous eyes.

"'Suit yourself' was my answer. I really didn't know what else to say. And so, four hours later he walked me home. I agreed to see him again, 'Only so I can check on your forehead,' I told him.

"Now, to make a long story short, we fell in love. Our dilemma was that he had to leave to start classes for his master's degree at Vanderbilt University. In those days, cars didn't go so fast, so we would've been a good 10 – 11 hours apart. We just knew we were meant for each other, so, we got married."

Dottie fixed her eyes upon the floor. A soft smile spread across her face. "And we've been together ever since."

Rina contemplated Dottie's story and tried to relate the circumstances to her own. In no way could she imagine having married Seth only three weeks after they met. Not even after the fourth week, when they knew their relationship was more than just a fleeting romance.

"Now," Dottie said as she began to flip through the dresses again, "I would in no way encourage someone to do such a thing in this day and age. Things are much different than they used to be. If my boy had come back from Israel with a little wife, I would've been none too happy 'bout it. I'd give him a good little smackin' around, ask him just what in the world he was thinking."

Dottie came to the end of her rack. "I do admit," she said and twisted her lips, "Chuck and I were a bit foolish, and maybe we should've waited a while. Everything worked out, though. We had our tough times, sure, but we've held strong through it all."

"I'm happy you and dad got married when you did," Rina said and pushed some hangers aside to look at a dress. "If not, you may have grown apart and never gotten back together."

"True, true. That's somethin' we've said all along." Dottie pulled out the dress of Rina's interest and inspected it front and back. "So, sweetness, now you heard my hasty marriage story, do you feel so bad now?"

"Oh, no," Rina said and held the mermaid style dress with a low-cut back close to her body. "Not that I felt bad about it, anyway. It was just a thought."

"My, oh, my," Dottie said. "What do ya think about that dress?"

"This is the one."

WEDDING AND DEPARTURE

We had a simple candlelight ceremony in the gazebo on Friday evening at seven-thirty. In attendance were your father's closest family members and a few friends. I'd say a total of forty guests were there. A lone violinist played the "Wedding March" as I walked toward your father who awaited me in the gazebo. It was the perfect evening. A wedding more beautiful than I ever imagined.

For our honeymoon, we stayed five days at a beachfront villa on Anna Maria Island, located off the east coast of Florida. It is the most stunning coastal area I have seen in my life. During our flight back to Trent Lott International Airport in Pascagoula, we talked about our plans after my return to Israel. We only had three days left together.

The cold window would need to be cleaned after Rina had been pressing her forehead and nose on it to stare at the Gulf of Mexico below. Her fascination with flying contrasted with Seth's fear of heights. He focused on the sky publication instead.

"I have some good news," Seth said and bumped Rina's elbow.

Rina turned toward her husband, still refreshed from the honeymoon. "Tell me."

"Well," Seth smiled with all his teeth showing, "right before you got here, I found out the documentary is going to be aired on primetime TV next month."

"Great!" Rina was puzzled. "But why didn't you tell me sooner?"

"I don't know." Seth shrugged. "Haven't been thinking about it, I guess. My mind's been occupied with other things." Seth grasped Rina's hand, drew it to his mouth and softly kissed her knuckles.

"I can't believe I didn't even think to ask about it."

"Now we're both guilty," Seth joked. "My plan is to visit you after it airs, Sunday, August 12th. I'm thinking the following Saturday."

"How long will you be able to stay?"

"Since I'll be there as your husband, I can stay ninety days without getting a visa."

Rina marveled at how much time they would be spending together. In the four months they'd known each other, the time had been little. "Do you think we'll have to stay that long?"

"I don't know. It'll depend on the embassy. I'm hoping to find a lawyer who'll be able to help us expedite the process to bring you back." Seth briefly glanced out the window, then sighed. "I'm trying not to think too much on this and just take it a day at a time. It's hard to do that with our situation, though. I'm going to be lost when you leave."

"I don't even want to think about it." Rina squeezed Seth's hands.

After their final three days had passed, they found themselves at the airport once again.

"This is the sixth time we've been at an airport together," Rina whispered as they said their goodbyes.

"The last time to part ways, though. Next time there'll be no goodbyes."

Rina hid the pain she felt in the depths of her heart. "I think these will be the longest five weeks of my life."

"Four weeks and six days, to be exact," Seth countered as he caressed his bride's arm and pulled her close. "Time will fly, and we'll be together again before we know it."

CHRISTIAN SCENES

For several years, my intention was to publish *Charge of the Beast* for the Christian market. This is what led me to enter the American Christian Fiction Writer's Genesis Contest in which I landed a spot in the semifinals.

With the objective to reach a greater audience, I decided to publish the novel as mainstream fiction. The remaining bonus content was extracted from early manuscripts.

Regardless of your spiritual beliefs, I encourage you to read these deleted chapters. You'll get a deeper look into Rina and Seth's romance and embark on a trip to historic Israel!

SURPRISE

Following the Passover Feast at Naomi's, Rina and Seth went for a walk and stopped at a nearby hill where a conversation ensued about Easter. After Seth shared his Christian beliefs, Rina took him to a surprise destination in Jerusalem.

RINA

Rina ground the clutch as she wedged through the tour buses, groups, and busy streets.

"Where are you taking me?" Seth hung his head out the window like a dog exhilarated by the incessant change of scenery.

"I never told you before, but I was trained as a tour guide. Everyone at the agency is required to do so, even if it's not what we intend to do. The place I'm taking you is a historical site." The phone rang, and Rina chattered in Hebrew to distract Seth. She purposely popped the clutch to scatter the tourists who were too overwhelmed to pay attention to anything but the sights. To Rina's surprise, they arrived with ample time for the secret meeting.

Seth had succumbed to a light sleep, but there was no time to waste.

"We're here!" She beeped the horn to interrupt the peace of his power nap.

Seth flinched and sat upright.

"Let's go look around," Rina said. "It's going to be crowded right now, but after the sun sets in about an hour, there will be less people."

After a short walk along a narrow street, Seth and Rina passed through a gate situated in a stone wall. Inside, well-kept gardens hosted a gathering of odd-looking trees. Their eerie assemblage in the pristine beds harkened tourists to join other admirers.

"What kind of trees are these?" Seth said when they approached the garden. "I've never seen anything like 'em."

Rina hesitated. A bit of suspense would strengthen Seth's subdued curiosity. "As you observe the enormous trunks, I'm sure you know by now that these trees are very old."

"Yeah, I figured they must be from ancient times. Too bad there's a gate. I'd like to get a closer look. I'm still waiting on your great revelation." Seth winked.

"Okay, okay. If you look across the way there, you'll also notice that we're at a low point on a hill. The view of Jerusalem from this site is spectacular."

"Um hum."

Rina pointed down the hill. "Now, look below. That's the Kidron Valley where many Christian and Muslim tombs are located. On the other side of that is the sacred Temple Mount: one of the major centers of attention in the Palestinian-Israeli conflict. Both countries claim dominion over the site. The path leading to the Temple Mount is said to be one of the many places where Jesus and his disciples followed paths to enter and leave Jerusalem."

The crammed roads below made it hard to concentrate. Seth paid no attention. He nodded as he began to understand their location.

"Behind us is a building." Rina turned and pointed to the structure. "It's the Church of All Nations. Over the years, many people have claimed the church resides on the site where Jesus prayed the night of his arrest. The trees you see all around are olive trees."

Seth's stare intensified as he scoped the perimeter of the grounds. "Is this the Garden of Gethsemane? Are we on the Mount of Olives?" He made brief eye contact with Rina.

"Yes, that's exactly where we are. We'll be able to stay here for a little while after the garden closes to the public. I know someone who will let us in beyond the fence so we can get closer to the trees."

"Incredible. I had thought about trying to visit some sites while I was here, but my focus remained solely on my project. Now, I'm standing in the place where the Lord spent his final moments of freedom almost two thousand years ago."

The crowd diminished. Tranquility kindled a fire of relief as the sun reached its lowest point on the horizon. The refraction of the sunlight upon the atmosphere created a striking sunset. Veiled with hues of light pink and pale orange, long wispy clouds layered the darkening blue sky.

Seth's quietude revealed a sweep of awestruck emotion.

Standing on these ancient grounds did not touch Rina in the same way. Seth had given her a detailed explanation of the man who many claimed was the only born Son of God. He claimed Jesus was the Messiah many Jews rejected, Naomi being one of them.

A heavy clank of thick metal resounded.

"There's the gate keeper," Rina said and bumped elbows with Seth to pull him out of a trance. "He's going to let us in."

An old man robed in a long, black tunic shuffled past without acknowledgement.

Seth and Rina followed in silence.

"Please, careful," the man said with a thick accent and waved them in. "Not ruin plants in ground, not step on border stones."

"I'll be careful," Seth said. "Can I touch the trees?"

"Very delicate, very soft," the old man whispered as if he were afraid to awaken the ancient trees. "Please respect sacred ground."

"Yes, sir," Seth replied. "Thank you, sir."

Long walkways composed of white pebbles created a maze through finely landscaped beds. Sparse red poppy plants and tall grasses bowed in homage to the grandiose patriarchs who stood watch over the grounds of their ancestors. Small olives danced with the wind on branches, then slumped when the breeze passed.

"How many do you think there are?" Seth squinted as he scanned the grounds.

"There are eight olive trees which are said to originate from the time of Jesus," Rina said and followed Seth's lead into the gardens.

"Are they really that old?"

"There is no proof, but olive trees can survive that long." The venerable trunks boasted secret insight into past generations. Rina reflected on the historical events the trees witnessed over the centuries. "Another scenario is that the original trees may have burned when the Romans destroyed Jerusalem in 70 A.D. The roots could have survived the fires and produced what we see today."

"I'm standing in the footsteps of the Lord." Seth took a few steps toward the nearest tree. "Wait, I'm not going to the trees yet."

"What?" Seth guided Rina as if he were already familiar with the grounds.

"Look over there," he said and pointed to a shiny, black monument near one of the younger olive trees. When they approached the stone, Seth read it aloud:

> "'MY FATHER, IF IT BE POSSIBLE, LET THIS CUP PASS FROM ME: NEVERTHELESS, NOT AS I WILL, BUT AS THOU WILT. Matthew 26:39.
>
> "O Jesus, in deepest night and agony You spoke these words of trust and surrender to God the Father in Gethsemane. In love and gratitude I want to say in times of fear and distress, My Father, I do not understand You, but I trust You.'"

For the first time in years, Rina traveled back to the day her mother died. She had fortified her soul in preparation for the lonely future ahead. With all the strength she gathered over time, she could not get past the demise of her family's fate. Both parents and her sister died early. If God did this to her family, how could she trust him?

Daylight offered limited visibility when Seth approached one of the ancient olive trees. "Here we are," he said. "Best for last."

Rina studied the gnarled trunk contorted by time. Young branches launched out in sharp slopes in defiance of the progenitors who gorged the sun's feeding light. Long, pointy leaves unique to the olive tree brushed the top of Rina's head.

Seth sat in a nook where the trunk wedged in two places.

Rina allowed Seth privacy for this special experience and wandered to another part of the garden. The prismatic façade on the Church of All Nations depicted an obscure scene of characters. During her training, Rina learned it represented Jesus Christ as the intermediary between God and mankind. The longer she rested in the tranquility of the garden, the more she thought about what Seth revealed to her about God.

"There you are."

Rina jumped. "Yes, here I am. So, what do you think?"

"I'm pretty speechless right now. What about you?"

Rina shrugged her shoulders. The façade of the church glistened in the subtle moonlight. The answer was right in front of her, but she wasn't ready to decide. "You got me to thinking earlier. I'll say that much for now."

"Good." Seth bowed his head and nodded. "Just let me know if you have any questions or want to talk about it."

RINA AND SETH'S VACATION IN ISRAEL

These scenes give more insight about Rina and Seth's time together during their early courtship. There is a strong Christian theme in these chapters, but also historical material I believe anyone will like!

When I wrote this, I was experimenting with a different literary style. I recognized I didn't have the talent with the technique, so I decided to not pursue it. While the writing is amateur, I wanted to include this for the meaningful subject matter.

RINA'S VACATION ENDS

Each evening after work, I rushed home to get ready for dinner with Seth. Our time together was short—two hours, three at the most. There were distractions every which way at the restaurants, so our full attention was not upon one another. During our parting moments and long embraces, neither of us was ready to say goodbye.

On Friday night, at the end of my first week back at work, I picked Seth up at his hotel just as I had the previous four nights. I was so happy that the weekend would bring me uninterrupted time with Seth.

"Tonight, we're doing something different," Rina said when Seth brushed his lips upon her hand.

"Oh, good." Seth stretched after buckling up. "I like change. Fill me in."

The click of Seth's seatbelt granted Rina permission to hasten her plans. "Rather than going to a restaurant, we're going to my condo for a home-cooked meal."

Seth leaned back onto the head rest as if he were ready for sleep. "Sounds perfect. You know I love Israeli home-cooking. A relaxing evening is just what I need."

"I hope you like what I made. It requires simmering for twenty-four hours, so I started preparing last night."

"Wow, I like it already. What kind of treat am I in for?"

"It's called hamin. In English, the best word to describe it is stew." Rina shuddered at the insult. "That's an understatement. It's a dish that practicing Jews generally eat on the Sabbath, because the cooking process begins the day before. No flame is to be lit on the Sabbath, but a fire lit on the previous day is acceptable to continue to burn in order to keep food warm." Rina sped into a parking spot near her apartment building.

"Whoa!" Seth said. "In a hurry?"

"Sort of." The down time with Seth could not come soon enough.

"What's all in this stew?"

"Most everyone has their own unique recipe." Rina whipped off the seatbelt after the loud click of emergency brake. She should not have described hamin as stew. "Mine follows the Sephardi style. The Sephardi Jews were expelled from Spain in the fifteenth century. When they immigrated to Israel, they brought along with them their own customs, traditions, and... food!"

"Spanish-Israeli food? What a combination."

"Centuries have passed, so it's purely Jewish. My recipe contains whole peppers, whole tomatoes and whole zucchini cut in half. All of these vegetables are stuffed with a beef and rice filling, then placed alongside chicken pieces and cut potatoes in a large pot. I also add barley, chickpeas, and a few other secret ingredients which make the recipe mine."

"My mouth's watering." Seth grimaced when his stomach grumbled. "Is it ready already?"

"When we get upstairs to my place, we'll find out."

"I can't wait to finally see where you live," Seth said as they approached the building.

Rina smiled. "It's small, but cozy. You get to meet my cat as well."

In spite of Rina's warning not to eat too much of the filling hamin, Seth ate two bowls full. The uncommonly cold April evening made the hot meal even more enticing, not to mention Rina's surprise—an excellent bottle of Sion Creek red wine from the Golan Heights winery.

Rather than the customary immaculate cleanup, Rina allowed the dishes to soak. Soap bubbles orchestrated a philharmonic sonata of burbles as steamy water gushed from the faucet. Chirpy meows from the hallway joined the symphony.

Mr. Big was happy.

Rina tiptoed to the doorway where Seth sprawled on the cold tile with her cat. Mr. Big was a large, long-haired, black beast. As ominous as he appeared, he was the epitome of what anyone could want in a feline friend. Mr. Big responded to Seth's silly tones and caresses with loud purrs. After a series of cheek rubs on Seth's head and shoulders, Mr. Big rolled onto his back to expose the fluff on his belly.

"Mr. Big likes you," Rina said and stooped down to scratch his head. "He doesn't do this with anyone."

"He's a gorgeous animal." Seth did not take his eyes off Mr. Big while he continued to pet the full length of the feline's silky coat.

A thorny sensation of thick metal studs gnawed at Rina's feet. "I have to sit down," she said and shuffled to the sofa.

"You know," Seth said as Rina propped her legs sideways, "I'm an expert foot masseuse."

"Really? I didn't know there existed such a thing."

"There does. A good foot massage can bring relief to the entire body if done properly."

How can he be so talented? "How much do you charge?"

Seth stroked the length of Mr. Big one last time with an unwilling expression to leave his new friend. "I'm not really a foot masseuse, but I've been the recipient of a few reflexology sessions."

As Seth lifted Rina's calves and feet, the tinge of pressure spurred an immediate release of tension.

"Hang on a sec," Seth said. "May as well make the most of this. Who knows when I'll be able to give you a foot massage again?"

Rina allowed Seth to lift the full weight of her legs. Springs from the old couch popped in rebuke as the warmth of his body vacated the cushions. Hushed activity sounded from the kitchen followed by a strong flow of water from the sink.

"Where are your towels?" Seth inched into the room with the bulky roasting pan. Swishes of water and slices of lemon seesawed when he set the dish on the floor. A proud gleam illuminated his expression. "Here's your footbath. The lemon is for detox."

The warmth of the water on Rina's feet triggered a race of chills throughout her body. As the nippy shivers decelerated, warm embers quelled the chill bumps on her arms. "The towels are in the hallway armoire," she huffed and melted into the couch. Seth initiated a series of peculiar processes beginning with a lemon wedge scrub while her feet still rested in the footbath. A soaked washcloth served as a sponge, which Seth squeezed above her knees to send gentle cascades of water down her calves. The spa-like cleansing was only a prelude to a relaxing and exotic massage. Ankle and toe rotations preceded a host of thumb circles on the heels and pads of her feet. Seth ushered in a finale of toe squeezes and total foot strokes with flat palms.

"How was that?" Seth whispered and stretched Rina's legs along the couch.

How could Rina describe his mysterious ability to uncoil the knots of tension throughout her body with just the touch of his hands on her feet? "No words."

"I'll take that as a compliment. Relax a few minutes while I clean up and get you some water." Seth covered Rina's legs and feet with a velvety throw. The cold, dirty footbath sloshed as Seth carried the roasting pan out of the room. Splashes of water licked the tile floor in the hallway. "I'll clean that up," Seth said with a facetious huff.

Mr. Big's loud purr from the floor created the white noise Rina loved to carry her to slumber. A snap of her fingers summoned his presence and subsequent massage as he kneaded her legs in feline bliss. Rina forced the burden of sleep from commandeering her mind, but her eyelids succumbed to the force of their weight.

An unfamiliar smell of cooking food coaxed Rina from sleep. Mr. Big's loud summons and extended head bumps indicated a need for attention. "Okay, okay. I'm up," she said. Memories of last night's short evening with Seth echoed as she slid out of bed. How did I get here? Mr. Big bounded toward the doorway. His classic question mark tail and body slides along the doorframe signaled his desire for her to follow. Rather than his usual saunter to the food and water bowls in the hall, he rounded the corner into the kitchen.

Seth hunched over the low sink with a soapy sponge in one hand and a foamy skillet in the other. "Morning," he said after he united the pan with other clean dishes on a towel.

Rina could not grasp the reality that a man stood in her kitchen. That he cleaned. That he held a chair out so she could sit down at the small breakfast table to eat the meal he prepared. Who now wrapped his arms around her as she stood, unable to move due to her stupor.

"Not awake yet?" He leaned back and pushed what was surely a tangled mess from her face.

"How did I get in my bed?"

"You don't remember? I picked you up and tucked you in. You told me to take the couch, so I did."

A man who spent the night…

"Come on, let's eat." Seth led her to the table and said a prayer of thanksgiving for the food.

"Amen," Rina repeated out of respect. The American egg sandwich for breakfast presented Rina with enough protein, carbohydrates, and dairy to last until dinner. "I have something to tell you," she said after a sip of tea to wash the saltiness from her mouth.

"What, that you just had the best breakfast of your life?" Seth winked.

A man who is holding my hand... The mid-morning blaze of the sun further rendered the reality of Seth's presence as it exposed his every feature. Could she tell him this was the first time she experienced this with a man?

"You need some coffee," he said and pulled her up from the chair.

"No." An uninhibited slide of her hands upon his tight waistline magnified her desire to savor each second. "I'm very much awake. It's just that I'm not…I'm not used to this. You're the only man who has been here. Ever." The scent and feel of his breath on her face bound her into a spell as he pulled her into his chest.

"I'm honored."

Rina held her breath as Seth eased the strength of his embrace. The warmth of his eyes drew her in to discover the true beauty of his soul. It seemed the perfect time for their first kiss, but too soon. Rina let the crown of her forehead fall into his chest. "How much work did you complete on your script this week?"

"About ninety percent." Seth's tone bespoke disappointment in the change of subject.

"What I wanted to tell you is that I don't have to work next week."

Confusion, surprise, and happiness interfused upon Seth's face. "But you were just off for two weeks."

"My boss called me into his office yesterday morning to express his concern about my peculiar behavior this week.

Rina pictured Mr. Lively's smirk as he explained what taboo questions were in the United States. "We're in a country where lawsuits aren't taken for granted like they are back home where money-hungry people will do just about anything for an extra coin in their pocket," he had said.

"He has this ability to sense change," Rina said. "His first guess was that I had fallen in love."

Seth's cheeks reddened. It was the first time he demonstrated shyness during their courtship.

"I told him about how we met and a little about the documentary. He asked about us, but I only told him we went on a few dates."

"You mean, you didn't tell him you'd fallen for an American country boy from Mississippi?" Seth's straightforward humor spoke hopes of undisguised revelation.

I don't know what it feels like to fall in love. Insecurity blocked Rina's will to express her feelings. A playful slap on the arm took the place of the answer Seth wanted to hear. "He's really interested in the documentary and thinks you should see more of the good parts of Israel. The more you know about our country, the better it will be for your documentary. I could take you some places and make sure you still have time for your work. I'll even help if I can."

Seth's reticent stare at the ceiling was not the response Rina expected.

"If you don't want to, I—"

"Of course I want to," Seth cut in. "There's nothing I want more than to spend time with you." He broke eye contact and hung his head. "It just gives me more time to fall in love with you."

Rina tried to restrain the flare of emotion that manifested in the rapid rise and fall of her chest.

"It's going to make it that much harder to leave you."

Seth flooded Rina with emotion as his eyes exposed everything he felt. He was right. They lived thousands of miles apart. In a week, he would be gone. Maybe they would never see each other again. "Yes, it will make it harder." Rina's voice broke. "Is it selfish of me to want to do it anyway?"

"There's no doubt we're doing this." Seth sat down and held his arms out. "Come here."

Rina slumped into Seth's lap and looped her arms around his shoulders. She didn't understand how she could feel such an inexplicable yearning for someone in only three weeks. A heavy ache of thirst for him swelled in the hollow of her stomach.

HISTORIC ISRAEL

The itinerary Rina created consisted of twelve locations she knew Seth would appreciate. The Sea of Galilee in Northern Israel welcomed them with sun and wind when they boarded a boat modeled after ancient fishing vessels. Seth focused his attention upon the various sights they passed as a tour guide explained geographical locations when Jesus Christ performed miracles.

"In chapter five of the Gospel of Mark," the female guide said as they passed a shoreline, "it is recorded that Jesus Christ healed a man who was indwelled by two-thousand demons who called themselves Legion. After a short conversation with the demons, Jesus forced them to exit the man's body and sent them to a herd of pigs feeding nearby on a steep bank. When this miraculous event transpired, the entire stock rushed down into the lake and drowned."

All tourists remained silent as the guide stood firm on the boat jostled by wind and wave. She projected her words, so each passenger heard her account of the historical sites from the days of the Lord's ministry.

A family who owned a bed and breakfast on the eastern shore of the lake at the Ein Gev kibbutz secured a two-bedroom apartment for Rina since she sent them a lot of business. A rocky drive down the private road led them to the main house where the family presented them with snacks for their stay. As eventide spawned sparkles of gold on the water, Rina and Seth picnicked on the beach near the kibbutz.

"This is such a miraculous place," Seth said after they finished the syrupy baklava for dessert. "The Lord spent so much time in and around the Sea of Galilee. As I look out into the middle of the lake, I imagine a great storm. A storm which, just by three simple words, immediately ceases to exist."

"What do you mean?" Rina searched the lake for the object of Seth's imagination.

"Jesus Christ spoke the words 'hush, be still' when he demanded a storm to cease. He and his disciples were traveling from Capernaum to the other side of the lake. While the Lord slept, winds from the hills formed a sudden storm. His newfound disciples determined that the boat was going to sink. In a frenzy, they woke him in desperation. As soon as he spoke those simple words, there was absolute calm on the lake."

Rina envisioned a violent, spontaneous storm across the breadth of the water. "You really believe that?"

"I do," Seth stressed. "Three of his disciples wrote about it in their epistles."

Rina pictured heavy wind, rain, billowing surges, and then instantaneous calm. "How can you know it really happened? How do you know they didn't make it up?"

"I know," Seth said with an expression similar to the day he explained the meaning of Easter, "because it's in the Bible. The Word of God is absolute truth. You're not gonna get more legitimate facts about history or a clearer explanation of our purpose in life anywhere else."

The waters of the lake stilled with only a few ripples on the glassy surface. Rina felt her eyes widen in unison with Seth's. Did God just give a sign that Seth was right? Thousands of people from all over the world journeyed to Israel every year due to their same beliefs. Could all of these people be wrong? Could their faith in one man as the savior of humanity be in vain? Two thousand years after the death of Jesus of Nazareth, billions of people put their faith in him over time. Why should I reject him?

"I miss our sunset walks in Gaza," Seth said and pushed off the sandy shore. "Come on."

Rina took Seth's outstretched hands and hopped to her feet. "This is much nicer than Gaza. Who knows, maybe Jesus walked here." The words came from Rina's mouth before the thought processed in her mind. The lake exhaled a fresh breeze as Rina and Seth padded barefoot in the sand. Waves swooshed in reply.

"I think God just answered your questions." Seth pointed to the lake.

"Does he really do that? Was he communicating with us when he stilled the water a few minutes ago and now with this wind that came from nowhere?"

Seth shrugged. "I don't know. It does seem like a coincidence, but I believe he uses unique ways to grab the attention of someone to whom he wants to give his love."

At last, Seth removed his gaze from the lake and looked up at Rina. "You wanna check out the apartment?"

"Sure. You know, I could use one of those foot massages again." Rina winked as she gathered the picnic basket.

"Yeah, and I need to teach you how to do it so you can give me one, too."

RESPECT

Once they entered the welcoming apartment, Rina felt a little awkward. Here she was with this man, alone in a quiet residence. No TV, just a small sitting room, kitchenette and two bedrooms.

"It'll do," Seth said while scoping the cozy quarters. "You want to take turns showering, and then meet back here in the den?"

"Alright." Rina forced a bashful smile as she turned toward the closest bedroom.

"Don't take too long. I know how you women can be."

"I'll try. The water heater is small, so the warm water will run out fast. I might conserve a little so you have a splash or two of warm water!"

After half an hour, Rina met Seth in the sitting area and took a chair next to the sofa where he sat.

"Thanks for that splash of cold water," he said while running his fingers through his wet hair.

"Sorry, I went as fast as I could." Rina sat straight with her hands squeezed between her knees. "Us women have much more to do in the shower than men, especially with long hair like mine."

"Why are you sitting over there? And why so shy all of a sudden?" Seth stood, took Rina's hand, and pulled her to sit next to him.

"I don't know. I'm not used to this. It's all new to me."

"Well, I have news for ya. It's new to me, too. Let's enjoy the newness, so to speak, together."

"I can do that." Rina held her breath when Seth threaded his fingers through hers.

"Do you think we might be able to find a treat at the main house where the owners live? I could go for some chocolate."

"Good idea. I think chocolate will make me relax a little."

"Why do you need to relax? I won't bite, you know."

"I do know you won't bite me. I guess I'm just a little unsure what to expect. Chocolate will be a good distraction, so let's go get acquainted with our hosts."

After visiting with the family of five for an hour, Seth and Rina headed to the back patio of the main house.

"What did you say those chocolate balls are called? I couldn't understand with the lady speaking so quickly. She's not at all like Mrs. Shalev."

"No," Rina laughed. "Quite the opposite. They're called kadori shokolad. She and her young daughter made them from scratch today."

"They taste like truffles. That's what we call 'em, anyway. Homemade at a family home in a foreign country makes all the difference for me." Seth squeezed Rina's shoulders. "So, do you feel better now?"

"Anything chocolate always makes things better, so yes. Not that there was anything wrong, but well, you know what I mean…"

For two hours, Rina and Seth relaxed side-by-side in a wide lounge chair and soaked in the beauty of the moonlight glimmering on the waters. The crisp, spring air and warmth from Seth enlivened Rina's spirits.

Once they returned to the apartment, Rina's emotions were quite the opposite as they had been a few hours prior. She wanted to be close to Seth. Closer than they'd ever been.

"Are you tired?" Rina said as Seth set the key on a counter in the kitchenette.

"Actually, I am. Between his self-grooming, grooming me, head-butting and purring, Mr. Big kept me awake last night."

"So I noticed. For years he's slept by my side every single night, except for last night. What a traitor!"

"Please, feel free to lock him up in your room at night when we get back."

"He'll miss you as much as I will when you leave." Rina approached Seth and waited for his embrace.

"I'll miss him, too." Seth wrapped Rina's arms around his waist and paused. "Oh, and I'll miss you as well."

"I'm not ready to part ways with you for the evening, Seth." Rina caressed Seth's back and held him tightly around his waist."

"I know, Lady Love. I'm not ready either. Let's go to the couch."

Rina followed Seth's lead, not caring about anything except being close to him. He sat down, then guided her in lying down and resting the back of her head in his lap.

Seth began to stroke the top of Rina's head. "You comfortable?"

Staring into his eyes, Rina nodded and pulled his arm in to hug it. "Lay down next to me."

Grasping Rina's hand, Seth said, "You don't know how much I want to, but it's not a good idea. It could lead to more than what's right."

"I don't mean that. I just want to be close to you."

"I know what you mean. There's a mutual attraction between us, though. I know it's stronger on my part."

Rina furrowed her eyebrows. "That doesn't mean anything is going to happen."

"True, but I don't trust myself right now." Seth huffed and leaned his head back. "You're hard to resist," he said as he looked back down to Rina. "That's why I need to protect you. Protect your soul."

"I don't understand," Rina said, frustrated.

Seth took Rina's hand and played with her fingers. "This whole experience with you has caused my emotions to soar. I've been attracted to you since the night we met. Can you believe I was nervous about seeing you the next day?"

Rina grinned. "I was, too."

"You were nervous about seeing you the next day?"

"No, silly!" Rina playfully smacked Seth's arm. "About seeing you!"

Seth's face became serious again. "Our first two weeks together were rough but experiencing it with you sort of evened everything out. I know this is going to sound corny," Seth said and twisted his mouth, "but you were my light in the darkness."

Not corny, Rina thought. Sweet.

"Then," Seth continued, "our time since last Saturday. Whew! Being in this land. This place with you. It's all so romantic, enticing…"

Seth gently began to rub and squeeze the top of Rina's shoulders near her collarbone, then continued down her arms to her hands.

Rina inhaled deeply. Okay, okay, I understand now…

"Listen to me," Seth said in a bashful tone, "I sound like some kind of suave womanizer."

"I like it," Rina whispered. "Tell me more."

Seth's touch let up. "I already desire you, and I'm trying my hardest to suppress it."

Me too.

"You deserve nothing less than utmost respect," Seth said and returned his touch to Rina's hair and hand. "I'll be damned if I'm going to compromise your purity. It is for this reason, my little Lady Love, that I must resist the temptation to feel your warm body stretched alongside mine right now."

At that moment, Rina knew this was no ordinary man. He was extraordinary. Beyond measure. Prepared. She never imagined that something so simple could lead to more than an innocent embrace. But Seth's explanation made sense.

Before she knew it, her mind drifted into sleep. Every so often she'd feel her body flinch, then temporarily gain a few seconds of consciousness only to find Seth staring at her.

The next morning, she awoke early and found herself in bed. This time, it was Seth who slept late.

Rina decided to surprise Seth with breakfast, just as he had done Saturday morning. She anticipated that Seth's appetite would be insatiable, so she prepared what was an unusual breakfast for her – fried eggs, fresh bread, and cream cheese.

She then slipped through the half-open door of Seth's room and watched him sleep, taking advantage of the view of his semi-muscular chest and arms before speaking to him.

"Seth," she whispered close to his ear. "Wake up."

Seth stirred and fervently turned away from her.

"Your eggs are going to get cold," Rina said as she leaned over further, touching her lips to his ear.

Bolting upright, Seth took a few seconds to recognize his whereabouts, then grinned when he saw Rina.

"Thank you for last night," Rina said.

"You're welcome." Seth stretched then fell back onto the mattress. "What did I do?"

"You protected me."

Seth nodded his head, took Rina's hand and kissed it. "I'll meet you in the kitchen in just a few minutes."

REFLECTIONS

Seth's reactions to the places they visited during their journeys over the next two days varied from silent emotion to sudden excitement. Many times, he closed his eyes in an attempt to envision an occurrence from the Bible.

The sporadic descriptions were what Rina enjoyed the most.

"Somewhere along these shores," Seth explained while they walked near the Sea of Galilee in Capernaum, "a woman was healed simply by touching the hem of the Lord's garment. She had been wasting away from an incurable hemorrhaging disease for twelve years. Knowing that Jesus was the Son of God and able to perform miracles, she somehow pushed her way through the massive crowd surrounding Jesus. He was distracted, though. An official from the synagogue requested the Lord's presence at his home to heal his dying daughter. Just as Jesus was about to walk away, the woman reached through and touched the hem of his robe. Because of her faith, the Lord told her, she was healed."

"How do you know all of this?" Rina said, captivated by Seth's detailed accounts.

"I give the credit to my parents. They began to teach me about God when I was two years old. At that time, it was all about what God made: the stars, earth, animals, trees, and other things of nature a toddler understands. Then they introduced the creation of Adam and Eve, the first sin, and a wonderful place called Heaven. Mom kept everything I brought home from church as well as the books she read at bedtime."

"What about your father?"

"Dad did plenty with me during the day," Seth said with a reminiscent smile. "The evenings were his time for work. It's when he thinks the best."

"Do you think all that time they spent teaching you as a small child did anything? Surely you don't remember it?"

"What matters is that I grew up knowing about God, that he had a son named Jesus, and that Jesus went to the Cross for our sins so we could go to Heaven. I grew up a believer in Christ. It's what I've always known."

Rina followed Seth's lead as he slid his fingers through hers and headed back to the bed and breakfast. He did not ask about her thoughts. Instead, he comforted her with squeezes and playful smiles. Dizzying notions of a new purpose in life subdued her customary cheer. If the Bible had all the facts she needed to know about her existence, then she was in total ignorance.

"Hey," Seth stopped to face her. "Don't think on this too hard. The answer is easy. You just need faith to accept the truth."

Rina diverted her attention to the owner at the main house who summoned them to dinner. "Can we resume another time?"

"Just let me know when you're ready."

BELIEF

"If we were going to Jerusalem," Rina said as they neared Modi'in on Wednesday night, "what would you want to see more than anything else?"

"Golgotha, where Christ was crucified."

"That's what I hoped." Rina clenched her tight jaw when Seth turned onto her street. An image of Mr. Big sprawled across the bed made her want to run inside. "My plan for tomorrow is to walk the Via Dolorosa up to the Church of the Holy Sepulcher."

"What's the significance of the church?"

"You don't know?"

"Nope."

"The Church of the Holy Sepulcher was built upon the location where many believe the Cross stood. There is a hole in the ground that's said to be the place where the Cross was raised."

Bright rays of the morning sun ignited the path of the Via Dolorosa where Christ carried the cross. Chatter from small groups disrupted the silence at the first station, the Lion's Gate, where Pontius Pilate handed Jesus over to be tortured and crucified. Throughout the thirty-minute ascent, Rina explained what she knew of each station. Seth's responses consisted of head nods, forehead crinkles, and an occasional huh.

The ninth station marked the end of the path and the entrance to the church. Seth turned to look down the street. "It's hard to picture what happened," he said with a huff. "There's too much going on."

Blaring church bells greeted the tourists who entered the sacred grounds that led to the final stations of the Via Dolorosa. An overabundance of candles and people generated stifling conditions as the throng increased with each station. As they ascended the smoothed steps of the Stairway to Calvary, Rina sensed the climax of Seth's disappointment.

After a glance at the extravagant Rock of Calvary, he turned his back on the spectacle. "You ready?"

"Sure." Rina held her hand out waiting for Seth to take it.

"That wasn't what I expected," he said when they left the dark confines of the church. "I just wanted to see the hill where Jesus was crucified, not some elaborate get-up. Everything else in that place feels meaningless to me. It was as if I were at a museum."

"It's a good thing my plans don't end here," Rina said. "Next stop is The Garden Tomb."

Rocks crunched under their feet as they walked a stone path lined with clay flowerpots. Red and pink blooms contrasted with diverse greenery in the earthy garden. "Look, that must be it," Rina said. Pedestrians lingered around a rocky wall with an opening that resembled a doorway. "Many believe this is the tomb where Jesus was buried."

"What about that thing in the church? I thought that was the tomb?" Seth walked down the wide stone steps that led to the level of the tomb. "This looks more like a burial place to me," Seth said and dipped his head through the door.

"It's a big controversy with no real proof." Rina followed Seth into the right section of the spacious tomb. A carved bed level with the floor revealed the location where the body of Jesus would have been placed.

Seth slid his hands along the smooth walls. "This makes more sense."

Rina drew in the earthy scents of the room as she observed a portion at the far end of the stone bed that resembled a pillow.

"Imagine him there, covered in burial cloths." Seth drew the outline of a body with his finger.

Rina pictured a corpse wrapped in white like a mummy.

"Now imagine the cloths in the same position, but without a body. Unmoved, untouched."

The visualization in the tomb reminded Rina of their conversation at the Mount of Rest Cemetery. "Easter."

"That's right."

Rina leaned into Seth when he pulled her close to his body.

"Two angels would have been here. Bright, celestial beings who delivered the news of Christ's resurrection to Mary Magdalene."

Shivers pulsed through Rina's body as she tried to absorb the significance of Seth's words. It seemed unreal but fathomable with the detailed descriptions.

"This is the perfect way to visualize what happened," Seth said and guided Rina outside, "even if it isn't the true burial sight."

Rina kept pace with Seth as they ascended the wide steps. "This isn't the only place I want to show you." A cobblestone walkway revealed an ancient cistern and winepress. The gardens presented an oasis of greenery and florals that accompanied them to their destination.

"What's that?" Seth pointed to a small, rocky hill.

"That," she paused as they approached the ledge, "is what I want to show you."

Seth turned down the corners of his mouth and questioned Rina with his expression.

"Can you make out a shape in the rocky cliff? Perhaps that of a skull?" Rina traced what appeared to be the hollows of eyes and a flat nose in the steep, white stone cliff.

Seth's eyes widened. "No way. Could it be the place described by Matthew, Mark, Luke and John as The Skull?"

"It is another theory, yes."

"Now this is more like it. Much more believable than the get-up at the church. I can picture everything happening here."

"One of the reasons some believe this to be the location of the crucifixion is that it is in a highly visible site, which was customary for Roman executions. This was a major intersection of an ancient trade route from Damascus to Jericho and would have been filled with numerous passers-by on a daily basis."

"My father covered that several times over the years. It was advantageous for those who watched our Lord's crucifixion, especially for those who witnessed the supernatural phenomena." Seth shook his head. "How could they not believe after seeing sudden darkness in the middle of the day?"

"Sudden darkness?" A rowdy group of teenagers followed their tour guide to the far end of the viewing area.

"Let's go over there." Seth pointed to the opposite end. "Now let's go back in time. Wipe out everything you see and hear," Seth said with a sweep of his hand across the span of their vision. "Imagine the scene 2,000 years ago. The grand temple still boasts its beauty on the hill. Three crosses stand erect there at the Place of the Skull. On one cross, a man with a strong, healthy frame hangs in anguish. His skin is tarnished with lashes and bruises. Fresh blood drips from his hands and trickles from his toes where he has been nailed to the thick beams."

Subtle notes of emotion spawned hot moisture in Rina's eyes. The vision Seth created became reality as Rina absorbed his words.

"The wailing of women who watch in the distance can be heard by all. Roman soldiers and religious Jews insult him with blasphemous mockery."

Rina restrained the flow of tears cradled by her lower lids as Seth's voice cracked.

"He was known as the King of the Jews." The flare of his nostrils alluded to anger. "They said if he really were the Son of God that he would be able to get down from the cross on his own. The thing is," Seth said with a smirk, "they were right. He probably had 10,000 angels standing by to take him down and care for him."

"Why didn't he call them for help?"

"It wasn't the will of his Father in Heaven. He knew what he had to do to accomplish salvation for fallen man. He even prayed aloud for the Roman soldiers who treated him so badly. He asked, 'Father, forgive them; for they know not what they do.' What mercy and grace."

"Then what happened?"

"During the final three hours of the Lord's crucifixion, God the Father didn't want anyone to see how His Son suffered." Seth affixed his eyes on the cliff. "That's when God shut off the lights."

Rina returned to the vision of Christ on the cross. "Am I supposed to imagine dark skies or a complete blackout?"

"No light whatsoever. Maybe God allowed torches to burn. I don't know. This happened at noon! Imagine the mayhem."

"When did God turn the lights back on?"

"Three hours later, when the Lord exhaled his final breath. Then there was an earthquake and other supernatural events. Many people believed in him as the Son of God at that moment. Even a Roman Centurion and some of the soldiers.

"The ones who mocked him?"

Seth nodded as he squinted at the top of the hill. "Incredible, isn't it?"

Rina struggled to envision the latter portion of Seth's account. Absolute blackness in the middle of the day was incredible. An earthquake at the moment of Christ's death was incredible. Belief in Jesus as God's Son after witnessing these events is what seemed credible to Rina. "I would have believed if I had been there."

Seth turned away from the cliff. A solemn sense of worry etched into every crevice of his expression implored Rina to heed his words.

"It doesn't have to be that way, Rina. You can believe without seeing," Seth expressed as he clutched Rina's hands. "Do you believe all the other facts we know about antiquity? How about King Tut? Do you believe he was an ancient Egyptian Pharaoh?"

Rina shrugged. She didn't know much about him other than the fact that his tomb was excavated. "Sure, I believe it."

"Why?"

"It's recorded in historical documents. They found his tomb."

Seth raised his voice as he continued. "You've got the same thing for Jesus Christ. We just came from what may be his tomb. You're standing in what is most likely the very place where everything happened. It's just a matter of believing the longest surviving historical document that describes in detail what went down that day."

"The Bible," Rina's fingers tingled from Seth's tight grip.

"The very words of God." Seth's tone softened as he released Rina's hands and cupped her shoulders. "Everywhere we've been. Everything we've seen. All I've told you. What's not to believe?"

"I have no reason to reject your words, Elijah's words, or those of the Bible," Rina said without reluctance. "I believe it all. I know Jesus is God's Son. He's my Savior." A rising tide of harmony washed over the shores of Rina's soul, and Seth pulled her into his embrace. The beat of his heart grasped her emotions as she flattened her head upon his chest. Suspired whispers perished through his lips as a single body of words that could only be prayer.

The hollowed eyes of the skull in the cliff called her in to the reality of her temporary existence on earth. Now she became aware of a new destiny as she began her journey into the world of Christianity. "What do I do now? Do I have to be baptized?"

"Not necessary." The firm resolve in Seth's comportment gave Rina the certitude to trust his direction. "You proclaimed your trust in Christ for salvation. No work needs to be done other than belief. You're now a member of the family of God. The best thing you can do now is pray. It's a wonderful gift God has given us to communicate with Him."

"How do I? What am I supposed to say?"

"Just let it come naturally, say what comes to mind. Thank Him for His Son. Tell Him what you just told me. He'll listen no matter how little or how much you say."

The moments following my salvation included prayer in a secluded area in the gardens between the tomb and the Skull. I began slow and unsure. Was there really someone listening to me? I continued, and a calm set in. The words came naturally. I didn't feel any different other than a newfound meaning in life. As we enjoyed a relaxing dinner at a kosher sushi restaurant, Seth paid more attention to me than ever. I couldn't get enough of his new type of smile and expressions. Our relationship became even more meaningful and special with each minute that passed.

END BONUS CONTENT

Did you enjoy the bonus chapters? Email me your thoughts and sign up for my newsletter. In return, you will get a free copy of my short story, *Healed.*

Thank you for reading until the end!

Rosalie@rosalieking.com

www.ingramcontent.com/pod-product-compliance
Lightning Source LLC
Chambersburg PA
CBHW020606310726
48979CB00008B/1362/J

* 9 7 8 1 7 3 5 1 4 3 2 1 7 *